The Good Lord Bird

The
Good
Lord
Bird

JAMES McBRIDE

RIVERHEAD BOOKS

New York

RIVERHEAD BOOKS
Published by the Penguin Group
Penguin Group (USA) LLC
375 Hudson Street, New York, New York 10014, USA

USA · Canada · UK · Ireland · Australia · New Zealand · India · South Africa · China

penguin.com

A Penguin Random House Company

The Library of Congress has catalogued the Riverhead hardcover edition as follows:

McBride, James, date.
The good lord bird / James McBride.
P.   cm.
ISBN 978-1-59448-634-0
1. Fugitive slaves—United States—Fiction.   2. Brown, John, 1800–1859—Fiction.
3. Abolitionists—Fiction.   4. Harpers Ferry (W. Va.)—History—John Brown's Raid, 1859—
Fiction.   I. Title.
PS3613.C28G66   2013   2013004014
813'.6—dc23

First Riverhead hardcover edition: August 2013
First Riverhead trade paperback edition: August 2014
Riverhead trade paperback ISBN: 978-1-59463-278-5

PRINTED IN THE UNITED STATES OF AMERICA

10   9

Cover design and illustration by Oliver Munday
Book design by Michelle McMillian

FOR MA AND JADE,

WHO LOVED A GOOD WHOPPER

Contents

The Good Lord Bird

Prologue

Rare Negro Papers Found
by A. J. Watson

Wilmington, Del. (AP) June 14, 1966—*A fire that destroyed the city's oldest Negro church has led to the discovery of a wild slave narrative that highlights a little-known era of American history.*

The First United Negro Baptist Church of the Abyssinia at 4th and Bainbridge Streets was destroyed by fire last night. Fire officials blamed a faulty gas heater. No one was injured in the blaze. But among the scorched remains were several charred notebooks belonging to a late church deacon that have attracted national academic interest.

Charles D. Higgins, a congregation member since 1921, died last May. Higgins was a cook, but also an amateur historian who apparently recorded the account of another elderly United Baptist congregation member, Henry "the Onion" Shackleford, who claimed to have been the only Negro to survive the American outlaw John Brown's raid on Harpers Ferry, Va., in 1859. Brown, a white abolitionist, attempted to capture the nation's largest arsenal to start a war on slavery. The failed raid caused a national panic and prompted the start of America's Civil War. It led to Brown's hanging, as well as the deaths of most of his 19 accomplices, including four Negroes.

Until now, no full account of Brown or of his men has ever been found or known to exist.

The account was contained in a metal fireproof box hidden under the floorboards of the deacon's chair behind the pulpit, where Higgins held court faithfully every Sunday for more than 43 years. Also in the box was an envelope containing 12 Confederate dollars, a rare feather from an ivory-billed woodpecker, a nearly extinct bird species, and a note from Mr. Higgins's late wife which read, "If I ever see you again, I'll send your ass hooting and hollering out my damn door."

Mr. Higgins had no children. He worked as a cook for Mrs. Arlene Ellis of Chadds Ford, Pa., for 29 years. He was the eldest member of the First United Baptist, where he was known affectionately to congregation members as "Mr. Whopper" and "Deacon Shimmy Wimmy." His exact age at his death was unknown, but congregation members guessed it at close to 100. He was also something of an attraction at local city council meetings, where he often attended sessions dressed in Civil War regalia and petitioned the council to rename the Dupont Highway the "John Brown Road."

His neatly bound notebooks claim that he gathered the facts of Mr. Shackleford's life in a series of interviews conducted in 1942. According to Mr. Higgins, he first made the acquaintance of Mr. Shackleford when they both served as Sunday school teachers at First United in the early '40s, until Shackleford was tossed from the church in 1947 for what Mr. Higgins writes as "scoundreling and funny-touching a fast li'l something named Peaches. . . ."

Apparently, according to Mr. Higgins's papers, the church members believed Mr. Shackleford was a woman before that incident. He was apparently a small man, according to Mr. Higgins, "with girly features, curly hair . . . and the heart of a rascal."

Mr. Higgins claims Mr. Shackleford was 103 years old when the account was recorded, though he writes, "It could be more. Onion had me by at least 30 years."

While Mr. Shackleford is listed in the 1942 church registry, which survived the fire, no one in the current congregation is old enough to recall him.

The congregation has announced plans to pass the account of Mr. Shackleford to a Negro history expert for verification, and later sell the notebooks for publication, with the proceeds going toward the purchase of a new church van.

PART I

FREE DEEDS

(Kansas)

I

Meet the Lord

I was born a colored man and don't you forget it. But I lived as a colored woman for seventeen years.

My Pa was a full-blooded Negro out of Osawatomie, in Kansas Territory, north of Fort Scott, near Lawrence. Pa was a barber by trade, though that never gived him full satisfaction. Preaching the Gospel was his main line. Pa didn't have a regular church, like the type that don't allow nothing but bingo on Wednesday nights and women setting around making paper-doll cutouts. He saved souls one at a time, cutting hair at Dutch Henry's Tavern, which was tucked at a crossing on the California Trail that runs along the Kaw River in south Kansas Territory.

Pa ministered mostly to lowlifes, four-flushers, slaveholders, and drunks who came along the Kansas Trail. He weren't a big man in size, but he dressed big. He favored a top hat, pants that drawed up around his ankles, high-collar shirt, and heeled boots. Most of his clothing was junk he found, or items he stole off dead white folks on the prairie killed off from dropsy or aired out on account of some dispute or other. His shirt had bullet holes in it the size of quarters. His hat was two sizes too small. His trousers come from two different-colored pairs sewn together in the middle where the arse met. His hair was nappy enough to strike a match on. Most women wouldn't go near him, including my Ma, who closed her eyes in death bringing me to this life. She was said to be a gentle, high-yaller woman. "Your Ma was the only woman in the world man enough to hear my holy thoughts," Pa boasted, "for I'm a man of many parts."

Whatever them parts was, they didn't add up to much, for all full up and dressed to the nines, complete with boots and three-inch top hat, Pa only come out to 'bout four feet eight inches tall, and quite a bit of that was air.

But what he lacked in size, Pa made up for with his voice. My Pa could outyell with his voice any white man who ever walked God's green earth, bar none. He had a high, thin voice. When he talked, it sounded like he had a Jew's harp stuck down his throat, for he spoke in pops and bangs and such, which meant speaking with him was a two-for-one deal, being that he cleaned your face and spit-washed it for you at the same time—make that three-for-one, when you consider his breath. His breath smelled like hog guts and sawdust, for he worked in a slaughterhouse for many years, so most colored folks avoided him generally.

But white folks liked him fine. Many a night I seen my Pa fill up on joy juice and leap atop the bar at Dutch Henry's, snipping his scissors and hollering through the smoke and gin, "The Lord's coming! He's a'comin' to gnash out your teeth and tear out your hair!" then fling hisself into a crowd of the meanest, low-down, piss-drunk Missouri rebels you ever saw. And while they mostly clubbed him to the floor and kicked out his teeth, them white fellers didn't no more blame my Pa for flinging hisself at them in the name of the Holy Ghost than if a tornado was to come along and toss him across the room, for the Spirit of the Redeemer Who Spilt His Blood was serious business out on the prairie in them days, and your basic white pioneer weren't no stranger to the notion of hope. Most of 'em was fresh out of that commodity, having come west on a notion that hadn't worked out the way it was drawed up anyway, so anything that helped them outta bed to kill off Indians and not drop dead from ague and rattlesnakes was a welcome change. It helped too that Pa made some of the best rotgut in Kansas Territory—though he was a preacher, Pa weren't against a taste or three—and like as not, the same gunslingers who tore out his hair and knocked him cold would pick him up afterward and say "Let's liquor," and the whole bunch of 'em would wander off and howl at the moon, drinking Pa's giddy sauce. Pa was right proud of his friendship with the white race, something he claimed he learned from the Bible. "Son," he'd say, "always remember the book of Heziekial, twelfth chapter, seventeenth verse: 'Hold out thy glass to thy thirsty neighbor, Captain Ahab, and let him drinketh his fill.'"

I was a grown man before I knowed there weren't no book of Heziekial in the Bible. Nor was there any Captain Ahab. Fact is, Pa couldn't read a lick, and only recited Bible verses he heard white folks tell him.

Now, it's true there was a movement in town to hang my Pa, on account of his getting filled with the Holy Ghost and throwing hisself at the flood of westward pioneers who stopped to lay in supplies at Dutch Henry's—speculators, trappers, children, merchants, Mormons, even white women. Them poor settlers had enough to worry 'bout what with rattlers popping up from the floorboards and breechloaders that fired for nothing and building chimneys the wrong way that choked 'em to death, without having to fret 'bout a Negro flinging hisself at them in the name of our Great Redeemer Who Wore the Crown. In fact, by the time I was ten years old in 1856, there was open talk in town of blowing Pa's brains out.

They would'a done it, I think, had not a visitor come that spring and got the job done for 'em.

Dutch Henry's sat right near the Missouri border. It served as a kind of post office, courthouse, rumor mill, and gin house for Missouri rebels who come across the Kansas line to drink, throw cards, tell lies, frequent whores, and holler to the moon 'bout niggers taking over the world and the white man's constitutional rights being throwed in the outhouse by the Yankees and so forth. I paid no attention to that talk, for my aim in them days was to shine shoes while my Pa cut hair and shove as much johnnycake and ale down my little red lane as possible. But come spring, talk in Dutch's circled 'round a certain murderous white scoundrel named Old John Brown, a Yank from back east who'd come to Kansas Territory to stir up trouble with his gang of sons called the Pottawatomie Rifles. To hear them tell it, Old John Brown and his murderous sons planned to deaden every man, woman, and child on the prairie. Old John Brown stole horses. Old John Brown burned homesteads. Old John Brown raped women and hacked off heads. Old John Brown done this, and Old John Brown done that, and why, by God, by the time they was done with him, Old John Brown sounded like the most onerous, murderous, low-down son of a bitch you ever saw, and I resolved that if I ever was to run across him, why, by God, I would do him in myself, just on account of what he done or was gonna do to the good white people I knowed.

Well, not long after I decided them proclamations, an old, tottering Irishman teetered into Dutch Henry's and sat in Pa's barber chair. Weren't nothing special 'bout him. There was a hundred prospecting prairie bums wandering around Kansas Territory in them days looking for a lift west or a job rustling cattle. This drummer weren't nothing special. He was a stooped, skinny feller, fresh off the prairie, smelling like buffalo dung, with a nervous twitch in his jaw and a chin full of ragged whiskers. His face had so many lines and wrinkles running between his mouth and eyes that if you bundled 'em up, you could make 'em a canal. His thin lips was pulled back to a permanent frown. His coat, vest, pants, and string tie looked like mice had chewed on every corner of 'em, and his boots was altogether done in. His toes stuck clean through the toe points. He was a sorry-looking package altogether, even by prairie standards, but he was white, so when he set in Pa's chair for a haircut and a shave, Pa put a bib on him and went to work. As usual, Pa worked at the top end and I done the bottom, shining his boots, which in this case was more toes than leather.

After a few minutes, the Irishman glanced around, and, seeing as nobody was standing too close, said to Pa quietly, "You a Bible man?"

Well, Pa was a lunatic when it come to God, and that perked him right up. He said, "Why, boss, I surely is. I knows all kinds of Bible verses."

The old coot smiled. I can't say it was a real smile, for his face was so stern it weren't capable of smiling. But his lips kind of widened out. The mention of the Lord clearly pleased him, and it should have, for he was running on the Lord's grace right then and there, for that was the murderer Old John Brown his-self, the scourge of Kansas Territory, setting right there in Dutch's Tavern, with a fifteen-hundred-dollar reward on his head and half the population in Kansas Territory aiming to put a charge in him.

"Wonderful," he said. "Tell me. Which books in the Bible do you favor?"

"Oh, I favors 'em all," Pa said. "But I mostly like Hezekiel, Ahab, Trotter, and Pontiff the Emperor."

The Old Man frowned. "I don't recollect I have read those," he said, "and I have read the Bible through and through."

"I don't know 'em exact," Pa said. "But whatever verses you know, stranger, why, if it would please you to share them, I would be happy to hear 'em."

"It would please me indeed, brother," said the stranger. "Here's one: Whosoever stoppeth his ear at the cry of the Lord, he also shall cry himself."

"Hot goodness, that's a winner!" Pa said, leaping into the air and clapping his boots together. "Tell me another."

"The Lord puts forth his hand and touches all evil and kills it."

"That warms my soul!" Pa said, leaping up and clapping his hands. "Gimme more!"

The old coot was rolling now. "Put a Christian in the presence of sin and he will spring at its throat!" he said.

"C'mon, stranger!"

"Free the slave from the tyranny of sin!" the old coot nearly shouted.

"Preach it!"

"And scatter the sinners as stubble so that the slave *shall forever be free!*"

"Yes, sir!"

Now, them two was setting dead center in Dutch Henry's Tavern as they went at it, and there must've been ten people milling 'bout within five feet of them, traders, Mormons, Indians, whores—even the Old John Brown hisself—who could'a leaned over to Pa and whispered a word or two that would have saved his life, for the question of slavery had throwed Kansas Territory into war. Lawrence was sacked. The governor had fled. There weren't no law to speak of. Every Yankee settler from Palmyra to Kansas City was getting his duff kicked from front to back by Missouri roughriders. But Pa didn't know nothing 'bout that. He had never been more than a mile from Dutch's Tavern. But nobody said a word. And Pa, being a lunatic for the Lord, hopped about, clicking his scissors and laughing. "Oh, the Holy Spirit's a'comin'! The blood of Christ! Yes indeedy. Scatter that stubble! Scatter it! I feel like I done met the Lawd!"

All around him, the tavern had quieted up.

And just then, Dutch Henry walked into the room.

Dutch Henry Sherman was a German feller, big in feature, standing six hands tall without his boots. He had hands the size of meat cleavers, lips the color of veal, and a rumbling voice. He owned me, Pa, my aunt and uncle, and several Indian squaws, which he used for privilege. It weren't beyond old Dutch to use a white man in that manner, too, if he could buy his goods that way. Pa was Dutch's very first slave, so Pa was privileged. He come and go as he pleased. But at noon every day, Dutch came in to collect his money, which Pa faithfully kept in a cigar box behind the barber's chair. And as luck would have it, it was noon.

Dutch walked over, reached behind Pa's barber chair to the

cashbox, removed his money, and was about to turn away when he glanced at the old man setting in Pa's barber chair and saw something he didn't like.

"You look familiar," he said. "What's your name?"

"Shubel Morgan," the Old Man said.

"What you doing 'round these parts?"

"Looking for work."

Dutch paused a moment, peering at the Old Man. He smelled a rat. "I got some wood out back needs chopping," he said. "I'll give you fifty cents to chop wood half a day."

"No, thanks," the Old Man said.

"Seventy-five cents."

"Naw."

"How about a dollar, then?" Dutch asked. "A dollar is a lot of money."

"I can't," the Old Man grunted. "I'm waiting on the steamer to come down the Kaw."

"That steamer don't come for two weeks," Dutch said.

The Old Man frowned. "I am setting here sharing the Holy Word with a brother Christian, if you don't mind," he said. "So why don't you mind your marbles, friend, and saw your wood your own self, lest the Lord see you as a fat sow and a laggard."

Dutch carried a pepperbox in them days. Tight little gun. Got four barrels on it. Nasty close up. He kept it in his front pocket for easy pickings. Not in a holster. Right in his front pocket. He reached in that pocket and drawed it out, and held it, barrel down, all four barrels pointed to the floor, talking to that wrinkled Old Man with a gun in his hand now.

"Only a white-livered, tit-squeezing Yankee would talk like that," he said. Several men got up and walked out. But the Old

Man sat there, calm as an egg. "Sir," he said to Dutch, "that's an insult."

Now, I ought to say right here that my sympathies was with Dutch. He weren't a bad feller. Fact is, Dutch took good care of me, Pa, my aunt and uncle, and several Indian squaws, which he used for rootin'-tootin' purpose. He had two younger brothers, William and Drury, and he kept them in chips, plus he sent money back to his maw in Germany, plus fed and clothed all the various squaws and assorted whores his brother William drug in from Mosquite Creek and thereabouts, which was considerable, for William weren't worth a shit and made friends with everybody in Kansas Territory but his own wife and children. Not to mention Dutch had a stall barn, several cows and chickens, two mules, two horses, a slaughterhouse, and a tavern. Dutch had a lot on him. He didn't sleep but two or three hours a night. Fact is, looking back, Dutch Henry was something like a slave himself.

He backed off the Old Man a step, still holding that pepperbox pointed to the floor, and said, "Get down off that chair."

The barber's chair was set on a wood pallet. The Old Man slowly stepped off it. Dutch turned to the bartender and said, "Hand me a Bible," which the bartender done. Then he stepped up to the Old Man, holding the Bible in one hand and his pepperbox in the other.

"I'm gonna make you swear on this Bible that you is for slavery and the U.S. Constitution," he said. "If you do that, you old bag, you can walk outta here none the worse. But if you're a lying, blue-bellied Free Stater, I'mma bust you across the head so hard with this pistol, yellow'll come out your ears. Place your hand on that," he said.

Now, I was to see quite a bit of Old John Brown in the coming years. And he done some murderous, terrible things. But one thing the Old Man couldn't do good was fib—especially with his hand on the Bible. He was in a spot. He throwed his hand on the Bible and for the first time, looked downright tight.

"What's your name?" Dutch said.

"Shubel Isaac."

"I thought you said it was Shubel Morgan."

"Isaac's my middle name," he said.

"How many names you got?"

"How many I need?"

The talk had stirred up an old drunk named Dirk, who was asleep at a corner table nearby. Dirk sat up, squinted across the room, and blurted, "Why, Dutch, that looks like Old John Brown there."

When he said that, Dutch's brothers, William and Drury, and a young feller named James Doyle—all three would draw their last breath in another day—got up from their table near the door and drawed their Colts on the Old Man, surrounding him.

"Is that true?" Dutch asked.

"Is what true?" the Old Man said.

"Is you Old Man Brown?"

"Did I say I was?"

"So you ain't him," Dutch said. He seemed relieved. "Who are you then?"

"I'm the child of my Maker."

"You too old to be a child. You Old John Brown or not?"

"I'm whoever the Lord wants me to be."

Dutch throwed the Bible down and pushed that pepperbox

right on the Old Man's neck and cocked it. "Stop shitting around, you God-damned potato-head! Old Man Brown. Is you him or not?"

Now, in all the years I knowed him, Old John Brown never got excitable, even in matters of death—his or the next man's— unless the subject of the Lord come up. And seeing Dutch Henry fling that Bible to the floor and swearing the Lord's name in vain, that done a number on him. The Old Man plain couldn't stand it. His face got tight. Next when he spoke, he weren't talking like an Irishman no more. He spoke in his real voice. High. Thin. Taut as gauge wire.

"You bite your tongue when you swear about our Maker," he said coolly, "lest by the power of His Holy Grace, I be commanded to deliver redemption on His behalf. And then that pistol you holding there won't be worth a cent. The Lord will lift it out your hand."

"Cut the jitter and tell me your name, God dammit."

"Don't swear God's name again, sir."

"Shit! I'll swear his cock-dragging God-damn name whenever I God-damn well please! I'll holler it up a dead hog's ass and then shove it down your shit-eating Yank throat, ya God-damned nigger turned inside out!"

That roused the Old Man, and quick as you can tell it, he throwed off that barber's bib and flashed the butt end of a Sharps rifle beneath his coat. He moved with the speed of a rattler, but Dutch already had his pistol barrel at the Old Man's throat, and he didn't have to do nothing but drop the hammer on it.

Which he did.

Now that pepperbox is a fussy pistol. It ain't dependable like a Colt or a regular repeater. It's a powder cap gun. It needs to be dry, and all that sweating and swearing must've sprouted water on Dutch's big hands, is the only way I can call it, for when Dutch pulled the go switch, the gun hollered "Kaw!" and misfired. One barrel exploded and peeled sideways. Dutch dropped it and fell to the floor, bellowing like a calf, his hand nearly blowed off.

The other three fellers holding their Colts on Old Brown had stepped back momentarily to keep their faces clear of the Old Man's brains, which they expected to splatter across the room any minute, and now all three found themselves gaping at the hot end of a Sharps rifle, which the old fart coolly drawed out all the way.

"I told you the Lord would draw it out your hand," he said, "for the King of Kings eliminates all pesters." He stuck that Sharps in Dutch's neck and drawed the hammer back all the way, then looked at them three other fellers and said, "Lay them pistols down on the floor or here goes."

They done as he said, at which point he turned to the tavern, still holding his rifle, and hollered out, "I'm John Brown. Captain of the Pottawatomie Rifles. I come with the Lord's blessing to free every colored man in this territory. Any man who stands against me will eat grape and powder."

Well, there must've been half a dozen drummers bearing six-shooters standing 'round that room, and nary a man reached for his heater, for the Old Man was cool as smoke and all business. He throwed his eyes about the room and said calmly, "Every Negro in here, those of you that's hiding, come on out. You is now free. Follow me. Don't be afraid, children."

Well, there was several coloreds in that room, some on errands or tending to their masters, most of 'em hiding under the tables, shaking and waiting for the blasting to start, and when he spoke them words, why, they popped up and took off, every single one of 'em. Out the door they went. You didn't see nothing but the backs of their heads, hauling ass home.

The Old Man watched them scatter. "They is not yet saved to the Lord," he grumbled. But he weren't finished in the freeing business, for he wheeled around to Pa, who stood there, trembling in his boots, saying "Lawdy, Lawdy . . ."

This the Old Man took to be some kind of volunteering, for Pa had said "Lawd" and *he'd* said "Lord," which I reckon was agreement enough. He clapped Pa on the back, pleased as punch.

"Friend," he said, "you has made a wise choice. You and your tragic octoroon daughter here is blessed for accepting our blessed Redeemer's purpose for you to live free and clear, and thus not spend the rest of your lives in this den of iniquity here with these sinning savages. You is now free. Walk out the back door while I hold my rifle on these heathens, and I will lead you to freedom in the name of the King of Zion!"

Now, I don't know about Pa, but between all that mumbling about kings and heathens and Zions and so forth, and with him waving that Sharps rifle around, I somehow got stuck at the "daughter" section of that speech. True, I wore a potato sack like most colored boys did in them days, and my light skin and curly hair to boot made me the fun of several boys about town, though I evened things out with my fists against those that I could. But everybody in Dutch's, even the Indians, knowed I was a boy. I weren't even partial to girls at that age, being that I was raised in a tavern where most of the women smoked cigars, drunk gut sauce, and stunk to high heaven like men. But even those lowly types, who was so braced on joy juice they wouldn't know a boll weevil from a cotton ball and couldn't tell one colored from the other, knowed the difference between me and a girl. I opened my mouth to correct the Old Man on that notion, but right then a wave of high-pitched whining seemed to cover the room, and I couldn't holler past it. It was only after a few moments that I realized that all that bellowing and wailing was coming from my own throat, and I confess here I lost my water.

Pa was panicked. He stood there shaking like a shuck of corn. "Massa, my Henry ain't a—"

"We've no time to rationalize your thoughts of mental dependency, sir!" the Old Man snapped, cutting Pa off, still holding the rifle on the room. "We have to move. Courageous friend, I will take you and your Henrietta to safety." See, my true name is Henry Shackleford. But the Old Man heard Pa say "Henry ain't a," and took it to be "Henrietta," which is how the Old Man's mind worked. Whatever he believed, he believed. It didn't matter to him whether it was really true or not. He just changed the truth till it fit him. He was a real white man.

"But my s—"

"Courage, friend," he said to Pa, "for we has a ram in the bush. Remember Joel first chapter, fourth verse: 'That which the palmerworm hath left, hath the locust eaten. And that which the locust hath left, hath the cankerworm eaten. And that which the cankerworm hath left, hath the caterpillar eaten.'"

"What's that mean?" Pa asked.

"You'll be eaten alive if you stay here."

"But my child here ain't no gi—"

"Shush!" said the Old Man. "We can't tarry. We can talk raising her to the Holy Word later."

He grabbed my hand and, still holding that Sharps at the

ready, backed toward the rear door. I heard horses charging down the back alley. When he got to the door, he released my hand for a moment to fling it open, and as he did, Pa charged him.

At the same time, Dutch lunged for one of the Colts laying on the floor, snatched it up, pointed the hot end at the Old Man, and fired.

The bullet missed the Old Man and struck the edge of the door, sending a sliver of wood about eight inches long out sideways. The sliver jutted out the side of the door like a knife, straight horizontal, about chest high—and Pa runned right into it. Right into his chest it went.

He staggered back, dropped to the floor, and blowed out his spark right there.

By now the clabbering of horses making their way down the alley at hot speed was on us, and the Old Man kicked the door open wide.

Dutch Henry, setting on the floor, hollered, "Nigger thief! You owe me twelve hundred dollars!"

"Charge it to the Lord, heathen," the Old Man said. Then he picked me up with one hand, stepped into the alley, and we was gone.

2

The Good Lord Bird

We drove hard out of town, left the beaten California Trail, and headed straight into Kansas flatlands. There was three of them, the Old Man and two young riders. The two riders charged ahead of us on pintos, and the Old Man and me bounced behind them atop a painted horse with one blue eye and one brown eye. That horse belonged to Dutch. So the Old Man was a horse thief as well.

We rode hard for a couple of hours. The cottonwoods showed some distance off, and the hot wind beat against my face as we flew along. Kansas Territory is flat, wide-open hot earth to the sight, but when you making hot speed atop a horse, it's hard riding. My arse took a pretty strong beating bouncing atop that horse's back, for I had never ridden one before. It knotted up to about the size of a small bun, and just when I thought I couldn't bear it no more, we hit the top of a rise and stopped at a crude camp. It was a clearing with a three-sided tent held up by sticks, stretched along a rock wall with the remnants of a campfire. The Old Man stepped off the horse and helped me down.

"Time to water these horses and rest, my child," he said. "We can't tarry. The others is coming soon." He looked at me for a moment, his wrinkled face frowned up. I reckon he felt guilty for kidnapping me and getting my Pa kilt, for he seemed a little funny about the eyes, and stared at me a long time. Finally he begun ransacking his flea-bitten coat pocket. He rummaged through it and pulled out what appeared to be a ball covered with feathers. He dusted it off and said, "I reckon you is not feeling righteous about what has just transpired thereabouts, but in the name of freedom we is all soldiers of the cross and thus the enemy of slavery. Like as not, you now believes you has no family or may ne'er see what family you has ever again. But the fact is, you is in the human family and is welcome to this one as any. I like that you might hold this, my child, as a token of your newfound freedom and family, joining us as freedom fighters, even though you is a girl and we need to get rid of you as soon as possible."

He held the thing out to me. I didn't want whatever it was, but, being that he was white and hurrumped and hawed over the dang thing so much, I reckon I had to take it. It was an onion. Dried, dusty, covered with feathers, cobwebs, lint, and other junk from his pocket. That thing looked worse than dried mule shit. The Old Man had a high tolerance for junk, and in later years, I was to see him produce from his pockets enough odds and ends to fill a five-gallon barrel, but, being that this had been a scouting expedition to Dutch's, he'd been traveling light.

I took the thing and held it, frightened and afraid, so, not knowing what he wanted, I reckoned he wanted me to eat it. I didn't want to, of course. But I was hungry from the long ride and I was also his prisoner, after all, so I bit into it. That thing tasted foul as the devil. It went down my gullet like a stone, but I got the job done in seconds.

The Old Man's eyes widened, and for the first time I seen a look of sheer panic run across his old face, which I took for displeasure, though in later years I learned a look from him could mean just about anything you could render it to.

"That there's my good-luck charm you just swallowed," he grunted. "I had that thing for fourteen months and nar a knife has nicked me nar bullet touched my flesh. I reckon the Lord must mean it to be a sign for me to lose it. The Bible says it: 'Hold no idle objects between thouest and me.' But even a God-fearing man like myself has a pocketful of sins that flagellate betwixt my head—and my thighs too, truth be to tell it, for I has twenty-two children, twelve of them living, Little Onion. But my good luck lives between your ears now; you has swallowed in your gut my redemption and sin, eatin' my sin just like Jesus Christ munched on the sins of the world so that you and I might live. Let that be a lesson to me, old man that I am, for allowing sacrilegious objects to stand between me and the great King of Kings."

I didn't make head nor tails of what he was saying, for I was to learn that Old John Brown could work the Lord into just about any aspect of his comings and goings in life, including using the privy. That's one reason I weren't a believer, having been raised by my Pa, who was a believer and a lunatic, and them things seemed to run together. But it weren't my place to argue with a white man, especially one who was my kidnapper, so I kept my lips closed.

"Since you has shown me the way of the Maker and is now

my good-luck charm, Little Onion, I will give you good fortune as well, and hereby absolve myself of all these trickera-
tions and good-luck baubles which is the devil's work." And
here he dug in his pockets and produced a thimble, a root, two
empty tin cans, three Indian arrowheads, an apple peeler, a
dried-up boll weevil, and a bent pocketknife. He throwed them
all in a sack and gived it to me.

"Hold these things, and may they bring you good fortune
till you come along and meet the soul that shows you the way
of the Maker, Onion. For the prophet may cometh in the form
of man, boy, or a woman-child, as in the case of you, and each
person must attain his wisdom of the Almighty when they
meets their own prophet maker of the word who holds the
sign to redemption at the ready, and that includes you, Little
Onion." Then he throwed in there, "And may you meet another
Little Onion in your travels, so that *she* might be your good-
luck charm and thus rid you of these baubles and make you
truly free like me."

Here he produced the last from his pocket, an odd, long
black-and-white feather, and throwed the feather in my head,
tucked it right in my curly napped hair, then paused a moment,
reflecting, staring at that feather in my head. "Feather of a
Good Lord Bird. Now, that's special. I don't feel bad about it
neither, giving my special thing to you. The Bible says: 'Take
that which is special from thine own hand, and giveth to the
needy, and you moveth in the Lord's path.' That's the secret,
Little Onion. But just so you know, you ought not to believe
too much in heathen things. And don't stretch the Great Rul-
er's word too much. You stretch it here, stretch it there, before
you know it, it's full-out devilment. We being fighters of His
righteous Holy Word, we is allowed a few indulgences, like

charms and so forth. But we ought not take too much advantage. Understand?"

I didn't know what the hell he was talking about, but, being he was a lunatic, I nodded my head yes.

That seemed to please him, and he thrust his head toward the sky and said, "Teach thy children the ways of our King of Kings, and they shall not depart from it. I hear Thee, oh great Haymaker, and I thank Thee for blessing us every minute of every day."

I don't know but that God said to him aye-aye and proper, for after that, the Old Man seemed satisfied with the whole bit and forgot about me instantly. He turned away and pulled a huge canvas map from his saddlebag. He clopped to the canvas lean-to in his worn boots, plopped down on the ground under it, and stuck his head in the map without saying another word. As an afterthought, he motioned for me to sit on the ground next to him, which I done.

By now the two other riders had dismounted and come up, and by the look of it, they was the Old Man's sons, for they was nearly ugly as him. The first was a huge, strapping youth about twenty years old. He was taller than Dutch, six feet four inches tall without his boots. He had more weapons hanging off him than I ever seen one man carry: two heavy seven-shot pistols strapped to his thighs by leather—that was the first I ever saw such a thing. Plus a broadsword, a squirrel gun, a buckshot rifle, a buck knife, and a Sharps rifle. When he moved around, he rattled like a hardware store. He was an altogether fearsome sight. His name, I later come to know, was Frederick. The second was shorter, more stocky, with red hair and a crippled arm, a good bit older. That was Owen. Neither one of 'em spoke, but waited for the Old Man to speak.

"Water these horses and scare us up a fire," he said.

The Old Man's words got them movin' while I sat in the lean-to next to him. I was frightfully hungry despite being kidnapped, and I must say my first hours of freedom under John Brown was like my last hours of freedom under him: I was hungrier than I ever was as a slave.

The Old Man settled his back against the wall under the canvas tent and kept his face to the map. The camp, though empty, had been used heavily. Several guns and effects lay about. The place was odorous, downright ripe, and the smell brung mosquitoes, which swarmed about in thick black clouds. One of them clouds settled on me and the mosquitoes had at me right away something terrible. As I swatted at them, several mice scurried about in a rock crevice on the wall behind the Old Man, just over his shoulder. One of the mice fell off the rock crevice directly onto the Old Man's map. The Old Man studied it a moment, and *it* studied him. The Old Man had a way with every animal under God's creation. Later I was to see how he could pick up a baby lamb and lead it to slaughter with kindness and affection, could tame a horse just by gently shaking and talking to it, and could lead the most stubborn mule out of mud stuck up to its neck like it was nothing. He carefully picked up the mouse and gently placed it back in the rock crevice with the rest of its brother mice, and they set there quiet as pups, peeking over the Old Man's shoulder as he stared at his map. I reckoned they was like me. They wanted to know where they was, so I asked it.

"Middle Creek," he grunted. He didn't seem in a talking mood now. He snapped at his boys, "Feed this child."

The big one, Frederick, he moved 'round the fire and come up to me. He had so many weapons on him, he sounded like a marching band. He looked down, friendly, and said, "What's your name?"

Well, that was a problem, being that I didn't have no time to think of a girl one.

"Henrietta," the Old Man blurted out from his map. "Slave but now free," he said proudly. "I calls her Little Onion henceforth for my own reasons." He winked at me. "This poor girl's Pa was killed right before her eyes by that ruffian Dutch Henry. Rascal that he is, I would have sent a charge through him, but I was in a hurry."

I noted the Old Man hadn't said a word about scrapin' by with his own life, but the thought of Pa being run clean through with that wood pike made me weepy, and I wiped my nose and busted into tears.

"Now, now, Onion," the Old Man said. "We're gonna straighten you out right away." He leaned over and dug out his saddlebag again, rumbled through it, and brung out yet another gift, this time a rumpled, flea-bitten dress and bonnet. "I got this for my daughter Ellen's birthday," he said. "It's store-bought. But I reckon she'd be happy to give it to a pretty girl like you, as a gift to your freedom."

I was ready to give up the charade then, for while I weren't particular about eating the flea-bitten onion that lived in his pocket, ain't no way in God's kingdom was I gonna put on that dress and bonnet. Not in no way, shape, form, or fashion was I gonna do it. But my arse was on the line, and while it's a small arse, it do cover my backside and thus I am fond of it. Plus, he was an outlaw, and I was his prisoner. I was in a quandary, and my tears busted forth again, which worked out perfect, for it moved them all to my favor, and I seen right off that crying and squalling was part of the game of being a girl.

"It's all right," the Old Man said, "you ain't got but to thank the Good Lord for His kindnesses. You don't owe me nothing."

Well, I took the dress, excused myself, and went into the woods a ways and throwed that nonsense on. The bonnet I couldn't tie proper atop my head, but I mashed it on some kind of way. The dress come down to my feet, for the Old Man's children was stout giants to the last. Even the shortest of his daughters stood nearly six feet fully growed without her shoes, and head and shoulders above yours truly, for I followed my Pa in the size department. But I got the whole business fixed right as I could, then emerged from behind the tree and managed to say, "Thank you, marse."

"I ain't master to you, Onion," he said. "You just as free as the birds run." He turned to Frederick and said, "Fred, take my horse and teach Onion here to ride, for the enemy will be hurrying our way soon. There's a war on. We can't tarry."

That was the first I heard the word *war*. First I ever heard of it, but at the moment my mind was on my own freedom. I was looking to jump back to Dutch's.

Fred led me to Dutch's old pinto, the one me and the Old Man was riding, prompted me on it, then led my horse along by the reins, holding it steady, while riding his. As we rode, Fred talked. He was a chatterbox. He was twice my age, but I seen right off that he had half a loaf, if you get my drift; he was slow in his mind. He had a bubble in his head. He chatted about nothing, for he couldn't fix his mind on one thing more than a minute. We plodded along like that for a while, him blabbing and me quiet, till he piped up, "You like pheasant?"

"Yes, massa," I said.

"I ain't your massa, Onion."

"Yes, sir," I said, for I was of the habit.

"Don't call me sir."

"Yes, sir."

"Okay. Then I'll call you missy."

"Okay, sir."

"If you keep calling me sir, I'll keep calling you missy," he said.

"Yes, sir."

This went on for several minutes, us sirring and missying one another, till finally I got so hot I wanted to take a rock and bust him across the head with it, but he was white and I was not, so I busted into tears again.

My tears throwed Fred. He stopped the horse and said, "I am sorry, Henrietta. I takes back every word I said."

I quit bawling and we headed forth again, pacing slowly. We rode about a half mile down the creek where the cottonwood thickets stopped. The clearing met woods near a set of rocks and wide trees. We dismounted and Fred looked around the area. "We can leave the horses here," he said.

I seen a chance to jump. My mind was on escape, so I said, "I got to toilet, but a girl needs a bit of privacy." I near choked calling myself a member of the opposite nature, but lying come natural to me in them times. Truth is, lying come natural to all Negroes during slave time, for no man or woman in bondage ever prospered stating their true thoughts to the boss. Much of colored life was an act, and the Negroes that sawed wood and said nothing lived the longest. So I weren't going to tell him nothing about me being a boy. But everybody under God's sun, man or woman, white or colored, got to go to the toilet, and I really did have to answer nature's call. Since Fred was slow as gravy in his mind, I also seen a chance to jump.

"'Deed a girl does need her privacy, Little Onion," he said. He tied our horses to a low-hanging tree branch.

"I hopes you is a gentleman," I said, for I had seen white women from New England speak in that manner when their wagon trains stopped off at Dutch's and they had to use his outdoor privy, after which they usually come busting out the door coughing with their hair curled like fried bacon, for the odor of that thing could curdle cheese.

"I surely am," he said, and walked off a little while I slipped behind a nearby tree to do my business. Being a gentleman, he walked off a good thirty yards or so, his back to me, staring off at the trees, smiling, for he never weren't nothing but pleasant in all the time I knowed him.

I ducked behind a tree, done my business, and busted out from behind that tree running. I come out flying. I leaped atop Dutch's cockeyed pinto and spurred her up, for that horse would know the way home.

Problem was, that beast didn't know me from Adam. Fred had led her by the reins, but once I was on her myself, the horse knowed I weren't a rider. She raised up and lunged hard as she could and sent me flying. I went airborne, struck my head on a rock, and got knocked cold.

When I come to, Fred was standing over me, and he weren't smiling no more neither. The fall had throwed my dress up around my head, and my new bonnet was turned 'round backward. I ought to mention here that I had never known nor worn undergarments as a child, having been raised in a tavern of lowlifes, elbow benders, and bullyboys. My privates was in plain sight. I quickly throwed the dress back down to my ankles and sat up.

Fred seemed confused. He weren't all the way there in his mind, thank God. His brains was muddy. His cheese had pretty much slid off his biscuit. He said, "Are you a sissy?"

"Why, if you have to ask," I said, "I don't know."

Fred blinked and said slowly, "Father says I ain't the sharpest knife in the drawer, and lots of things confuse me."

"Me too," I said.

"When we get back, maybe we can put the question to Father."

"'Bout what?"

"'Bout sissies."

"I wouldn't do that," I said quickly, "being that he's got a lot on his mind, fighting a war and all."

Fred considered it. "You're right. Plus, Pa don't suffer foolishness easily. What do the Bible say 'bout sissies?"

"I don't know. I can't read," I said.

That cheered him. "Me neither!" he said brightly. "I'm the only one of my brothers and sisters who can't do that." He seemed happy I was dumb as him. He said, "Follow me. I'mma show you something."

We left the horses and I followed him through some dense thickets. After pushing in a ways, he shushed me with his finger and we crept forward silent. We followed a thick patch of bushes to a clearing and he froze. He stood silent like that, listening. I heard a tapping noise. We moved toward it till Fred spotted what he wanted and pointed.

Up at the top of a thick birch, a woodpecker hammered away. He was a good-sized feller. Black and white, with a touch of red around him.

"Ever seen one of them?" he asked.

"I wouldn't know one bird from the next."

Fred stared up at it. "They call that a Good Lord Bird," he said. "It's so pretty that when man sees it, he says, 'Good Lord.'"

He watched it. That stupid thing darn near hypnotized him, and I had a mind to break for it then, but he was too close. "I can catch or trap just about any bird there is," he said. "But that one there . . . that's an angel. They say a feather from a Good Lord Bird'll bring you understanding that'll last your whole life. Understanding is what I lacks, Onion. Memories and things."

"Whyn't you catch it, then?"

He ignored me, watching through the thick forest as the bird hammered away. "Can't. Them things is shy. Plus, Father says you ought not to believe in baubles and heathen stuff."

How do you like that? Stuffed in my pocket was the very sack his own Pa gave me with his own baubles and charms, including a feather that looked like it come off that very creature we was staring at.

I had my eye on jumping, and since he was loony, I figured to confound him further and keep his mind off seeing I was a boy, and also give me a better chance to get away. I rummaged through my small gunnysack and pulled out that very same feather his Pa gave me and offered it to him. That floored him.

"Where'd you get that?"

"I ain't allowed to say. But it's yours."

Well, that just knocked him flat. Now, truth is, I didn't know whether that thing come from a Good Lord Bird or not. His Pa *said* it did, but I didn't know whether his Old Man told the truth or not, for he was a kidnapper, plus white folks was full of tricks in them days, and I was a liar myself, and one liar don't trust another. But it seemed close enough. It was black, had a bit of red and white in it. But it could'a come from an eagle or a plain hummingbird for all I know. Whatever it was, it pleased Fred something terrible and he aimed to return the favor. "Now I'mma show you something special," he said. "Follow me."

I followed him back to the horses, whereupon he dumped his seven-shooters, his sword, gun belt, and rifles all on the ground. He pulled out from his saddlebag a blanket, a handful of dried corn, and an oak stick. He said, "We can't shoot out here, for the enemy might hear. But I'll show you how to catch pheasant without firing a shot."

He led me to a hollowed-out tree stump. He laid the corn along the ground in a straight line leading into the stump. He throwed a few pieces inside, then chose a spot not too far from the stump to sit. With his knife, he cut two peepholes in the blanket—one for him and one for me—then throwed it over us. "Every game bird in the world is afraid of man," he whispered. "But with a blanket over you, you ain't a man anymore."

I wanted to say I weren't feeling like a man no matter how the cut came or went, but I kept my peace. We sat like that under the blanket, staring out, and after a while I growed tired and leaned on him and fell asleep.

I was awakened by Fred stirring. I peeked through my hole and, sure enough, a pheasant had dropped by to help himself to Fred's corn. He followed that line of dried corn just as you please right into the tree hollow. When he stuck his head inside it, Fred snapped the oak twig he was holding. The pheasant froze at the sound, and quick as I can tell it, Fred throwed the blanket on him, grabbed him, and snapped his neck.

We caught two more pheasants in this manner and headed back to camp. When we arrived, Owen and the Old Man was busy arguing about the Old Man's map, and sent us to ready

our catch for dinner. As we readied the birds at the campfire, I
got worried about Fred blabbing about what he seen and said,
"Fred, you remembers our deal?"

"'Bout what?"

"'Bout nothing," I said. "But you probably ought not tell nobody what I gived you," I murmured.

He nodded. "Your gift's giving me more understanding even
as I speak it, Onion. I am grateful to you and won't tell a soul."

I felt bad for him, thin-headed as he was, and him trusting
me, not knowing I was a boy and planned to jump. His Pa
already gived that feather to me and told me not to tell it.
And I gived that feather to his son and told *him* not to tell.
They didn't know what to believe, is how I figured it. Back in
them days white folks told niggers more than they told each
other, for they knowed Negroes couldn't do nothing but say,
"Uh-huh," and "Ummmm," and go on about their own troubled
business. That made white folks subject to trickeration in my
mind. Colored was always two steps ahead of white folks in
that department, having thunk through every possibility of
how to get along without being seen and making sure their lies
match up with what white folks wanted. Your basic white man
is a fool, is how I thought, and I held Fred in that number.

But I was wrong, for Fred weren't a complete fool. Nor was
his Pa. The bigger fool turned out to be yours truly, for thinking they was fools in the first place. That's how it goes when
you place another man to judgment. You get stretched out
wrong to ruination, and that would cost me down the road.

3

The Old Man's Army

No sooner had we roasted those pheasants than the rest of the Old Man's men straggled in. Old John Brown's fearsome army which I heard so much about weren't nothing but a ragtag assortment of fifteen of the scrawniest, bummiest, saddest-looking individuals you ever saw. They were young, and to a man skinny as horsehair in a glass of milk. There was a Jew foreigner, an Indian, and a few other assorted no-gooders. They were downright ugly, poor men. They'd been on a raid of some sort, for they clattered into camp on a wagon that clanged like a dry-goods store, with pots, cups, saucers, furniture, card tables, spindles, leather strips, bits of this and that hanging off the sides.

They brung everything but food, and the aroma of the birds drawed them to the fire right off. They stood around it in a circle. One of 'em, the Jew named Weiner, a thin, taut, lean feller wearing suspenders, was bearing a newspaper which he gived to Owen. "Hold it till after we eat," he said, staring at the fire. "Otherwise the Captain will want to ride off directly."

But the Old Man come up and seen him and he snatched the newspaper. "Mr. Weiner, no doubt the news from Lawrence is pressing," he said. "But worry not, for I has had a vision on it already." He turned to the others and said, "Men, before you stuff your gullets, let us thank our Holy Provider for these victuals, since we is after all spreading freedom in His name."

The men stood in a circle with their heads bowed while the Old Man stood in the center, hat in hand, bowing his wrinkled old face over the roasted birds and the fire.

Thirty minutes later the fire was out, the dinner as cold as Dick's ice house, and he was still prattling on. I ought to give you a full sample of Old John Brown's prayers, but I reckon they wouldn't make sense to the dear reader who's no doubt setting in a warm church basement a hundred years distant, reading these words wearing Stacy Adams shoes and a fake fur coat, and not having to do no more than waddle over to the wall and flick a button to warm his arse and heat his coffee. The Old Man's prayers was more sight than sound, really, more sense than sensibility. You had to be there: the aroma of burnt pheasant rolling through the air, the wide, Kansas prairie about, the smell of buffalo dung, the mosquitoes and wind eating at you one way, and him chawing at the wind the other. He was a plain terror in the praying department. Just when he seemed to wrap up one thought, another come tumbling out and crashed up against the first, and then another crashed up against that one, and after a while they all bumped and crashed and commingled against one another till you didn't know who was who and why he was praying it, for the whole thing come together like the tornadoes that whipped across the plains, gathering up the sagebrush and boll weevils and homesteads and tossing them about like dust. The effort of it drawed his sweat, which poured down his leathery neck and runned down his shirt, while he spouted about burnt offerings and blood from the lamp stand of Jesus and so forth; all the while that dress of mine itched to high heaven and the mosquitoes gnawed at my guts, eating me alive. Finally Owen murmured, "Pa! We got to get up the trail! There's a posse riding!"

That brung the Old Man to his senses. He coughed, throwed out a couple more Hail Marys and Thank You Lords, then wound the whole business down. "I ought to give Thee a full prayer," he grumbled, "rather than just a few bumbling words to our Great Redeemer Who hath paid in blood and to Whose service we is obliged." He was given to saying "thees" and "thous" in his talks.

The men collapsed on their haunches and ate while the Old Man read the newspaper. As he done so, his face darkened, and after a few moments he balled the newspaper up in a large, wrinkled fist and shouted, "Why, they attacked our man!"

"Who's that?" Owen asked.

"Our man in Congress!" He uncrinkled the newspaper and read it aloud to everyone. From what I could gather, two fellers got into a wrangle about slavery in the top hall of the U.S. government in Washington, D.C., and one of them knocked the other cold. Seemed like a feller from Massachusetts named Sumner got the worst end of it, being that a feller from South Carolina broke his cane over Sumner's head and got a bunch of new canes in the mail from people that liked his side of the whole bit.

The Old Man throwed the newspaper down. "Roust up the horses and break down the tent. We shall strike back tonight. Hurry, men, we have work to do!"

Well, them men was in no hurry to leave, being they'd just

got there and was busy stuffing their faces. "What difference do it make," one feller said. "It can wait a day."

"The Negro has waited two hundred years," the Old Man said.

The feller snorted. "Let 'em wait. There ain't enough food in this camp." He was a raggedy-dressed feller like the rest, but he was a thick man, bearing a six-shooter and real riding pants. He had a thick, wrinkled neck of a turkey buzzard, and he kept his mouth movin' on that pheasant as he talked.

"We is not out here to eat, Rev. Martin," the Old Man said.

"Just because two fools have a fight in Congress don't mean nothing," he said. "We has our own fights out here."

"Rev. Martin, you is on the wrong side of understanding," the Captain said.

The Reverend munched away and said, "I aim to better my reading so I don't have to hear your interpretations of things, Captain, which I is no longer sure of. Every time I ride out and come back to your camp, you got another face rooting around, eating. We ain't got enough food for the men here already." He nodded at me. "Who's that there?"

I was stuffing my face with bird fast as I could, for I had my own plan on escaping.

"Rev. Martin, that's Onion," Frederick announced proudly.

"Where'd she come from?" he asked.

"Stolen from Dutch Henry's Tavern."

The Reverend's eyes widened and he turned to the Old Man. "Of all the troublemakers in this country, why'd you pick a fight with him?"

"I didn't pick no fight," the Old Man said. "I went to scout his territory."

"Well, you done scouted trouble. I wouldn't pick a fight

with Dutch for a box of crackers. I ain't come to this country to shoot it out with him."

"Nobody's shooting nothing," the Old Man said. "We are riding for redemption, and the Bible says it, 'Hold truth to thine own man's face, and the Lord shall deliver.'"

"Don't pick no boil with me about the Bible," the Reverend snorted. "I know more about it than any man here."

He bit off the wrong end then, for in my 111 years on God's green earth, I never knowed a man who could spout the Bible off better than Old John Brown. The Old Man straightened up, reared back, and throwed off half a dozen Bible verses right in the Reverend's face, and when the Reverend tried to back-fire with a couple of his own, the Old Man drowned him out with half dozen more that was better than the first. Just mowed him down. The Rev was outgunned.

"All right already," he snapped. "But you sporting trouble. Dutch got a mess of Missouri redshirts 'round his place. You just gived him a reason to set 'em loose. He'll come after us hard."

"Let him come," the Old Man said. "Onion's part of my family, and I aim to keep her free."

"She ain't part of mine," the Reverend said. He sucked a pheasant bone and tossed it down coolly, licking his fingers. "I'm fighting to free Kansas, not to steal oily-headed niggers like this one."

The Old Man said icily, "I thought you was a Free State man, Reverend."

"I *am* a Free State man," the Reverend said. "That ain't got nothing to do with getting aired out for stealing somebody's nigger."

"You shouldn't'a rode with this company if you were planning to peck and hoot 'bout the colored being free," Old Man Brown said.

"I rode with you out of common interest."

"Well, my interest is freeing the colored in this territory. I'm an abolitionist through and through."

Now as them two was wrangling, most of the men had finished up eating and sat on their haunches watching.

"That's Dutch's nigger. Bought and paid for!"

"He'll forget about it soon enough."

"He won't forget that kind of wrong."

"Then I'll clear his memory of it when he comes."

The Indian, Ottawa Jones, stepped to the Captain and said, "Dutch ain't a bad sort, Captain. He done some work for me before he got his tavern. He weren't for slavery then. He should have the chance to change his mind."

"You just defending him 'cause you had a slave or two yourself," another man piped up.

"You're a liar," Jones said.

That started more disruption, with several leaning this way and that, some with the Old Man, others with the Reverend. The Old Man listened in silence and finally waved 'em quiet.

"I aim to strike a blow at the slavers. We know what they done. They killed Charles Dow. They sent Joe Hamilton to our Maker right in front of his wife. They raped Willamena Tompkin. They're rapists. Pillagers. Sinners, all. Destroying this whole territory. The Good Book says, 'Hold thine enemy to his own fire.' Dutch Henry is an enemy. But I'll allow if he don't get in the way, he won't suffer injury from me."

"I ain't going up against Dutch," Reverend Martin said. "I got no hank with him."

"Me neither," another man said. "Dutch gave me a horse on

credit. Plus this here army's got too many angles to it. I didn't
come all the way from Connecticut to ride with Jews."

The Jew Weiner, standing next to Jones, stepped toward the
man with his fists balled. "Peabody, you open your mouth sideways again, I'll bust you straddle-legged."

"That's enough," the Old Man said. "We riding on Osawatomie tomorrow night. That's where Pro Slavers are. Whoever
wants to ride, come on. Whoever don't want to can go home.
But go north by way of Lawrence. I don't want anyone riding
south to warn Dutch."

"You wanna ride against Dutch, go 'head," the Reverend
said. "I won't get in the way. But nobody tells me where to
ride—especially not over a nappy-headed, bird-gobbling nigger." He placed his hand on his shooter, which hung on his left
side. Peabody and a couple of other men stepped aside with
him, and suddenly, just like that, the Old Man's army split in
half, one side standing with the Old Man, the other angling
behind the Rev.

There was a rustle in the crowd behind the Old Man, and
the Reverend's eyes growed to the size of silver dollars, for Fred
came at him and he was hot, drawing his hardware as he come.
He handled them big seven-shooters like twigs. Quick as you
can tell it, he was on the Reverend and mashed both his seven-
shooters on the Reverend's chest. I heard the cocks snap back
on both of them.

"If you say another word about my friend Onion here, I'll
bust a charge in your chest," he said.

The sound of the Old Man's voice stopped him. "Frederick!"
Fred froze, pistols drawn out.

"Leave him be."

Frederick stepped away. The Reverend huffed and glared,

but he didn't pull his metal, and he was wise not to, for Owen had stepped out the crowd, and so had two of Brown's other sons. They was a rough bunch, them Browns. They was holy as Jesus to a man. They didn't swear, didn't drink. Didn't cuss. But God help you if you crossed 'em, for they didn't take no back-water off nobody. Once they decided something, it was done.

The Reverend gathered his rifle and things, got on his horse, and hit off without a word. Peabody and two others followed. They rode north out the campgrounds, the way the Captain told 'em to do.

The Old Man, Ottawa Jones the Indian, and the Jew Weiner stood together and watched Reverend Martin and his men leave.

"You ought to duck-hunt that Reverend in his back while you got the chance," Weiner said. "He won't be out of sight five minutes before he turns south and heads to Dutch's Crossing. He'll hoot and holler to Dutch loud as he can."

"Let him holler," the Old Man said. "I want everyone to know what I aim to do."

But he made a mistake letting the Reverend go that day, and it would cost him down the line.

4

Massacre

The Old Man's plan to attack Osawatomie got delayed, like most things he done, and we spent the next few days wandering the county, stealing from Pro Slavers so we could eat. The Old Man was always broke and delayed in everything. For one thing, he had a lot of men to feed, twelve in all. That's a lot. I sometimes reckon that Old John Brown wouldn't have started no trouble at all if he didn't have to feed so many people all the time. Even at home he had twelve children there, not to mention his wife and various neighbors who throwed in with him, from what I'm told. That's a lot to feed. That'll make anyone mad at anything. Weiner fed us at his trade store in Kinniwick. But after two days, his wife was done with the slavery fight and throwed us out. "We'll be slaves ourselves once this is done," she growled.

Them first few days of wandering the territory gived me time to get a read on things. From the Old Man's side of things, new atrocities was occurring all up and down Kansas Territory, the business in Congress being the last straw. From his point of view, the Yank settlers was being plundered regular by the Kickapoo Rangers, the Ranting Rockheads, the Border Ruffians, Captain Pate's Sharpshooters, and a number of such bloodthirsty, low-down drunks and demon outfits bent on killing off abolitionists or anyone being suspected of being one. Many of them types was personal favorites of mine, truth be told, for I growed up at Dutch's and knowed many a rebel. To them the Old Man's Yanks was nothing more than a bunch of high-siddity squatters, peddlers, and carpetbaggers who came west stealing property with no idea 'bout how things was, plus the Yanks wasn't fighting fair, being that they got free guns and supplies from back east which they used against the poor plainsmen. Nobody asked the Negro what he thunk about the whole business, by the way, nor the Indian, when I think of it, for neither of their thoughts didn't count, even though most of the squabbling was about them on the outside, for at bottom the whole business was about land and money, something nobody who was squabbling seemed to ever get enough of.

I weren't thinking them thoughts back then, of course. I wanted to get back to Dutch's. I had an aunt and uncle back there, and while I weren't close to them, anything seemed better than starving. That's the thing about working under Old John Brown, and if I'm tellin' a lie I hope I drop down a corpse after I tell it: I was starving fooling with him. I was never hungry when I was a slave. Only when I got free was I eating out of garbage barrels. Plus, being a girl involved too much work. I spent my days running around, fetching this or that for these young skinflints, washing their clothes, combing their hair. Most of 'em didn't know their heads from their arses and liked having a little girl to do this and that for 'em. It was all, "Fetch me some water, Onion," and "Grab that gunnysack and bring it yonder," and "Wash this shirt in the creek for me, Onion," and "Heat me some water, dearie." Being free weren't worth shit. Out of all of 'em, only the Old Man didn't demand girl chores, and that's mostly 'cause he was too busy praying.

I was done in with that crap and almost relieved when he announced after a few days, "We is attacking tonight."

"You ain't gonna tell us where it is?" Owen grumbled.

"Just sharpen your broadswords."

Well, that kind of talk goes down fine when you giving orders to a Negro. But them men was white, and there was some grousing from them about not knowing exactly what they was supposed to attack and so forth. The Old Man's army was brand new, I found that out. They hadn't been in a war before, none of 'em, not even the Old Man. The hell-raisin' they'd done was mostly stealing food and supplies. But now the game turned serious, and he still wouldn't tell 'em where they was going to fight. He ignored 'em when they asked. He never gived out his plans to nobody in all the years I knowed him. Then, on the other hand, looking back, maybe he didn't know his own self, for he was prone to stop on his horse in the middle of the afternoon, cup his hand to his ear, and say, "*Shh.* I'm getting messages from our Great Redeemer Who stoppeth time itself on our behalf." He'd set several minutes, setting on his horse with his eyes closed, meditating, before movin' on.

After he announced the attack for the night, the men spent the day sharpening their broadswords on stones and getting ready. I spent the day looking for a chance to run off, but Fred was on me. He kept me busy tending the fire and learning to sharpen broadswords and clean rifles. He wouldn't give me two minutes on my own and kept me close to him. Fred was a good teacher in them things but a pain in the neck, for he had adopted me, and it pleased him to see his little girl catch on so quickly riding a horse and ignoring the mosquitoes and being so adaptable, he said, "almost like a boy." The dress itched me something terrible, but as the days wore into the cold nights, it growed right warm and comfortable. And I ought to say it here—I ain't proud to report it—it also kept me from the fight. Somebody was gonna get their head blowed off, and I had no interest in that business.

Afternoon turned to dusk, and the Old Man announced, "The hour is near, men." No sooner did he say it when, one by one, the men begun to peel off and make excuses to quit. This one had to tend to his livestock. That one had to cut crops. That one had a sick child at home, another had to run home to fetch his gun, and so on. Even Ottawa Jones begged off at the last second, promising to meet us later.

The Old Man let them go with a shrug. "I'd rather have five dedicated, trained fighters than an army of frightened ninnies," he scoffed. "Why, take Little Onion here. A girl and a Negro besides, tending to her duties like a man. That," he pointed out proudly to Fred and Owen, "is dedication."

By evening, the company of twelve had whittled down to eight, not counting yours truly, and the pep had gone out of them that stayed. There was a new color to the thing now, for it growed serious, and hunger struck again. The Old Man hardly ever ate, so his needs for food wasn't great. But them others was dying of hunger, as was yours truly. Seemed like the closer the hour came to mounting the attack, the hungrier I got, till midnight rolled past, and the hunger changed to fear, and I forgot all about being hungry.

Well into the wee hours, the Old Man gathered what was left of the Pottawatomie Rifles 'round him to pray—I'd say on average he prayed about twice an hour, not counting meals and including the times when he went to the privy, for which he uttered a shortie even before he ducked into the woods to remove his body's impurities. They gathered 'round him, and the old man rousted it up. I can't recollect all what he said—the terrible barbarity that followed stayed in my mind much longer—though I do recall standing in my bare feet while the Old Man called on the spirit of Jesus with an extra long spell of Old Testament and New Testament workings, hollering about the Book of John and so forth. He barked and prayed and howled at God forward and backward a solid forty-five minutes, till Owen called out, "Pa, we got to roll. It'll be light in three hours."

That rousted the Old Man, who came out his spell grumbling, "Course you would interrupt my reckonings to our dear departed Savior upon Whose blood our lives rest," he said, "but I reckon He understands the impatience of children and is partial to their youth and recklessness. C'mon, men."

They gathered in a wagon with horses tied to follow, and I hoisted myself aboard. There was but eight souls left aboard now from the original Pottawatomie Rifles, and only on the wagon as we rolled did I come to the knowledge that five of those was the Old Man's sons: Owen and Fred, course, then Salmon, Jason, and John Jr., plus one son-in-law, Henry Thompson. The other two were James Townsley and Theo Weiner, the Jew.

We stayed off the California Trail, the main trail which runs clear through Kansas, and rode an old logging path for about an hour, then veered off to a trail that led toward a group of houses. Not a one of them fellers lost a breath or showed any hesitation as we moved, but I overheard them fussin' about where Dutch lived, them guessing he wanted to attack Dutch's, and there was some confusion about where it was, for it was dark, and there weren't much of a moon, and new settlements was popping up along the California Trail every day, changing the look of things. Course I knowed Dutch's place and everything within a mile of it, but I weren't quite sure of where we was, either. I know we wasn't in his country just yet. Wherever we was, we was off the California Trail, clear on the other side of Mosquite Creek. I believe we would'a ended up in Nebraska if the Old Man allowed it, for he didn't know where he was, either.

I didn't say a word while they rode back and forth, trying to figure it, and after a while when I looked over at the Old Captain to hear his word on it, I seen he'd fallen asleep in the wagon. I reckon they didn't want to wake him. He lay there snoring as the others led us 'round in circles for about an hour. I was happy he was asleep, and thought he'd sleep through the whole business and forget it. I was to learn later Old John Brown could stay up for days at a time without eating a crumb, then shut down and sleep for five minutes before waking up to do any kind of task under God's sun, including killing man or beast.

He awoke in good time sure enough, sat up, and barked out, "Stop near that cabin in clearing yonder. Our work is here."

Now he was as lost as the rest of us, and didn't know his way out of the particular patch of woods and that homestead any more than a bird knows his way out of a privy with the door closed, but he was the leader, and he had found what he wanted.

He stared at the cabin in the dim moonlight. It weren't Dutch's place at all, but no one, not even Owen or Frederick, said a wrong thing about it, for no one wanted to back-talk him. Truth be told, Brown's Station, the farmstead where he and his boys stayed, was within ten miles of Dutch's place, and some of his boys had to know we was at the wrong spot, but none said a word. They was afraid to cross their father. Most of 'em would speak up against Jesus Christ Himself before they took on the Old Man, except Owen, who was the least religious of all his boys and the most sure of hisself. But Owen too looked unsure, at the moment, for this whole conundrum attack and warring in the middle of the night was his Pa's idea, not his, and he followed his Pa like the rest, right to the brink.

The Old Man was sure, he spoke with the strength of a man who knowed hisself. "To the cause," he whispered. "Dismount and tie off the two trailing horses." The men done it.

It was dark but clear. The Old Man leaped out the back of the wagon and led us behind some thickets, peering at the cabin.

"I do believe we'll catch him by surprise," he said.

"Are you sure this is Dutch's?" Owen asked.

The Old Man ignored that. "I can smell slavery within it," he declared. "Let us strike quickly with the Lord's vengeance. Broadswords only. No guns."

He turned to me and said, "Little Onion, you are a courageous child, and while I knows you wants to strike a blow for freedom yourself, tonight is not the time. Stay here. We'll be back shortly."

Well, he didn't have to tell me twice. I weren't going nowhere. I stood by the wagon and watched them go.

The moon peeked from behind the clouds and it allowed me to see them approach the cabins, spread out in a line. Several switched to guns, despite what the Old Man told 'em, as they approached the front door.

When they were almost on the front door, and a good thirty yards from me, I turned around and ran.

I got no more than five steps and runned right into two four-legged mongrels who jumped at me. One knocked me down and the other barked holy hell and would'a tore me apart had not something dropped on him and he fell. The other mutt ran off howling into the woods.

I looked up to see Fred standing over the slain dog with his broadsword and the Old Man and the rest standing over me. The Old Man looked grim, and the sight of them tight, gray eyes boring into me made me want to shrivel up to the size of a peanut. I thought he was going to chastise me, but instead he turned and glared at the others. "It's Lucky Onion here had the mind to look out for watchdogs behind us, which none of you had the mind to consider. I reckon you can't prevent someone from fighting for their freedom. So come on, Little Onion. I knows you want to come. Stay back from us, and be very quick and quiet."

Well, he done me a worse service, but I done as he said. They trotted toward the cabin. I followed at a safe distance.

Owen and Fred stepped up to the front door, guns bared, and knocked politely, while the Old Man stood back.

A voice inside said, "Who's there?"

"Trying to get to Dutch's Tavern," Old Man Brown called out. "We're lost."

The door opened and Owen and Fred cold-kicked the man inside the house and stepped in behind him. The rest tumbled inside.

I went to a side window and watched. The cabin was but a room, lit by a dim candle. The Old Man and his sons stood over none other than James Doyle, who had been in the tavern and held his .45 Colt on the Old Man, and Doyle's three sons and his wife. Doyle and his boys were pressed to the wall, facing it, while the Old Man's boys held Sharps rifles and swords at their necks. The Old Man stood over them, shuffling one foot to the other, his face twitching, searching in his pockets for something.

I don't reckon he knowed what to do at first, for he had never taken nobody prisoner before. He dug in his pockets a good five minutes before he finally pulled out a piece of yellowed, rumpled paper and read from it in a high, thin voice: "I'm Captain Brown of the Northern Army. We come here from back east to free the enslaved people of this territory under the laws of our Redeemer the Lord Jesus Christ Who spilt His blood for you and me." Then he balled up the paper, stuck it in his pocket, and said to Doyle, "Which one of you is Dutch Henry?"

Doyle was white-faced. "He don't live here."

"I know that," the Old Man said, though he didn't know it. He had just learnt it. "Is you related to him?"

"None of us here is."

"Is you Pro Slavers or against?"

"I don't own no slaves myself."

"I ain't ask that. Ain't I seen you at Dutch Henry's?"

"I was just passing through," Doyle said. "He lives down the road a piece, don't you remember?"

"I don't recollect every step I take in doing my duties as the Almighty directs me to them," the Old Man said, "for I am commingling with His spirit almost every minute. But I do recollects you being one of them ruffians wanting to blast me over there."

"But I'm not Dutch," Doyle said. "Dutch's Tavern is two miles east."

"And a heathen's haven it is," the Old Man said.

"But I didn't fire on you," Doyle pleaded. "I could have but didn't."

"Well, you should have. You kin to Dutch, by the way?"

"Absolutely not."

"Well, I ask you again. Is you for slavery or not?"

"You won't find one slave 'round here," Doyle said. "I got nar one."

"Too bad, for this is a big homestead," Old Brown said. "It's a lot of work to keep it going."

"You telling me," Doyle said. "I got more plowing than me and my boys can handle. I could use a couple of niggers around here. You can't make it in Kansas Territory without help. Why, just yesterday—"

And then he stopped, for he knowed he made a mistake. Old Brown's face changed. The years dropped off him, and a youngness climbed into him. He straightened up and his jaw poked out. "I come to deliver the Redeemer's justice to free His people. And to exact the Lord's revenge on the murdering and kidnapping of the Negro people by slavers and them like yourself who has robbed and stole in the name of that infernal institution. And all that it involves, and all who's involved in it, who has partaken in its spoils and frivolities. There ain't no exceptions."

"Do that mean you don't like me?" Doyle said.

"Step outside," the Old Man said.

Doyle growed white as a sheet and pleaded his case. "I

meant you no harm at Dutch's," he said. "I'm just a farmer try-ing to make a dollar change pockets." Then he suddenly swiv-eled his head, glanced at the window—my face was stuck dead in it and the window was right there—and saw me peering in, wearing a dress and bonnet. A puzzled look come across his face, which was stone-cold frightened. "Ain't I seen you before?" he asked.

"Save your howdys for another time. I'm doing the talking here," Brown said. "I'll ask you for the last time. Is you Free State or Slave State?"

"Whatever you say," Doyle said.

"Make up your mind."

"I can't think with a Sharps under my chin!"

The Old Man hesitated, and Doyle was almost off the hook, till his wife hollered out, "I told you, Doyle! This is what you get for running with them damn rebels."

"Hush, Mother," he said.

It was too late then. The cat was out the bag. Brown nod-ded to his boys, who grabbed Doyle and throwed him and his two older boys out the door. When they reached for the last, the youngest, the mother throwed herself at Old Brown.

"He's just sixteen," the missus pleaded. "He ain't had noth-ing to do with them law-and-order people. He's just a boy."

She pleaded with the Old Man something terrible, but he weren't listening. He was lost. Seemed like he went to a differ-ent place inside his head. He looked past her head, beyond her, like he was looking to heaven or something far off. He got downright holy when it was killing time. "Take thine own hand and split an ax with it," he said. "That's Eucclestsies twelve seven or thereabouts."

"What's that mean?" she asked.

"This one's coming with me, too."

Well, she fell on her knees and howled and pleaded and scratched some more, so much she threw the Old Man out of his killing stupor for a minute, and he said, "All right. We'll leave him. But I'm keeping a man with a muzzle trained on this door. If you or anybody else pokes their head outside it, they gonna chew a powder ball."

He left a man to watch the door and split the rest, half taking Doyle to one part of the thickets, the other half a few yards off with Doyle's two boys. I followed Fred, Owen, and the Old Man, who took Doyle a few steps into the thicket, stopped, and placed him standing with his back to a large tree. Doyle, barefoot, quaked like a knock-kneed chicken and begun moaning like a baby.

The Old Man ignored that. "Now, I'mma ask you for the last time. Is you Pro Slavery or Free State?" Brown said.

"It was just talk," Doyle said. "I didn't mean nothing by it." He commenced to shaking and crying and begging for his life. His sons, several feet away, couldn't see him, but they heard him bellowing like a broke calf and begun to moan and howl as well.

The Old Man didn't say nothing. Seem like he was hypnotized. He didn't seem to see Doyle. I couldn't stand it, so I moved out the thicket, but not fast enough, for Doyle seen me in the glint of the moonlight and suddenly recognized me. "Hey," he said suddenly. "Tell 'em I'm all right! You know me! Tell 'em. I never done you no wrong."

"Shush," Brown said. "I'll ask you for the last time. Is you a Pro Slaver or not!"

"Don't hurt me, Captain," Doyle said. "I'm just a man trying to make a living slinging wheat and growing butter beans."

He might as well have been singing to a dead hog. "You didn't say that to Lew Shavers, and them two Yankee women you ravaged outside Lawrence," the Old Man said.

"That weren't me," Doyle murmured quietly. "Just those I knowed."

"And you wasn't there?"

"I was. But that . . . was a mistake. It weren't me that done that."

"I'll beg the Lord your forgiveness, then," Brown said. He turned to Fred and Owen and said, "Make quick work of it."

By God, them two raised their swords and planted them right in the poor man's head, and down he went. Doyle wanted to live so bad he fell down and got up in the same motion, with Fred's broadsword still planted in his skull, scrambling for life. Owen struck him again and knocked his head nearly clean off, and this time he went down and stayed there, still twitching as he lay on his side, legs running sideways, but even with his head half sheared off, Doyle hollered like a stuck hog long enough for his sons, not more than ten yards off in the thickets, to hear. The sound of their Pa's getting murdered and bellowing spooked them to howling like coyotes, till the thud of swords striking their heads echoed out the thicket and they was quieted up. Then it was done.

They stood in the thicket, the whole bunch of 'em panting and exhausted for a minute, then a terrible howling emerged. I jumped in my skin, thinking it was from the dead themselves, till I saw a soul running off through the woods and seen it was one of Brown's own sons, John. He ran toward the cabin clearing, squawking like a madman.

"John!" the Old Man hollered, and took off after him, the men following.

There weren't going to be another chance. I turned into the thickets where the wagon and two horses were tethered. One of them, Dutch's old pinto, had been ridden over by one of the Old Man's men. I leaped atop it, turned it toward Dutch's, and put it to work as fast as it would go. Only when I was clear of the thickets did I look behind me to see if I was clear, and I was. I'd left them all behind. I was gone.

5

Nigger Bob

I made it to the California Trail as fast as that horse could stand it, but after a while she tired down and moved to a trot, so I ditched her, for light was coming and me riding her would attract questions. Niggers couldn't travel alone in them days without papers. I left her where she was and she trotted on ahead while I moved on foot, staying off the road. I was a mile from Dutch's Tavern when I heard a wagon coming. I jumped into the thickets and waited.

The trail curved around and dipped before it hit an open wood area near where I was, and around the curve, up over the dip, came an open-back wagon driven by a Negro. I decided to take a chance and hail him down. I was about to jump out when, around the curve behind him, a posse of sixteen red-shirts on horses in columns of twos appeared. They was Missourians, and traveling like an army.

Sunlight was laying across the plains now. I laid in the thickets, crouched behind a row of bramblers and thick trees, waiting for them to pass. Instead, they halted at the clearing just a few feet from me.

In the back of the wagon was a prisoner. An elderly white feller in a beard, dirty white shirt, and suspenders. His hands was free but his feet was roped to a metal circular hook built into the floor of the wagon. He looked downright tight. He sat near the back flap of the wagon, while the rest passed a bottle of joy juice among them, regarding him.

A man rode to the front of them, a sour-looking feller with a face like molded bread, pock-faced. I reckon he was their leader. He dismounted his horse, swayed, two sheets to the wind, then suddenly swerved around and staggered right toward me. He stepped to the woods not two feet off from where I crouched hidden. He swayed so close to my hiding place I saw the inside of his ear, which looked like the cross-section of a cucumber. But he didn't spot me for he was clean soused. He leaned against the other side of the tree where I hid, and emptied his bladder, then staggered into the clearing again. From his pocket he brung out a rumpled piece of paper and addressed the prisoner.

"Okay, Pardee," he said. "We gonna try you right here."

"Kelly, I already told you I weren't a Yank," the old man said.

"We's see," Kelly mumbled. He held the rumpled piece of paper up to the sunlight. "I got several resolutions here saying the Free State men is liars and law-breaking thieves," he said. "You read them out loud. Then sign them all."

Pardee snatched the paper. He held it close to his eyes, then far off at arm's length, then close again, straining to see. Then he thrust it back at Kelly. "My eyes ain't what they once was," he said. "You g'wan and read it."

"You ain't got to follow it to the dot," Kelly barked. "Just put your mark on it and be done with it."

"I ain't scratching my name to nothing till I know what it is," Pardee grumbled.

"Stop making it tough, ya stupid idiot. I'm making it easy for ya."

Pardee throwed his eyes to the paper again and started reading.

He took his time about it. Five minutes passed. Ten. The sun shone full overhead and the liquor bottle the men passed around was emptied and tossed. Another liquor bottle appeared. They passed that. Twenty minutes passed. He was still reading.

Several fellers dozed off while Kelly sat on the ground, doodling with his gun belt, drunk as a fish. Finally he looked up at Pardee. "What you waiting on, the steamboat?" he snapped. "Just sign it. It's just a few declarations."

"I can't read 'em all at once," Pardee said.

Well, it occurred to me that Pardee probably couldn't read at all. But he acted like he could. The men begun to curse him. They cursed him for the better part of ten minutes. He kept on reading. One man went up to Pardee and blowed cigar smoke in his face. Another come up and yelled into his ear. A third come up, hawked, and spit right on his face. That made him put the paper down.

"Hatch, I'm gonna bust you across the jibs once I get clear here," Pardee growled.

"Just finish!" Kelly said.

"I can't read with your cousin screwing up my figuring. Now I got to start all over again."

He threwed the paper to his face again. The men grew

more furious. They threatened to tar and feather him. They promised to hold an auction and let the Negro driver sell him. Still, Pardee kept reading. Wouldn't look up. Finally Kelly stood up.

"I'mma give you one last chance," he said. He looked serious now.

"Okay," Pardee said. He thrust the paper out to Kelly. "I'm finished. I can't sign it. It's illegal."

"But it's signed by a bona fide judge!"

"I don't care if it's signed by Jesus H. Christ. I ain't signing nothin' that I don't know what it is. I don't understand nothin' in it."

Now Kelly got mad. "I'm giving you a break, ya watery-mouth, yellow-livered Free Stater. Sign it!"

"That's some way to treat a feller who rode cattle with you for two years."

"That's the only reason you're drawing air now."

"You lyin', bowlegged cockroach. You just tryin' to stake my claim!"

That stirred the men. Suddenly the thing went the other way. Claim jumpers in Kansas, folks who throwed themselves on another's land who already made a claim on that land, why, they was almost worse than horse and nigger thieves.

"Is that true, Kelly?" one of them asked. "You trying to stake his land?"

"Course not," Kelly said hotly.

"He's straight out been aiming on my land since we got here," Pardee said. "That's why you calling me a Yank, ya leech!"

"You's a blue-bellied, pet house-paupin' liar!" Kelly roared. He snatched the paper from Pardee and gave it to the driver of the wagon, a Negro.

"Nigger Bob, you read it out loud," he said. He turned to Pardee. "And whatever that nigger reads off here, if you don't agree and sign off on it, I'm gonna bust a charge into your neck and be done with you."

He turned to the Negro. "G'wan and read it, Nigger Bob."

Nigger Bob was a hardy, tall, fit Negro, not more than twenty-five, setting atop the driver's bench on the wagon. He took the paper with shaking hands, his eyes wide as silver dollars. That nigger was panicked. "I can't read, boss," he stammered.

"Just read it."

"But I don't know what it says."

"G'wan and read it!"

That Negro's hands shook and he stared at the paper. Finally he blurted nervously, "Een-y. Mean-y. Mine-y. Moe. One-two-three."

Several men burst out laughing, but Kelly was hot now, as was several others, for the men growed impatient.

"Kelly, let's hang Pardee and get up the road," one said.

"Let's tar and feather him."

"What you fooling 'round for, Kelly? Let's go."

Kelly waved them to silence, then blew out his cheeks, hemming and hawing. He didn't know whether to shit or go blind. Being full of gulp sauce weren't helping him, neither. He said, "Let's vote on it. All in favor of hanging Pardee for being a nigger-loving Free State Yankee and an agent of the New England Emigrant Yellow Belly Society, raise your hand."

Eight hands were raised.

"All in favor of not hanging?"

Eight more hands went up.

I counted sixteen men. It was a tie.

Kelly stood there swaying, drunk, in a quandary. He tottered over to Nigger Bob, who sat in the wagon driver's seat, trembling. "Since Pardee here's an abolitionist, we'll let Nigger Bob decide. What's your vote, Nigger Bob? Hang Pardee here or not?"

Pardee, setting in the back of the wagon, suddenly leaped up in a snit. "Hang me then!" he howled. "I'd rather hang than have a nigger vote on me!" he cried, then tried to leap out the wagon, but fell flat on his face, for his feet were tied.

The men howled even more. "You pukin' abolitionist egghead," Kelly said, laughing, as he helped Pardee up. "You should'a read them resolutions like I told you."

"I can't read!" Pardee said.

That stopped Kelly cold and he took his hands off Pardee like he was electrified. "What? You said you could!"

"I was lying."

"What about that land title at Big Springs? You said it was . . ."

"I don't know what that was. You wanted it so damn bad!"

"You blockhead!"

Now it was Kelly's turn to be on the spot while the other men laughed at him! "You should'a said something, ya damn dummy," he growled. "Whose land is it then?"

"I don't know," Pardee sniffed. "But you been told. Now. You read these resolutions to me and I'll sign 'em." He thrust the paper out to Kelly.

Kelly hemmed and hawed. He coughed. He blew his nose. He flustered around. "I ain't much on reading," he muttered. He snatched the paper from Pardee and turned to the posse. "Who here reads?"

Weren't a man among them spoke. Finally a feller in the

back said, "I ain't setting here watching you fiddle with your noodle a minute more, Kelly. Old Man Brown's hiding out near here somewhere, and I aim to find him."

With that he galloped off, and the men followed. Kelly rushed to follow them, staggering to his mount. When he swung his horse around, Pardee said, "At least gimme my gun back, ya knobhead."

"I sold it in Palmyra, ya mule-face abolitionist. I oughta kick your teeth out for screwing up that land title," Kelly said. He rode off with the rest.

Pardee and Nigger Bob watched him leave.

When he was out of sight, Nigger Bob moved from the driver's seat to the back and untied Pardee's ankles without a word.

"Ride me home," Pardee fumed. He said it over his shoulder as he rubbed his ankles, setting in back of the wagon.

Nigger Bob hopped into the driver's seat, but didn't move. He sat atop the wagon and looked straight ahead. "I ain't riding you no place," he said.

That floored me. I had never heard a Negro talk to a white man like that before in my entire life.

Pardee blinked, stunned. "What you say?"

"You heard it. This here wagon belongs to Mr. Settles and I'm taking it home to him."

"But you got to pass Palmyra! That's right where I live."

"I ain't going nowhere with you, Mr. Pardee. You can go where you want, however you please. But this here wagon belongs to Marse Jack Settles. And he ain't give me no permission to ride nobody in it. I done what Mr. Kelly said 'cause I had to. But I ain't got to now."

"Git down off that seat and come down here."

Bob ignored him. He sat in the driver's seat, staring off into the distance.

Pardee reached for his heater, but found his holster empty. He stood up and glared at Nigger Bob like he was fit to whup him, but that Negro was bigger than him and I reckon he thought better of it. Instead, he jumped down off the wagon, stomped down the road a piece, picked up a large stone, walked back to the wagon, and chinked out the wood cotter pin on one of the wagon wheels. Just banged it right out. That pin held the wheel on. Bob sat there as he chinked. Didn't move.

When Pardee was done, he throwed the pin in the thickets. "If I got to walk home, you walking too, ya black bastard," he said, and stomped up the road.

Bob watched him till he was out of sight, then climbed down from the wagon and looked at the wheel. I waited several long minutes before I finally come out the woods. "I can help you fix that if you take me up the road a piece," I said.

He stared at me, startled. "What you doing out, little girl?" he said.

Well, that throwed me, for I forgot how I was done up. I quick tried to untie the bonnet. But it was tied tight. So I went at the dress, which was tied from behind.

"Good Lord, child," Bob said. "You ain't got to do that to get no ride from Nigger Bob."

"It ain't what it looks like," I said. "In fact, if you'd be so kind as to help me take this thing off—"

"I'll be heading out," he said, backing away.

But I had my chance and I weren't going to lose it. "Wait a minute. Help me. If you don't mind, just untie—"

Good God, he jumped atop the wagon, hustled onto the driver's seat, called up that horse to trotting, and was off, pin or no pin. He got about ten yards before that back wheel got to wobbling so bad—it just about come clean off—before he stopped. He jumped down, pulled a stick from the thickets, stuck it into the pin hole, and commenced to banging it into place. I ran up on him.

"I got business, child," he said, chinking away at the wheel. He wouldn't look up at me.

"I ain't a girl."

"Whatever you think you is, honey, I don't think it's proper that you unstring that dress from 'round yourself in front of ol' Nigger Bob—a married man." He paused a minute, glanced around, then added, "Less'n you want to, of course."

"You got a lot of salt talking that way," I said.

"You the one asking for favors."

"I'm trying to get to Dutch's Crossing."

"For what?"

"I live there. I'm Gus Shackleford's boy."

"That's a lie. Old Gus is dead. And he ain't have no girl. Had a boy. Wasn't worth shit neither, that child."

"That's a hell of a thing to say 'bout somebody you don't know."

"I don't know you, child. You a sassy thing. How old are you?"

"It don't matter. Take me back to Dutch's. He'll give you a little something for me."

"I wouldn't ride to Dutch's for a smooth twenty dollars. They'll kill a nigger in there."

"He won't bother you. It's Old John Brown he's after."

At the mention of that name, Bob glanced around, taking stock up and down the trail, making sure nobody was rolling toward us. The trail was empty.

"*The* John Brown?" he whispered. "He's really 'round these parts?"

"Surely. He kidnapped me. Made me wear a dress and bonnet. But I escaped that murdering fool."

"Why?"

"You see how he got me dressed."

Bob looked at me closely, then sighed, then whistled. "There's killers all up and down these plains," he said slowly. "Ask the red man. Anybody'll say anything to live. What would John Brown want with you anyhow? He need an extra girl to work his kitchen?"

"If I'm tellin' a lie I hope I drop down dead after I tell it. I ain't a girl!" I managed to pull the bonnet back off my head.

That shook him some. He peered at me close, then stuck his face into mine and it hit him then. His eyes got wide. "What the devil got into you?" he said.

"Want me to show you my privates?"

"Spare me, child. I takes your word for it. I wouldn't want to see your privates any more than I'd want to stick my face in Dutch Henry's Tavern. Why you paddling 'round like that? Was John Brown gonna run you north?"

"I don't know. He just murdered three fellers up about five miles from here. I seen that with my own eyes."

"White fellers?"

"If it look white and smell white, you can bet it ain't buzzard."

"You sure?"

"James Doyle and his boys," I said. "Deadened 'em with swords."

He whistled softly. "Glory," he murmured.

"So you'll take me back to Dutch's?"

He didn't seem to hear me. He seemed lost in thought. "I heard John Brown was about these parts. He's something else. You ought to be grateful, child. You met him and all?"

"Met him? Why you think I'm dressed like a sissy. He—"

"Shit! If I could get Old John Brown to favor me and carry me to freedom, why, I'd dress up as a girl every day for ten years. I'd be thoroughly a girl till I got weak from it. I'd be a girl for the rest of my life. Anything's better than bondage. Your best bet is to go back with him."

"He's a murderer!"

"And Dutch ain't? He's riding on Brown now. Got a whole posse looking for 'em. Every redshirt within a hundred miles is rolling these plains for him. You can't go back to Dutch nohow."

"Why not?"

"Dutch ain't stupid. He'll sell you south and git his money for you while he can. Any nigger that's had a sip of freedom ain't worth squat to the white man out here. High-yellow boy like you'll fetch a good price in New Orleans."

"Dutch wouldn't see me sold."

"You wanna bet?"

That gived me pause then. For Dutch weren't too sentimental.

"You know where I can go?"

"Your best bet is to go back to Old Brown. If you ain't lyin' 'bout being with his gang and all. They say they're fearsome. Is it true he carries two seven-shooters?"

"One of 'em does."

"Ooh, wee, that just tickles me," he said.

"I'd rather blow my brains out than run around dressed like a girl. I can't do it."

"Well, save yourself the bullet and go on back to Dutch, then. He'll send you to New Orleans and death'll be knocking shortly. I never heard of a nigger escaped from there."

That done me in. I hadn't considered none of that. "I don't know where the Old Man is now," I said. "I couldn't find him by myself nohow. I don't know these parts."

Bob said slowly, "If I help you find him, you think he could lead me to freedom, too? I'll dress like a girl for it."

Well, that sounded too complicated. But I needed a ride. "I can't say what he'll do, but he and his sons got a big army. And more guns than you ever saw. And I heard him say it clear, 'I'm an abolitionist through and through, and I aims to free every colored in this territory.' I heard him say that many times. So I expect he would take you."

"What about my wife and children?"

"I don't know about that."

Bob thunk on it a long moment.

"I got a cousin down near Middle Creek who knows everything in these parts," he said. "He'll know where the Old Man's hideout is. But if we set here too long, another posse's gonna roll up, and they might not be drunk like the last. Help me tie that wagon wheel back."

I hopped to work. We rolled a fallen tree stump under the wagon. He harred the horse up so it pulled the wagon high enough to free the bottom, then tied the rope to a tree and harred the horse up again, creating a winch. We piled planks

and stones under it to keep it up. I searched the thickets and
found that cotter pin and helped him put the wheel back on
and chink it in. The sun was near to noon when we finished,
and we was hot and sweaty by the time we got the thing done,
but we got that wagon wheel spinning like new, and I hopped
aboard the driver's seat next to him, and we was off in no time.

6

Prisoner Again

We didn't get two miles down the road before we runned into patrols of every type. The entire territory was in alarm. Armed posses crisscrossed the trail every which way. Every passing wagon had a rider setting up front with a shotgun. Children acted as lookouts for every homestead, with Pas and Mas setting out front in rocking chairs holding shotguns. We passed several wagons pulling terrified Yankees going in the opposite direction, their possessions piled high, hauling ass back east fast as their mules could go, quitting the territory altogether. The Old Man's killings terrified everyone. But Bob got safe passage, for he was riding his master's wagon and had papers to show it.

We followed the Pottawatomie Creek on the California Trail toward Palmyra. Then we cut along the Marais des Cygnes River toward North Middle Creek. A short way along the river, Bob stopped the wagon, dismounted, and tied off the horse. "We got to walk from here," he said.

We walked down a clean-dug trail to a fine, well-built house on the back side of the river. An old Negro was tending flowers at the gate, turning dirt on the walkway as we come. Bob howdied him and he hailed us over.

"Good afternoon, Cousin Herbert," Bob said.

"What's good about it?"

"The Captain's good about it."

At the mention of the word "Captain," Herbert glanced at me, shot a nervous look at his master's house, then fell to turning that dirt again on his hands and knees, getting busy on that dirt, looking down. "I don't know nothing about no Captain, Bob."

"C'mon, Herbert."

The old feller kept his eyes on that dirt, turning it, busy, tending flowers, talking low as he worked. "Git on outta here. Old Brown's hotter than a pig in shit. What you doing fooling with him? And whose knock-kneed girl is that? She too young for you."

"Where's he at?"

"Who?"

"Stop fooling. You know who I'm talking about."

Herbert glanced up, then back down at his flowers. "There's posses from here to Lawrence combing this whole country for him. They say he throwed the life spark outta ten white fellers up near Osawatomie. Knocked their heads clean off with swords. Any nigger that mentions his name'll be shipped outta this territory in pieces. So git away from me. And send that girl home and run on home to your wife."

"She belongs to the Captain."

That changed things, and Herbert's hands stopped a moment as he considered it, still looking down at the dirt, then he started digging again. "What that got to do with me?" Herbert said.

"She's Captain's property. He's running her out this country, outta bondage."

The old man stopped his work for a minute, glancing at me. "Well, she can suck her thumb at his funeral, then. Git. Both of y'all."

"That's a hell of a way to treat your third cousin."

"Fourth cousin."

"Third, Herbert."

"How's that?"

"My Aunt Stella and your Uncle Beall shared a second cousin named Melly, remember? She was Jamie's daughter, second cousin to Odgin. That was Uncle Beall's nephew by his first marriage to your Mom's sister Stella, who got sold last year. Stella was my cousin Melly's second cousin. So that makes Melly your third cousin, which puts your Uncle Jim in the back behind my uncles Fergus, Cook, and Doris, but before Lucas and Kurt, who was your first cousin. That means Uncle Beall and Aunt Stella was first cousins, which makes me and you third cousins. You would treat your third cousin this way?"

"I don't care if you is Jesus Christ and my son together," Herbert snapped. "I don't know nothing 'bout no Captain. 'Specially in front of her," he said, nodding at me.

"What you gettin' in a knot over her for? She's just a child."

"That's just it," Herbert said. "I ain't gonna eat tar and feathers over that high-yellow thing there who I don't even know. She don't look nothing like the Old Man, whatever he do look like."

"I didn't say she was his kin."

"Whatever she is, she don't belong with you, a married man."

"You ought to check yourself, cousin."

He turned to me. "Is you colored or white, miss, if you don't mind my asking?"

"What difference do it make?" Bob snapped. "We got to find the Captain. This little girl is rolling with him."

"Is she colored or not?"

"Course she's colored. Can't you see?"

The old man stopped his digging to stare at me a moment, then started digging again, and snorted, "If I didn't know no better, I'd say she was kin to old Gus Shackleford, who they say got his spark blowed out on account of talking to John Brown in Dutch's Tavern four days past, bless his soul. But Gus had a boy, that trifling Henry. He worried Gus to devilment, that one. Acting white and all. He needs a good spanking. I ever catch that little gamecock nigger outside Dutch's I'll warm his little buns with a switch so hard, he'll crow like a rooster. I expect his devilment is what sent his Pa to his rewards, for he was as lazy as the devil. Children these days is just going to hell, Bob. Can't tell 'em nothing."

"Is you done?" Bob said.

"Done what?"

"Fluffling your feathers and wasting time," Bob snapped. "Where's the Captain? Do you know or not?"

"Well, Bob. A jar of peaches'll go far in this kind of weather."

"I ain't got no peaches, Herbert."

Herbert straightened. "You work your mouth awful good for a feller who never gived his cousin a penny in this world. Driving 'round in your high-siddity wagon with your high master. My marse is a poor man, like me. Go find yourself a bigger fool."

He turned away and dug more dirt into his flower bed.

"If you won't tell it, cousin," Bob said, "I'll go inside and ask your marse. He's a Free Stater, ain't he?"

The old man glanced back at the cabin. "I don't know what he is," he said dryly. "He come out to this country Free State, but them rebels is changing these white folks' mind fast."

"I'll tell you this, cousin. This here girl do belong to John Brown. And he's looking for her. And if he *do* find her, and she tells him you was pushing the waters against him, he's liable to ride down here and place his broadsword on your back. And if he sets his mind to that kind of blood frolic, nothing'll stop him. Who's gonna look after you then?"

That done it. The old man grimaced a bit, glanced up at the woods beyond the cabin behind him, then returned to digging his flowers. He talked with his face to the ground. "Circle 'round the cabin and move straight back into the woods, past the second birch tree beyond the cornfield yonder," he said. "You'll find an old whiskey bottle stuck between two low branches on that tree. Follow the mouth of that bottle due north two miles, just the way the mouth is pointed. Keep the sun on your left shoulder. You'll run into an old rock wall somebody built and left behind. Follow that wall to a camp. Make some noise 'fore you roll in there, though. The Old Man's got lookouts. They'll pull the trigger and tell the hammer to hurry."

"You all right, cousin."

"Git outta here 'fore you get me kilt. Old Brown ain't fooling. They say he roasted the skulls of the ones he kilt. That's the Wilkersons, the Fords, the Doyles, and several folks on the Missouri side. Ate their eyeballs like they was grapes. Fried the brains like chitlins. Used the scalps for wick lamps. He's the devil. I ain't never seen white folks so scared," he said.

That's the thing about the Old Man back in them days. If he done a thing, it got whipped up into a heap of lies five minutes past breakfast.

Herbert covered his mouth and chortled, licking his lips. "I want my jar of peaches, cousin. Don't forget me."

"You'll git 'em."

We bid leave of him and headed toward the woods. When we reached them, Bob stopped. "Little brother," he said, "I got to cut you loose here. I'd like to go, but I'm getting shaky. Being that Old John Brown has chopped off eyeballs and heads and all, I don't think I can make it. I'm fond of my head, since it do cover the top of my body. Plus, I got a family and can't leave 'em just yet, not unless they has safe passage. Good luck, for you is going to need it. Stay a girl and go with it till the Old Man's dead. Don't worry 'bout old Nigger Bob here. I'll catch up to you later."

Well, I couldn't assure him of nothing about whether or not the Old Man would take his head or be deadened, but there weren't nothing to do but take my leave of him. I followed old Herbert's directions, walking through the tall pines and thickets. A short while later, I recognized a piece of the rock wall—that was the same wall the Old Man had leaned on to follow the map when he first kidnapped me, but the camp was gone. I followed that wall along till I seen smoke from a fire. I went behind the wall, on the far side, intending to go behind the Old Man and holler at him and his men so they'd recognize me. I made a wide circle, snaking through trees and thickets, and after I was sure I was far back off 'em, I rose up, stepped behind a wide oak, and sat down to gather myself. I didn't know what kind of excuse I would cook up for 'em and needed time to think of one. Before I knew it, I fell asleep, for all that trekking and running around in the woods got me exhausted.

When I woke, the first thing I saw was a pair of worn boots with several toes sticking out of them. I knowed them toes, for just two days previous, I'd seen Fred throw a needle and thread at them things as we set by the fire salting peanuts. From where I lay, them toes was looking none too friendly.

I looked up into the barrel of two seven-shooters, and behind Frederick was Owen and several more of the Old Man's army, and none was looking too happy.

"Where's Pa's horse?" Fred asked.

Well, they brung me to the Old Man and it was like I hadn't gone no place. The Old Man greeted me like I had just come back from an errand to the general store. He didn't mention the missing horse, me running off, or none of them things. Old Brown never cared about the details of his army. I seen fellers walk off from his army one day, stay away a year, and a year later walk back into his camp and set down by the fire and eat like they had just come back from hunting that morning, and the Old Man wouldn't say a word. His abolitionist Pottawatomie Rifles was all volunteers. They came and went just as they pleased. In fact, the Old Man never gave orders unless they was in a firefight. Mostly he'd say, "I'm going this way," and his sons would say, "Me too," and the rest would say, "Me too," and off they went. But as far as giving orders and checking attendance and all, the abolitionist army was a come-one, come-all outfit.

He was standing over a campfire in his shirtsleeves, roasting a pig, when I walked up. He glanced up and seen me.

"Evening, Onion," he said. "You hungry?"

I allowed that I was, and he nodded and said, "Come hither

and chat whilst I roast this pig. Afterward, you can join me in praying to our Redeemer to give thanks for our great victory to free your people." Then he added, "Half your people, since on account of your fair complexion, I reckon you is one half white or thereabouts. Which in and of itself, makes this world even more treacherous for you, sweet dear Onion, for you has to fight within yourself and outside yourself, too, being half a loaf on one side and half the other. Don't worry. The Lord don't have no contention with your condition, for Luke twelve, five says, 'Take not the breast of not just thine own mother into thy hand, but of both thy parents.'"

I didn't know what he was talking about, course, but figured I'd better explain about his horse. "Captain," I said. "I got scared and run and lost your horse."

"You ain't the only one that run." He shrugged, working that pig expertly. "There's several 'round here who's shy to putting God's philosophy into action." He glanced around at the men, several of whom looked away, embarrassed.

By now the Old Man's army had gotten bigger. There were at least twenty men setting about. Piles of arms and broadswords were leaned up against trees. The small lean-to tent I first saw was gone. In its place was a real tent, which, like everything there, was stolen for it was painted in the front with a sign that read Knox's Fishing, Tackle, and Mining Tools. Out near the edge of camp, I counted fourteen horses, two wagons, a cannon, three woodstoves, enough swords to supply at least fifty men, and a box marked Thimbles. The men looked exhausted, but the Old Man looked fresh as a daisy. A week's worth of white beard had growed on his chin, bringing it closer down to his chest. His clothes were soiled and torn worse than ever, and his toes protruded so far from his boots, they looked like slippers. But he moved spry and sprite as a spring creek.

"The killing of our enemies was ordained," he said aloud, to no one in particular. "If folks 'round here read the Good Book, they wouldn't lose heart so easily when pressing forth in the Lord's purpose. Psalms seventy-two, four, says, 'He shall judge the poor of the people, and save the children of the needy, and break into pieces the oppressor.' And that, Little Onion," he said sternly, pulling off the fire the pig that was now roasted clean through, and glancing around at the men who looked away, "tells you all you need to know. Gather 'round a moment as I pray, men, then my brave Little Onion here will help me serve this ragged army."

Owen stepped forward. "Let me pray, Pa," he said, for the men looked to be starving, and I reckoned they couldn't stand an hour of the Captain doodling at the Almighty. The Old Man grumbled but agreed, and after we prayed and ate, he huddled with the others around his map, while Fred and I stayed away from them and cleaned up.

Fred, short as he was in his head, was terrific glad to see me. But he seemed worried. "We done a bad thing," he said.

"I know it," I said.

"My brother John who run off, we never found him. My brother Jason, too. We can't find neither."

"Where you think they gone?"

"Wherever they are," he said glumly. "We gonna fetch 'em."

"Do we got to?"

He glanced furtively at his Pa, then sighed and looked away. "I missed you, Little Onion. Where'd you run off to?"

I was about to tell him when a horse and rider charged into

camp. The rider cornered the Old Man and spoke to him, and a few moments later, the Captain called us to order, standing in the middle of the camp by the fire while the men gathered around.

"Good news, men. My old enemy Captain Pate has a posse raiding homes on the Santa Fe Road and planning to attack Lawrence. He got Jason and John with him. They are likely to drop 'em at Fort Leavenworth for imprisonment. We going after them."

"How big is his army?" Owen asked.

"A hundred fifty to two hundred, I'm told," Old Man Brown said.

I looked around. I counted twenty-three among us, including me.

"We only got ammo for a day's fight," Owen said.

"Doesn't matter."

"What we gonna use when we run out? Harsh language?"

But the Old Man was already movin', grabbing his saddle-bags. "Lord's riding on high, men! Remember the army of Zion! Mount up!"

"Tomorrow's Sunday, Father," Owen said.

"So what?"

"What say we wait till Monday and catch Pate then. He's likely headed to Lawrence. He won't attack Lawrence on a Sunday."

"In fact, that's *exactly* when he'll attack," the Old Man said, "knowing I'm a God-fearing man and likely to rest on the Lord's day. We'll ride up by way of Prairie City and cut him off at Black Jack. Let's pray, men."

Well, there weren't no stopping him. The men gathered around him in a circle. The Old Man dropped to his knees, stretched out his hands, palms toward the sky, looking like Moses of old, his beard angling down like a bird's nest. He commenced to praying.

Thirty minutes later Fred lay on the ground snoring, Owen stared into space, and the others milled about, smoking and doodling with saddlebags and scrawling letters home while the Old Man carried on, hollering up to the Anointed One with his eyes closed, till Owen finally piped out, "Pa, we got to ride! Jason and John is prisoner and headed to Fort Leavenworth, remember?"

That broke the spell. The Old Man, still on his knees, opened his eyes, irritated. "Every time I gets to the balance of my words of thanks to my Savior, I gets interrupted," he grumbled, getting to his feet. "But I expect the God of Gods has understanding about the patience of the young, who don't favors Him to the necessary ends so as to give Him proper thanks for blessings which He giveth so freely."

With that, we saddled up and rode due north, to meet Captain Pate and his posse, and I was full-blown back in his army and the business of being a girl again.

7

Black Jack

Like most things the Old Man planned out, the attack against Captain Pate's Sharpshooters didn't work out the way he drawed it up. For one thing, the Old Man always got bad information. We rode out against Captain Pate on a Saturday in October. Come December, we still hadn't found him . . . Everywhere we went, the story changed. We'd roll toward Palmyra and a settler on the trail would holler, "There's a fight with the rebels yonder in Lawrence," and off we'd go toward Lawrence, only to find the fight two days past and the rebels gone. A few days later a woman on her porch would exclaim, "I seen Captain Pate over near Fort Leavenworth," and the Old Man would say, "We have him now! Go men!" and off we'd bust out again, full of pluck, riding two days, only to find out it weren't true. Back and forth we went, till the men was plumb wore out. We went like that all the way into February, the Old Man spoiling for a fight, and getting none.

We picked up another dozen or so Free Staters this way

though, wandering around southern Kansas near the Missouri border, till we growed to about thirty men. We was feared, but the truth is, the Pottawatomie Rifles weren't nothing but a bunch of hungry boys with big ideas running 'round looking for boiled grits and sour bread to stuff their faces with in late February. Winter come full on then, and it growed too cold to fight. Snow blanketed the prairie. Ice formed eighteen inches deep. Water froze in pitchers overnight. Huge trees, covered with icicles, crackled like giant skeletons. Those in the Old Man's army who could stand it stayed in camp, huddled under the tent. The rest, including me and the Old Man and his sons, spent the winter keeping warm wherever we could. It's one thing to say you's an abolitionist, but riding for weeks on the plains in winter, with no spare victuals, you weeding a bad hoe for satisfaction to test a man's principles that way. Some of the Old Man's men was turned toward slavery by the time winter was over.

But truth be to tell it, it weren't killing me to be with the Old Man. Lazy slob that I was, I growed used to being outside, riding the plains looking for ruffians, stealing from Pro Slavers, and not having no exact job, for the Old Man changed the rules for girls in his army after he seen how I'd been put to scrubbing back and forth. He announced, "Henceforth every man in his company has to shift for himself. Wash your own shirts. Do your own mending. Fix your own plate." He made it clear that every man was there to fight slavery, not get his washing done by the only girl in the outfit who happened to be colored. Fighting slavery is easy when you ain't got that load. Fact is, it was pretty easy altogether, unless you was the slave, course, for you mostly rode around and talked up how wrong the whole deal was, then you stole whatever you could from the

Pro Slavers, and off you went. You weren't waking up regular to cart the same water, chop the same wood, shine the same boots, and hear the same stories every day. Slave fighting makes you a hero, a legend in your own mind, and after a while the thought of going back to Dutch's to be sold down to New Orleans, and barbering and shining shoes and my skin smacking against that rough old potato sack I wore versus the nice soft, warm wool dress I had begun to favor, not to mention the various buffalo hides I covered myself with, growed less and less sweet. I weren't for being a girl, mind you. But there was certain advantages, like not having to lift nothing heavy, and not having to carry a pistol or rifle, and fellers admiring you for being tough as a boy, and figuring you is tired when you is not, and just general niceness in the way folks render you. Course in them days colored girls had to work harder than white girls, but that was by normal white folks' standards. In Old Brown's camp, *everyone* around him worked, colored or white, and fact is, he busied all of us so much that at times slavery seemed no different than being free, for we was all on a schedule: The Old Man woke everyone at four a.m. to pray and mumble and blubber over the Bible for an hour. Then he put Owen on me to teach me letters. Then he throwed Fred on me to teach me the way of the woods, then he throwed me back to Owen again, who showed me how to throw a bullet into a breechloader and fire it. "Every soul has got to learn to defend God's word," the Old Man said. "And these is all defenses of it. Letters, defense, survival. Man, woman, girl, boy, colored or white, and Indians, needs to know these things." He teached me himself how to make baskets and bottom chairs. How you do it is simple: You take white oak, split it, and then it's just a manner of folding. Inside a month I could make any kind of basket you wanted:

musket basket, clothes basket, feed basket, fish basket—I caught catfish big and wide across as your hand. On long afternoons while we waited for the enemy to cross the trail, Fred and I went and made sorghum syrup from sugar maple trees. There weren't nothing to it. You sap it out the tree, pour it in a pan, fire it over a fire, skim them skimmings off the top with a stick or fork, and you done. Most of your job is to put the syrup away from the skimmings on the top. When you cook it right, you got the best sugar there is.

I come to enjoy that first winter with the Old Man's army, especially with Fred. He was as good a friend as a feller—or a girl who was really a feller—could want. He was more like a child than a man, which meant we fit together well. We never run short on playthings. The Old Man's army stole everything from the Pro Slavers a child could want: fiddles, saltshakers, mirrors, tin cups, a wooden rocking horse. What we couldn't keep, we used for target practice and blasted up. It weren't a bad life, and I growed used to it and forgot all about running off.

Spring came on like it always did, and one morning the Old Man went out scouting by himself, looking for Pate's Sharpshooters, and come back driving a big schooner wagon instead. I was setting by the campfire, making a fish basket when he rolled in. I looked up at the wagon as it rolled past and saw it had a busted-up back wheel with the hardwood brake shorn off. I said, "I knows that wagon," and no sooner had I said it than Nigger Bob and five Negroes tumbled out the back.

He seen me right off, and while the rest tumbled out to follow the Old Man to the campfire to eat, he cornered me.

"I see you is still working your show," he said.

I had changed over the winter. I had been out some. Seen a

little bit. And I weren't the meek little thing he had seen the fall before. "I thought you said you weren't going to join this army," I said.

"I come to live large like you," he said happily. He glanced 'round, seen nobody was close, and then whispered, "Do they know you're . . . ?" and he done his hand in a wiggly way.

"They don't know nothing," I said.

"I won't tell," he said. But I didn't like him having that on me.

"You plan on riding with us?" I asked.

"Not hardly. The Captain said he had but a few things to do and then we's gone to freedom."

"He's riding against Captain Pate's Sharpshooters."

That floored Bob. "Shit. When?"

"Whenever he finds 'em."

"Count me out. There's two hundred in Pate's army. Probably more. Pate got so many rebels wanting to join you'd think he was selling Calpurnia's flapjacks. He's turning 'em away. I thought Old Brown was working the freedom train. Riding north. Ain't that what you said last fall?"

"I don't know what I said then. I don't remember."

"That's what you said. Said he was riding for freedom. Gosh darnit. What other surprises is around here? What's his plan?"

"I don't know. He don't tell me. Whyn't you ask him?"

"He favors you. You ought to ask."

"I ain't gonna ask him them things," I said.

"Ain't you angling on freedom? What you routin' 'round here for then?"

I didn't know. Up till then, escaping back to Dutch's was in my plans. Once that changed, it was day-to-day living. I never was one to look too far past angling meat and gravy and biscuits down my throat. Bob, on the other hand, mostly had a family to consider, I reckon, and he had his mind on the freedom line, which weren't my problem. I growed used to the Old Man and his sons. "I reckon being practiced on a sword and a pistol is what I been learning 'round here," I said. "And reading the Bible. They do lots of that, too."

"I ain't come here to read nobody's Bible and fight nobody's slavery," Bob said. "I come to get myself out from under it." He looked at me and frowned. "I guess you don't have to worry about it, the way you playing it, being a girl and all."

"You the one that told me to do it."

"I ain't tell you to get me kilt!"

"You come here 'cause of me?"

"I come here 'cause you said the word 'freedom.' Sheesh!" He was mad. "My wife and children's still in bondage. How I'm gonna plan on earning money to buy them if he's monkeying 'round, fighting the Missourians?"

"You didn't ask him?"

"There weren't no asking," Bob said. "My marse and I was rolling to town. I heard a noise. Next thing I know, he stepped out the woods holding a rifle in marse's face. He said, 'I'm taking your wagon and freeing your colored man.' He didn't ask me if I wanted to be free. Course I come along 'cause I had to. But I thought he was gonna free me to the north. Nobody said nothing about fighting nobody."

That was the thing. The Old Man done the same to me. He reckoned every colored wanted to fight for his freedom. It never occurred to him that they would feel any other way.

Bob stood there, fuming. He was hot. "I done gone from the frying pan to the fire. Captain Pate's rebels is gonna burn us up!"

"Maybe the Captain'll find somebody else to fight. He ain't the only abolitionist 'round these parts."

"He's the only one that counts. Cousin Herbert said there's two companies of U.S. dragoons combing this country, looking for this outfit. That's U.S. Army, I'm talking. From back east. That ain't no posse. They gonna blame us for whatever he does when he's caught, you can bet on it."

"What we done wrong?"

"We here, ain't we? If we's caught, you can bet whatever they do to him, they'll double the potion on the niggers. We'll be in deep grease. You never thunk that, did you?"

"You didn't sing that song when you told me to run with him."

"You didn't ask it," Bob said. He got up, looking toward the campfire, where the smell of food beckoned. "Fight for freedom," he said, sucking his teeth. "Sheesh." He turned and spotted the bevy of stolen horses tied to the outer barrier, where several scouts stood. Looked to be at least twenty horses there and a couple of wagons to boot.

He looked at them and back to me. "Whose horses is those?"

"He always got a bunch of stolen horses around."

"I aim to take one of them and get gone. You can come if you want."

"Where to?"

"Jump across the Missouri, then find Tabor, Iowa. They say there's a gospel train there. Underground Railroad. That'll run you north to Canada. Distant country."

"You can't run a horse that far."

"We'll take two, then. The Old Man won't mind one or two missing."

"I wouldn't snatch a horse from him."

"He ain't gonna live long, child. He's crazy. He thinks the nigger's equal to the white man. He showed that on the way here. Calling the coloreds in the wagon 'mister' and 'missus' and so forth."

"So what? He does that all the time."

"They gonna kill him for being so dumb. He ain't right in his mind. Ain't you seen that?"

Well, he had a point, for the Old Man weren't normal. For one thing, he rarely ate, and he seemed to sleep mostly atop his horse. He was old compared to his men, wrinkled and wiry, but nearly as strong as every one of them except Fred. He marched for hours without stopping, his shoes full of holes, and was overall gruff and hard generally. But at night he seemed to soften some. He'd pass Frederick sleeping in his roll, lean over, and tuck the giant's blanket roll tightly with the gentleness of a woman. There weren't a dumb beast under God's creation—cow, ox, goat, mule, or sheep—that he couldn't calm or tame to touch. He had nicknames for everything. Table was "floor tacker," walking was "tricking." Good was "dowdy." And I was "the Onion." He sprinkled most of his conversation with Bible talk, "thees" and "thous" and "takest" and so forth. He mangled the Bible more than any man I ever knowed, including my Pa, but with a bigger purpose, 'cause he knowed more words. Only when he got hot did the Old Man quote the Bible exact to the letter, and then it was trouble, for it meant someone was about to walk to the quit line. He was a lot to deal with, Old Brown.

"Maybe we ought to warn him," I said.

"'Bout what?" Bob said. "About dying for niggers? He made that choice. I ain't getting into no hank with no rebels about slavery. We'll be colored when the day's done, no matter how the cut comes or goes. These fellers can go back to being Pro Slavers anytime they want."

"If you stealing from the Old Man, I don't want to know about it," I said.

"Just keep shut 'bout me," he said, "and I'll keep quiet 'bout you." And with that he got up and headed over to the campfire to eat.

I decided to warn the Old Man about Bob the next morning, but no sooner did I consider it than he marched into the middle of camp and shouted, "We found 'em boys! We found Pate! He's close by. Mount up! On to Black Jack!"

The men tumbled out of their rolls, grabbed their weapons, and staggered to their horses, tripping over pots and pans and junk, getting ready to roll outta camp, but the Old Man halted 'em and said, "Wait a minute. I got to pray."

He done it quick—twenty minutes, which was fast for him, sawing away at God for His goodwill, advice, benefit, and so forth, while the men stood around, jumping on one foot to keep warm, which gived Bob a chance to prowl the camp and arm himself with every little bit of foodstuff that was left, which weren't much. I seen him on the outside of the circle, nobody bothering him, for the Old Man's camp was full of every abolitionist and colored who needed a gun or a hot meal. The Captain didn't mind it a bit, for while he was big on stealing swords, guns, pikes, and horses from Pro Slavers, he didn't mind anyone in his camp helping themselves to one of them things, so long as they was all for the good cause of the abolitionists. Still, Bob rooting around a bunch of rifles lined against a tree while everyone else was looking for food perked his interest, for he thought Bob wanted to arm himself. After his prayer, while the men broke camp and placed pikes, Sharps rifles, and broadswords in a wagon, the Captain marched over to Bob and said, "Good sir, I see you is ready to strike a blow for your own freedom!"

That hemmed Bob up. He pointed to the rifles and said, "Sir, I don't have no knowledge of how to use them things."

The Captain thrust a sword into Bob's hands. "Swinging this high is all the knowledge you need," he grunted. "Come now. Onward. Freedom!"

He hopped into the rear of an open-back wagon driven by Owen, and poor Bob had to follow. He looked downright unsettled, and set there, quiet as a mouse, while we rode. After a few minutes, he uttered, "Lord, I'm feeling weak. Help me, Jesus. I need the Lord is what I need. I need the blood of Jesus!"

This the Old Man took as a sign of friendship, for he grabbed Bob's hands in his and jumped into a roaring prayer about the Almighty in the book of Genesis, then washed it down with several more verses from the Old Testament, then throwed some New Testament in there, and tossed that about for a good while. A half hour later Bob was dead asleep and the Old Man was still prattling on. "The blood of Jesus binds us as brothers! The Good Book says, 'Hold thine own hand to the blood of Christ and you will see the coming of thine own intervention.' Onward, Christian soldiers! Glorious redemption!"

He got just plain joy hollering out the Bible, and the closer we got to the battlefield, the more redeemed he got, and his words made my insides quiver, for he had prayed like that at Osawatomie when he knocked them fellers' heads off. I weren't for no fighting, and neither was some of his army. As we drawed closer to Black Jack, his herd, which had growed to nearly fifty by that time, thinned out just like they done at Osawatomie. This one had a sick child, that one had to tend crops. Several in the column on their horses let their mounts slow-trot till they faded to the back of the column, then turned around and scooted. By the time we got to Black Jack, about only twenty remained. And them twenty was exhausted from the Old Man's prayer, which he throwed out to full effect en route, and them mutterings had a way of putting a man to sleep on his feet, which meant the only person awake and fired by the time we reached Black Jack was the Old Man himself.

Black Jack was a boggy swamp with a ravine cutting through it and woods sheltering either side. When we reached it, we proceeded to a ridge outside the village, where it sheered off the trail and cut straight into the woods. The Old Man waked the troops in the wagon and ordered the rest on horse to dismount. "Follow my orders, men. And no talking."

It was hot and broad daylight. Early morning. No night charge here. We proceeded on foot for about ten minutes to a clearing, then he crawled up a ridge to look over the crest to the valley of Black Jack below to see where Pate's Sharpshooters was. When he come back off the ridge he said, "We're in a good position, men. Take a look."

We crawled to the edge of the ridge and looked over into the town.

By God, there was three hundred men swilling around on the other side of the ravine if there was one. Several dozen had lined up as shooters, laying on the ridge that defended the town. The ridge overlooked a creek in a ravine with a small river. Beyond it was the town. Since they was beneath us, Pate's shooters hadn't seen us yet, for we was hidden by the thickets above them. But they was ready, sure enough.

After reconnoitering the enemy, we headed back to where the horses were tied, whereupon the Old Man's sons began to wrangle about what came next. None of it sounded pleasant. The Old Man was keen for a frontal attack by coming down one of the ridges, for they was protected by rocks and the slope of the land. His boys preferred a sneak surprise attack at night.

I walked off from 'em a bit, for I was nervous. I walked out and down the trail a bit, heard the sound of hoofbeats, and found myself staring at another Free State rifle company that galloped past me and into our clearing. There were about fifty, in clean uniforms, all spit and shine. Their captain rode up in a smartly dressed military outfit, leaped off his horse, and approached the Old Man.

The Old Man, who always kept himself deep in the woods, away from his horses and wagon lest a surprise attack come, popped out the woods to greet them. With his wild hair, beard, and chewed-up clothes, he looked like a mop dressed in rags compared to this captain, who was all shined up from his buttons to his boots. He marched up to the Old Man and said, "I'm Captain Shore. Since I got fifty men, I'll command. We can go straight at them from the ravine."

The Old Man weren't keen on taking orders from nobody. "That won't do," he said. "You're wide open that way. The ravine circles them all the way around. Let's work our way to the side and kill off their supply line."

"I come here to kill 'em, not starve 'em," Captain Shore said. "You can work your way 'round the side all you want, but I ain't got all day." With that he mounted up, turned to his men, and said, "Let's take them," and sent his fifty men on their horses straight down the ravine toward the enemy.

They hadn't got five steps down that ravine before Pate's Sharpshooters met them with a hail of bullets. Knocked five or six clean off their mounts and diced, sliced, and chopped every one of the rest that was stupid enough to follow their captain down that ridge. The rest that could make off their mounts hotfooted it up that ridge fast as the devil on foot, with their captain running behind them. Shore collapsed at the top and took cover, but the remainder of his men that got up there kept going, right past their captain, taking off down the road.

That Old Man watched 'em, irritated. "I knew it," he said. He ordered me and Bob to guard the horses, sent a few men to a distant hill to take aim at the enemy's horses, then sent a few more to the far edge of the ravine to block the enemy's escape. To the rest he said, "Follow me."

Now, yours truly weren't following him no place. I was happy to guard the horses, but a few of Pate's men decided to fire on our horses, which put me and Bob in the hothouse. Shooting suddenly erupted everywhere on the ridge where we was, and the Old Man's army broke apart. Truth be to tell it, much of the grapeshot whistling past my ears was from our side as come from the enemy, for neither side was coolheaded about what they was doing, loading and firing fast as they could, the devil keeping score. You had as much chance getting killed by your neighbor blowing your face off in them days as you did the enemy hitting you from a hundred yards distant. A bullet's a bullet, and there was so many of 'em snapping and pinging against the trees and limbs, there weren't no place to hide. Bob cowered under the horses, which was heavy taking fire and rearing in panic, and staying with them didn't seem

safe to me, so I followed the Old Man down the hill. He seemed
the safest bet.

I got halfway down the hill when I realized I had lost my
mind, so I throwed myself to the ground and cowered behind
a tree. But that wouldn't do, for there was lead slapping up
against the bark 'round my face, so I found myself rolling down
the crest into the ravine right behind the Old Man, who had
plopped down next to about ten of his men in a line behind a
long log they used for cover.

Well, that charged up the Old Man when he seen me land
down there behind him, for he said to the others, "Look! 'And
a child shall lead them!' The Onion's here. Look, men. A girl
among us! Thanks be to God to inspire us to glory, to bring us
luck and good fortune."

The men glanced at me, and while I can't say whether they
was inspired or not, for they was taking fire, I will say this:
When I looked down that line of fellers, weren't a single man
from Captain Shore's company there, except Captain Shore
himself. He had somehow got the nerve to come back. His
clean uniform and shiny buttons was muddied up now, and
his face was drawed-out nervous. His confidence was spent.
His men had turned and cut clean out on him. Now it was just
the Old Man and his fellers running the show.

The Old Man looked down the line at his men who lay
there in the ravine firing and barked, "Halt. Down." They done
as he said. He used his spyglass to inspect the Missourians'
pickets who was firing from their side. He ordered his men to
load up, told 'em exactly where to aim their fire, then said,
"Don't fire till I say so." Then he got up, and paced back and
forth along the log, tellin' 'em where to shoot as balls whizzed
past his head, talking to his men who were reloading and fir-

ing. He was cool as ice in a glass. "Take your time," he said. "Line 'em up in your sights. Aim low. Don't waste ammunition."

Pate's Sharpshooters wasn't organized and they was scared. They blowed a lot of ammunition firing willy-nilly and exhausted themselves after a few minutes. They started falling back in numbers on their ridge. The Old Man shouted, "The Missourians are leaving. We must compel them to surrender." He ordered Weiner and another feller named Biondi to move down the side of the ravine to flank them and shoot their horses, which they done. This caused cussing and more firing from the Missouri side, but the Old Man's men was confident, shooting dead-on and putting a hurting on 'em. Pate's men took a lot of bad hits, and several runned off without their horses to avoid capture.

An hour later, the fight had gone clean out of them. The Old Man's fellers was organized, whereas Pate's forces wasn't. By the time the shooting stopped, there weren't but thirty or so of Captain Pate's men left, but it was still a stalemate. Nobody could hit nobody. Each side was tucked behind ridges, and anybody on either side stupid enough to stand up got their balls blowed off, so nobody done it. After about ten minutes of this, the Old Man got impatient. "I will advance some twenty yards by myself," he said, crouching in the ravine and cocking his revolver, "and when I wave my hat, you all follow."

He stepped out into the ravine to run forward, but a sudden wild shout in the air stopped him.

Frederick, riding a horse, galloped straight past us, down the ravine, across the bottom of the ravine, and up the hill toward the Missourians, waving a sword and screaming, "Hurrah, Father! We got 'em surrounded! Come on, boys! We cut 'em off!"

Well, he was light as a feather in his mind, and dotty as they come, but the sight of Fred rolling at 'em, huge as he was, hollering to beat the band, wearing enough guns to arm Fort Leavenworth, it was too much for 'em, and they stone quit. A white flag come up from their ravine, and they surrendered. They come out with their hands up.

Only when they was disarmed did they learn to whose hands they had fallen in, for they hadn't known it was the Old Man they was shooting at. When the Old Man walked up and grumbled, "I'm John Brown of Osawatomie," several panicked and looked to sprout tears, for the Old Man in plain view was a frightening sight. After months in the cold woods, his clothes was tattered and worn, so you could see the skin underneath. His boots was more toes than anything. His hair and beard were long and scraggly and white and nearly to his chest. He looked mad as a wood hammer. But the Old Man weren't the monster they thought he was. He lectured several on their cussing and gived them a word or three on the Bible, which plain wore 'em out, and they calmed down. A few even bantered with his men.

Me and Bob tended to the wounded while the Old Man and his boys disarmed Pate's troops. There was a great many of them rolling on the ground in agony. One feller received a bullet through the mouth that tore away his upper lip and shattered his front teeth. Another, a young boy no more than seventeen or so, lay in the grass, moaning. Bob noticed he was wearing spurs. "You think I can have them spurs, since you won't be needing them no more?" Bob asked.

The boy nodded, so Bob stooped down to take them off, then said, "There's only one spur here, sir. Where's the other?"

"Well, if one side of the horse goes, the other must," said the boy. "You won't need but one."

Bob thanked him for his kindness, took his one spur, and the feller expired.

Up at the top of the ravine, the rest of the men had gathered their prisoners, seventeen in all. Among them was Captain Pate himself and Pardee, who had it out with Bob after he was tried by Kelly and his gang near Dutch's. He spotted Bob among the Captain's men and couldn't stand it. "I should'a beat the butt covers off you before, ya black bastard," he grumbled.

"Hush now," the Old Man said. "I'll have no swearing 'round me." He turned to Pate. "Where is my boys John and Jason?"

"I ain't got 'em," Pate said. "They are at Fort Leavenworth, under federal dragoons."

"Then we will go there directly and I will exchange you for them."

We set off for Fort Leavenworth with the prisoners, their horses, and the rest of the horses that Pate's men left behind. We had enough horses to stock a horse farm, maybe thirty in all, along with mules, and as much of Pate's booty as we could carry. Myself, I made off with two pairs of pants, a shirt, a can of paint, a set of spurs, and fourteen corncob pipes I was aiming to trade. The Old Man and his boys didn't take a thing for themselves, though Fred helped hisself to a couple of Colts and a Springfield rifle.

It was twenty miles to Fort Leavenworth, and on the way Pate and the Old Man chatted easily. "I'd just as soon aired you out," Pate said, "if I had known that was you standing down there in that ravine."

The Old Man shrugged. "You missed your chance," he said.

"We ain't gonna reach the fort," Pate said. "This trail is full of rebels looking for you, aiming to collect on your reward."

"When they come, I'll make sure my first charge is in your face," the Old Man said calmly.

That quieted Pate up.

Pate was right, though, for we got about ten miles down the road, near Prairie City, when an armed sentinel in uniform approached. He rode right at us, shouting, "Who goes there?"

Fred was in the lead and he hollered out, "Free State!"

The sentry spun his horse 'round, hurried back down the trail, and reappeared with an officer and with several U.S. dragoons, heavily armed. They was federal men, army men, dressed in flashy colored uniforms.

The officer approached the Old Man. "Who are you?" he asked.

"I'm John Brown of Osawatomie."

"Then you are under arrest."

"For what?"

"For violating the laws of Kansas Territory."

"I don't abide by the bogus laws of this territory," the Old Man said.

"Well, you will abide by this," the officer said. He drawed his revolver and pointed it at the Old Man, who stared at the revolver in disdain.

"I don't take it personal your threats on my life," the Old Man said calmly. "For you are given orders to follow. I understand you have a job to do. So go ahead and drop the hammer on that thing if you want. You will be a hero to some in this territory if you do it. But should you burst a cap into me, your life won't be worth a plugged nickel. You will be food for the wolves come evening, for I got a charge to keep from my Maker, Whose home I hope to make my own someday. I done no harm to you and will not. I will let the Lord have you, and that is a far worse outcome than any that you can put forth with what you holding in your hand, which compared to the will of our Maker, ain't worth a fingernail. My aim is to free the slaves in this territory no matter what you do."

"On whose authority?"

"The authority of our Maker, henceforth and forevermore known as the King of Kings and Lord of Lords."

I don't know what it is, but every time the Old Man started talking holy, just the mention of his Maker's name made him downright dangerous. A kind of electricity climbed over him. His voice become like gravel scrapin' a dirt road. Something raised up in him. His old, tired frame dropped away, and in its place stood a man wound up like a death mill. It was most unsettling thing to see, and the officer got unnerved by it. "I ain't here to debate you on the premise," he said. "Tell your men to lay down their arms, and there won't be no trouble."

"Don't want none. Does your work include taking prisoners and exchanging them?" the Old Man asked.

"Yes, it does."

"I got seventeen prisoners here from Black Jack. I could have killed them directly, for they was intent on taking my life. Instead I am bringing them to Fort Leavenworth for your justice. That ought to be worth something. I want my boys who is held there and nothing more. If you will take these prisoners in exchange for them, I will call it a square deal and hand myself over to you without a fight or harsh word. But if you don't, you will be worm food, sir. For I am in service of a Greater Power. And my men here will aim for your heart and no one else's. And while we are outnumbered here two to one, your death will be certain, for they will aim for you alone, and after that, you will suffer the death of a thousand ages, having to explain to your Maker the support of a cause that has enslaved your fellow human beings and entrapped your soul in a way you know not. I have been chosen to do His special work and I aim to keep that charge. You, on the other hand, have not been chosen. So I am not going with you to Fort Leavenworth today, nor am I leaving this territory, until my boys are freed."

"Who are they?"

"They are Browns. They had nothing to do with any killings in this area. They came here to settle the land and have lost everything, including their crops, which were burned by the very rebels you see before you."

The officer turned to Pate. "Is that true?" he asked.

Pate shrugged. "We did burn these nigger-stealer's crops. Twice. And we will burn their homes if we get the chance, for they are lawbreakers and thieves."

That changed up the officer, and he said, "That sounds like a pretty rotten piece of business."

"Is you Pro Slave or Free State?" Pate asked.

"I'm U.S. State," the officer snapped. "Here to enforce the territorial laws of the United States government, not Missouri or Kansas." He now turned his gun on Pate and said to Brown, "If I carry your prisoners back to Leavenworth, can I trust you to stay here?"

"So long as you bring my sons back in exchange for 'em."

"I cannot promise that, but I will speak to my superior officer about it."

"And who would that be?"

"Captain Jeb Stuart."

"You tell Captain Stuart that Old John Brown of Osawatomie is here at Prairie City awaiting his sons. And if they are not back here in exchange for these prisoners in three days, I will burn this territory."

"And if they do come back? Would you surrender yourself?"

The Old Man folded his hands behind his back.

"I would do that," he said.

"How do I know you're not lying?"

The Old Man held up his right hand. "You have it here before God that I, John Brown, will not leave here for three days while I wait for you to bring my boys back. And I will surrender myself to the will of Almighty God upon their return."

Well, the officer agreed and set off.

The Old Man was lying, of course. For he didn't say nothing about surrendering himself to the U.S. government. Anytime he said something about the will of God, it meant he weren't going to cooperate or do nothing but as he saw fit. He had no intentions of leaving Kansas Territory or turning himself in or paying attention to what any white soldier told him. He would tell a fib in a minute to help his cause. He was like everybody in war. He believed God was on his side. Everybody got God on their side in a war. Problem is, God ain't tellin' nobody who He's for.

8

A Bad Omen

The Old Man said he'd wait three days for the federals to bring his boys back. He didn't get to wait that long. The very next morning, a local feller, friendly to our side, come charging in on his horse, breathless, and told him, "The Missourians got a column heading to burn down your homestead." That was Brown's Station, where the Old Man and his boys had staked out claims and built homes, near Osawatomie.

The Old Man considered it. "I can't leave till the federals come back with John and Jason," he said. "I gived my word. I can't go back home and face their wives with empty palms." Some of his son's wives wasn't too fond of the Old Man for pulling their husbands into the war and getting 'em damn near kilt—in fact, before it was over, some of 'em was kilt outright—over the slavery question.

He turned to Owen and said, "Take Fred, Weiner, Bob, the Onion, and the rest of the men to Osawatomie. See what you see and report back with the men. But leave the Onion in

Osawatomie with your sister-in-law Martha or the Adairs, for she has seen enough killing. Don't tarry."

"Yes, Father."

He turned to me and said, "Onion, I is sorry I am taking you out the fight. I knows how much you like fighting for your freedom, having seen you in action at Black Jack"—I ain't done a thing there that I recall other than cower and holler in that ravine when we was taking fire, but the Old Man looked over there and saw me down there with the best of his men, and I reckon he claimed that as bravery. That was the thing with the Old Man. He seen what he wanted to see, for I knowed I was square terrified, and unless you count hollering uncle and curling up into a ball and licking your toes signs of courage and encouragement, there weren't nothing too courageous about what I done down there. Anyway, he went on: "Brave as you are, we involved here is men, even Bob here, and it is best that you stay in Osawatomie with my friends the Adairs till things calm down, then think about heading north to your freedom where it is safer for a girl to be."

Well doggone it I was ready to hit out hooting and hollering that minute. I was done with the smell of gunpowder and blood. Him and his men could pick fights and spur their horses into shoot-outs for the rest of their days as far as I was concerned. I was finished. But I tried not to show too much joy about the whole bit. I said, "Yes, Captain, I will honor your wishes."

Osawatomie was a full day's ride from Prairie City, and Owen decided to lead his men on the main California Trail, which was a little more risky for chance meetings with Pro Slave patrols, but he wanted to get back to his Pa in quick fashion. The Adairs who I was set to stay with lived off that trail too, in the same general direction as Osawatomie, so all the more reason to take the trail. It worked out well at first. As we rode, I gave a thought or two to where I'd slip off to once Owen and the Old Man's men left. I had a few boy's items I'd picked up in my travels, and a few little items. But where to go? North? What was that? I didn't know north in any way, shape, fashion, or form in them days. I was considering this thought as I rode along with Fred, which always made me feel better about myself, for Fred didn't require but a half a mind to talk to, being that he weren't but half a glass, which made him a good talking partner, for I could think one thing to myself and chat to him about another, and he generally was agreeable to anything I said.

Me and him lingered in the rear of the column, with Weiner and Owen leading up front, and Bob in the middle. Fred seemed blue.

"I heard Owen say you know all your letters now," he said.

"I do," I said. I was proud of it.

"I'm wondering why I can't hold a letter in my head," he said drearily. "I learns one at a time and forgets 'em right off. Everybody else can hold their letters in their head except me. Even you."

"Knowing letters ain't all it's cracked up to be," I said. "I ain't read but one book. It's a Bible picture book I got from the Old Man."

"You think you could read it to me?"

"Why, I'd be happy to," I said.

When we stopped to water the horses and eat, I got my book out and throwed a few words at Fred. I gived him my version of it anyway, for while I knowed my letters, I didn't know more than a few words, so I cooked up what I didn't know. I gave him the book of John, and John's tellin' the people of Jesus's coming and Jesus being so great that John weren't even worthy to fasten his slippers. The story growed to the size of an elephant in my retelling of it, for when's the last time you read in the Bible 'bout a horse named Cliff pulling his wagon 'round into the city of Jerusalem wearing slippers? But Fred never said a cross or contrary word as he listened. He liked it fine. "It's the most dandy reading of the Bible I ever heard," he declared.

We mounted up and followed the trail that crossed to the north side of the Marais des Cygnes River, which cuts through Osawatomie. We were passing close to the Brown settlement but not quite at it, when the smell of smoke and hollering suddenly drifted into the wind.

Owen rode ahead to look, then returned at full gallop. "The Missourians is having it out with a bunch of Free State Indians, looks like. Maybe we should run back and fetch Father."

"No. Let's join the Indians and attack the rebels," Weiner said.

"We got orders from our Pa," Owen said.

Them two argued about it, with Weiner favoring joining the Indians and attacking the redshirts, and Owen in favor of obeying the Old Man's orders and movin' on to check on Osawatomie, or at least run back and fetch the Old Man. "By the time we get anywhere, the redshirts will have burned them Indians out and moved into Osawatomie," Weiner said.

"We got my orders to ride on," Owen said.

Weiner was itching mad but kept quiet. He was a stout, stubborn man who loved a good fight, and you couldn't tell him nothing. We rode closer and seen the Free State Indians and Missourians engaging through the thin pine trees of the wooded area in the clearing. It weren't a big fight, but them Indians defending their free settlement was outnumbered, and when Weiner spied it, he couldn't help hisself. He rode off, busting through the woods on his horse, leaning low. The other men followed him.

Owen watched them go, frowning. He turned on his horse and said, "Fred, you and Onion ride forward toward Osawatomie and wait outside the settlement while we chase off these Missourians. I'll be back shortly." And off *he* went.

Now, Bob was setting there on his mount and he watched them ride off. And nobody said nothing to him. And *he* rode off in another direction. Said, "I'm gone," and took off. That nigger ran off a total of seven times, I believe, from John Brown. Never did get free from the Old Man right off. He had to run all the way back to slavery—to Missouri territory—to get free. But I'll get to that in a minute.

That left me and Fred setting there on our stolen ponies. Fred looked itching for a fight, too, for he was a Brown, and them Browns liked a good gunfight. But no way in God's kingdom was I gonna go over there and fight it out with the Missourians. I was done. So I said, just to distract him, "Gosh, this little girl is hungry."

That snapped him right to me. "Ohhh, I will get you some eatings, Little Onion," he said. "Nobody lets my Little Onion go hungry, for you is halfway to being growed now, and you needs your rest and victuals so you'll grow into a great big sissy." He didn't mean nothing by it and I took no offense from it, for neither of us knowed what the word really meant, though the leanings of it from what I knowed weren't flattering. Still, it was the first time he said the word *sissy* since he first come to knowing of my secret some time back. And I took note of it and was glad to be leaving him before he gived me away.

We rode forward into a patch of thick woods about a mile farther up the trail, then cut off it to follow an old logging trail. It was peaceful and quiet, once we drawed away from the shooting. We crossed a creek and come to where the old logging trail picked up again on the other side and tied our horses off there. Fred pulled off his hardware and got his blanket and hunting things out—beads, dried corn, dried yams. Took him several minutes to unstrap them guns, for he was loaded. Once he done that, he give me a squirrel rifle and took one for hisself. "Normally I wouldn't use this," he said, "but there's enough shooting 'round here so it won't draw no attention, not if we hurry."

It weren't dark yet but evening was coming. We walked about a half mile along the creek bank, with Fred showing me the markings and the likes of where a beaver family was busy making a dam. He said, "I'll cross the creek and work him from the other side. You come up this way, and when he hears you coming, that'll flush him out, and we'll just meet yonder near where the creek bends to get him."

He crept over on the other side and disappeared in the thickets, while I come up on the other side of it. I was about halfway to where we was to meet when I turned and seen a white man standing about five yards off, holding a rifle.

"What you doing with that rifle, missy?" he said.

"Nuthin', sir," I said.

"Put it down, then."

I done like he said, and he come up on me, snatched my rifle from the ground, and, still holding his rifle on me, said, "Where's your master?"

"Oh, he's 'cross the creek."

"Ain't you got a sir in your mouth, nigger?"

I was out of practice, see. I hadn't been 'round normal white folks in months, demanding you call 'em sir and what all. The Old Man didn't allow none of that. But I righted up. I said, "Yes, sir."

"What's your marse's name?"

I couldn't think of nothing, so I said, "Fred."

"What?"

"Just Fred."

"You call your marse Fred or just Fred or Marse Fred or Fred sir?"

Well, that tied me in knots. I should'a named Dutch, but Dutch seemed a long way away, and I was confused.

"Come with me," he said.

We started off through the woods away from the creek, and I followed on foot. We hadn't gotten five steps when I heard Fred holler. "Where you going?"

The man stopped and turned. Fred was standing dead in the middle of the creek, his squirrel gun cocked to his face. He was a sight to see, big as he was, frightening to look at with dead intent, and he weren't no more than ten yards off.

"She belong to you?" the man said.

"That ain't your business, mister."

"You Pro Slave or Free State?"

"You say one more thing, and I'mma deaden where you is. Turn her loose and git your foot up that road."

Well, Fred could'a burned him, but he didn't. The feller turned me loose and trotted off, still holding my squirrel rifle.

Fred climbed out of the water and said, "Let's come off this creek and head back toward where the others is. It's too dangerous out here. There's another creek on the other side from where they left."

We went back to where the horses were tied off, mounted, and rode a half hour or so north, this time to a clearing near where another, bigger creek widened out. Fred said, "We can catch a duck or a pheasant or even a hawk here. It's gonna be dark soon and they'll be collecting their last vittles of the day. Stay here, Little Onion, and don't make a sound." He dismounted and left, still holding his squirrel rifle.

I stuck close to the spot where he left me and watched him move through the woods. He was smooth business out there, quiet as a deer, not a sound come out of him. He didn't go far. Maybe thirty yards off, I could see his silhouette in the trees, then he spotted something up in a long birch that stretched skyward. He raised his rifle and let a charge go, and a huge bird fell to the earth.

We run up on it and Fred paled. It was a fat, beautiful catch, black, with a long red-and-white stripe on its back, and a strange, long beak. It was a nice bird, plenty meat, about twenty inches long. Wingspan must've been nearly a yard. Big as any bird you'd want to eat. "That's a hell of a hawk," I said. "Let's move away from here just in case somebody heard the shot." I moved to grab it.

"Don't touch it!" Fred said. He was pale as a ghost. "That ain't no hawk. That's a Good Lord Bird. Lord!"

He sat on the ground, just ripped up. "I never saw it clear. I only had one shot. See that?" He held up the squirrel rifle.

"Damn thing. Only got one shot. Don't take much. Man sins without knowing, and sins come without warning, Onion. The Bible says it. 'He who sins knows not the Lord. He does not know Him.' You think Jesus knows my heart?"

I growed tired of his mumbling confusion 'bout the Lord. I was hungry. I was supposed to be getting away from the fighting and here I was held up by more of the same. I was irritated. I said, "Stop worrying. The Lord knows your heart."

"I got to pray," he said. "That's what Father would do."

That wouldn't do. It was almost dark now, and the others hadn't caught up to us yet, and I worried that the shot would draw somebody. But there ain't nothing to tell a white man, or any man, who's made up his mind to a prayerful thing. Fred set there on his knees and prayed just like the Old Man, fluffering and blubbering to the Lord to come to his favor and this and that. He weren't nearly as good as his Pa in the praying department, being that he weren't able to attach one thought to the next. The Old Man's prayers growed up right before your eyes; they was all connected, like stairways running from one floor to another in a house, whereas Fred's prayers was more like barrels and clothing chests throwed about a fine sitting room. His prayers shot this way and that, cutting hither and yon, and in this way an hour passed. But it was a precious hour which I'll tell you about in a minute. After he gave up them various mumblings and jumblings he gently picked up the bird, gived it to me, and said, "Hold it for Pa. He'll pray on it and favor God to fix the whole thing up righteously."

I grabbed it, and as I done, we heard horses coming fast on the other side of the creek. Fred snapped over his shoulder, "Hide quick!"

I had just enough time to jump into the thickets holding

that bird as several horses splashed across the creek, came straight up the bank, and busted through the thickets and to where Fred was standing. They came straight on him.

There wasn't nowhere to run, for we had tied our horses a quarter mile off, and they'd come from that very direction, which meant they likely found our mounts anyway. I had just enough time to dive deep into the thickets before they sloshed up the bank and marched up to Fred. He stood there smiling, wearing all his hardware, but his seven-shooters wasn't drawn. The only gun he had in his hand was that squirrel gun, and it was spent.

They sloshed up the bank right to him quick as you can tell it. There were maybe eight of 'em, redshirts, and riding in the lead of 'em was Rev. Martin, the feller Fred drawed on back at the Old Man's camp.

Now Fred was thick, but he weren't an altogether fool. He knowed how to survive in the woods and do lots of outdoor things. But he weren't a quick thinker, for if he was, he'd'a drawed his heater. But two or three thoughts at once was more than he could handle. Plus he didn't recognize the Reverend right off. That cost him.

The Reverend was riding with two men on either side of him bearing six-shooters and the rest behind him heavily armed. The Rev hisself wore his two shiny pearl-handled numbers on his belt, which he likely stole off some dead Free Stater, for he hadn't had them things before.

He rode right up to Fred while his men surrounded Fred, cutting off his escape.

But still Fred didn't get it. Fred said, "Morning." He was smiling. That was his nature.

"Morning," the Reverend said.

Then Fred's mind checked itself. You could see his head cock to the side, something whirring in there. He stared at the Reverend. He was trying to figure out whether he knowed him.

He said, "I know you . . . ," and quick as you can tell it, without a word, the Reverend, setting atop his horse, drawed his shooter and took him. Blasted Fred right in the chest, buttered him with lead and powder, and the blessed God, the ground caught him. Fred twitched a few times and breathed his last.

"That'll teach you to draw on me, you apple-headed, horse-thieving, nigger-loving bastard," the Reverend said. He come down off his horse and took every single gun Fred was wearing. He turned to the others. "I got me one of Brown's boys," he said proudly. "Got the biggest one."

Then he throwed his eyes to the woods 'round him, where I was hiding. I held tight to where I was. Didn't move an inch. He knowed I was close.

"Look for the second rider," he barked. "There was two horses."

Just then another feller spoke up, a feller sitting on a horse behind the Rev. "You ain't had to shoot him cold-blooded like that," he said.

Rev. Martin turned to the man. It was the feller that had caught me in the woods just a while before. He was still holding my squirrel gun, and he weren't pleased.

"He would'a returned the favor," the Reverend said.

"We could'a exchanged him for one of ours," the feller said.

"You wanna change out prisoners or fight a war?" the Rev said.

"He could'a aired me out an hour ago back down the creek there and he didn't," the man said.

"He was Free State!"

"I don't give an owl's ass if he was George Washington. The man didn't draw on you and he's deader'n a turnip. You said you was looking for a cattle rustler and nigger thieves. He ain't no cattle rustler. And the nigger he had weren't nobody's nigger I know. What kind'a war rules is we fighting under here?"

This started a hank between 'em, with several taking this feller's side and others holding with the Reverend. Several minutes gone by as they wrangled, and by the time they finished, dusk had come. Finally Rev. Martin said, "Brown won't tarry when he finds his boy dead out here. You wanna wait till he comes?" That done it. That silenced 'em all, for they knowed there was consequences to the whole bit. They took off on their horses without another word.

I come out the clearing in the dusk, and took a long look at my old friend in the growing darkness. His face was clear. He still had a little smile on his face. I can't say whether his super-stition about that Good Lord Bird done him in or not, but I felt low, standing there holding that dumb bird. I wondered if I should wander someplace and fetch a shovel with the aim of burying Fred and the bird together, since he called it an angel and all, but I quit that idea and decided to run off instead. Weren't nothing to this life of being free and fighting slavery, was how I thunk of it. I was so bothered by the whole bit I can't tell it. I didn't know what to do. The idea of running back home to Dutch and trying to work it out, that worked in there, too, truth be to tell it, and I aimed on seeing to that, for Dutch was all I knowed outside the Old Man. But to be hon-est, I was broke up by the way the whole deal added up, me running 'round as a girl and not knowing what to do. I couldn't think of nothing to do at the moment, and as usual, the whole business just wore me out. So I set on the ground next to Fred and curled into a ball and fell asleep next to him, holding that Good Lord Bird. And that's how the Old Man found me the next day.

9

A Sign from God

I woke up to the sound of cannon fire and the Old Man standing before me. "What happened, Little Onion?"

I gently set the Good Lord Bird on Fred's chest and explained to him who done the deed. He listened, his face grim. Behind him the sound of gunfire and artillery cannon boomed and sent grapeshot slinging through the woods right over his head. Me and Fred had wandered right near Osawatomie, and the fight that Weiner and them had joined in had spilled over into there just as Weiner said it would, with blasting full out. The men ducked low on their horses and held on while the grape whipped past, but none of 'em moved off their mount as the Old Man stood over me. I noted Jason and John among them, but nobody weren't explaining how they got there and why the Old Man weren't in federal prison. They was all hot, staring at Fred, especially his brothers. He was still wearing his little cap, with the Good Lord Bird now perched on his chest where I had rested it.

"Is you gonna find the Reverend?" I asked.

"We ain't got to," the Old Man said. "He has found us. Stay with Fred till we get back." He mounted his horse and nodded toward the sound of the fighting. "Let's go!"

They dashed toward Osawatomie. The town weren't but a short distance off, and I cut through the woods a few steps to a high knoll, where I could see the Old Man and his men take the trail that circled 'round and led to the river and the town on the other side of it. I didn't want to set 'round with Fred and that dead bird asleep in death, and there weren't nothing to say to him nohow.

From where I was, I could see the town. The bridge crossing the Marais des Cygnes River leading to Osawatomie was swarming with rebels who had hauled two cannons over it. A few hundred yards off was the first cannon, which was perched downstream, along a grassy ridge, where you could wade across the water. There were several Free Staters firing on our side, trying to make it across there, but rebels on the other side was holding them off, and every time a group of Free Staters got close in, that cannon cleaned them out.

The Old Man and his boys busted right through them and charged down the hill and into the shallow water like wild men. They come up on the other side firing, and just like that sent the rebels on the other bank scrambling.

This fight was hotter than Black Jack. The town was in a state of panic and there were women and children about, scattering every which way. Several homesteaders was desperately trying to douse the fires on their homes, for the Reverend's riders had torched several houses, and the Rev's men shot them as they tried to put out the flames, which gave the busy homesteaders one less task to do, being that they was deadened. Altogether the Free Staters in town was badly organized. The

Missourians' second cannon was on the other side of town, blasting away, and between that one barking on one end of town, and the other barking at the riverbank on the other end, they was cleaning up the Free Staters.

The Old Man and his men charged out the water with guns blazing and cut to the right toward the first cannon that was downstream. The Free Staters who couldn't cross on account of that cannon took courage when the Old Man's army come and runned past them to take the bank, but the rebels at the cannon held. The Old Man's men hacked and shot their way halfway to the cannon working alongside the creek, which ridged up as it reached the cannon. They pushed the enemy back, but more enemy arrived on horses, dismounted, regrouped, and swung that cannon to bear on them. That thing blowed off to deadly effect and halted the Old Man's charge cold. Sent grapeshot whistling into the trees and cut down several Free Staters, who fell down the riverbank into the creek and didn't get up. The Old Man mounted a charge again, but the cannon sent another volley that sent the Old Man and his men backward again, this time several falling halfway down the riverbank. And this time the rebels leaped out from behind the cannon and charged.

The Old Man's men was outgunned and his boys fell back farther to the ridge, the creek right at their backs now, no place else to back up. There was a line of timber at the riverbank there, and he shouted quickly to his fellers to mount a line, which they did, just as the rebels charged the riverbank again.

I don't know how they held it. The Old Man was stubborn. The Free Staters was badly outnumbered, but they held on until a second party of rebels flanked them from the rear, on the same side of the stream. A few of the Old Man's team turned 'round to fight them off while the Old Man held his boys on the line, urging his men on. "Hold men. Steady. Aim low. Don't waste ammunition." He walked up and down the line shouting directions as bullets and cannon shot tore the leaves and limbs off the trees 'round him.

Finally, behind him, the Free Staters trying to hold off the rebels in that direction quit and run for it across the river, eating lead the whole way, and several of them breathed their last in the river. It was just too many enemy. The Old Man was cut off from a clean retreat now, taking fire from two sides, with the cannon blasting grape at him and rebels closing from the other way, with the creek behind him. He weren't going to make it. He was defeated, but he wouldn't give in. He held his men there.

The Missourians, cussing and hollering, quit for a minute to move their cannon closer, and took some lead from the Old Man's men. But they got it mounted up again within fifty yards or so of the Old Man's line and blowed a big hole in the line, sending several of his men into the water. Only then did he give up. He was done. He hollered, "Back across the river!" The men gladly did it, scrambling fast, but not him. He stood, big as you want, firing and reloading until the last man got out the tree line, hit the bank, and waded across. Owen was the last to go, and when he was at the riverbank and seen his Pa weren't there, he turned back, hollering, "Come, Father!"

The Old Man knowed he was defeated, but couldn't stand it. He squeezed off one more blast from his seven-shooter, turned to run, and as he did, a cannon volley whipped through the tree line and got him. He was hit square in the back and went down like a rag doll, knocked clean off the ridge and back into the bank. He rolled off the ridge down to the river's edge and didn't move. He was done.

Dead.

He weren't dead, though, only stunned, for that ball had spent itself before it got to him. It plunked a hole in his coat and pierced the skin of his back and lost juice right as it got to him. The Old Man's skin was thicker than a mule's ass, and while that ball drawed blood, it didn't go deep. He jumped up quick as you can tell it, but the sight of him falling off that ridge toward the water drawed a cheer from the Missourians at the top of the bank who smelled red meat but couldn't see him at the water's edge, and several jumped down to the bank after him, only to find the Old Man waiting with that seven-shooter which was still dry and loaded. He busted a cap into the face of the first man, cracked the skull of the second man with the butt of that thing—that gun is heavy as the dickens—and sent a third to his Maker with his broadsword just as easy as you please. A fourth feller ran down toward him, and when the poor bastard got over the ridge and seen the Old Man still living, he tried to stop hisself and scramble back to safety. But Owen had scrambled back to the bank to help his Pa and busted a shot at him and blowed out his spark.

It was just them two going at it close, and the sight of them two fighting off rebels attacking 'em from all sides now caused a round of cursing and swearing from the Free Staters who made it to the other side of the river, and they blowed several rounds into the rest of the charging Missourians, who was at the top of the ridge near the tree line. The rebels scattered and fell back. This gived the Old Man and Owen time to get across the river.

I had never seen the Old Man retreat before. He seemed a queer figure there in the river, in a broad straw hat and linen duster, his coattails flung out behind him, arms outspread on the water, as he waded over, a revolver held high in each hand. He climbed onto the opposite bank, out of range of the rebels now, mounted atop his horse, and scrambled his horse up the bank to where I was, followed by the other men, all of 'em joining me on the knoll.

From that knoll you could see Osawatomie clear, the town blazing brightly in the afternoon sun, every house burning to the ground, and every Free Stater stupid enough to hang 'round and try to put out the fire eating his house getting shot to shit by Reverend Martin and his men, who were drunk, laughing and whooping it up. They defeated the Old Man and hollered it all across Osawatomie, several shouting that he was dead and claiming to be the one who done it, whooping that they'd burned his house to the ground, which they'd done.

Most of the other Free Staters who survived had taken the tall timber once they got across the creek to our side. Only the Old Man and his sons remained on our side, watching the rebels celebrate: Jason, John, Salmon, the two younger ones Watson and Oliver, who had joined us, Owen course, all of 'em atop their mounts, staring angrily at the town, for their houses was burning up, too.

But the Old Man didn't look at it once. When he reached the knoll, he slowly paced his horse back to Frederick and got off it. The rest followed him over.

Fred was where we left him, his little cap atop his head, the Good Lord Bird atop his chest. The Old Man stood over him.

"I should'a come out of hiding to help him," I said, "but I don't know how to shoot."

"And shoot you should not," the Old Man said. "For you is a girl soon to be a woman. You was a friend to Fred. He was fond of you. And for that I am grateful to you, Little Onion."

But he might as well have been talking to a hole in the ground, for even as he spoke, his mind was somewhere else. He knelt over Fred. He looked at him several minutes, and for a moment, the old gray eyes softened and it seemed like a thousand years had washed over the Old Man's face. He sighed, gently pulled Fred's cap off his head, pulled a feather off the Good Lord Bird, and rose. He turned and stared at the town grimly, burning in the afternoon sun. He could see it plain, the smoke spiraling up, the Free Staters fleeing, the rebels firing at them, whooping and hollering.

"God sees it," he said.

Jason came up to him. "Father, let's bury Frederick and let the federals have the fight. They'll be here soon enough. I don't want to fight no more. My brothers and me, we had enough. We're decided on it."

The Old Man was silent. He fingered Fred's cap and eyed his sons.

"Is that how you want it, Owen?"

Owen, setting atop his horse, looked away.

"And Salmon. And John?"

Six of his sons was there: Salmon, John, Jason, Owen, and the young ones, Watson and Oliver, plus their kin, the Thompson brothers, two of them. They all looked down. They was spent. Not a one of 'em spoke up. Didn't say a word.

"Take Little Onion with you," he said. He tossed Fred's cap into his saddlebag and made ready to get on his horse.

"We've done enough for the cause, Father," Jason said. "Stay with us and help us rebuild. The federals will find Rev. Martin. They'd catch him and put him in jail, try him for Fred's killing."

The Old Man ignored him and mounted his horse, then stared out at the land before him. He seemed to be someplace else in his head. "This is beautiful country," he said. He hold out the feather from the Good Lord Bird. "And this is this beautiful omen that Frederick left behind. It's a sign from God." He stuck it in his weathered, beaten straw cap. It stuck straight up in the air. He looked ludicrous.

"Father, you are not hearing me," Jason said. "We are done! Stay with us. Help us rebuild."

The Old Man stretched his lips in a crazy fashion. It weren't a real smile, but as close as he could come. Never saw him out and out smile up to that point. It didn't fit his face. Stretching them wrinkles horizontal gived the impression of him being plumb stark mad. Seemed like his peanut had poked out the shell all the way. He was soaked. His jacket and pants, which was always dotted full of holes, was a mass of torn and ripped clothing. On his back was a bit of blood where he'd taken a grape ball. He paid it no attention. "I have only a short time to live," he said, "and I will die fighting for this cause. There will be no more peace in this land until slavery is done. I will give these slaveholders something to think about. I will carry this war into Africa. Stay here if you want. If you're lucky, you'll find a cause worth dying for. Even the rebels have that."

He turned his horse 'round. "I have to go and pray and commingle with the Great Father of Justice upon whose blood we live. Bury Fred right. And take care of Little Onion."

With that, he turned on his horse and rode off east. I wouldn't see him again for two years.

PART II

SLAVE DEEDS

(Missouri)

10

A Real Gunslinger

The brothers started haggling not two minutes after the Old Man departed. They stopped their wrangle long enough to bury Frederick atop a knoll that looked down on the town from across the river, plucking some of his Good Lord Bird feathers and giving them out to each of us. Then they hanked among themselves some more about who said this or that, and who shot who and what to do next. It was decided they'd split up and I'd be tagged up with Owen, though Owen weren't particular about the idea. "I'm going to Iowa to court a young lady, and I can't move fast with the Onion on me."

"You weren't saying that when you kidnapped her," Jason said.

"It was Father's idea to take a girl on the trail!"

On it went some more, just fussin'. There weren't no clear leader between them once the Old Man had gone. Nigger Bob was standing 'round as they quarreled. He had run and been plumb gone and disappeared during all the fighting—that nigger had a knack for that—but now that the shooting stopped, he showed up again. I guess wherever he run to weren't good or safe enough. He stood behind the brothers as they went at it. Hearing them fussin' 'bout me, he piped up, "I will ride the Onion to Tabor."

I weren't particular about riding with Bob no place, for it was his pushing me along that helped me to my situation of playing girl for the white man. Plus Bob weren't a shooter, which Owen was. I'd been on the prairie long enough to know that being with a shooter counted a whole mess out there. But I didn't say nothing.

"What do you know about girls?" Owen said.

"I know plenty," Bob said, "for I have had a couple of my own, and I can look after the Onion easily if it pleases you. I can't go back to Palmyra nohow."

He had a point there, for he was stolen property and was tainted goods no matter how the cut go or come. Nobody would believe nothing he said about his time with John Brown, whether he actually fought with the Old Man or not. He'd likely get sold to New Orleans if, according to his word, things went the way they did among the Pro Slavers, with white folks believing that a slave who tasted freedom weren't worth a dime.

Owen groused about it a few minutes but finally said, "All right. I'll take you both. But I'm going back across the river first to scrounge what's left of my claim first. Wait here. We'll head out soon's I get back." Off he went, harring up his horse and riding straight into the thickets.

Course the brothers one by one reckoned they too would scrounge what they could from their claims, and followed him along. John Jr. was the oldest of the Old Man's sons, but Owen was more like the Old Man, and it was his notions that the rest

followed. So Jason, John, Watson and Oliver, and Salmon—
they all had different notions 'bout fighting slavery, though all
was against it—they followed him out. They rode off, tellin' me
and Bob to wait and watch from across the river and holler a
warning if I seen some rebels.

I didn't want to do it, but it seemed like the danger had
passed. Plus it brought me some comfort being near where
Fred slept. So I told 'em I'd holler loud and clear for sure.

It was afternoon now, and from the knoll where we sat, Bob
and I could see clear across the Marais des Cygnes River into
Osawatomie. The rebels had mostly cleared out, the last loot-
ers hurrying out of town whooping and hollering, with a few
bullets of a few early Free Staters who had started to make
their way back across the river whistling in their ears. The fight
had mostly gone out of everybody.

The brothers took the logging trail that looped out of our
sight for a minute, heading to the shallow part of the river to
wade across. From my position, I could see the bank, but after
several long minutes of leaning over the knoll to watch them
cross the river, I still didn't see them reach the other side.

"Where they at?" I asked. I turned 'round but Bob was gone.
The Old Man always had a stolen wagon and horse or two
tied about, and every firefight usually ended up with all kinds
of items laying about as folks scrambled to duck lead. As
luck would have it, there was an old fat mule and a prairie
wagon setting there among the stolen booty in the thickets
just beyond the clearing where we stood. Bob was back there
and he was in a hurry, digging out lines and traces from the
back of the wagon. He slapped the lines onto the mule, hitched
it to the wagon, hopped atop the driver's seat, and harred that
beast up.

"Let's scat," he said.

"What?"

"Let's git."

"What about Owen? He said to wait."

"Forget him. This is white folks' business."

"But what about Frederick?"

"What about him?"

"Reverend Martin shot him. In cold blood. We ought to level things out."

"You can seek that if you want, but you ain't gonna come out clear. I'm gone."

No sooner did he utter them words than a bunch of hollering and shooting came from the same direction as the brothers disappeared to, and two horseback-riding rebel riders in red shirts busted through the thicket and into the clearing, circling 'round the long row of trees and coming right at us.

Bob jumped down from the driver's seat and commenced to pulling the mule. "Wrap that bonnet tight on your little head," he said. I done it just as the redshirt riders come through the clearing, saw us in the thicket of trees, and charged us.

Both of them were young fellers in their twenties, their Colts drawed for business, one of them pulling a mule behind his horse loaded with gunnysacks. The other feller, he seemed to be the leader. He was short and thin, with a lean face and several cigars stuffed in his shirt pocket. The feller pulling the mule was older and had a hard, sallow face. Both their horses was loaded with goods, rolling fat, with bags stuffed busting to the limit with booty taken from the town.

Bob, trembling, tipped his hat to the leader. "Morning, sir."

"Where you going?" the leader asked.

"Why, I'm taking the missus here to the Lawrence Hotel," Bob said.

"You got papers?"

"Well, suh, the missus here got some," Bob said. He looked at me.

I couldn't explain nothing and didn't have paper the first. That set me back. God-damned fool put me on the spot. Oh, I stuttered and bellowed like a broke calf. I played it as much as I could, but it weren't that good. "Well, I don't need papers in that he is taking me to Lawrence," I stuttered.

"Is the nigger taking you?" the leader said, "Or is you taking the nigger?"

"Why, I'm taking him," I said. "We is from Palmyra and was passing through this country. There was quite a bit of mess with all the shooting, so I drug him 'round this way."

The leader moved in close on his horse, staring. He was a ripe, good-looking drummer, with dark eyes and a rowdy look to him. He stuck a cigar in his mouth and chewed it. His horse clunked like a marching band as he plopped his mount 'round me, circling me. That pinto was loaded down with so much junk it was a pity. She looked ready to shut her eyes in death. That beast was carrying a house worth of goods: pots and pans, kettles, whistles, jars, a miniature piano, apple peelers, barrels, dry goods, canned goods, and tin drums. The older feller behind him pulling the mule had twice as much junk. He had the nervous, rough look of a gunfighter, and hadn't said nothing.

"What are you?" the leader asked. "Is you part nigger or just a white girl with a dirty face?"

Well, I was fluffed, wearing that bonnet and dress. But I

had some practice being a girl by then, having been one for the several months past. Besides, my arse was on the line, and that'll unstring your guts quick when you're in a tight spot. He throwed me a bone and I took it. I mustered myself up and said as proudly as I could, "I am Henrietta Shackleford and you ought not to talk 'bout me like I am a full-blooded nigger, being that I am only half a nigger and all alone in this world. The best part of me nearly as white as you, sir. I just don't know where I belongs, being a tragic mulatto and all." Then I busted into tears.

That boo-hooing moved him. That just stuck him! Whirled him backward! His face got soft and he throwed his Colt in its sleeping place, and nodded at the other feller and told him to do the same.

"All the more reason to run these Free Staters out of this country," he said. "I'm Chase." He motioned to his partner. "That's Randy."

I howdied 'em.

"Where's your Ma?"

"Dead."

"Where is your Pa?"

"Dead. Dead, dead, dead. They all dead." I boo-hooed again.

He stood there watching. That throwed him some more. "Quit crying for God's sake, and I'll give you a peppermint," he said.

I stood sniffling while he reached in one of them bags on his horse and throwed me a candy. I throwed it down my little red lane without hesitation. It was my first time tasting one of them things, and by God, the explosion in my mouth gived me more pleasure than you can imagine. Candy was rare in them days.

He seed the effect of it and said, "I has plenty more of them, little missus. What's your business in Lawrence?"

He had me there. I hadn't no business in Lawrence, and wouldn't know Lawrence from Adam. So I commenced to choking and fluttering on that candy to give me a minute to think, which made Chase leap off his horse and pound my back—but that didn't work, neither, for he slammed me so hard, the candy got throwed out my mouth and hit the dust, and that gave me a reason to pretend to be sorry about that, which I was in a real way, so I bawled a little more, but this time it didn't move him, for we both stared at the candy on the ground. I reckon we was both trying to decide a good way to get it up, clean, and eat it as it should be eaten. After a minute or so, I still hadn't come up with nothing.

"Well?" he said.

I glanced at the thicket, hoping Owen would come back. Never had I wanted to see his sour face so much. But I heard shots from the woods where he and the brothers had departed, so I figured they'd had their own troubles. I was on my own.

I said, "My Pa left me this sorry nigger Bob here, and I told him to take me to Lawrence. But he got to giving me so much trouble—"

By God, why did I do that? Chase drawed out his heater again and stuck it in Bob's face. "I'll beat this nigger cockeyed if he's giving you trouble."

Bob's eyes widened big as silver dollars.

"No, sir, that's not it," I said hurriedly. "This nigger's actually been a help to me. It would do me great harm if you hurt him, for he is all I have in this world."

"All right then," Chase said, holstering his six-shooter. "But lemme ask you, honey. How can a part-way nigger own a full-way nigger?"

"He's paid for fair and square," I said. "They do that in Illinois all the time."

"I thought you said you was from Palmyra," Chase said.

"By way of Illinois."

"Ain't that a Free State?" Chase said.

"Not for us rebels," I said.

"What town in Illinois?"

Well, that stumped me. I didn't know Illinois from a mule's ass. I couldn't think of a town there to save my life, so I thunk of something I heard the Old Man say often. "Purgatory," I said.

"Purgatory," Chase laughed. He turned to Randy. "That's the right name for a Yankee town, ain't it, Randy?"

Randy stared at him and didn't say a natural word. That man was dangerous.

Chase looked 'round and seen Frederick's grave where we'd buried him.

"Who's that?"

"Don't know. We been hiding in this thicket while the Free Staters was scouting 'round here. I heard 'em say it was one of theirs."

Chase pondered the grave thoughtfully. "It's a fresh grave. We ought to see if who'sever in there got on boots," he said.

That threw me, for last thing I wanted to do was for them to dig up Frederick and pick all over his parts. I couldn't bear the thought of it, so I said, "I heard 'em say he got his face blowed off and it was all mush."

"Jesus," Chase mumbled. He backed away from the grave. "Damn Yanks. Well, you ain't got to fear them now, little angel. Chase Armstrong done drove 'em off! Wanna ride with us?"

"We is going to the Lawrence Hotel to get a job, and Bob is a help to me. We was waylaid, see, when you all whipped up on them darn Free Staters. But thanks to you, the danger is gone. So I reckon we'll be off."

I motioned to Bob to har up the mule, but Chase said, "Hold on now. We're going to Pikesville, Missouri. That's in your general direction. Why not come with us?"

"We'll be fine."

"These trails is dangerous."

"They ain't that bad."

"I think they is bad enough that you ought not ride alone," he said. It weren't no invitation the way he said it.

"Bob here is sick," I said. "He got the ague. It's catching."

"All the more reason to roll with us. I know a couple of nigger traders in Pikesville. Big nigger like that would draw some good money, sick or not. A couple thousand dollars, maybe. Give you a good start."

Bob shot a wild look at me.

"I can't do that," I said, "for I promised my Pa never to sell him."

I motioned for him again to har up the mules, but Chase grabbed the traces this time and held them tight. "What's waiting for you in Lawrence? Ain't nothing but Free Staters there."

"There is?"

"Surely."

"We'll go to the next town, then."

Chase chuckled. "Ride our way."

"I weren't going that way. Plus Old John Brown's riding these woods. They're still dangerous."

I motioned Bob to har up the mule one more time, but

Chase held 'em tight, looking at me out the corner of his eye. He was serious now.

"Brown is done. The redshirts is shooting up what's left of his boys in the woods yonder. And he's dead. I seen him with my own eyes."

"That can't be!"

"Yep. Deader than yesterday's beer."

That floored me. "That's a low-down, rotten, dirty piece of luck!" I said.

"How's that?"

"I mean it's rotten luck that . . . I ain't never seen him dead, him being a famous outlaw and all. You seen him surely?"

"He's stinking to high heaven right now, the nigger-stealing thief. I seen him hit at the bank and fall into the Marais des Cygnes myself. I would'a run down there and chopped his head off myself but"—he cleared his throat—"me and Randy had to run 'round to protect the flank. Plus there was a hardware store on the back end of town that needed cleaning out, if you get my drift, being that them Free Staters won't be needin' this stuff . . ."

I knowed he was wrong about the Old Man's whereabouts then, and I was relieved. But I had to take care of myself too, so I said, "I am so glad he is gone, for this territory is now safe for good white folks to live free and clear."

"But you ain't white."

"Half-white. Plus we got to take care of the coloreds here, for they needs us. Right, Bob?"

Bob looked away. I knowed he was mad.

I reckoned Chase decided I was close enough to white for him, for Bob's manner sullied him. "You's a sour-faced coon," he muttered, "and I ought to bust you 'cross the jibs for attitude."

He turned to me. "What kind of work you seeking in Lawrence that you carry 'round such a sour nigger?"

"Trim's my business," I said proudly, for I could cut hair.

He perked up. "Trim?"

Now, having growed up with whores and squaws at Dutch's, I should'a knowed what that word "trim" meant. But the truth is, I didn't.

"I sell the best trim a man can get. Can do two or three men in an hour."

"That many?"

"Surely."

"Ain't you a little young to be selling trim?"

"Why, I'm twelve near as I can tell it, and can sell trims just as good as the next person," I said.

His manner changed altogether. He polited up, wiping his face clean with his neckerchief, fluffing his clothes, and straightening out his ragged shirt. "Wouldn't you rather have a job waiting or washing?"

"Why wash dishes when you can do ten men in an hour?"

Chase's face got ripe red. He reached in his sack and drawed out a whiskey bottle. He sipped it and passed it to Randy. "That must be some kind of record," he said. He looked at me out the corner of his eye. "You want to do me one?"

"Out here? On the trail? It's better to be in a warm tavern, with a stove cooking and heating your victuals, while you enjoys a toot and a tear. Plus I can clip your toenails and soak your corns at the same time. Feet's my specialty."

"Ooh, that stirs my britches," he said. "Listen, I know a place there that's perfect for you. I know a lady who'll give you a job. It's in Pikesville, not Lawrence."

"That ain't in our direction."

For the first time, Randy opened his talking hole. "Sure it is," he said. "Unless you playing us for a fool. You all could be lying. 'Cause you ain't showed us no papers—'bout you or him."

He looked rough enough to scratch a match off his face. I didn't have no choice, really, for he had called me out so I said, "You is not a gentleman, sir, to accuse a young lady of my background of lying. But, being that it's dangerous on this trail for a girl like myself, I reckon Pikesville is as good a place to go as any. And if I can make money there selling trims as you claims, why not?"

They ordered Bob to help unload their horses and mules, then spotted some knickknacks among the stolen goods the Old Man's sons had left about. They jumped off their horses to gather that stuff.

The moment they was out of earshot, Bob leaned over from the driver's seat and hissed, "Aim your lies in a different direction."

"What I done?"

"Trim means 'tail,' Henry. Birds and the bees. All that."

When they come back I seen the glint in their eyes, and I was tied in a knot. I'd have given anything to see Owen's sour face come charging, but he didn't come. They tied their beasts to ours, throwed what they gathered up in the wagon, and we rolled off.

11

Pie

We followed the trail half a day northeast, dead into Missouri slave territory. I sat behind Bob in the wagon while Chase and Randy followed on horseback. On the trail, Chase did all the talking. He talked about his Ma. Talked about his Pa. Talked about his kids. His wife was half cousin to his Pa and he *talked about that*. There weren't nothing about himself he didn't seem to want to talk about, which gived me another lesson on being a girl. Men will spill their guts about horses and their new boots and their dreams to a woman. But if you put 'em in a room and turn 'em loose on themselves, it's all guns, spit, and tobacco. And don't let 'em get started on their Ma. Chase wouldn't stop stretching his mouth about her and all the great things she done.

I let him go on, for I was more concerned with the subject of trim, and what my doings was gonna be in that department. After a while them two climbed in the back of the wagon and opened a bottle of rye, which helped commence me to singing right away, just to keep them two off the subject. There ain't nothing a rebel loves more than a good old song, and I knowed several from my days at Dutch's. They rode happily back there, sipping moral suasion while I sang "Maryland, My Maryland," "Please, Ma, I Ain't Coming Home," and "Grandpa, Your Horse Is in My Barn." That cooled them for a while, but dark was coming. Thankfully, just before true night swallowed the big prairie sky, the rolling plains and mosquitoes gived way to log cabins and squatters' homes, and we hit Pikesville.

Pikesville was rude business back in them days, just a collection of run-down cabins, shacks, and hen coops. The streets were mud, with rocks, tree stumps, and gullies lying about the main road. Pigs roamed the alleyways. Ox, mules, and horses strained to pull carts full of junk. Piles of freight sat about uncollected. Most of the cabins was unfinished, some without roofs. Others looked like they were on the verge of collapse altogether, with rattlesnake skins, buffalo hide, and animal skins drying out nearby. There were three grog houses in town, built one on top of the other practically, and every porch railing on 'em was thick with tobacco spit. That town was altogether a mess. Still, it was the grandest town I'd ever seen to that point.

We hit the town to a great hubbub, for they'd heard rumors about the big gunfight at Osawatomie. No sooner had we pulled up than the wagon was surrounded. An old feller asked Chase, "Is it true? Is Old John Brown dead?"

"Yes, sir," Chase crowed.

"You killed him?"

"Why, I threwed every bullet I had at him sure as you standing there—"

"Hoorah!" they hollered. He was pulled off the wagon and clapped and pounded on the back. Randy got sullen and didn't say a word. I reckon he was wanted and there was a reward for him somewhere, for the minute they pulled Chase off the wagon howling, Randy slipped on his horse, grabbed his pack mule, and slipped off. I never seen him again. But Chase was riding high. They drug him to the nearest grog house, sat him down, pumped him full of whiskey, and surrounded him, drunks, jackals, gamblers, and pickpockets, shouting, "How'd you do it?"

"Tell us the whole thing."

"Who shot first?"

Chase cleared his throat. "Like I said, there was a lotta shooting—"

"Course there was! He was a murdering fool!"

"A jackal!"

"Horse thief, too! Yellow Yank!"

More laughter. They just throwed the lie on him. He weren't aiming to lie. But they pumped him full of rotgut as he could stand it. They bought every bit of his stolen booty, and he got soused, and after a while he couldn't help but to pump the thing up and go along with it. His story changed from one drink to the next. It growed in the tellin' of it. First he allowed that he shot the Old Man hisself. Then he killed him with his bare hands. Then he shot him twice. Then he stabbed and dismembered him. Then he throwed his body into the river, where the alligators lunched on what was left. Up and down he went, back and forth, this way and that, till the thing stretched to the sky. You'd a thunk it would'a dawned on some of them that he was cooking it all up, the way his story growed legs. But they was as liquored up as him, when folks wanna believe something, the truth ain't got no place in that compartment. It come to me then that they feared Old John Brown something terrible; feared the idea of him as much as they feared the Old Man hisself, and thus they was happy to believe he was dead, even if that knowledge was just five minutes long before the truth would come about to it and kill it dead.

Bob and I set quiet while this was going on, for they weren't paying us no mind, but each time I stood up to step toward the door and slip away, catcalling and whistling drove me back to my chair. Women or girls of any type was scarce out on the prairie, and even though I was a mess—my dress was flattened out, my bonnet torn, and my hair underneath it was a wooly mess—the men offered me every kind of pleasure. They outworked a cooter in the nasty chattering department. Their comments come as a surprise to me, for the Old Man's troops didn't cuss nor drink and was generally respecters of the woman race. As the night wore on, the hooting and howling toward me growed worse, and it waked Chase, who ended up with his head on the bar, lubricated and stewed past reason, out his stupor.

He rose from the bar and said, "Excuse me, gentlemen. I am tired after killing the most dastardly criminal of the last hundred years. I aim to take this little lady across the road to the Pikesville Hotel, where Miss Abby is no doubt holding my room for me on the Hot Floor, on account of having heard of my late rasslings with that demon who I wrestled the breath from and fed him to the wolves in the name of the free living state of Missoura! God bless America." He pushed me and Bob out the door and staggered across the street to the Pikesville Hotel.

The Pikesville was a high-class hotel and saloon compared to the previous two shitholes that I aforementioned, but I ought to say here that looking back, it weren't much better.

Only after I seen dwellings in the East did I learn that the finest hotel in Pikesville was a pigsty compared to the lowliest
flophouse in Boston. The first floor of the Pikesville Hotel was
a dark, candlelit drinking room, with tables and a bar. Behind
it was a small middle room with a long dining table for eating.
On the side of that room was a door that led to a hall leading
to a back alley. At the back of the room was a set of stairs leading to the second floor.

There was a great hubbub when Chase came in, for word
had proceeded him. He was pounded on the back and hailed
from one corner of the room to the other, drinks shoved into
his hands. He hailed everyone with a great big howdy, then
proceeded to the back room, where several men seated at the
dining table howdied him and offered to give him their seats
and more drinks. He waved them off. "Not now, fellers," he
said. "I got business on the Hot Floor."

On the stairs at the back of the room, several women of the
type that frequented Dutch's place sat along the bottom rungs.
A couple were smoking pipes, shoving the black tobacco down
into the cups with wrinkled fingers and shoving the pipes into
their mouths, clamping down with teeth so yellow they looked
like clumps of butter. Chase staggered past them and stood at
the bottom of the stairs, hollering up, "Pie! Pie darling! C'mon
down. Guess who's back."

There was a commotion at the top of the stairs, and a
woman made her way from the darkness and stepped halfway
down the stairs into the dim candlelight of the room.

I once pulled a ball from the ham of a rebel stuck out near
Council Bluffs after he got into a hank out there and someone
throwed their pistol on him and left him bleeding and stuck. I
cleared him, and he was so grateful, he drove me to town after-

ward and gived me a bowl of ice cream. That was something I never had before. Best thing I ever tasted in my life.

But the feeling of that ice cream running down my little red lane in summertime weren't nothing compared to seeing that bundle of beauty coming down them stairs that first time. She would blow the hat off your head.

She was a mulatto woman. Skin as brown as a deer's hide, with high cheekbones and big brown dewy eyes as big as silver dollars. She was a head taller than me but seemed taller. She wore a flowered blue dress of the type whores naturally favored, and that thing was so tight that when she moved, the daisies got all mixed up with the azaleas. She walked like a warm room full of smoke. I weren't no stranger to nature's ways then, coming on the age of twelve as I believe I was more or less that age, and having accidentally on purpose peeked into a room or three at Dutch's place, but the knowing of a thing is different from the doing of it, and them whores at Dutch's was generally so ugly, they'd make the train leave the track. This woman had the kind of rhythm that you could hear a thousand miles down the Missouri. I wouldn't throw her outta bed for eating crackers. She was all class.

She surveyed the room slowly like a priestess, and when she seen Chase, her expression changed. She quick-timed to the bottom of the stairs and kicked him. He toppled off the stair like a rag doll as the men laughed. She came down to the bottom landing and stood over him, her hands on her hips. "Where's my money?"

Chase got up sheepishly, dusting himself off. "That's a hell of a way to treat the man who just killed Old John Brown with his bare hands."

"Right. And I quit buying gold claims last year. I don't care who you killed. You owe me nine dollars."

"That much?" he said.

"Where is it?"

"Pie, I got something better than nine dollars. Look." He pointed at me and Bob.

Pie looked right past Bob. Ignored him. Then she glared at me.

White fellers on the prairie, even white women, didn't pay two cents' worth of attention to a simple colored girl. But Pie was the first colored woman I seen in the two years since I started wearing that getup, and she smelled a rat right off.

She blew through her lips. "Shit. Whatever that ugly thing is, it sure needs pressing." She turned to Chase. "You got my money?"

"What about the girl?" Chase said. "Miss Abby could use her. Wouldn't that square us?"

"You got to talk to Miss Abby about that."

"But I carried her all the way from Kansas!"

"Must'a been some party, ya cow head. Kansas ain't but half a day's ride. You got my money or not?"

Chase got up, brushing himself off. "Course I do," he muttered. "But Abby'll be hot if she finds out you let this tight little thing shimmy across the road and work for the competition."

Pie frowned. He had her there.

"And I ought to get special favor," he throwed in, "on account of I had to kill John Brown and save the whole territory and all, just to get back to you. So can we go upstairs?"

Pie smirked. "I'll give you five minutes," she said.

"I take ten minutes to whiz," he protested.

"Whizzes is extra," she said. "Come on. Bring her, too." She moved upstairs, then stopped, glaring at Bob, who had started up the stairs behind me. She turned to Chase.

"You can't bring that nigger up here. Put him in the nigger pen out back, where everybody parks their niggers." She pointed to the side door of the dining hall. "Miss Abby'll give him some work tomorrow."

Bob looked at me wild eyed.

"Excuse me," I said, "but he belongs to me."

It was the first thing I said to her, and when she threwed them gorgeous brown eyes on me, I like to have melted like ice in the sun. Pie was something.

"You can sleep out there with him, too, then, you high-yellow, cornlooking ugler-ation."

"Wait a second," Chase said. "I drug her all this way."

"For what?"

"For the men."

"She's so ugly, she'd curdle a cow. Look, you want me to job you or not?"

"You can't leave her in the pen," Chase said. "She said she ain't a nigger."

Pie laughed. "She's close enough!"

"Miss Abby wouldn't like that. What if she gets hurt out there? Let her come upstairs and send the nigger to the pen. I got a stake in this, too," he said.

Pie considered it. She looked at Bob and said, "G'wan to the back door out there. They'll fetch you some eatings in the yard. You." She pointed to me. "C'mon up."

There weren't nothing to do. It was late and I was exhausted. I turned to Bob, who looked downright objectable. "Sleepin' here's better'n the prairie, Bob," I said. "I'll come get you later."

I was good to my word, too. I did come for him later, but he never forgave me for sending him out the door that day. That was the end of whatever closeness was between us. Just the way of things.

We followed Pie upstairs. She stopped at a room, throwed open the door, and pushed Chase inside. Then she turned to me and pointed to a room two doors down. "Go in there. Tell Miss Abby I sent you, and that you come to work. She'll see you get a hot bath first. You smell like buffalo dung."

"I don't need no bath!"

She grabbed my hand, stomped down the hall, knocked on a door, flung it open, throwed me into the room, and closed the door behind me.

I found myself staring at the back of a husky, well-dressed white woman setting at a vanity. She turned away from the vanity and rose up to face me. She was wearing a long white fancy scarf 'round her neck. Atop that neck was a face with enough powder on it to pack the barrel of a cannon. Her lips was thick and painted red and clamped a cigar between them. Her forehead was high, and her face was flushed red and curdled in anger like old cheese. That woman was so ugly, she looked like a death threat. Behind her, the room was dimly lit by candles. The smell of the place was downright infernal. Come to think of it, I have never been in a hotel room in Kansas but that didn't smell worse than the lowliest flophouse you could find in all of New England. The odor in that place was ripe enough to peel the wallpaper off the worst sitting room in Boston. The sole window in the room hadn't been disturbed by water for years. It was dotted with specks of dead flies that clung to it like black dots. Along the far wall, which was lit up by two burning candles, two figures lounged on two beds that set side by side. Between the beds sat a tin bathtub that, to my reckoning, in the dim light, appeared to be filled with water and what looked to be a naked woman.

I started to lose consciousness then, for as my eyes took in the sight of these two figures, two young ones setting on the bed, one combing the other one's hair, and the older one setting in the tub smoking a pipe, her love bags hanging low into the water, my fluids runned clear out of my head and my knees gived way. I slipped to the floor in a dead faint.

I was awakened a minute later by a hand slapping my chest. Miss Abby stood over me.

"You flat as a pancake," she said dryly. She flipped me over onto my stomach, gripped my arse with a pair of hands that felt like ice tongs. "You small in that department, too," she grunted, feeling my arse. "You young *and* homely. Where'd Pie get you?"

I didn't wait. I leaped to my feet, and in doing so, that pretty white scarf of hers caught my arm and I heard it tear as I took off. I ripped that thing like paper and hit the door running and scampered out. I hit the hallway at full speed and made for the stairs, but two cowboys were coming up, so I busted into the closest door, which happened to be Pie's room—just in time to see Chase with trousers down and Pie sitting on her bed with her dress pulled down to her waist.

The sight of them two chocolate love knobs standing there like fresh biscuits slowed my step, I reckon, long enough for Miss Abby, who was hot on my tail, to grab at my bonnet and rip it in half just as I dove under Pie's bed.

"Git out from under there!" she hollered. It was a tight squeeze—the bedsprings was low—but if it was tight for me, it was tighter for Miss Abby, who was too big to lean over all the way and get at me. The smell under that feather bed was pretty seasoned though, downright rank, the smell of a thousand dreams come true, I reckon, being that its purpose was for nature's deeds, and if I wasn't worried 'bout getting broke in half, I would'a moved out from under it.

Miss Abby tried pulling the bed from side to side to expose me, but I clung to the springs and moved with the bed as she slung it.

Pie come 'round to the other side of the bed, leaned on all fours and placed her head on the floor. It was a tight fit down there but I could just see her face. "You better come out here," she said.

"I ain't."

I heard the click of a Colt's hammer snapping back. "I'll get her out," Chase said.

Pie stood up and I heard the sound of a slap, then Chase hollered, "Ow!"

"Put that peashooter up before I beat the cow-walkin' hell outta you," Pie said.

Miss Abby commenced to razzing Pie something terrible for me ripping her scarf and causing a ruckus in her business. She cussed Pie's Ma. She cussed her Pa. She cussed all her relations in all directions.

"I'll fix it," Pie protested. "I'll pay for the scarf."

"You better. Git that girl out, or I'll have Darg come up here."

It growed silent. From where I lay, it felt like all the air had left the room. Pie spoke softly—I could hear the terror in her voice—"You don't have to do that, missus. I'll fix it. I promise. And I'll pay for the scarf, missus."

"Get busy counting your pennies, then."

Miss Abby's feet stomped toward the door and left.

Chase was standing there. I could see his bare feet and his boots from where I was. Suddenly Pie's hand snatched up his boots, and I reckon she handed them to him, for she said, "Git."

"I'll straighten it out, Pie."

"Skinflint! Dumbass. Who told you to bring me that snaggle-mouth headache here? Git out!"

He put on his boots, grumbling and muttering, then left. Pie slammed the door behind him and stood against it, sighing in the silence. I watched her feet. They slowly came toward the bed. She said softly, "It's all right, honey. I ain't gonna hurt ya."

"You sure?" I said.

"Course, baby. You a young thing. You don't know nuthin'. Sweet thing, ain't got nobody in the world, coming here. Lord have mercy. It's a shame, Miss Abby hollering about some silly old scarf. Missouri! Lord, the devil's busy in this territory! Don't be scared, sweetie. You gonna suffocate down there. C'mon out, baby."

The soft tenderness of that woman's voice moved my heart so much, I slipped out from under there. I come out on the opposite side of the bed, though, just in case she weren't good for her word, but she was. I could see it in her face when I stood up, watching me from across the bed now, smiling, warm, dewy. She gestured to me with an arm. "C'mon over here, baby. Come 'round the side of the bed."

I melted right off. I was in love with her right from the first. She was the mother I never knowed, the sister I never had, my first love. Pie was all woman, one hundred percent, first rate, grade A, right-from-the-start woman. I just loved her.

I said, "Oh, Mama," and runned 'round the bed to nestle my head between them big brown love knockers, just cram my head in there and sob out my sorrows, for I was but a lonely boy looking for a home. I felt that in my heart. And I was aiming to tell all my story to her and let her make it right. I throwed myself at her and put my heart in hers. I went over there and put my head on her chest, and just as I done so, felt myself being lifted like a pack of feathers and throwed clear across the room.

"God-damn, cockeyed idiot!"

She was on me before I could get up, picked me up by the collar, and whomped me twice, then throwed me on the floor on my stomach, and put a knee on my back. "I'mma send you hooting and hollering down the road, ya goober-faced tart! Ya lying lizard." She whomped me twice more on the head. "Don't move," she said.

I stayed where I was as she got up, frantically pushed the bed aside, then dug at the floorboards underneath it, pulling them out till she found what she was looking for. She reached in and pulled out an old jar. She opened it, checked its contents, seemed satisfied, throwed the jar back in there, and put the whole assembly of floorboards back in place. She slid the bed back in place and said, "Git outta here, cow face. And if any of my money's missing while you're in this town, I'll cut your throat so wide, you'll have two sets of lips working at the top of your neck."

"What I done?"

"Git."

"But I don't have no place to go."

"What do I care? Git out."

Well, I was hurt, so I said, "I ain't going no place."

She marched over to me and grabbed me up. She was a strong woman, and while I resisted, I weren't no match for her. She throwed me over her knee. "Now, you high-yellow heifer, think you so high-siddity? Got me paying for a damn scarf I ain't never had! I'mma warm your two little buns the way your Ma should'a," she said.

"Wait!" I hollered, but it was too late. She throwed my dress up, and seed my true nature dangling somewhere down there between her knees at full salute, being that all that wrestling and tugging was a wonderment to the fringlings and tinglings of a twelve-year-old who never knowed nature's ways firsthand. I couldn't help myself.

She yelped and throwed me to the floor, her hands cupped her face as she stared. "You done put me in the fryer, you God-damned pebble-mouthed, wart-faced sip of shit. You heathen! Them was *women* you was in that room with. . . . Was they working? Lord, course they was!" She was furious. "You gonna get me hanged!"

She leaped at me, throwed me over her knee, and went at it hard again.

"I was kidnapped!" I hollered.

"You lyin' lizard!" She spanked me some more.

"I ain't. I was kidnapped by Old John Brown hisself!"

That stopped her flinging and flailing for a second. "Old John Brown's dead. Chase killed him," she said.

"No, he's not," I hollered.

"What do I care!" She throwed me off her lap and set on the bed. She was cooling off now, though still hot. Lord, she looked prettier burnt up than she did regular, and the sight of them brown eyes boring into me made me feel lower than dirt, for I was plumb in love. Pie just done something to me.

She sat thinking for a long moment. "I knowed Chase was a liar," she said, "or he would'a gone on and collected that money on Old John Brown's head. You likely lying, too. Maybe you working with Chase."

"I ain't."

"How'd you get with him?"

I explained how Frederick was killed and how Chase and Randy rolled up on me and Bob when the Old Man's sons went to town to collect their belongings.

"Randy still here?"

"I don't know."

"I hope not. You'll end up in an urn buried in somebody's yard fooling with him. There's a reward out on him."

"But the Old Man's alive surely," I said proudly. "I seen him get up out the river."

"What do I care? He'll be dead soon enough, anyway."

"Why does every colored I meet say that?"

"You ought to worry about your own skin, ya little snit. I had a feeling about you," she said. "God-damned Chase! Damn cow turd!"

She cussed him some more, then sat a moment, thinking. "Them rebels find out you was on the Hot Floor, peeking at them white whores, they'll cut out them little grapes hanging between your legs and stick them down your gizzard. Might pull me in on it, too. I can't take no chances with you. Plus you seen where my money is."

"I ain't interested in your money."

"That's touching, but everything on this prairie's a lie, child. Ain't nothing what it looks like. Look at you. You's a lie. You

got to go. You ain't gonna make it on the prairie as a girl nohow.
I know a feller drives a stagecoach for Wells Fargo. Now *he's* a
girl. Playing like a man. But whatever she fancies herself, girl or
boy, she's a white thing. And she's going from place to place as
a stagecoach driver. She ain't setting in one place, selling tail.
And that's what you'd do here, child. Miss Abby got a business
here. She got no use for you. Unless you wanna service . . . can
you still service as a boy? Do that interest you?"

"The only service I know is washing dishes and cutting hair
and such. I can do that good. Me and Bob can work tables,
too."

"Forget him. He's gonna get sold," she said.

It didn't seem proper to remind her that she was a Negro
herself, for she was ornery, so I said, "He's a friend."

"He's a runaway like you. And he's getting sold. And you
too, unless you let Miss Abby work you. She might work you
to death, *then* sell you."

"She can't do that!"

She laughed. "Shit. She can do whatever she wants."

"I can do other things," I pleaded. "I knows working 'round
taverns. I can clean rooms and spittoons, bake biscuits, do all
manner of jobs, till maybe the Captain comes."

"What Captain?"

"Old John Brown. We call him Captain. I'm in his army.
He's gonna ride on this town once they find out I'm here."

It was a lie, for I didn't know whether the Old Man was living or not, or what he was gonna do, but that peaked her feathers some.

"You sure he's living?"

"Sure as I'm standing here. And the fur's gonna fly if he
comes here and finds out Bob's sold, for Bob's his'n, too. For all

we know, Bob's likely spreading the word among them niggers downstairs right now, saying he's a John Brown man. That gets certain niggers rowdy, y'know, talking 'bout John Brown."

Fear creased that pretty little face of hers. Old Brown scared the shit outta every living soul on the prairie. "That's all I need," she said. "Old John Brown riding here, screwing things up and whipping them pen niggers into a frenzy. It'll drive these white folks crazy. They'll wail away on every nigger in sight. If it was up to me, every nigger in that pen would be sold down the river."

She sighed and sat down on the bed, then flattened her hair, and pulled her dress up tighter 'round them love lumps of hers. Lord, she was beautiful. "I don't want no parts of what Old John Brown's selling," she said. "Let him come. I got my own plans. But what I'm gonna do with you?"

"If you take me back to Dutch's Tavern, that might help me."

"Where's that?"

"Off Santa Fe Road on the border with Missouri. West of here. About thirty-five miles. Old Dutch might take me back."

"Thirty-five miles? I can't go thirty-five feet out this hotel without papers."

"I can get you papers. I can write 'em. I know my letters."

Her eyes widened, and the hardness fell away from her face. For a moment she seemed fresh as a young child on a spring morning, and the dew climbed back into her face again. Just as fast, though, the dew hit the road, and her face hardened again.

"I can't ride no place, child. Even with a pass, too many people 'round here know me. Still, it'd be nice to pass the time reading dime books like the other girls. I seen it done," she said.

She smirked at me. "Can you really read? Knowing your letters is something you can't lie about, y'know."

"I ain't lying."

"I expect you can prove that out. Tell you what. You teach me letters, and I'll girl you up and work it out with Miss Abby so you start out cleaning beds and emptying piss pots and things to pay off her scarf and your keep. That'll give you a little time. But keep away from the girls. If these rebels find out about that little nub swinging between your legs, they'll pour tar down your throat. I reckon that'll work for a while till Miss Abby decides you old enough to work the trade. Then you on your own. How long'll it take me to learn my letters?"

"Not long."

"Well, however long that takes, that's how much time you got. After that, I'm done with you. Wait here while I fetch you another bonnet to cover them nigger naps and a clean something to wear."

She rose, and by the time she disappeared out the door and shut it behind her, I missed her already, and she hadn't been gone but a few seconds.

12

Sibonia

I settled into Pikesville pretty easy. It weren't hard. Pie set me up good. She done me up like a real girl: Cleaned me up, fixed my hair, sewed me a dress, taught me to curtsey before visitors, and advised me against smoking cigars and acting like the rest of them walking hangovers who worked Miss Abby's place. She had to twist Miss Abby into keeping me, for the old lady didn't want me at first. She weren't anxious to have another mouth to feed. But I knowed a thing or two about working in taverns, and after she seen how I emptied spittoons, cleaned up tables, scrubbed floors, emptied chamber pots, carted water up to the girls all night, and gived haircuts for the gamblers and jackals in her tavern, she growed satisfied with me. "Just watch the men," she said. "Keep 'em liquored up. The girls upstairs will do the rest," she said.

I know this was a whorehouse, but it weren't bad at all. Fact is, I never knowed a Negro from that day to this but who couldn't lie to themselves about their own evil while pointing out the white man's wrong, and I weren't no exception. Miss

Abby was a slaveholder true enough, but she was a good slave-holder. She was a lot like Dutch. She runned a lot of businesses, which meant the businesses mostly runned her. Whoring was almost a sideline for her. She also runned a sawmill, a hog pen, a slave pen, kept a gambling house, had a tin-making machine, plus she was in competition with the tavern across the street that didn't have a colored slave like Pie to bring in money, for Pie was her main attraction. I was right at home in her place, living 'round gamblers and pickpockets who drank rotgut and pounded each other's brains out over card games. I was back in bondage, true, but slavery ain't too troublesome when you're in the doing of it and growed used to it. Your meals is free. Your roof is paid for. Somebody else got to bother themselves about you. It was easier than being on the trail, running from posses and sharing a roasted squirrel with five others while the Old Man was hollering over the whole roasted business to the Lord for an hour before you could even get to the vittles, and even then there weren't enough meat on it to knock the edges off the hunger you was feeling. I was living well and clean forgot about Bob. Just plain forgot about him.

But you could see the slave pen from Pie's window. They had couple of huts back there, a canvas cover that stretched over part of it that was fenced all 'round, and once in a while, between my scamperings 'round working, I'd stop, scratch out a clean spot on the glass, and take a peek. If it weren't raining, you could see the colored congregated and bunched up out in the yard near a little garden they put together. Otherwise, if it was raining or cold, they stayed under the canvas. From time to time I'd take a look out the window to see if I could spot old Bob. Never could, and after a few weeks I got to wondering about him. I spoke to Pie about it one afternoon while she sat on her bed combing her hair.

"Oh, he's around," she said. "Miss Abby ain't sold him. Let him be, darling."

"I thought I might bring him some victuals to eat."

"Leave them niggers in the yard alone," she said. "They're trouble."

I found that confusing, for they done her no wrong, and nothing they could do would hurt Pie's game. She was right popular. Miss Abby gived her the run of the place, let her choose her own customers more or less, and live as she wanted. Pie even closed down the saloon at times. Them coloreds couldn't hurt her game. But I kept quiet on it, and one evening I couldn't stand it no more. I slipped down to the slave pen to see about Bob.

The slave pen was in an alley behind the hotel, right off the dining room back door. Soon as you opened that door you stepped into an alley, and two steps across it and you was there. It was a penned-in area, and beside it was a little open area in the back where the colored set on crates, played cards, and had a little vegetable garden. Behind that was a hog pen, which opened right to the colored pen for easy tending of Miss Abby's hogs.

Inside both them pens combined—the pen where they fed the pigs and the pen where the slaves lived and kept a garden— I reckon it was about twenty men, women, and children in there. Up close it weren't the same sight that it was from above, and right then I knowed why Pie kept away and wanted me off from it. It was evening, for most of 'em was out working during the day, and the dusk settling on that place, and the swill of them

Negroes—most of 'em dark-skinned, pure Negroes like Bob—
was downright troubling. The smell of the place was infernal.
Most was dressed in mostly rags and some without shoes. They
wandered 'round the pen, some setting, doing nothing, others
fooling 'round a bit in the garden, and there in the middle of 'em,
they kinda circled 'round a figure, a wild woman cackling and
babbling like a chicken. She sounded like her mind was a little
soft, babbling like she was, but I couldn't make out no words.

I walked to the fence. Several men and women were working along the back end of it, feeding hogs and tending the garden there, and when they seed me they glanced up, but never
stopped working. It was twilight now. Just about dark. I stuck
my face to the fence and said, "Anybody see Bob?"

The Negroes gathered at the back of the pen working with
shovels and rakes kept working and didn't say nary a word. But
that silly fool in the middle of the yard, a heavyset, settle-aged
colored woman setting on a wooden box, cackling and babbling, she got to cackling louder. She had a large, round face.
She was really off her knob the closer you got to her, for up
close, the box she set on was pushed deep into the muddy
ground nearly up to its top, it was wedged so deep, and she set
on it, commenting and cackling and warbling about nothing.
She seen me and croaked, "Pretty, pretty, yeller, yeller!"

I ignored her and spoke generally. "Anybody seen a feller
named Bob?" I asked.

Nobody said nothing, and that feebleminded thing clucked
and swished her head 'round like a bird, gobbling like a turkey.
"Pretty, pretty, yeller, yeller."

"He's a colored feller, 'bout this high," I said to the others.

But that crazy thing kept her mouth busy. "Knee-deep,
knee-deep, goin' 'round, goin' 'round!" she cackled.

She was feebleminded. I looked to the other Negroes in the pen. "Anybody see Bob?" I said. I said it loud enough for all of 'em to hear it, and nar soul looked at me twice. They busied themselves on with them hogs and their little garden like I weren't there.

I climbed the first rung of the fence and stuck my face high over it and said louder, "Anybody see B—" and before I could finish, I was struck in the face by a mud ball. That crazy fool woman setting on the box scooped up another handful of mud by the time I looked, and throwed that in my face.

"Hey!"

"Goin' 'round. Goin' 'round!" she howled. She had got up from her box, came to the edge of the fence where I was, picked up another mud ball, and throwed that, and that one got me in the jaw. "Knee-deep!" she crowed.

I flew hot as the devil. "Damn stupid fool!" I said. "Git! Git away from me!" I would have climbed in there and dunked her head in the mud, but another colored woman, a tall, slender slip of water, broke off from the rest on the other side of the pen, dug the crazy woman's box out the mud, and come over. "Don't mind her. She's feebleminded," she said.

"Don't I know it."

She set the crazy woman's box down by the edge of the fence, set her own down, and said, "Sit by me, Sibonia." The crazy coot calmed down and done it. The woman turned to me and said, "What you need?"

"She needs a flogging," I said. "I reckon Miss Abby would flog her righteous if I was to tell it. I works inside, you know." That was privileged, see, to work inside. That gived you more juice with the white man.

A couple of colored men pushing that hog slop 'round with

rakes and shovels glanced over at me, but the woman talking to me shot a look at them, and they looked away. I was a fool, see, for I didn't know the dangerous waters I was treading in.

"I'm Libby," she said. "This here's my sister, Sibonia. You awful young to be talking about flogging. What you want?"

"I am looking for Bob."

"Don't know no Bob," Libby said.

Behind her, Sibonia hooted, "No Bob. No Bob," and chucked a fresh mud ball at me, which I dodged.

"He's got to be here."

"Ain't nar Bob here," Libby said. "We got a Dirk, a Lang, a Bum-Bum, a Broadnax, a Pete, a Lucious. Ain't no Bob. What you want him for anyway?"

"He's a friend."

She looked at me a long minute in my dress. Pie had fixed me up nice. I was dressed warm, clean, in a bonnet and warm dress and socks, living good. I looked like a real high-yeller girl, dressed damn near white, and Libby set there dressed in rags. "What a redbone like you need a friend in this yard for?" she asked. Several Negroes working shovels behind her leaned over them and chuckled.

"I ain't come out here for you to sass me," I said.

"You sassing yourself," she said gently, "by the way you look. You own Bob?"

"I wouldn't own him with your money. But I owes him."

"Well, you ain't got to fret about paying him what you owe, so you should be happy. 'Cause he ain't here."

"That's strange, 'cause Miss Abby said she hadn't sold him."

"Is that the first lie you heard from white folks?"

"You sure got a smart mouth for an outside nigger."

"And you got a smarter one for a big-witted, tongue-beating, mule-headed sissy. Walking 'round dressed as you is."

That flummoxed me right there. She knowed I was a boy. But I was an inside nigger. Privileged. The men in Miss Abby's liked me. Pie was my mother, practically. She had the run of things. I didn't need to bother with no mealymouth, lowlife, no-count, starving pen nigger who nobody wouldn't pay no attention to. I had sauce, and wouldn't stand nobody but Pie or a white person sassing me like that. That colored woman just cut me off without a wink. I couldn't stand it.

"How I covers my skin is my business."

"It's your load. You carry it. Ain't nobody judging you out here. But dodging the white man's evil takes more than a bonnet and some pretty undergarments, child. You'll learn."

I ignored that. "I'll give you a quarter if you tell me where he is."

"That's a lot of money," Libby said. "But I can't use it where I'm at now."

"I know my letters. I can show you some."

"Come back when you ain't full of lies," she said. She picked up Sibonia's box and said, "Come on, sister."

Sibonia, standing there holding a dripping mud ball in her hand, then did something strange. She glanced at the hotel door, saw it was still closed, then said to Libby in a plain voice, "This child is troubled."

"Let the devil have him, then," Libby said.

Sibonia said to her softly, "Go on over yonder with the rest, sister."

That just about dropped me, the way she was talking. She and Libby looked at each other for a long moment. Seemed like some kind of silent signal passed between 'em. Libby handed Sibonia her wooden crate and Libby slipped away without a word. She stepped clean away to the other side of the fence with the rest of the Negroes who was bent over, tending to the garden and the hogs. She never said a word to me again for the rest of her life, which as it turned out weren't very long.

Sibonia sat on her box again and stuck her face through the fence, looking at me close. The face peeking through the slats with mud on her cheeks and eyelashes didn't sport an ounce of foolishness in it now. Her manner had flipped inside out. She had brushed the madness off her face the way you'd brush a fly away. Her face was serious. Deadly. Her eyes glaring at me was strong and calm as the clean barrel of a double-barreled shotgun boring down at my face. There was power in that face.

She runned her fingers in the ground, scooped up some mud, shaped it into a ball, and set it on the ground. Then she made another, wiping her face with her sleeve, keeping her eyes on the ground, and set that new mud ball next to the first. From a distance she looked like a fool setting on a box, piling up mud balls. She spoke with them shotgun eyes staring at the ground, in a voice that was heavy and strong.

"You sporting trouble," she said, "playing folks for a fool."

I thought she was talking 'bout the way I dressed, so I said, "I'm doing what I got to do, wearing these clothes."

"I ain't talking 'bout that. I'm talking 'bout the other thing. That's more dangerous."

"You mean reading?"

"I mean lying about it. Some folks'll climb a tree to tell a lie before they'll stand on the ground and tell the truth. That could get you hurt in this country."

I was a little shook about how she was so tight in her mind, for if I played a girl well, she played a fool even better. There weren't no fooling somebody like her, I seen that clear, so I said, "I ain't lying. I'll get a piece of paper and show you."

"Don't bring no paper out here," she said quickly. "You talk too much. If Darg finds out, he'll make you suffer."

"Who's Darg?"

"You'll see soon enough. Can you write words?"

"I can draw pictures, too."

"I ain't studying no pictures. It's the words I want. If I was to tell you about your Bob, would you write me something? Like a pass? Or a bill of sale?"

"I would."

She had her head to the ground, busy, her hands deep in the mud. The hands hesitated and she spoke to the ground. "Maybe you best think on it first. Don't be a straight fool. Don't sign no note you can't deliver on. Not out here. Not with us. 'Cause if you agrees to something with us, you gonna be held to it."

"I said I would."

She glanced up and said softly, "Your Bob's been bounded out."

"Bounded out?"

"On loan. Miss Abby loaned him out to the sawmill 'cross the village. For a price, of course. He been out there practically since the day he got here. He'll be back soon. How come he never spoke of you?"

"I don't know. But I'm worried Miss Abby's planning on selling him."

"So what? She's gonna sell us all. You, too."

"When?"

"When she's good and ready."

"Pie never said nothing about that."

"Pie," she said. She smiled grimly and said nothing more. But I didn't like the way she said it. That pulled at me some. She moved her hands in the mud and packed up another mud ball.

"Can you get word to me about Bob?"

"I might. If you do what you said you would."

"I said I would."

"When you hear tell of a Bible meeting for the colored out here in the yard, come on. I'll get you to your Bob. And I'll take you up about them letters."

"All right, then."

"Don't stretch your mouth to nobody about this, especially Pie. If you do, I'll know about it, and you'll wake up with a heap of knives poking out that pretty neck of yours. Mine's be the first. Loose talk'll have us all sleeping on the cooling board."

And with that she turned, picked up her box, and cackled her way across the yard, movin' into the center and setting that box deep in the mud again. She sat on it, and the Negroes gathered 'round her again, holding picks and shovels, working the ground all 'round her, glaring at me, picking at the mud 'round her while she set on her box in the middle of 'em, cackling like a chicken.

13

Insurrection

About a week later, a colored girl from the yard named Nose runned into the saloon carrying a pile of kindling, set it by the stove, and passed by me as she left, whispering, "Bible meeting's in the slave pen tonight." That evening I slipped out the back door and found Bob. He was standing near the front gate of the yard, leaning on the fence, alone. He looked tore up. His clothes was a ragged mess, but it was him and he was yet living.

"Where you been?" I asked.

"At the sawmill. They killing me out there." He glanced at me. "I see you living high."

"Why you giving me the evil eye? I ain't got run of this place."

He glanced nervously 'round the pen. "I wish they'd'a kept me at the sawmill. These niggers in here are gonna kill me."

"Stop talking crazy," I said.

"Nobody talks to me. They don't say nar word to me. Nothing." He nodded at Sibonia in the back corner, cackling and crowing on her wooden crate. The coloreds surrounded her, working the ground garden with rakes and shovels, making a silent wall 'round her, pushing dirt, slinging up rocks and weeding. Bob nodded at Sibonia. "That one there, she's a witch. She's under a mad spell."

"No, she ain't. I owe her now on account of you."

"You owe the devil, then."

"I done it for you, brother."

"Don't call me brother. Your favors ain't worth shit. Look where I got 'cause of you. I can't hardly bear to look at you. Look at you," he snorted. "All high-siddity, playing a sissy, eating well, living inside. I'm out here in the cold and rain. And you sportin' that new, fancy dress."

"You said running 'round this way was a good idea!" I hissed.

"I ain't say get me kilt!"

Behind Bob, a sudden hush come over the yard. The rakes and hoes moved quicker, and every head snapped down to the ground like they was tending work hard. Someone whispered in a hurried fashion, "Darg!" and Bob quickly slipped over to the other side of the yard. He got busy with the rest 'round Sibonia, pulling weeds in the garden.

The back door of a tiny hut on the other side of the slave pen opened up, and a huge colored feller emerged. He was nearly tall as Frederick, but just as wide. He had a thick chest, wide shoulders, and big, thick arms. He wore a straw hat and coveralls and a shawl around his shoulders. His lips was the color of hemp rope, and his eyes was so small and close together, they might as well have been shoved in the same socket. That fool was ugly enough to make you think the Lord put him together with His eyes closed, guessing. But there was power in that man, too, he was raw powerful, and looked big enough to pick up a house. He moved quick, slipping to the edge of the pen a minute and pausing there, peering in, air whooshing out huge nostrils, then he moved along the side to the gate to where I stood.

I backed off when he come, but when he got close, he removed his hat.

"Evening, pretty redbone," he said, "what you need at my pen?"

"Pie sent me here," I lied. I didn't think it was a good thing to bring Miss Abby up, just in case he said something to her about it, for while I had never seen him inside the saloon, knowing he was boss of that yard meant he could pass word to her some kind of way. I weren't supposed to be there and reckoned he knowed it.

He licked his lips. "Don't mention that high-siddity bitch to me. What you need?"

"Me and my friend here"—I pointed to Bob—"was just having a word."

"You soft on Bob, girl?"

"I ain't soft on him in no way, form, or fashion. I is here to merely visit him."

He smirked. "This is my yard," he said. "I tends to it. But if the missus say so, it's all right, it's all right. If she don't, you got to move on. You check with her and come back. Unless"—he smiled, showing a row of huge white teeth—"you can be Darg's friend. Do old Darg a sweet favor, give him a li'l sugar. You old enough."

I would step off to hell before I touched that monster-looking nigger with a stick. I backed off quick. "It ain't that important," I said, and I was gone. I took one last look at Bob before I cut inside. He had his back turned, pulling weeds in the garden fast as he could, the devil keeping score. I betrayed him, is how he felt. He didn't want no parts of me. And I couldn't help him. He was on his own.

I got nervous about the whole bit and told it to Pie. When she heard I was in the yard, she was furious. "Who told you to consort with them outside niggers?"

"I was looking in on Bob."

"Hell with Bob. You gonna bring trouble for us all! Did Darg say sumpthing 'bout me?"

"He didn't bring a word on you."

"You's a bad liar," she snapped. She cussed Darg for several minutes, then throwed me in for good measure. "Keep off them low-down, no-count niggers. Either that, or don't come 'round me."

Well, that done it. For I loved Pie. She was the mother I never had. The sister I loved. Course I had other ideas, too, 'bout who she was to me, and them ideas was full of stinkin', down-low thoughts which weren't all bad when I thunk them up, so that stopped me from thinking about Bob and Sibonia and the pen altogether. Just quit it altogether. Love blinded me. I was busy anyhow. Pie was the busiest whore on the Hot Floor. She had heaps of customers: Pro Slavers, Free Staters, farmers, gamblers, thieves, preachers, even Mexicans and Indians lined up outside her door. Me being her consort, I was privileged to line 'em up in order of importance. I come to know quite a few important people in this fashion, including a judge named Fuggett, who I'll get to in a minute.

My days was generally the same. Every afternoon when Pie got up, I brung her coffee and biscuits and we would set and talk about the previous night's events and so forth, and she'd laugh about some feller who'd made a fool of hisself on the Hot Floor one way or the other. Being that I cavorted all over the tavern and she spent the night working, she missed out on events in the saloon, which privileged me to give her the gossip on who done what and who shot John and the like downstairs. I didn't mention the slave pen to her no more, but it was always on my mind, for I owed Sibonia, and she didn't strike me as the type a body ought to owe something to. Every once in a while Sibonia would slip word for me through some colored or other to come out to see her and live up to my promise of teaching her letters. Problem was, getting out there was tough business. The pen could be seen from every window in the hotel, and the slavery question seemed to be putting Pikesville on edge. Even in normal times, fistfights was common out west on the prairie in them days. Kansas and Missouri drawed all types of adventurers—Irishman, German, Russian, land speculators, gold diggers. Between cheap whiskey, land claim disputes, the red man fighting for their land, and low women, your basic western settler was prone to a good dustup at any time. But nothing stirred up a row better than the slavery question, and that seemed to press in on Pikesville at that time. There was so much punching and stabbing and stealing and shouting on account of it, Miss Abby often wondered aloud if she ought to get out of the slave game altogether.

She often set up in the saloon smoking cigars and playing

poker with the men, and one night, while she threw cards at the table with a few of the more well-off fellers from town, she piped out, "Between the Free Staters and my niggers running off, slavery's getting to be a bother. The real danger in this territory is there's too many guns floating around. What if the nigger gets armed?"

The men at the table, sipping whiskey and holding their cards, laughed her off. "Your basic Negro is trustworthy," one said.

"Why, I'd arm my slaves," said another.

"I'd trust my slave with my life," said another. But not long after that, one of his slaves drawed a knife on him, and he sold every single slave he had.

I was mulling these things in my head, course, for I was smelling a rat in all of it. Something was happening outside of town, but word on it was thin. Like most things in life, you don't know nothing till you want to know it, and don't see what you don't want to see, but all that talk about slavery was drawing water for something, and not long after, I found out.

I was heading past the kitchen, drawing water, and heard a terrible hank coming from the saloon. I peeked in there to find the place packed with redshirts, three deep from the bar, armed to the teeth. Through the front window, I could see the road out front was full of armed men on horseback. The back door leading to the slave alley was shut tight. And before that stood several redshirts, and *they* was armed. The hotel bar was going full steam, packed tight with rebels bearing weapons of all kinds, and Miss Abby and Judge Fuggett—that same judge who was a good customer of Pie—them two was having a full-out fight.

Not a fistfight, but a real wrangle. I had to keep movin' as I worked, lest somebody stop me for lingering, but they was so hot that nobody paid me no mind. Miss Abby was furious. I believe if that room wasn't full of armed men surrounding Judge Fuggett, she'd'a drawed on him with the heater she carried around on her waistband, but she didn't. From what I could gather, them two was arguing about money, lots of it. Miss Abby was burning up. "I declare I won't go along with it," she said. "That's a loss of several thousand dollars for me!"

"I'll arrest you if I have to," Judge Fuggett said, "for that business needs doing." Several men nodded with him. Miss Abby took a backseat then. She backed off, fuming, while the judge took the center of the room and told the others. I lingered with my face behind a post and listened as he told it: There was a planned insurrection. It involved the Negroes from the pen, at least a couple dozen of 'em. They was planning on killing white families by the hundreds, including the town minister, who loved the Negro and preached against slavery. Several pen Negroes, some that belonged to Miss Abby and several others—for slave owners who come to town to do business often parked their Negroes in the yard—was all arrested. Nine was found out. The judge was planning to try all nine the next morning. Four of 'em was Miss Abby's.

I run back upstairs to Pie's room and busted in the door. "There's big trouble," I blurted out, and told her what I heard.

For the rest of my life, I would remember her response. She was setting on the bed as I told it, and when I was done, she didn't say a word. She got up from her bed, walked to the window, and stared down at the slave pen, which was empty. Then she said over her shoulder, "That's all? Only nine?"

"That's a lot."

"They should hang 'em all. Every one of them low-down, no-count niggers."

I reckon she saw my face, for she said, "Just be calm. This don't involve you and me. It'll pass. But I can't be seen talking to you right now. Two of us is a crowd. Git out and listen around. Come up when it's safe and tell me what you hear."

"But I ain't done nothing," I said, for I was worried about my own tail.

"Ain't nothing gonna happen to you. I already fixed it with Miss Abby for me and you. Just be quiet and listen to what's said. Tell me what you hear. Now get out. And don't be seen talking to any niggers. Nary a one. Lay low and listen. Find out who them nine is, and when it's safe, slip back in here and tell me."

She shoved me out the door. I ventured down to the saloon, slipped into the kitchen, and listened in as the judge told Miss Abby and the others what was to come. What I heard about made me nervous.

The judge revealed that he and his men questioned every slave in the yard. The coloreds denied the insurrection plans, but one colored was tricked into confessing or just told it some way or other, I reckon. Somehow they'd got the information about them nine coloreds from somebody, and they snatched them nine from the yard and throwed them in the jailhouse. The judge further explained that he and his men knowed who the leader of the whole thing was, but the leader weren't talking. They aimed to fix that problem straightaway, which was the reason for all the men and various town folks setting up shop in the saloon, armed to the gizzards, shouting down Miss Abby. For the leader of the insurrection was one of Miss

Abby's slaves, the judge said, downright dangerous, and when they brung Sibonia in twenty minutes later wearing chains on her ankles and feet, I weren't surprised.

Sibonia looked worn out, tired, and thin. Her hair was a mess. Her face was puffy and swollen, and her skin shiny. But her eyes shone calm. That was the same face I'd seen in the pen. She was calm as an egg. They slammed her into a chair before Judge Fuggett, and the men surrounded her. Several stood before her, cursing, as the Judge pulled up a chair before her. A table was throwed in front of him, and a drink was set before him. Somebody handed him a cigar. He settled himself behind the table and lit it, puffing and sipping his drink slowly. He weren't in a hurry, and neither was Sibonia, who sat there silent as the moon, even as several men around her cussed her up and down.

Finally Judge Fuggett spoke up and shushed everybody. He turned to Sibonia and said, "Sibby, we aims to find out about this murderous plot. We know you is the leader. Several people has said it. So don't deny it."

Sibonia was calm as a blade of grass. She looked straight at the judge and looked neither sideways nor over his head. "I am the woman," she said, "and I am not ashamed or afraid to confess it."

The way she spoke, talking straight at him, in a room crowded full of drunk rebels, that just floored me.

Judge Fuggett asked her, "Who else is involved?"

"Me and my sister, Libby, and I ain't confessing to no other."

"We got ways of getting you to tell it if you want."

"Do your wants, then, Judge."

Well that blowed his top. He went low-grade then, he got so hot it was a pity. He threatened to beat her, whip her, tar and feather her, but she said, "Go ahead. You can even get Darg if you want. But it can't be whipped out of me nor coerced in any way. I am the woman. I done it. And if I had the chance, I would do it again."

Well, the judge and the men around him stomped and hollered something grievous; they railed about how they was gonna grind her to a stump and rip her private parts off and feed her to the pigs if she didn't tell the names of the others. Judge Fuggett promised they'd start a bonfire in the middle of the town square and throw her in it, but Sibonia said, "Go ahead. You have me, and no other one shall you git through me."

I reckon the only reason they didn't string her up right then and there was them not being sure who the other traitors might be, and worried that there might be bunches more of 'em. That flummoxed 'em, so they harangued some more and threatened to hang her right then and there, told her they'd pull out her teeth and so forth, but at the end of it they got nothing from her and threw her back in jail. They spent the next few hours trying to figure matters through. They knowed her sister and seven others was involved. But there was twenty to thirty slaves that lived in the pen at various times, not to mention several that passed there every day, for the masters coming to town parked their slaves in the pen when they come to do business. That meant dozens of coloreds from near a hundred miles around might be involved in the plot.

Well, they argued into the night. It weren't just the principle of the thing neither. Them slaves was worth big money. Slaves in them days was loaned out, borrowed against, used as collateral for this, that, or the other. Several masters whose slaves was arrested upped and declared their slaves innocent and demanded to get Sibonia back and pull her fingernails out one by one till she gave up who was in the plot with her. One of 'em even challenged the judge, saying, "How is it you knows of the plot in the first place?"

"I was told in confidence by a colored," he said.

"Which one?"

"I ain't telling it," the judge said. "But it's a colored that told me—a trusted colored. Known to many of you."

That gived me the shivers, too, for there weren't but one colored in town known to many of them. But I throwed that thought from my mind at the moment, for the judge declared right then and there that it was already three days since they found out about the insurrection, and they had better find a way to make Sibonia give up more names, for he feared the insurrection had already gone past Pikesville. They all agreed.

That was the monkey wrench she throwed on 'em, and they couldn't stand it. They was determined to break her, so they thunk and thunk on it. They broke that night and met the next day and talked and thunk on it some more, and finally, late that night on the second day, the judge himself come up with a scheme.

He called on the town's minister. This feller ministered to the coloreds in the yard every Sunday evening. Since the plot was favored to murder him and his wife, the judge decided to ask the minister to go to the jailhouse and talk to Sibonia, 'cause the coloreds knowed him as a fair man, and Sibonia was known to respect him.

It was a master idea, and the rest agreed on it.

The judge summoned the minister to the saloon. He was a solid, firm-looking man in whiskers, dressed in a button-down jacket and vest. He was clean by prairie standards, and when they brung him before Judge Fuggett, who told him of the plan, the minister nodded his head and agreed. "Sibonia will not be able to lie to me," he announced, and he marched out the saloon and headed toward the jailhouse.

Four hours later he staggered back into the saloon exhausted. He had to be helped into a chair. He asked for a drink. A drink was poured for him. He throwed it down his throat and asked for another. He drunk that. Then he demanded another, which they brung him, before he could finally tell Judge Fuggett and the others what happened.

"I went to the jail as instructed," he said. "I greeted the jailer, and he led me to the cell where Sibonia was held. She was held in the very back cell, the last one. I went inside the cell and I sat down. She greeted me warmly.

"I said, 'Sibonia, I come to find out everything you know about the wicked insurrection'—and she cut me off.

"She said, 'Reverend, you come for no such purpose. Maybe you was persuaded to come or forced to come. But would you, who taught me the word of Jesus; you, the man who taught me that Jesus suffered and died in truth; would you tell me to betray confidence secretly entrusted to me? Would you, who taught me that Jesus's sacrifice was for me and me only, would you now ask me to forfeit the lives of others who would help me? Reverend, you know me!'"

The old minister dropped his head. I wish I could repeat the tale as I heard the old man tell it, for even in the retelling of it, I ain't tellin' it the way he rendered it. He was broke in spirit. Something in him collapsed. He bent forward on the table with his head in his hands and asked for another drink. They throwed that on him. Only after he flung it down his throat could he continue.

"For the first time in my ministerial life, I felt I had done a great sin," he said. "I could not proceed. I accepted her rebuke. I recovered from my shock at length and said, 'But, Sibonia, yours was a wicked plot. Had you succeeded, the streets would run red with blood. How could you plot to kill so many innocent people? To kill me? And my wife? What have my wife and I done to you?'

"And here she looked at me sternly and said, 'Reverend, it was you and your wife who taught me that God is no respecter of persons; it was you and your missus who taught me that in His eyes we are all equal. I was a slave. My husband was a slave. My children was slaves. But they was sold. Every one of them. And after the last child was sold, I said, "I will strike a blow for freedom." I had a plan, Reverend. But I failed. I was betrayed. But I tell you now, if I had succeeded, I would have slain you and your wife first, to show them that followed me that I could sacrifice my love, as I ordered them to sacrifice their hates, to have justice for them. I would have been miserable for the rest of my life. I could not kill any human creature and feel any less. But in my heart, God tells me I was right.'"

The reverend sagged in the chair. "I was overpowered," he said. "I could not answer easily. Her honesty was so sincere, I forgot everything in my sympathy for her. I didn't know what I was doing. I lost my mind. I grasped her by the hand and said, 'Sibby, let us pray.' And we prayed long and earnestly. I prayed to God as our common Father. I acknowledged that He would do justice. That those deemed the worst by us might be regarded the best by Him. I prayed for God to forgive Sibby, and if we was wrong, to forgive the whites. I pressed Sibby's hand when I was done and received the warm pressure of hers pressing mine in return. And with a joy I never experienced before, I heard her earnest, solemn 'Amen' as I closed."

He stood up. "I ain't for this infernal institution no more," he said. "Hang her if you want. But find someone else to minister to this town, for I am finished with it."

And with that he got up and left the room.

14

A Terrible Discovery

They didn't waste time roasting corn when it come to hanging Sibonia's coloreds. The next day, they started building the scaffold. Hangings was spectacles in them days, complete with marching bands, militia, and speeches and all the rest. On account of Miss Abby losing so much money, being that four of hers was going to the scaffold, they drug the thing out longer while she fussed about it. But it was already decided. It brought plenty money to the town. Business boomed the next two days. It kept me busy running drinks and food all day long for the folks who come from miles around to watch. There was a sense of excitement in the air. Meanwhile, any master who had slaves slipped out of town taking their colored, they disappeared with their colored and stayed away. Them folks wanted to keep their money.

News of that hanging drawed some other troubles, too, for there was a rumor that Free Staters got wind of it and was roaming around to the south. Several raids was said to have gone on. Patrols was sent out. Every settler walked around with a rifle. The town was locked up tight, with roads in and out closed off to everybody unless you was known to the townsfolk. What with the booming business, the rumors, and the sense of excitement in the air that runned everywhere, the actual thing took nearly a full week before they got to the show itself.

But they finally got to it on a sunny afternoon, and no sooner did the people assemble in the town square and the last militia arrive did they drag Sibonia and the rest of them out. They come out the jailhouse in a line, all nine of them, escorted on both sides by rebels and militia. It was a mighty crowd that came to witness it, and if them coloreds had any notions of being rescued by Free Staters at the last minute, all they had to do was look around to see it weren't going to happen. There was three hundred rebels armed to the teeth at formation around the scaffold, about a hundred of 'em being militia in uniform with bright bayonets, red shirts, and fancy trousers, even a real drummer boy. The colored from all the surrounding areas was brought in, too—men, women, and children. They lined 'em up right in front of the scaffold, to let them witness the hanging. To let them see what would happen if they tried to revolt.

It weren't a long distance from the jailhouse to the scaffold that Sibonia and them walked, but for some of 'em, I reckon it must've felt like miles. Sibonia, the one they'd all come to see hang, she come last in line. As the line walked to the steps leading to the scaffold, the feller in front of Sibonia, a young feller, he got timid and collapsed at the bottom of the scaffold stairs as they were led up to the hanging platform. He fell down on his face and sobbed. Sibonia grabbed him by his collar and pulled him to his feet. "Be a man," she said. He got hisself together and climbed up the stairs.

When all of 'em got to the top and was gathered there, the hangman asked which of them would go first. Sibonia turned to her sister, Libby, and said, "Come on, sister." She turned to the others and said, "We'll give you an example, then obey." She stepped up to the noose to let the rope get drawed around her neck first, and Libby followed.

I wish I could express for you the tension. It seemed like a rope had knotted itself around the sunlight in the sky to keep every leaf and fig in place, for not a soul moved nor did a breeze stir. Not a word was spoken in the crowd. The hangman weren't pushy nor rude, but rather polite. He let a few more words pass between Sibonia and her sister, then asked if they was ready. They nodded. He turned to reach for the hood to place over their heads. He moved to cover Sibonia's head first, and as he done so, Sibonia suddenly sprung away from him, jumped high as she could, and fell heavily through the galley hole.

But she only went halfway through. The knotted rope weren't adjusted right to make her drop all the way. It checked her fall. Instantly her frame, which was halfway down the opening, was convulsed. In her writhing, her feet kicked and instinctively tried to reach back for the landing where she had stood. Her sister, Libby, her face turned toward the rest of the coloreds, put her hand on Sibonia's side and, leaning forward, held Sibonia's wriggling body clear of the landing with her arm, and said to the rest, "Let us die like her." And after a few shaking, quivering moments, it was done.

By God, I would'a passed out, had not the thing gone in the wrong direction entirely, which made the whole of it a lot more interesting right away. Several rebels in the crowd started muttering they didn't like the business at all, others said it was a damn shame to hang them nine people in the first place, since one colored'll lie on another just as easily as you can snap your trousers, and nobody knows who done what, and it's better to hang them all. Still others said the Negroes hadn't done nothing, and it was all just a bunch of malarkey, 'cause the judge wanted to take over Miss Abby's businesses, and others said slavery ought to be done with, since it was so much trouble. What's worse, the colored watching the whole thing become so agitated after seeing Sibonia's courage that the military rushed up on them to cool them down, which caused even more of a stir. It just didn't go the way nobody expected it.

The judge seen the thing winging out of control, so they hung the rest of the convicted Negroes fast as they could, and in a few minutes Libby and all the rest was asleep on the ground together.

Afterward I stole off to seek a word of consolation on it. Since Pie hadn't seen it, I reckoned she'd want to know about it. She stayed in her room during the past few days, for the business of selling tail went on day and night, and in fact increased during times of trouble. But now that the thing was over, it gived me a chance to get back in her graces, passing the news to her, for she always enjoyed hearing gossip, and this was a hot one.

But she got strange on me. I come to the room and knocked. She opened the door, cussed me out a bit, told me to get lost, then slammed the door in my face.

I didn't think too much of it at first, but I ought to say here while I weren't for the hanging, I weren't totally against it neither. Truth is, I didn't care too much either way. I got plenty chips from it in the way of food and tips for it was a spectacle.

That was fine. But the upshot was Miss Abby had lost a great deal of money. Even before the insurrection, she had come to hinting that I could make more money on my back than on my feet. She was preoccupied with the hanging, course, but now that it was done, I should have been worried about her next intentions for me. But they didn't bother me in the least. I weren't worried about the hanging, nor Sibonia, nor the whoring, not Bob neither, who didn't get hanged. My heart was aching only for Pie. She wouldn't have nothing to do with me. She cut me off.

I didn't make much of it at first. There was a lot of discombobulation, for it was a troublesome time anyway, for colored and whites. They had hung nine coloreds, and that's a lot of folks—even for coloreds, that's a lot of folks. A colored was a lowly dog during slave time, but he was a *valuable* dog. Several owners whose slaves hung fought against the hanging till the end, for it weren't never clear who did what and who planned what and what Sibonia's real plan was and who told who. There was just plain fear and confusion. Some of them Negroes that was hung confessed one way before they died, then turned around confessed another, but their stories banged up against each other, so no one ever knew who to believe, for the ringleader never told it. Sibonia and her sister Libby never sung their song, and left the place more of a mess than it was when they was living, which I reckon was their intent. The upshot was that several slave traders showed up and done a little business for a few days after the hanging, but not much, for slave traders was generally despised. Even Pro Slavers didn't favor them much, for men who traded cash for blood wasn't considered working people, but more like thieves or traders in souls and your basic superstitious pioneer didn't take to them types. Besides, no busy slave trader wanted to journey all the way to Missouri Territory to get a troublesome slave, then run them all the way to the Deep South and sell them, for that troublesome Negro could start an insurrection down south in New Orleans just as easy as he could up here, and word would get back, and that slave trader had a reputation to keep. Them colored from Pikesville was marked as bad goods. Their trading price gone down, for nobody knowed who among them was in the insurrection and who weren't. That was Sibonia's gift to them, I reckon. For otherwise, every one of them would'a been gone south. Instead, they stuck where they was, nobody wanting them, and the slave traders left.

But the stink of the thing lingered. Especially with Pie. She had wanted the hanging, but now seemed put out by it. I knowed what she done, or suspected it, tellin' the judge of the insurrection, but truth is, I didn't blame her for it. Colored turned tables on one another all the time in them days, just like white folks. What difference does it make? One treachery ain't no bigger than the other. The white man put his treachery on paper. Niggers put theirs in their mouth. It's still the same evil. Someone from the pen must've told Pie that Sibonia was planning a breakout, and Pie told it to the judge for some kind of favor, and when the stew got boiled down and shared out, why, it weren't a breakout at all, but rather murder. Them's two different things. Pie had opened a shit bag, I reckon, and didn't know it till it was too late. The way I figure it, looking back, Judge Fuggett had his own interests. He didn't have no slaves, but wanted some. He had everything to gain by Miss Abby going broke, for I'd heard him say later on that he wanted to open his own saloon, and like most white men in town, he was scared and jealous of Miss Abby. The loss of them slaves cost her big time.

I don't think Pie figured on all that. She wanted to get out. I reckon the judge had made some kind of promise to her to escape, is the way I figure it, and never owned up to it. She never said it, but that's what you do when you in bondage and aiming on getting out. You make deals. You do what you got to. You turn on who you got to. And if the fish flips out the bucket and on you and jumps back in the lake, well, that's too bad. Pie had that jar of money under her bed and was learning her letters from me, and turned on Sibonia and them who hated her guts for being yellow and pretty. I didn't blame her. I was sporting life as a girl myself. Every colored did what they had to do to make it. But the web of slavery is sticky business. And at the end of the day, ain't nobody clear of it. It whipped back on my poor Pie something terrible.

It deadened her. She'd let me into her room to clean and tidy and give her water and empty bedpans and so forth. But soon as I was done, out I went. She wouldn't say more than a few words to me. Seemed like she was emptied out, like a glass of water poured onto the ground. Her window looked over the slave yard—you could just see the edge of it, and it gradually filled back up—and many an afternoon I'd walk in on her and find her staring down there, cussing. "They ruined everything," she said. "God-damn niggers." She complained the hanging throwed her business off, though the lines of customers out-side her room was still long. She'd stand at the window, cussing about the whole business, and would throw me out on one pre-text or another, leaving me to sleep in the hallway. She kept her door closed always. When I come by offering to teach her let-ters, she weren't interested. She simply stayed inside that room and humped them fellers dry, and some of 'em even took to complaining she fell asleep right in the middle of the action, which wouldn't do.

I was lost. And also—and I ought to say it here—I growed so desperate for her, I gived some thought to stop playing a girl. I didn't want it no more. Watching Sibonia changed me some. The remembrance of her picking that feller up at the scaffold, saying, "Be a man," why, that just stuck in my craw. I weren't sorry she was dead. That's the life she chose to get rid of, in her own form and fashion. But it come to me that if Sibonia could stand up like a man and take it, even if she was a woman, well, by God, I could stand up like a man, even if I weren't acting like one, to declare myself for the woman I loved. The whole damn thing was jippity in my head, but there was a practical side, too. Miss Abby had lost four slaves to that hanging—Libby, Sibonia, and two men, fellers named Nate and Jefferson. And while she'd been hinting my time on my back was coming, I figured she could use another man or two to replace them that was hung. I figured I would fit the bill. At age twelve, I weren't quite a man, and I never was a big man, but I was a man still, and now that she had lost a lot of money, Miss Abby might see things my way and take me as a man, since I was a hard worker no matter how the cut comes or goes. I reckon I decided I didn't want to play like a girl no more.

This is what happens when a boy becomes a man. You get stupider. I was working against myself. I risked being sold south and losing everything 'cause I wanted to be a man. Not for myself. But for Pie. I loved her. I was hoping she would understand me. Accept me. Accept my courage about throwing off my disguise and being myself. I wanted her to know I weren't going to play girl no more, and for that reason, I was expecting she'd love me. Even though she weren't being good to me, she never turned me away outright. She never said, "Don't come back." She always let me in her room to clean up and tidy a little bit, and I took that to be encouragement.

I had them thoughts in my head one afternoon and decided I was done with the whole charade. I went up to her room with the words ready in my mouth to say 'em. I opened the door, closed it tight, for I knowed her chair sat behind the dressing partition, which set by the window, so that she could look out, for you could set there and see the slave pen and past the alley outside, and she favored setting in that chair, looking out into the alley.

When I come into the room I couldn't see her from the door, but I knowed she was there. I couldn't quite face her, but my mind was set, so I spoke to the partition and declared what was in my heart. "Pie," I said, "no matter how the cut goes or comes, I'm gonna face it. I'm a man! And I'm gonna tell Miss Abby and everybody else in this tavern who I am. I'll explain everything to 'em."

It was quiet. I looked behind the partition. She weren't there. That was unusual. Pie hardly ever left her room, 'specially since she had that money hidden under her bed.

I checked the closet. The back stairs. Under the bed. She was gone.

I stole around to the kitchen to look for her, but she weren't there, either. I went to the saloon. The outhouse. Gone. I went back to the slave pen and didn't find her there, neither. It was empty, for the few slaves that was held out there spent most days loaned out or working elsewhere. I looked up and down the alley by the pen. Not a soul. I turned and was about to head back inside the hotel when I heard a noise from Darg's hut, on the other side of the alley, directly across from the slave yard. It sounded like struggling and fighting, and I thought I heard Pie squawking in there, in pain. I whipped over there quick.

As I hurried over, I heard Darg cursing and the sound of skin hitting skin, and a yelp. I rushed to the doorway.

It was fastened by a nail from the inside, but you could push it open a crack and peer inside. I peeked in there and seen something I would not soon forget.

From the sliver of lights in the broken shutter I seen my Pie in there on a straw bed on the floor, buck naked, on all fours, and behind her was Darg, holding a little tree switch about six inches long, and he was just doing her something terrible, just having his way with her and striking her with that whip at the same time. Her head was throwed back and she was howling while he rode her and called her a high-yellow whore and turncoat for turning in all them niggers and revealing their plot. He whipped her with that switch and called her every name he could think of. And she was hollering that she was sorry and had to confess it to someone.

I kept a two-shot pepperbox revolver under my dress, fully loaded, and I would'a busted in there and put both loads in his head right then, but for her look of liking the whole business immensely.

15

Squeezed

I never said nothing to nobody about what I seen. I done my duties around the Pikesville Hotel like normal. Pie come to me a few days later and said, "Oh, sweetie, I been so terrible to you. Come on back to my room and help me out, for I wants to work on my letters."

I didn't have the spirit for it, to be honest, but I tried. She seen I weren't shining up to her like normal, and got mad and frustrated and throwed me out as usual, and that was the end of it. I was turned out in a way, changing, and for the first time was coming to some opinions of my own about the world. You take a boy and he's just a boy. And even when you make him up like a girl, he's still a boy deep down inside. I was a boy, even though I weren't dressed like one, but I had my heart broke as a man, and 'cause of it, for the first time I had my eye on freedom. It weren't slavery that made me want to be free. It was my heart.

I took to spilling a little rotgut down my throat in them times. It weren't hard. I growed up around it, seen my Pa go his way with it, and I went with it. It was easy. The men in the tavern liked me, for I was a good helper. They let me help myself to the suds at the bottom of their mugs and glasses, and when they found out I had a good singing voice, throwed me a glass of rye or three for a song. I sung "Maryland, My Maryland," "Rebels Ain't So Hard," "Mary Lee, I'm Coming Home," and religious songs I heard my Pa and Old John Brown sing. Your basic rebel was as religious as the next man, and them songs moved 'em to tears every time, which encouraged them to throw more happy water in my direction, which I put to good use, sousing myself.

It weren't long before I found myself the life of the party, two sheets to the wind, staggering around the saloon, singing each night and tellin' jokes and making myself handy the way my Pa done. I was a hit. But a girl in them times, colored or white, even a little one, who drinks and carouses with men and acts a fool, is writing an IOU that's got to be cashed in sooner or later, and them pinches on my duff and old-timers chasing me 'round in circles at closing time was getting hard to take. Luckily, Chase appeared. He'd tried his hand at cattle rustling in Nebraska Territory and got broke at it, and he come back to Pikesville heartsick about Pie as I was. We spent hours setting on the roof of Miss Abby's, drinking joy juice and pondering the meaning of all things Pie as we stared out over the prairie, for she wouldn't have squaddly to do with neither of us now. Her room on the Hot Floor was for only those who paid now, no friends, and we two was clean out of chips. Even Chase, feeling low and lonely, tried his hand at getting fresh with me. "Onion, you is like a sister to me," he said one night, "even more than a sister," and he groped at me like the rest of them old-timers in the tavern, but I avoided him easily and he fell flat on his face. I forgived him course, and we went on like sister and brother from then on, my kidnapper and me, and spent many a night drunk together, howling at the moon, which I generally enjoyed, for there ain't nothing better when you sunk to the bottom to have a friend there.

I would'a gone whole hog with it and been a pure dee bum, but Sibonia's hanging brung more trouble. For one thing, several of them dead Negroes was owned by masters who wasn't agreed to Judge Fuggett's rulings. A couple of fistfights got started on account of it. Miss Abby, who had argued against it, got called an abolitionist, for she runned her mouth about it considerable too, and that caused more wrangling. Judge Fuggett quit town and run off with a girl named Winky, and reports that Free Staters was causing trouble down in Atchinson was becoming more frequent, and that was troublesome, for Atchinson was cold rebel territory, and it meant the Free Staters was making headway against the shirts, which made everybody nervous. Business at the hotel dropped off, and the town's business slowed up generally. Work got hard to find for everyone. Chase declared, "Ain't no more claims to be had around here," and he quit town to head west, which left me on my own again.

I thought about running, but I'd gotten soft living indoors. The thought of riding on the prairie by myself, with the cold, the mosquitoes, and the howling wolves, weren't useful. So one night I went to the kitchen and clipped some biscuits and a mug of lemonade and slipped out to see Bob at the slave pen, being that he was the only friend I had left.

He was setting on a crate at the edge of the pen by himself

when I come, and he got up and moved off when he seen me coming. "Git away from me," he said. "My life ain't worth a plugged nickel 'cause of you."

"These is for you," I said. I reached in the pen with the biscuits, which was in a handkerchief, and held them out to him, but he glanced at the others and didn't touch them.

"Git off from me. You got a lot of nerve comin' 'round here."

"What I done now?"

"They say you gived up Sibonia," he said.

"What?"

Before I could move, several Negro fellers watching from the far side of the pen slipped over closer to us. There was five of them, and one, a young, strong-looking feller, broke off the pack and come over to the fence where I was. He was a stout, handsome, chocolate-skinned Negro named Broadnax who done outside work for Miss Abby. He was wide around the shoulders, with a firm build, and seemed an easygoing feller most times, but he didn't look that way now. I backed off the fence and moved along the rail quick back to the hotel, but he moved quicker and met me just at the corner of the fence and stuck a thick hand through the fence rail, grabbing my arm.

"Not so fast," he said.

"What you need me for?"

"Set a minute and talk."

"I got to go work."

"Every nigger in this world got to work," Broadnax said. "What's your job?"

"What you mean?"

He had my arm tight, and his grip was strong enough to snap my arm in two. He leaned against the fence, speaking calm and evenly. "Now, you could be sproutin' a lie 'bout what you knowed about Sibonia and what you didn't know. And 'bout what you said and didn't say. You could say it to your friend here, or you could say it to me. But without a story, who knows what your job is? Every nigger got the same job."

"What's that?"

"Their job is to tell a story the white man likes. What's your story?"

"I don't know what you're talking about."

Broadnax squeezed my arm harder. His grip was so tight, I thought my arm might break off. Holding my arm, he peered around to make sure the way was clear. From where we was, you could see the hotel, the alley, and Darg's house behind the pen. Nobody was about. In normal times, three or four people would wander down that alleyway during the day. But Pikesville had thinned out since Sibonia died. That woman was a stone witch.

"I'm talking letters," he said. "Your job was to come back and write Sibonia some letters and passes and be quiet about it. You agreed to it. I was here. And you didn't do it."

I had stone-cold forgot about my promise to Sibonia by then. By now Broadnax's friends had slipped up to the fence behind Broadnax and stood nearby holding shovels, movin' dirt, looking busy, but listening in close.

"There weren't time to get out here. The white folks was watching me close."

"You awful close to Pie."

"I don't know nothing 'bout Pie's business," I said.

"Maybe she told it."

"Told what?"

"About Sibonia."

"I don't know what she done. She don't tell me nothing."

"Why would she, you frittering around dressed as you is."

"You ain't got to pick my guts about it," I said. "I'm just trying to make it along like you. But I never had nothing against
Sibonia. I wouldn't stand in the way of her jumping."

"That lie ain't worth a pinch of snuff out here."

The fellers behind Broadnax edged to the corner of that
fence, close now. A couple of 'em had plain stopped working altogether. Weren't no pretense to them working now. I had that
two-shot pepperbox sleeping under my dress, and a free hand,
but it wouldn't do nothing against all of them. There was five of
them altogether, and they looked mad as the devil.

"God hears it," I said. "I didn't know nothing 'bout what she
was aiming to do."

Broadnax peered at me straight. Didn't blink once. Them
words didn't move him.

"Miss Abby's selling off the souls in this yard," Broadnax
said. "Did you know that? She's doing it slow, thinking nobody
notices. But even a dumb nigger like me can count. There's
ten souls left in this yard. Two weeks ago there was seventeen.
Three of 'em's been sold off in the past week. Lucious there"—
here he pointed to one of the men standing behind him—
"Lucious lost both his children. And them children ain't never
been inside Miss Abby's hotel, so *they* couldn't'a told it. Nose,
the girl who gived you the word about the Bible meeting, she
was sold off two days ago, and *Nose* didn't tell it. That makes
just us ten left here. We all likely be sold off soon, 'cause Miss
Abby thinks we is trouble. But I aim to find out who sung
about Sibonia before I leave. And when I do, they gonna suffer.
Or their kin. Or"—he glanced at Bob—"their friends."

Bob stood there trembling. Didn't say a word.

"Bob ain't been inside the hotel since Miss Abby throwed him out here," I said.

"He could'a talked at the sawmill, where he works every day. Told one of them white folks over there. That kind of word'll pass fast."

"Bob couldn't know—'cause I didn't know. Plus he ain't one to run his mouth at white folks. He was scared of Sibonia."

"He should'a been. She didn't trust him."

"He ain't done no wrong. Neither did I."

"You just trying to save your skin."

"Why not? It covers my body."

"Why should I believe a sissy who frolics 'round in a frock and a bonnet?"

"I'm tellin' you, I didn't tell nobody nothing. And neither did Bob."

"Prove it!"

"Bob rode with Old John Brown. So did I. Why didn't you tell him, Bob?"

Bob was silent. Finally he piped up. "Ain't nobody gonna believe me."

That stopped Broadnax. He glanced around at the others. They'd all gathered in close now, they didn't care who was watching from the hotel. I certainly hoped somebody from the hotel would bust out the back door, but nar soul come. Glancing over to the hotel back door, I seen they'd posted a lookout anyway. A Negro was over there, sweeping the dirt around with his back to the door, so if somebody come busting through, he'd hold that door closed a minute to give 'em all a chance to pop back into place. Them pen colored fellers was organized.

But I had their attention now, for Broadnax looked interested. "Old John Brown?" he said.

"That's right."

"Old John Brown's dead," Broadnax said slowly. "He was killed at Osawatomie. Your friend killed him. The feller you get soused with, which is all the more reason to skin you."

"Chase?" I would'a laughed if I weren't feeling so chickenhearted. "Chase ain't killed nobody. Two hundred drunks like him couldn't deaden the Old Captain. Why, at Black Jack, there was twenty rebels there with dead aim and they couldn't hurt the Old Man. Turn me loose and I'll tell it."

He wouldn't turn me loose all the way, but he motioned them fellers to back off, which they done. And right there, standing at the fence, with him gripping my arm tight as a raccoon trap, I gived it to him. Quickly told them everything: About how the Old Man come to Dutch's and took me. How I run off and met Bob near Dutch's Crossing. About how Bob refused to ride Pardee home once the rebels rode off. How Bob helped me get back to the Old Man and was stolen along with his master's wagon by the Old Man hisself and brung into camp. How Chase and Randy brung us there after Old Man Brown run off after Osawatomie, where Frederick was murdered. I left out the part about not knowing for sure if the Old Man was alive.

It moved him enough not to kill me right there, but he weren't moved enough to turn me loose. He considered what I spoke on though, then said slowly, "You had the run of things in the hotel for months. How come you never took off?"

I couldn't tell him about Pie. I still loved her. He could'a put it all together and suspected what I knowed. They would'a deadened Pie right off, though I suspected they planned as such anyway, and I didn't want that. I hated her guts but I still loved her. I was in a tight spot all the way around.

"I had to wait on Bob," I said. "He got cross with me. Wouldn't run. Now the trap's sprung. They watching everybody close now. Ain't nobody going nowhere."

Broadnax pondered it thoughtfully, and he softened some, letting go of my arm. "That's a good thing for you, for these fellers here is game to send their knives rambling across your pretty little face and throw you in the hog pen without instructions. I'll give you a chance at redemption, for we got bigger game. Turncoat like you, you'll get reward for your labor from us or somebody else down the road one way or the other."

He backed off the fence and allowed me to straighten myself out. I didn't turn and run. Weren't no use in that. I had to hear him through.

"This is what I want you to do," he said. "We hear word the Free Staters is riding this way. Next time you get wind of where they are, come out here and pass it to me. That'll even us."

"How I'm gonna do that? I can't get out here easy. The missus is watching me close. And Darg's out here."

"Don't you study ol' Darg," Broadnax said. "We'll take care of him. You just pass the word on what you hear 'bout the Free Staters. Do that, and we'll leave your Bob alone. But if you tarry, or we get word about them Free Staters from some corner other than you? Well, you'll be overdue. And you won't have to sneak out here with lemonade and biscuits for Bob no more, 'cause we'll bust him so hard across the head, he'll have a headache that'll deaden him right where he is. As it is, only reason he's drawing air right now is 'cause of me."

With that, he snatched the handkerchief holding the biscuits and the mug of lemonade I brung out for Bob, shoved the biscuits down his mouth, drunk down the lemonade, and handed me the mug. Then he turned and walked back to the other side of the pen, and the others followed.

Oh, I was stuck tight then. Love will hang you up in many a direction. I thunk on it quite a while that day, thunk about Broadnax busting Bob's brains out and coming into the hotel after me, and that was a worrisome notion. That Negro was determined. A man would have to pump a bunch of iron into a feller like that to stop him. He had a purpose, and that strangled the hope outta me. I fretted on it quite a bit that night and the next morning, then decided to run outta town, quit the idea right off, then thunk on it again all afternoon, decided to run again, waited all night, quit on the idea again, then runned the same whole bit around my head in the same fashion the next day. The third day I got tired of spinning 'round and fretting in that fashion, and gone back and done what I normally done in them days, ever since I lost Pie really: I got drunker with greater purpose.

The fourth night after Broadnax made his threat, I went on a bender with a redshirt who'd stumbled into the saloon full of trail dust, and we was having a good go at it—me more than him, to be honest. He was a young feller, broad-chested feller, more thirsty for water than liquor it seemed. He sat at a table in a big hat pulled close over his face, a long beard, and his arm in a sling. He stared at me in silence while I laughed and joked at him and threw his rotgut down my red lane while double-talking him and switching glasses so as to jug him more water than his whiskey. I overserved myself and he didn't seem to mind it a bit. In fact he seemed to enjoy watching me get out my skull, which, on the prairie, if you can't please a man one way, why you can always please him another. I seen Pie do that a million times. I took this big young feller for one of those, and after several toots and tears and swipes at his glass with him watching and saying nothing, I flat out asked him if I could polish off the entire bottle of whiskey which he had purchased, as it sat on the table hardly getting used by him in the proper manner and it was a waste of breakfast, lunch, and dinner and mother's milk to let such a precious thing go to waste.

He remarked, "You drinks a lot of rotgut for a girl. How long has you worked here?"

"Oh, long enough," I said, "and if you allows me to finish that bottle of bleary on the table there, sir, why, this lonely colored girl will fillet your ears with a song about fish."

"I will do just that if you tells me where you is from, dear maiden," he said.

"Many places, stranger," I said, for I was of the habit about lying about myself, and the "dear maiden" part of his talking meant that he was prone to perhaps buy me a second bottle of that buttercup whiskey after we finished the first. Fact is, when I thunk on it, seemed like he hadn't drunk much at all, and seemed to enjoy watching me do all the sipping and soaking of the alkie for him, which at that point was more than a thrill, for I was already two sheets to the wind and wanted more. I said, "If you buy us a second bottle of moral suasion, I'll give you the whole sad story, plus a haircut, stranger. Then I'll sing 'Dixie Is My Home' for you, which will stir your spirits and put you right to sleep."

"I will do that," the feller said, "but first I needs a favor. I got a saddlebag on my horse, which is tied outside on the alley side of the hotel. That saddlebag needs cleaning. On account of my arm"—and here he pointed to his arm, which was hung in a sling—"I can't lift it. So if I can trust you to go out and fetch that saddlebag and bring it inside and lather it up with saddle soap, why, I'll give you two bits or even three and you can buy your own whiskey. I rides the brown-and-white pinto."

"I will be happy to do that, friend," I said.

I went outside and untied his saddlebag from his pinto in a jiffy, but it was loaded up full, and that thing was heavy. Plus I was pixilated. I lost my grip on it when I got it loose from the horse and it fell to the ground, and the leather top flap popped open. When I bent to close the flap, I noticed in the moonlight an odd thing sticking out the top of that flap.

It was a feather. A long, black-and-white feather with a touch of red on it. Drunk as I was, I still knowed what it was. I hadn't seen a feather like that in two years. I seen a plume of them very same type feathers on Frederick Brown's chest when he was buried. A Good Lord Bird.

I quick stuffed it back into the saddlebag, turned to go inside, and walked straight into the feller who'd sent me out there. "Onion?" he said.

I was two sheets to the wind and seeing double, and he was so tall standing up there in that dark alley that I couldn't quite make out his face, and I was seeing threes anyway. Then he pulled off his hat, threw back his hair, leaned down to look at me close, and I seen past his beard into his face, and found myself staring at Owen Brown.

"I been seeking you for two years," he said. "What is you doing here, carousing around like a drunk?"

I was shocked out my petticoat, practically, and didn't know what to cook up to tell him on the spot, for lying takes wit, and that was on a high shelf in my brain on account of that essence, which tied up my tongue, so I blurted the truth: "I has fallen in love with someone who don't want no parts of me," I said.

To my surprise, Owen said, "I understands. I too has fallen in love with someone who don't want no parts of me. I went to Iowa to fetch a young lady but she said I am too grumpy. She wants prosperity and a man with a farm, not a poor abolitionist. But that didn't turn me into a drunk like you. Is I too grumpy, by the way?"

Fact is, there weren't a soul in Kansas Territory more grumpy than Owen Brown, who would grumble to Jesus Himself on account of just about anything that weren't to his liking. But it weren't for me to say. Instead I said, "Where was you at Osawatomie? We was waiting for you."

"We runned into some rebels."

"Whyn't you come back and get me and Bob?"

"I'm here, ain't I?"

He frowned, glanced up and down the alley, then picked up his saddlebag, and throwed it on his horse with one hand, tying it, using his teeth to hold one of the straps as he did so. "Set tight," he said. "We'll be ridin' here soon. And quit sipping that joy juice."

He mounted up on his horse. "Where's the Old Man?" I hissed. "Is he dead?"

But he had already turned his horse up the alley and was gone.

16

Busting Out

It was the next day before I got a chance to slip out to the pen. Someone had tipped off the town that the Free Staters was coming, and that made the white folks get busy and also watch the niggers close. The town loaded up all over again. They never really geared down after Sibonia's hanging, truth be told, but now the sure sign of Free Staters picked things up. The saloon bar was packed three deep with rebels and militia armed to the teeth. They made plans to block off the streets to the town, this time with cannons on both sides, facing outward. They posted watchouts on both ends and on the hills around the town. They knowed trouble was coming.

I was sent to draw water after lunch the next afternoon, and got out to the yard. I found Bob pining at the edge of the pen by himself as usual. He looked about low as a man can get, like a feller waiting for his execution, which I reckon he was. As I trotted to the gate, Broadnax and his men seen me and peeled away from their side, where they was working with the hogs, and come on over. Broadnax stuck his face inside the rails.

"I got news," I said.

The words hadn't left my mouth when the back door of the hut on the other side of the alley opened and Darg rolled out. That big Negro always moved fast. The slaves scattered when he came, except for Broadnax, who stood alone at the gate.

Darg stomped up to the gate and glared inside the pen. "Git along the back of the fence there, Broadnax, so I can make my count."

Broadnax took his face out the fence railing and stood up straight, facing Darg.

"Git along," Darg said.

"I ain't got to jump like a chicken every time you open that hole in your face," Broadnax said.

"What?"

"You heard me."

Without a word, Darg removed his shawl, pulled out his whip, and moved to unwire the gate and unlock the fence to go inside.

I couldn't stand it. There was rebels three deep in the saloon just inside. A dustup between them two would bring Miss Abby and twenty-five armed redshirts out of the back door ready to throw lead at every colored out there, including them two. I couldn't have that, not with freedom so close. Owen said he was coming, and his word was good.

I stepped in front of Darg and said, "Why, Mr. Darg, I am glad you is here. I come out here to check on my Bob, and Lord these niggers is ornery. I don't know how to thank you on account of your kindness and bravery for keeping these yard niggers in check. I just don't know how to thank you."

That tickled him. He chuckled and said, "Oh, I can think of many ways to thank me, high yeller, which I'll get to in a minute." He flung the gate open.

When he done that, I fell out. Fainted dead out right in the mud, just like I seen the white ladies do.

Gosh darnit, that done it. He hustled over to me, leaned over, and picked me up clear off the ground by the collar with one hand. He stuck his face close to mine's. I didn't want that, so I come out my swoon and said, "Lordy, don't do that. Pie might be looking out the window!"

Well, he dropped me to the ground like a hot potato, and I bounced in the mud and played dead again. He shook me a couple of times, but I didn't come to right off this time. I played possum good as I could for a few seconds. Finally I come to and said, "Oh, Lord, I is ill. Is it possible for a gallant gentleman like you to get a girl a glass of water? I'm ever so shook now with gratefulness, having been jooped and jaloped around by your kind protection."

That done him. He was right loopy over me. "Wait here, little sweetness," he grumbled. "Darg'll take care of you."

He bounced up and runned toward the alley of the hotel, for there was a big water barrel along the side of it that the kitchen used. The moment he scampered off, I pulled my head out the mud long enough to bark at Broadnax, who stood there, and he caught my words.

"Be ready," I said.

That's all I had the chance to do, for Darg came racing back holding a ladle. I played sick while he picked up my head and throwed a slug of nasty, putrid water down my gullet. It tasted so terrible I thought he'd poisoned me. Suddenly I heard a bang, and the ladle knocked into the fence post, which was right next to my head. The thing struck that fence post so hard, I thought that nigger had figured my ruse out and swung at me with it and missed. Then I heard another bang, and that fence post was nearly sheared off, and I knowed it weren't no ladle that busted that wood apart, but steel and powder. I heard more blasts. Them was bullets. The back door of the hotel suddenly flung open, and somebody from inside hollered, "Darg, come quick!"

There was blasting out front, a lot of it.

He dropped me and rushed inside the hotel. I picked myself out the mud and followed.

There was chaos inside. Soon as I hit the kitchen doorway, two Indian cooks knocked me over scrambling for the back door. I got up and scampered through the dining room, and hit the saloon just in time to see the front window blast inward and shower several rebels with pieces of glass. Several Free Staters followed the glass in, leaping into the room and blasting as they come. Behind them, outside the broken window, at least a dozen more could be seen charging on horses down Main Street, firing. At the front door, about the same number kicked their way inside.

They came in there in a hurry and all business, kicking over tables and throwing their pistols on every rebel dumb enough to reach for his hardware, and even those that tossed their guns to the floor was aired out, too, for it was a shooting frolic. A few rebels near the back of the room of the dining hall doorway managed to throw up a table as a barrier and fire back on the enemy, backing toward the doorway where I crouched. I stayed where I was once they got there, trying to get up enough guts to make a dash for the stairs in the dining room to check on Pie, for I could hear the girls on the Hot Floor screaming, and could see from my view out the window that several Free Staters had hopped to the second-floor roof from outside by standing on the backs of their horses. I wanted to go up them stairs, but couldn't bring myself to make a dash for 'em. It was too hot. We was overrun.

I stayed crouched where I was long enough to see the rebels in the saloon make a small comeback, for Darg had been pre-occupied somewhere else and come in the saloon fighting like a dog. He smashed a Free Stater in the face with a beer bottle, tossed another Free Stater out the window, and made the dash into the dining room without being hit, despite heavy fire. He took the back stairs to the Hot Floor on the quick. That was the last I ever saw of him, by the way. Not that it mattered, for no sooner had his back disappeared up the stairs than a fresh wave of Free Staters rushed in the front door to add to those that was chewing up the remaining rebels in the saloon, while yours truly was still cowering in the corner near the dining room, where I could see both rooms.

The rebels in the dining room put up a fight, but in the saloon they was outnumbered, and that room was already compromised. Most of the rebels in there was down or dead. In fact, several Free Staters had already given up the fight for the dining room and pillaged the bar, grabbing bottles and drinking them down. In the midst of that, a tall, rangy feller with a wide-brim hat walked into the busted front door of the saloon and announced, "I'm Captain James Lane of the Free State Militia, and you is all my prisoners!"

Well, there weren't hardly no prisoners to speak of in the

saloon where he spoke, for every Pro Slaver in there had gone across the quit line or was just about to, save for two or three souls squirming on the floor, giving their last kicks. But the rebels who had backed into the dining room caught their breath now and put up a fight. The size of the room favored them, for the dining room was tight and there weren't room for the superior numbers of Yanks, which made shooting at the remaining Pro Slavers in there sloppy business. There was some panic, too, for several drummers fired within ten feet of each other and missed. Still, a good number of the Free Staters took balls in that frolic and their friends, seeing that, weren't taking a liking to it. Their attack slowed. Their surprise was gone, and now it was just a hot fight. There was some crazy talk and laughing, too, for one Pro Slaver exclaimed, "God-damn fucker shot my boot," and there was more laughing. But them rebels done a good enough job to hold them Yanks out the dining room for the moment, and when I seen a path clear to the back door to the alley where the slave pen was, I made for it as quick as I could. I didn't make for the stairs to help Pie. Whether Darg, her new love, was there and got her out, I didn't know. But she was on her own. I never did see either of 'em again.

I busted out that back door running. I hustled over to the slave pen, where the Negroes was scrambling trying to break the lock, which was fastened from the outside. I quick undid it and flung open the gate. Broadnax and the rest run out there with hot feet. They didn't look at me twice. They vanished out the gate quick as you can tell it and hauled ass down the alley.

Bob, though, stood in the corner in the same spot where he always stood, gaping like a fool, his mouth hanging open.

"Bob, let's roll."

"I'm done running with you," he said. "G'wan 'bout your business and leave me be. This is one of your tricks."

"It ain't no trick. C'mon!"

Behind me, at the far end of the alley, a group of rebel townsmen on horses rounded the corner and charged the alleyway, hooping and hollering. They fired over our heads at the fleeing Negroes who was making it for the other end of the alley. The alley dead-ended at a T. You had to turn right or left to get to the road on either side. Them coloreds was making for that intersection something terrible.

I didn't wait. I took off after them. I reckon Bob looked over my shoulder and got a taste of them rebels' bullets singing over his head, for he jumped up like a rabbit and took off right behind me.

The escaped Negroes from the yard was only about twenty-five yards in front of us. They made it to the end of the alley on a dead run and split apart, some cutting right and the others left, out of sight. Me and Bob headed there, too, but didn't get no farther than halfway to the end of the alley when a rebel on horseback rounded the corner on that very same end from the main street side where several Negroes had disappeared to. He charged down the alley toward us. He had a Connor rifle in his hand, and when he seen me and Bob coming at him, he charged dead at us and raised his rifle to fire.

We stopped cold in our tracks, for we was caught. The red-shirt slowed his horse as it trotted on us, and as he pulled his traces on his horse he said, "Stay right there." Just as he said it—he weren't more than five feet from us—a feller stepped out from one of the doorways in the alley and swiped that rebel

clean off his horse with a broadsword. Knocked him clean
down. The rebel hit the ground cold.

Me and Bob made to hotfoot it around him. But the feller
who knocked him down throwed his foot out as I passed, and
I tripped clean over it and fell face-first in the mud.

I turned to get up, and found myself staring up into the barrel of an old seven-shooter, a familiar-looking one, and at the
end of it was the Old Man, and he didn't look none too pleased.

"Onion," he said. "Owen says you is a drunk, using tobacco
and swearing. Is that true?"

Behind him, slowly stepping out the alleyway door come his
boys: Owen, Watson, Salmon, Oliver, the new man Kagi, and
several men I didn't recognize. They stepped out that doorway
slow and steady, never rushing. The Old Man's army was trained
to be calm and cool in a fight as usual. They glanced at rebels
down at the other end of the alley firing at us, formed a firm
firing line, set up, and opened fire.

Several rebels fell. The rest who got a taste of that trained
army bucking lead at them hopped off their horses, and took
cover behind the slave pen, returning the favor.

Bullets whizzed back and forth down the alley, but the Old
Man, standing over me, paid them no mind. He stared at me,
clearly annoyed, waiting for an answer. Well, since he was waiting, I couldn't tell him a lie.

"Captain," I said. "It's true. I fell in love and had my heart
broke."

"Did you commingle with anyone in a fleshly way of nature
without being married?"

"No, sir. I am still clean and pure as the day I was born in
that fashion."

He nodded grumpily, then glanced down the alley as bullets zinged past him and struck the shingles of the building next to him, pinging the wood out into the alley in splinters. He was a fool when it come to standing around getting shot at. The men behind him ducked and grimaced as the rebels gived them fire, but the Old Man might as well been standing in a church at choir practice. He stood mute, as usual, apparently thinking something through. His face, always aged, looked even older. It looked absolutely spongy with wrinkles. His beard was now fully white and ragged, and so long it growed down to his chest and could'a doubled for a hawk's nest. He had gotten a new set of clothes someplace, but they were only worse new versions of the same thing he wore before: black trousers, black vest, frock coat, stiff collar, withered, crumpled, and chewed at the edges. His boots was worse than ever, crumpled like pieces of text paper, curled at the toes. In other words, he looked normal, like his clothes was dying of thirst, and he himself was about to keel over out of plain ugliness.

"That is a good thing, Little Onion," he said. "The Good Book says in Ezekiel sixteen, eight: 'When I passed by thee and looked upon thee behold, that was the time of love and the Lord spread his skirt over thee, and covered thy nakedness.' You has kept your nakedness covered?"

"Much as possible, Captain."

"Been reading the Bible?"

"Not too much, Captain. But I been thinking in a godly way."

"Well, that's something at least," he said. "For if you stand to the Lord's willingness, He will stand for you. Did I ever tell you the story of King Solomon and the two mothers with one baby? I will tell you that one, for you ought to know it."

I was aching for him to move, for the firing had ramped up even more. Bullets zinged high overhead and kicked around his boots and near my face, but he stood where he was a good five minutes, lecturing his thoughts on King Solomon and about me not reading the Good Book. Meanwhile, just behind him at the near end of the alley, which he couldn't see, Broadnax and his band from the slave yard had made their return. They somehow got hold of the rebels' cannon, which had been parked at the edge of town, and they plumb rolled that thing back to the end of the alley and swung the hot end to face the rebels. The barrel of that thing was just over the Old Man's shoulder. He didn't notice, course, for he was preaching. His sermon about the Holy Word and King Solomon and the two mothers with one baby was clearly important to him. He went on warbling about his sermon as one of Broadnax's Negroes flared a light and set fire to the cannon's fuse.

The Old Man didn't pay it a lick of mind. He was still bellowing on about King Solomon and the two mothers when Owen piped up, "Pa! We got to go. Captain Lane's riding outta town and gonna leave us."

The Old Man looked down the alley as bullets whizzed past his head and at the lit cannon over his shoulder, then down at the rebels firing and cussing at the other end of the alley gathered behind the slave pen, trying to mount up the nerve to charge. Behind him, the fuse of Broadnax's cannon was lit and was kicking out thick smoke as it headed home. The Negroes backed away from it in awe, watching the fuse burn. The Old Man, watching them, seemed straight-out irritated that they was taking the fight from him, for he wanted the glory.

He stepped out in the clear, right in the middle of the alley, and shouted to the rebels who was shooting at us from the slave pen. "I'm Captain John Brown! Now in the name of the Holy Redeemer, the King of Kings, the Man of Trinity, I hereby orders you to git. Git in His holy name! Git! For He is always on the right side of justice!"

Well, I don't know if it was that lit cannon belching smoke over his shoulder that done it, or them rebels losing heart when they seen the Old Man hisself in person standing in the clear, untouched with their bullets zinging past his face, but they turned and took the tall timber. They took off. And with that cannon fuse lit and burning home to its maker, the Old Man stood right next to it and watched the fuse burn to nothing and fizzle out. It didn't hit the hammer. The thing was dead.

Looking back, I reckon cannon fuses blowed out all the time. But that cannon not firing only gived the Old Man more reason to believe in divine intrusions, beliefs of which he weren't never short. He watched the fuse fizzle out and said, "Good Lord. God's blessing is eternal and everlasting, and now I sees yet another sign that His ideas which has come to me lately is on the dot and that He is speaking to me directly."

He turned to Owen and said, "I don't want to run behind Jim Lane no more. I come this far only to gather up Little Onion, who is a good-luck charm to me and this army and also a reminder of our dear Frederick, who lies sleeping in this territory. Now that I has got what I come for, our Redeemer has sprung forth yet another rain bucket of ideas for me to lead the way to freedom for the multitudes of His children, like Little Onion here. I have been making some hatchings of various sundry plans, with God's help, and after we help ourselves to some of God's gifts from the hardware and dry-goods stores of these heathen slave owners, we will gather our bees for hiving to a greater purpose. Kansas Territory don't need me no more. We have great work. To the east, men! Onward!"

And with that the Old Man plopped me on his horse, and we sped down that alley, right past that cannon, out of Pikesville, and into legend.

PART III

LEGEND

(Virginia)

17

Rolling into History

A blizzard set on top of us as we moved out of Pikesville with three men on horses and the rest on wagons. Snow fell for a straight day and covered the trail. It left snow nearly a foot high in every direction. A warm snap followed for a day, melting some of the snow, then a deep freeze came. Ice on trees was two inches thick. Water froze in canteens by morning. We lay out under canvases wrapped in roll blankets, with snow blowing over our faces and wolves howling nearby. The Old Man had a new army, a bigger one, and each man took turns keeping the fires going, though they didn't help much. The outdoors never bothered the Old Man, of course. He could sense a change in the weather like an old farmer, walk through the dead of night through a dark woods without nary a light, and step through a thunderstorm like it weren't there. But I was hitting the trail after two years of smooth, dry, easy living and shoving rotgut ale down my throat. The second day I come down with a bad case of the ague. Lucky for me, the Old Man fell ill with the ague, too, so he announced, during the middle of the third day when yet another snowstorm fell, "Men, I has word from on high that there is a slave or two that needs freeing here in Missouri. We is heading to Vernon County."

There weren't no arguing with him in that weather. He had changed considerably since I seen him two years hence. He was a fearsome sight. His face was wrinkled like a raisin. His gnarled old hands looked like leather claws. His face was stern as a rock. His eyes were like gray granite. His speech changed some, too. He declared he had moved to the woods alone to study the works of some feller named Cromwell, and I reckon it moved him mightily, for he sprinkled his talk with more "thees" and "thous" and "thithers" than ever. Sitting atop his horse with snow falling off his flecked wool coat, sticking to his beard, he looked even more like Moses of old. "I ought to be a general," he remarked one morning as we trudged through the freezing woods of Vernon County, "but our Redeemer of Trinity Who controlleth the weather and is Commander of all stations deems it fit to keep me at His feet. I was enjoined with nature for nearly a year, Onion, living in the woods on my own, studying my battle plans and commingling with our great King of Kings, I come away with the understanding that I serves His will as a Captain, Onion, that is the title He has charged me with. Nothing higher."

"Why don't God's Captain take us to warm shelter," Owen grumbled.

The Old Man snorted. "God protects us in winter, Owen. No Pro Slavers will be seen in this country till the grass grows green again. That allows us to do our work."

He was right about that, for no creature with a brain would venture out into that snow. We trudged along through southwest Missouri territory for four days that way, freezing, not finding no slaves to free, till finally the Old Man declared, "Slavery in Vernon County is vanquished. We will march east to Iowa by land."

"Whyn't we take the ferry?" Owen asked. "That's the fastest way east."

The Captain smirked. "The ferries are run by Pro Slavers, son. They don't take Yanks."

Owen brandished his sword and pistols, nodding at the men behind us, three on horses and the rest on wagons, all armed. "They'll take us."

The Old Man smirked. "Did Jesus take a chariot down Jericho Road from eight thousand feet to sea level? Did Moses circle the mountain with the scroll of the commandments on a horse? Or did he climb the swell with his own feet? We shall march to Iowa as cavalry, like David of old." Truth is, though, he couldn't take the ferry 'cause he was on the run. The price on the Old Man's head had gone up considerable in the two years since I'd been in Pikesville. Owen told me both Missouri and Kansas Territory had different prices on his head, and the folks back east had been stirred up considerable by their hearing of the Old Man's doings, which included removin' the head of Doyle and them others, not to mention freeing slaves wherever he went. Each week the Old Man sent one of his men to the nearby town of Cuddyville to get newspapers from back east, and them accounts was filled with all kinds of debates about the slave fight, not to mention the various wonderings about the prices on his head from various pickets, both territories, and Washington, D.C. To make matters worse, a federal company picked up our trail outside Nebraska City and chased us north, away from the ferry. They hung on through the snowstorm. We tried to ride away from them, but they hung back several miles, just out of sight. Each time we thought we'd lost them, the Old Man stopped and peered back through his looking glass and spotted them a few miles distant, struggling to keep up with us in the snow. This went on for days.

"Whyn't they just come on and make a fight of it," Owen murmured.

"They ain't gonna do that," the Captain said. "For Gideon told the people, 'I will not rule over you. My son will not rule over you. The Lord will rule over you.' Our Savior won't let 'em fight us."

After another three days of snow and freezing weather, the federals got tired of the game. They sent a horseman over to our camp bearing a white flag to speak to the Old Man. He was a rangy feller, with his uniform tucked neatly into his boots and his face beet-red from the cold. "I'm Lieutenant Beers," he announced. "I brings words from my commander, Captain Haywood. He says if you was to come in quietly and not resist, we will take you to Lawrence for a fair trial and leave your men alone."

The Old Man snorted. "Tell Captain Haywood to come and get me."

"He'll have to arrest you."

"For what?"

"I ain't certain of the charges, Captain," the lieutenant said, "but the governor of Kansas Territory throwed a three-thousand-dollar price for your capture. President Buchanan has offered another two hundred fifty. You'd be safer with us than riding these parts with all that money hanging on your head."

Sitting on his horse in the falling snow, the Old Man

laughed. He had the oddest laugh of any man I ever saw. He didn't make a sound, but rather crinkled his face and sucked in his breath. His shoulders heaved, he sucked in air, his face tightened up, and the wrinkles in his forehead would collapse around his eyes till they disappeared and all you could see was his yellow teeth, about to whoosh air out at you from what seemed like just about every hole in his head—his eyes, ears, and mouth. The overall effect was terrifying if you didn't know him. The lieutenant got right unsettled watching it, and at that particular moment the Old Man sneezed, which flipped his body off his saddle for a moment and sent his frock coat tails flipping up, showing the handles of one of them great, big seven-shooters he carried in holsters on either side.

"That's an insult," the Old Man finally snorted when he was done. "I am fighting the cause in the name of our Holy Redeemer, who can expunge the word of any nation with a mere cough. I ain't ruled by him. Deuteronomy thirty-two, thirty-five, says, 'Their foot shall slide in due time.'"

He turned around and said to his men, "I herebys offer any man in this here army two dollars and fifty cents for President Buchanan's head. He is presiding over a barbaric institution that does not answer to the throne of our most Holy Martyr."

The soldier turned around and rode back to his company in a hurry. After a day, the federals rode off, tumbling through the deep snowdrifts and long ridges of the prairie. "A wise move," the Old Man murmured, watching them leave through his peering glass. "They knows I have friends in high places."

"Where?" snorted Owen.

"Our most high God, son, whose call you'd do well to heed yourself."

Owen shrugged and didn't pay him no mind. He and his

brothers was used to the Old Man's proclamations. Most weren't nearly as religious as their Pa. In fact, when the Old Man was out of earshot, his sons gived full lip service to quitting the slave-fighting game altogether and returning to their homesteads. A couple of 'em, Jason and John, had already went and done it; they had enough living on the prairie the two years I was gone and quit and gone home, back to upstate New York, and most of his original crew from Kansas went home or was deadened. But he still had four sons with him, Watson, Oliver, Salmon, and Owen, plus he'd picked up some new men in his travels, and these fellers weren't like his earlier crew, which was mostly Kansas farmers, homesteaders, and Indians. This new batch of fellers was young gunfighters, rough adventurers, teachers and scholars, serious business, and would shoot the hair off your head. The most serious of 'em was Kagi, a smooth-faced drummer out of Nebraska City who'd come to Pikesville with Owen. Kagi fought at Black Jack with the Old Man, but I hadn't seen him there, being that my head was in the sand at the time. He was a schoolteacher by trade, and carried lectures and readings in a rolled-up paper bunch in his pocket, which he referred to from time to time. He seemed temperate enough, but he was wanted in Tecumseh for pulling out his Colt and throwing enough lead at a Pro Slavery judge to knock his face off and put the feller to sleep forever. The judge shot Kagi in the heart before Kagi deadened him. Kagi claimed the judge's ball was stopped from piercing his heart by a notebook he carried in his breast pocket. He kept that ragged notebook on his person for the rest of his life, which it turned out weren't very long. Next to him was John Cook, Richard Hinton, Richard Realf, a colored named Richard Richardson, and Aaron Stevens. The last was a tall, hulking grouse, a bad-tempered feller, well over six hands tall, dangerous business, always spoiling for a fight. He weren't religious in the least. These fellers weren't like the Old Man's earlier crew of farmers fighting for their land. They didn't smoke nor drink nor chew tobacco. They mostly read books and argued about politics and spiritual matters. The Old Man referred to 'em as "Mister This" and "Mister That," and had the aim of converting 'em to the Holy Word. He overthrowed 'em with God every chance he got, saying, "Mister So and So, you're doing the devil's work making light of God's salvation," but they'd become used to ignoring him on that affair. Slavery was the question. That's what bonded 'em. And they wasn't fooling.

They followed him like sheep, though. Smart as they was, nary a one of 'em challenged him on his orders or even knowed where we was going from day to day. The Old Man was stone-cold silent on his plans, and they trusted his word. Only thing he allowed was, "We going east, men. We are going east to fight the war against slavery."

Well, there is a lot of east. And there is a lot of slavery. And it is one thing to say you is gonna fight slavery and ride east to do it and take the war all the way to Africa and so forth. It is another to keep riding day after day in the cold to do it.

We drug and slung along one hundred fifty miles toward Tabor, Iowa—it took two months—freeing coloreds as we went. Tabor was free country in them days, but it was winter and tough going, in twelve degree weather, on a trail caked with six inches of ice, and the Old Man praying over burnt squirrel and old johnnycake the whole time. Luckily we had stolen a bunch of booty from Pikesville and a few slave owners along the way: ammo, guns, two Conestoga wagons, four horses, two mules, one ox, bedding, frying pans, tins, some trousers and

hats, coats, even a sewing table and apple barrel, but game on
the prairie in winter is scarce, and we was plumb out of food in
no time, so we traded with whomever we come across as we
plodded along, and survived that way. In that manner I was
also able to secret me a pair of trousers and a hat and under-
wear with nobody giving a hoot's notice, for it was too cold to
care what a person wore out there. By the time we hit Tabor,
Iowa, we was exhausted and hungry—except for the Captain,
who sprang up every morning bright as a bird, ready to go. It
seemed like he didn't need sleep. And food didn't interest him
in the least, 'specially anything revolving around butter. He'd
quit the living game altogether if it meant eating butter. Something about that delicacy just throwed him. But if it was turtle
soup or roasted bear, why, he'd rustle through a pigsty in his
drawers in the dead of winter just to get a whiff of that kind of
game. He was queer that way. An outdoor man to the limit.

He was all but enthusiastic the moment we hit town, which
was strangely quiet when we plodded into the village square.
He looked about and breathed deeply. "I am thankful we is in
abolitionist territory," he crowed as he sat atop his horse, gazing
about. "Even the air seems clearer. Freedom lives here, men. We
are home. We shall rest here through the winter months."

We stood there for an hour and that town stayed quiet as a
mouse fart. Not a door opened. Not a shutter moved. The
town folks was panicked. They wouldn't have nothing to do
with us. After a while we was so cold we knocked on doors
looking for shelter, but no homestead nor tavern wanted us.
"Murderer," a woman chirped, slamming the door. "Crazy old
man," said another. "Keep out." One man told him, "I am against
slavery, Captain, but I'm against killing. You and your men can't
stay here." It went like that all through town. Tabor was free

country in them days, and he was known to every abolitionist east of Missouri, but they was just stone chickenhearted about the whole business. Course the Old Man was hot, too, a wanted man with a price on his head. Every newspaper in the country crowed about how he knocked a few heads off back in Kansas Territory, so I guess that made 'em shy, too.

We went to just about every door in town, a parade of freezing, ragged men, beaten mules and starving horses, and when the last was slammed in his face, the Old Man was irritated but not downtrodden. "Talk, talk, talk," he muttered. "All the Christian can do is talk. And *that*, men," he said, as he stood in the middle of the deserted town, wiping the snow off his whiskers, "is our true battle. Your basic slave needs freedom, not talk. The Negro has listened to talk of moral suasion for two hundred years. We can't wait. Did Toussaint-Louverture, wait for the French in Haiti? Did Spartacus wait on the Roman government? Did Garibaldi wait on the Genovese?"

Owen said, "I am sure they are good people of whom you speak, Father. But it is cold out here."

"We ought to be like David of old," the Old Man grumbled, "living off the grace and nurturing of our King of Kings, who provides for all our needs and wants. I myself am not cold. But for your sakes I *do* have a few friends left in this world." He ordered the men to saddle up again and led us out to a few farmers in nearby Pee Dee who agreed to take us on—after the Old Man sold them most of his horses and wagons and made arrangements for us to help them shuck corn and tend their homesteads through the rest of the winter months. There was some grumbling, but the men was grateful to have food and shelter.

Soon as that was arranged, the Old Man announced, "I has

sold the wagons and our supplies for a purpose. I needs a train ticket to go back east. I will leave you here, men, in comparative warmth and safety, whilst I travel to Boston alone to seek out funds in the name of our Redeemer. For we needs to eat, and our fight requires money, of which there is plenty back east, which I will fetch from our many supporters there." They agreed, for a warm place to sleep was golden and we was exhausted, whereas the Old Man was kicking like a Texas mule.

As the Old Man made ready to go east, his men gived him a few things to take with him, letters for home, gifts for friends, and blankets to keep warm. As he gathered them things, he announced, "Kagi, you is my lieutenant, and you will be in charge of training the men in military exercises and the like that they'll need in our fight against slavery."

Kagi nodded his agreement. Then the Captain cast an eye at yours truly. "Onion, you will come with me."

Owen looked surprised. "Why her?" he asked.

"Onion is a good-luck charm. She is reminiscent of your dear brother Frederick, who lies sleeping in this territory and whose goodness attracted both beast and human. We need every tool now for our purpose, thus it is time to bring the Negro to the fore for his own liberation. I will need her to help hive the Negro. Both the Negro and our white supporters will see the innocence of her countenance and say, 'Yea, child, ye of the Blessed Father, we will inherit the kingdom. He has prepared for us, and we will join up to fight for the cause of our children!' They will come by the thousands!" And he clapped his hands and nodded his head. There weren't no stopping him in the way of enthusiasm on the matter of freedom.

I weren't against it, naturally. I wanted to get out the plains fast as possible. It was my intention to jump off soon as he looked the other way. But Bob was there. He'd clung on through the cold trek over the prairie, having been grabbed up by Owen in Pikesville and pulled along, like always. And just like always in the past, Bob laid low for his chance to cut, and when he seen the Old Man's intent to head east to free country, he spoke out.

"I can help you find Negro soldiers," he announced, "for the Negro is more inclined to listen to the saying of a colored man than a girl."

Before I could argue the point, the Old Man snorted. "God is no respecter of men over women, good Bob. If a man can't meet the needs of his own women or children, why, he's just half a man. You stay here with the rest, for the thousands of Negroes that will flock to our stead will need you to calm them and keep them from pounding the bushes until our war starts, for they will be anxious to go at it. Me and Onion will lay the groundwork, and then you, sir, will be our ambassador to welcome them into our army of men."

Bob sulked and stayed back and kept his peace, which, as it turned out, weren't long, for two weeks after we got back east, a letter come to the Captain that Bob had run off.

We took a train that hauled us from Chicago to Boston, which is what the Old Man said his plan was. Rolling behind that steam engine was a slam-banging, bumpy, clickety-clackety situation, but it was righteous warmer and more comfortable than the prairie. He traveled variously as "Nelson Hawkins," "Shubel Morgan," or "Mr. Smith," depending on what he could remember, for he often generally forgot his fake names and often asked me to remind him which one he was using.

He made various attempts to comb out his beard without success, but with me traveling incog-Negro, posing as a consort, he weren't tricking nobody. I looked raggedy as an old knot rope from weeks on the prairie, and the Captain was famous as bad whiskey. The Pro Slavery passengers cleared out the car when they saw him, and anytime he professed a need for food or drink on the train, why, the other Yankee passengers ponied up whatever food they had for his pleasure. He took these gifts without a blink. "These is not for ourselves, Onion, but rather in the name of our Great Haymaker and for the cause of liberty of our enslaved brothers and sisters." He ate only what he could eat and not a drop more. That was the ironical thing about the Old Man. He stole more wagons, horses, mules, shovels, knives, guns, and plows than any man I ever knowed, but he never took anything for hisself other than what he used personally. Whatever he stole was for the cause of fighting slavery. If he stole something and didn't use it, why, he'd run it back to the poor drummer he stole it from to return it, less'n course the feller was disagreeable, in which case he'd liable to find himself dead or roped to a pole, with the Old Man lecturing him on the evils of slavery. The Captain enjoyed lecturing captured Pro Slavers on the evils of slavery, so much so that a couple of 'em said, "Captain, I'd ruther you plugged me now and get it over with than lecture my ears one more second, for your words is drowning me. You is killing me here." Several prisoners quit the game altogether and dropped off to sleep as he lectured, for many of 'em was drunk, only to wake up sober to find the Old Man praying over them, which was even worse torture, being that they was now sober and the Old Man carried on his prayers longer when he had an audience.

It was on the train that I learned that John Brown was a poor man. He had a large family, even by prairie standards he birthed twenty-two children altogether with two wives. He outlived the first wife and still had the second one living in Elba, New York, along with twelve children, them that weren't killed off through sickness and disease. Most of his young'uns at home was knee-high children or girls, and he constantly scooped up small items and remembrances for them on the train to Boston, such as colorful paper and spools of thread he found tossed about on the passenger car floor, saying, "I'll give this one to Abby," and "This would delight my little Ellen." It was there that I come to understand how guilty he felt for my Pa getting kilt when he first kidnapped me two years prior. He'd given me a store-bought dress he'd got for his own daughter Ellen. The Old Man never bought his goods in any store. That store-bought dress had long wore out by then. I was sporting a fine embroidered number I'd gotten from Pie when he found me in Pikesville. But that gived way on the plains to trousers, undergarments, shirt, and hat, all stolen, course, which I was allowed to wear on account of the fierce weather. The Old Man seen I took to that clothing and it delighted him, for he figured me as being a tomboy of sorts, which generally amused him. Rough and gruff as he was, he was kindhearted to every child he come across. Many a time I seen him set up all night with a colicky colored child who was part of whatever exhausted band of runaway Negroes he was slinging along to freedom. He'd feed her as her tired parents slept, pouring hot milk or soup down her throat, and sing her to sleep. He pined for his own little children and wife, but seen that his fight against slavery was more important than them.

He spent most of the journey reading the Bible, studying

maps, and writing letters. You never seen a man write more letters than Old John Brown. He wrote letters to newspapers, politicians, enemies, his wife, his children, his old Pa, his brother, and several cousins. He received letters from his wife and creditors, mostly—considerable amounts from creditors, for he outworked a cooter in the borrowing department in the old days and owed money on every business he'd owned which gone belly-up and there was considerable numbers of them. He also got letters from Negroes on the run and even Indians asking for help, for he was partial to the red man as well. In most every town where the train stopped, he had some friend or other living there who could post letters for him, and, like as not, when the train stopped to pick up passengers, a child would leap aboard or hand him through the window a bunch of letters addressed to him, for which the Old Man passed him a shilling, then throwed a bunch of letters at him to mail. A few letters arrived with a bit of money in them, from his supporters back east. Which was one reason why letters was so important to him. When he weren't writing letters, he constantly scribbled on maps, several small ones and one big one. He carried that thing rolled up like a large scroll, and unscrolled it and scratched at it constantly in pencil, scrawling numbers and lines, muttering about troops and flanking maneuvers and so forth. He'd sometimes set it down and walk the railroad car, pacing back and forth, figuring. The other passengers was mostly finely dressed businessmen from Missouri, Pro Slavers, and to them, the Captain walking the aisle bearing two seven-shooters barely hidden inside his ragged frock coat and the broadsword sticking out his gunnysack, along with a colored child dressed in farm trousers and hat, was quite a sight. Other than a few Yanks who offered him a nibble or two for himself and his "consort," nobody much bothered him.

The journey to Boston was supposed to take four days, but on the third day, as we swung through Pittsburgh, Pennsylvania, the train stopped to take on water, and he announced, "We are getting off here, Onion."

"I thought we was going to Boston, Captain."

"Not directly," he said. "I suspect there might be a spy among my men in Iowa. I don't want the federal hounds to catch us."

We hopped another train in Pittsburgh for Philadelphia, and got off there for a day to wait for the next train to Boston which weren't due to leave till morning, whereupon the Old Man decided to walk about the city for he was an outdoor man and couldn't bear the thought of setting by a warm woodstove in the station and resting his feet. That city was right enjoyable. The sights and colors of it whirled up before my eyes like a peacock's feathers. Even the smallest street in Philadelphia made the biggest road in Kansas Territory seem like a rutted back alley, full of nags and chickens. Folks in fine clothing strutted about; and there were homes of red brick with perfect, straight chimneys. Telegraph wires, wooden sidewalks, and inside privies lined every street. The trading stores were loaded with fresh poultry, cooked fish, brass candles, ladles, cradles, warming pans, hot-water bottles, commodes, brass ware, even bugles. As I took it all in, I decided the Old Man was a fool to leave the east to fight on the prairie on behalf of the colored. Even the colored in Philadelphia didn't seem to care about their slave brothers. I seen a few of them strolling about, sporting pocket watches, walking canes, breast pins, and finger rings just like white folks, they were right dandy. In fact, they was dressed better than the Old Man.

The next morning, at the train station, the Old Man, he got into a wrangle with the ticket agent, for he was nearly out of money and had changed his mind about going to Boston straight off. Instead he wanted to stop off at Rochester, New York, first. That stretched him to the limit, and he spent his last money getting the tickets changed. "You perhaps question why I am spending my last before we get to Boston," he said. "Fret not, Onion. We will find more funds where we're going. It is worth the cost of ten tickets to Boston, for we are going to meet with the king of the Negro people. He is a great man and a dear friend. Have no doubt, Onion, that in the coming years his exploits will be heralded across this country for genera-tions, and you will be able to tell your children that you have met him. He has promised to fight with us to the end, and that is important, for we will need his help in our cause, to hive the bees. We will need thousands of Negroes, and with him, we will get them. So be kind to him. And polite. He has promised to fight with us. We must convince him to keep his promise to help us hive the bees."

We arrived at Rochester station in the early morning, and as the train pulled in, there upon the platform stood a Negro unlike any I'd ever seen. He was a stout, handsome mulatto with long dark hair parted in the middle. His shirt was starched and clean. His suit was pressed and flat. His boots spotless. His face was shaved and smooth. He waited still as a statue, proud, erect. He stood like a king.

The Old Man descended the train, and the two shook hands and embraced warmly. "Onion," he said, "meet Mr. Fred-erick Douglass, the man who will help lead our cause. Frederick, meet Henrietta Shackleford, my consort, who goes by the name of the Onion."

"Morning, Fred," I said.

Mr. Douglass looked at me coldly. Seemed like the bottom of his nose opened up two inches as he peered down.

"How old are you?"

"Twelve."

"Then where is your manners, young lady? What kind of a name is Onion for a young lady? And why are you dressed in that fashion? And why do you address me as Fred? Don't you know you are not addressing a pork chop, but rather a fairly considerable and incorrigible piece of the American Negro diaspora?"

"Sir?"

"I am Mr. Douglass."

"Why, howdy, sir. I am here to help hive the bees."

"And hive them she will," the Old Man said cheerily. I never seen him knuck to somebody the way he knucked to Mr. Douglass.

Mr. Douglass looked me over close. "I suspect there is a pretty little piece of pork chop under all them rags, Mr. Brown," he said. "And we will forthrightly teach her some manners to go with them fair looks. Welcome to Rochester, young lady."

"Thank you, Mr. Fred," I said.

"Mr. Douglass."

"Mr. Douglass."

"She a spritely little package, Douglass," the Old Man said proudly, "and has showed pluck and courage through many a battle. I reckon it is the highlight of her life to meet the man who is going to lift her people from the chains of the underling world. Onion," he said, clapping Mr. Douglass on the back, "I has been disappointed many times in my life. But this is one man on whom the Old Captain can always depend."

Mr. Douglass smiled. He had perfect teeth. The two of them stood there proudly, beaming there, standing on the train platform, white and colored together. It made for a pretty picture, and if I'd had one of them picture-taking contraptions that had just come out in them days, I'd have recorded the whole thing. But the fact is, like most things the Old Man done, his business didn't work out the way it was drawed up. He couldn't have been more wrong about Mr. Douglass. Had I knowed what was coming, I expect I'd have taken that little derringer I kept from my Pikesville days out my pants pocket and popped Mr. Douglass off in the foot, or at least cleaned him up with the handle of it, for he would short the Old Man something terrible going forward, at a time when the Captain needed him the most. And it would cost the Old Man a lot more than a train ticket to Rochester.

18

Meeting a Great Man

The Old Man laid up at Mr. Frederick Douglass's house for three weeks. He spent most of that time in his room, writing and studying. That weren't unusual for him, to set over paper and write, or walk about with a pocket full of compasses, scribbling notes and consulting maps and so forth. It never amounted to nothing, but three weeks was a long time for me to sit inside anybody's house, and for the Old Man, I expect it was worse. The Captain was an outdoor man. He couldn't sit at a hearth long, or sleep on a feather bed, or even eat food that was cooked for civilized people. He liked wild things: coons, possum, squirrel, wild turkeys, beavers. But food prepared inside a proper kitchen—biscuits, pie, jam, butter—he couldn't stand the taste of them things. So it was suspicious that he set there that long, for that's all they ate in that house. But he hunkered down in a bedroom by hisself, coming out only to use the privy. From time to time Mr. Douglass went in there, and I

overheard them two jawing with raised voices. I overheard
Mr. Douglass at one point say, "Unto the death!" but I made
nothing of it.

Three weeks gave me plenty of time to get acquainted with
the Douglass household, which was run by Mr. Douglass's two
wives—a white one and a colored one. That was the first time
I ever saw such a thing, two women married to one man, and
both of 'em being of a different race. Them two women hardly
spoke to one another. When they did, you'd a thunk a chunk
of ice dropped into the room, for Miss Ottilie was a German
white woman, and Miss Anna was a colored woman from the
South. They was polite enough to each other, more or less,
though I expect if they weren't civilized, they'd a punched each
other wobbly. They hated each other's guts, is the real picture,
and took their rage out on me, for I was uncouth in their eyes
and needing barbering and learning of proper manners, ways
to sit and curtsy and all them things. I gave them a lot of work
in that department, for what few manners and ways Pie taught
me out on the prairie was cow dung to these women, who
didn't use an outdoor privy, and never chewed tobacco or used
words like "haw" and "git." After Mr. Douglass introduced me
to them and retired to his own scribbling—he scribbled, too,
like the Old Man, them two scribbled in separate rooms—
them two women stood me before 'em in the parlor and studied me. "Take them pantaloons off," Miss Anna barked. "Throw
them boots out," Miss Ottilie throwed in. I allowed I'd do what
they asked but would do it in private. They fought over it,
which gave me time to slip off and change alone. But that
drove Miss Anna mad, and she made a comeback two days
later by dragging me into her kitchen to draw me a bath. I

scooted out to the drawing room and runned to the white wife, Miss Ottilie, who insisted *she* draw me a bath, and let them two wrangle over that. In that manner I kept them off me and let them catfight the whole business out.

Them two women would'a grinded each other up if I'd remained there long. But luckily they didn't have time to fool with me much, being that every inch of movement in that house, every speck of cleaning, cooking, dusting, working, writing, pouring of lye, and sewing of undergarments revolved around Mr. Douglass, who walked about the house like a king in pantaloons and suspenders, practicing his orations, his mane of dark hair almost wide as the hallways, his voice booming down the halls. I once heard the mighty marching band at Tuskegee in Tennessee beating at a parade, and that band of two hundred strong, with drums beating and trumpets wailing was an enjoyment. But it weren't nothing compared to the blasting of Mr. Douglass practicing his orations about the fate of the Negro race in his house.

Them women tried to outdo each other with the handling of him, even though he regarded them both like they was cooters and stink bombs. When he took meals, he took them alone at the big mahogany desk in his office. That man gobbled down more in one setting than I seen thirty settlers chunk down in three weeks out in Kansas Territory: steak, potatoes, collard greens, yams, sweet potatoes, cucumbers, chicken, rabbit, pheasant, buck meat, cake, biscuits, rice, cheeses of all types, and kneaded bread; he washed it down with milk, curd, peach juice, cow's milk, goat's milk, cherry juice, orange juice, grape juice. Neither did he turn away from alcohol libations and drinks of all sorts, of which several types was kept on hand at the house:

beer, lager, wine, seltzer, even bottled water from various springs out west. That man put a hurting on a kitchen.

I was exhausted with being a girl a week into the stay, for a damsel out west on the trail could spit, chaw tobacco, holler, grunt, and fart, and gather no more attention to herself than a bird would snatching crumbs off the ground. In fact, your basic Pro Slaver found them behaviors downright likable in a girl, for there weren't nothing better to a feller out on the plains than finding a girl who could play cards like a feller and clean up the bottom of a bottle of whiskey for him when he was pie-eyed. But in Rochester, by God, you couldn't so much as doodle your fingers without insulting somebody on the question of a lady behaving thus and so, even a colored lady—*especially* a colored lady, for the high-siddity coloreds up there was all tweet and twit and whistle. "Where's your bustle?" a colored lady snapped at me when I walked down the street. "Un-nip your naps!" piped up another. "Where's your wig, child?" asked another.

I couldn't stand it and retreated back to the house. All that blitzing and curtsying pressured me, and I got the thirst, needed a jag, a sip of whiskey, to clear me out. Sipping blisters at Miss Abby's had whetted my whistle for tasting the giddy water when things growed tight, and once I got off the freezing trail and fell into the good-eating life, I growed thirsty from all that squeezed-up, settled-down living. I had the thought of cutting out from the Old Man at that time, slipping off and working in a tavern of some type in Rochester, but them taverns there weren't nothing compared to taverns in Kansas Territory. They was more like libraries or thinking places, full of old farts in button-down frock coats setting around sipping sherry and wondering about the state of the poor Negro not prospering, or drunk Irishmen learning to read. Women and girls weren't allowed, mostly. I thunk about getting other jobs, too, for every once in a while a white woman in a bonnet would saunter up to me on the sidewalk and say, "Is you interested in earning three pennies to do laundry, dear?" I was twelve at the time, coming on thirteen or even fourteen is my guess, though I never knowed to be exact. I was still allergic to work no matter what age, so washing folks' drawers weren't an idea I was game to surrender to. I had trouble enough keeping my own clothes clean. I was growing short of temper from all this treatment, and I expect them women would'a found out my real nature once something broke wrong and I drawed my heater, which I still kept. For I had come to the notion that on account of my adventures out west with the Captain, I was a gunfighter of sorts, girl or not, and I felt above most of them citified easterners who ate toast with jam and moaned and crowed about not having no blueberries in the winter months.

But the lack of woozy water chewed at me, and one afternoon I couldn't stand it no more. I decided to drown my thirst with a taste of muddle sauce that Mr. Douglass kept in his kitchen pantry. He had bottles and bottles of it. So I slipped in there and grabbed a bottle, but no sooner did I take a quick drinkie-poo than I heard somebody coming. I quick put the bottle back just as Miss Ottilie, his white wife, appeared, frowning. I thought she'd busted me flat-footed, but instead she announced, "Mr. Douglass asks to see you in his study now."

I proceeded there and found him setting behind his spacious desk. He was a short man, the top of the desk was nearly

as high as he was. He had a big head for such a tiny person, and
his hair, standing on end like a lion's mane, loomed over the top
of the desk.

He seen me coming and bid me to close the door. "Since you
are in the employ of the Captain, I has got to interview you," he
said, "to make you aware of the plight of the Negro in whose
service you has been fighting."

Well, I was aware of that plight, being that I am a Negro
myself, plus I heard him bleating it about the house, and the
truth is, I weren't interested in fighting for nobody's cause. But
I didn't want to offend the great man, so I said, "Well, thank
you, sir."

"First of all, dear," he said, drawing himself up, "sit down."

I done that. Set in a chair just across from his desk.

"Now," he said, drawing hisself up. "The Negro comes in all
colors. Dark. Black. Blacker. Blackest. Blacker than night. Black
as hell. Black as tar. White. Light. Lighter. Lightest. Lighter
than light. White as the sun. And almost white. Take me, for
example. I am of a brown hue. You, on the other hand, is nearly
white, and comely, and that's a terrible dilemma, is it not?"

Well, I never thunk of it that way, but since he knowed everything, I gived him my best answer. "Yes, sir," I said.

"I'm a mulatto myself," he said proudly.

"Yes, sir."

"Being comely, we mulattoes have therefore various certain
experiences that define our existence and set us apart from the
other adherents of our racial congruities."

"Sir?"

"We mulattoes are different from most Negroes."

"We is?"

"Of course, my child."

"I reckon so, Mr. Douglass, if you say so."

"I deedy doody say so indeed-y," he said.

I reckoned he said that as a joke, for he chortled and looked at me. "Ain't that funny?"

"Yes, sir."

"Cheer up, little Henrietta. Where are you from, dear?"

"Why, Kansas, Mr. Douglass."

"No need to call me Mr. Douglass," he said, coming from behind his desk and approaching where I sat. "My friends call me Fred."

It didn't seem proper to call a great man like him Fred, for the only Fred I knowed was dumber than doughnuts and deader than yesterday's beer. Besides, Mr. Douglass was stout as a porcupine about the rules of me calling him "Mr. Douglass" at the train station before. But I didn't want to offend the great leader, so I said, "Yes, sir."

"Not sir. Fred."

"Yes, sir, Fred."

"Oh, come now. Get cheery. Here. Move. Have a seat here," he said. He moved to a tiny couch that was as cockeyed and cocky-mamy as anything I ever seen. One side faced one way. One side faced the other. I reckoned the carpenter was drunk. He stood before it. "This is a love seat," he said, motioning me over with his hands. He done it like he was in a hurry, impatient, like he was used to people listening to his thoughts, which I expect they was, him being a great man. "Would you like to sit here whilst I explain to you further the plight of our people?" he asked.

"Well, sir, I reckon that plight looks righteous bad now, till you furthers it."

"What's that mean?"

"Well, er, with people like you leading the way, why, we can't go wrong."

Here the great man laughed. "You are a country girl," he chortled. "I love country girls. They're fast. I'm from the country myself." He pushed me down in the love seat and sat down on the other side of it. "This love seat's from Paris," he said.

"Is she a friend of yours?"

"It's the city of light," he said, sneaking an arm around my shoulder. "You simply *must* experience the sunlight coming over the Seine River."

"Sunlight over a river? Oh, I seen it come over the Kaw many times. Every day in Kansas, in fact. It rains out there every day sometimes, too, just like it do here."

"My dear," he said. "You are a waif in the darkness."

"I am?"

"A tree of unborn fruit."

"I am?"

"Yet to be picked." Here he tugged on my bonnet, which I quickly pushed back in place.

"Tell me. Where were you born? What is your birthday?"

"I don't know exactly. Though I reckon to be about twelve or fourteen."

"That's just it!" he said, hopping up to his feet. "The Negro knows not where he was born, or who his mother is. Or who his father is. Or his real name. He has no home. He has no land. His station is temporary. He is guile and fodder for the slave catcher. He is a stranger in a strange land! He is a slave, even when he is free! He is a renter, an abettor! Even if he owns a home. The Negro is a perpetual lettor!"

"Like A, B, and C?"

"No child. A renter."

"You rent here?"

"No, dear. I buy. But that's not the point. See this?" He squeezed my shoulder. "That is merely flesh. You are natural prey to the carnal wisdom and thirst of the slave owner, that dastardly fiend of fiendishness. Your colored woman knows no freedom. No dignity. Her children are sold down the lane. Her husbands tend the field. While the fiendish slave owner has his way with her."

"He do?"

"Of course he does. And see this?" He squeezed the back of my neck, then stroked it with fat fingers. "This slender neck, the prominent nose—this, too, belongs to the slave owner. They feel it belongs to them. They take what is not rightfully theirs. They know not you, Harlot Shackleford."

"Henrietta."

"Whatever. They know not you, Henrietta. They know you as property. They know not the spirit inside you that gives you your humanity. They care not about the pounding of your silent and lustful heart, thirsting for freedom; your carnal nature, craving the wide, open spaces that they have procured for themselves. You're but chattel to them, stolen property, to be squeezed, used, savaged, and occupied."

Well, all that tinkering and squeezing and savaging made me right nervous, 'specially since he was doing it his own self, squeezing and savaging my arse, working his hand down toward my mechanicals as he spoke the last, with his eyes all dewy, so I hopped to my feet.

"I reckons your oration's done drove me to thirst," I said. "I wonders if you have some libations around in one of these cabinets here that would help loosen up my gibbles and put me in the right understanding of some of your deepest comminglings about our peoples."

"By God, pardon my rudeness! I've just the thing!" he said. "Would that I had thought of that first." He fair dived for his liquor cabinet and pulled out a tall bottle and two tall glasses, pouring me a tall one and a short one for himself. He didn't know but that I could drink like a man, having already gulped a bit of his hot sauce without his knowing and having absorbed rummy sauce with Pro Slave rebels out west who could hoist a barrel of whiskey down their throats and see double without a hitch. Even your basic pioneer settler church woman out west could outdrink any soft Yank who ate food stored in jars and cabinets and prepared in a hot stove. They could drink him right under the table on the spot.

He shoved the tall glass of whiskey at me and hoisted the short glass for himself.

"Here. Let us toast to the education of a country girl who learns about the plights of our people from its greatest orator," he said. "Careful now, for this is strong." He turned his glass to his talking hole and drunk it down.

The effect of that whiskey hitting his gizzards was altogether righteous. He sat up as if electrified. It throwed him. He shook and rattled a bit. His large mane of hair stood on end. His eyes growed wide. He seemed sotted right off. "Whew. That's a sip, a sot, and a mop!"

"Why, you is right," I said. I drunk mine's down and placed the empty glass on the table. He stared at the empty glass. "Impressive," he grumbled. "You means business, you little harlot." He filled both glasses again, this time filling both to the brim.

"How's about one for the plights of our people in the South who ain't here to hear your speech on 'em?" I said, for I aimed to get pixilated, and his whiskey was weak. He poured another and I drunk mine down again.

"Hear, hear," he said, and he followed suit, downing his a second time and looking bleary-eyed.

Mine's was gone, but I growed to like the taste. "What about the pets who is in slavery, too, suffering in all the heat and cold without your word on 'em?" I said. He poured and I downed it again.

Well, that surprised him, seeing me throw that essence down so easy. See, I learned my drinking out on the prairie of Kansas and Missouri with redshirts, Pro Slavers, and abolitionists, of which even the women could drain a gallon or three and not get two-fisted so long as somebody else was pouring. It pushed his confidence a bit, seeing a girl outdo him. He couldn't stand it.

"Surely," he said. He refilled both glasses again. "Preach it, my country waif, sing that they needs to hear me everywhere in the world!" He was getting addled now, all his fancy prattling started to drop off him like raindrops bouncing off a roof, and the country in him begun to come out. "Nothin' like a spree and a jag then a bout!" he barked, and he poured that weepy, sorry, tea-tasting willowy whiskey down his red lane one more time. I followed him.

Well, we just went on like that. We run through that bottle and then runned into a second. The more stupefied he got, the more he forgot about the hanky-panky he had in mind and instead germinated on what he knowed—orating. First he orated on the plight of the Negro. He just about wore the Negro out.

When he was done orating on them, he orated about the fowl, the fishes, the poultry, the white man, the red man, the aunties, uncles, cousins, the second cousins, his cousin Clementine, the bees, the flies, and by the time he worked down to the ants, the butterflies, and the crickets, he was stone-cold, sloppy, clouded-up, sweet-blind drunk, whereas yours truly was simply buzzing, for that tea was weaker than bird piss, though when you drunk it by volume, it growed more to your liking and tasted better each lick. By the third bottle of essence, he had gone to pot completely, tripping over his oration and skunking about the birds and bees, which was the point of it all, I reckon, for while I was not even half-mud-eyed, he was bent on not being outdrunk by a girl. But being the great leader that he was, he never let go of himself, though he seemed to lose his fancy for me. The more bleary-eyed he got, the more he talked like a right regular down-home, pig-knuckle-eatin' Negro. "I had a mule once," he bawled, "and she wouldn't pull the hat off your head. But I loved that damn mule. She was a stinkin' good mule! When she died, I rolled her in the creek. I would'a buried her, but she was too heavy. A fat thousand-pounder. By God, that mule could single-trot, double-trot. . . ." I rather fancied him then, not in the nature-wanting sort of a way, but knowing that he was a good soul, too muddled to be of much use. But after a while I seen my out, for he was off the edge, wasted and looped beyond redemption, and couldn't hurt me now. I got up. "I got to go," I said.

He was setting in the middle of the floor by then, his suspenders off, clasping the bottle. "Don't marry two women at once," he managed to burble. "Colored or white, it'll whip you scandalous."

I made for the door. He took one final dive for me as I made for it, but fell on his face.

He looked up at me, grinning sheepishly as I opened the door, then said, "It's hot in here. Open da winder." Then laid his mighty Negro head, with his mighty hair like a lion's mane, down flat on his face, and was out cold, snoring when I quietly took my leave.

19

Smelling Like Bear

I didn't tell the Old Man about his friend's exploits. I hated to disappoint him and it didn't seem proper. Besides, once the Old Man made up his mind about somebody, nothing could change him. If the Old Man liked somebody, it didn't matter whether they was heathen or reckless or a boy sporting life as a girl. So long as they was against slavery, that was good enough.

He left Mr. Douglass's house roaring pleased, which meant his face weren't scrunched up like a prune and his mouth weren't closed like a pair of tight britches. That was unusual for him. "Mr. Douglass gave me his word on something important, Onion," he said. "That is good news indeed." We loaded onto a westbound train to Chicago, which didn't make sense, for Boston was the other way, but I weren't going to question him. As we settled in for the ride, he proclaimed loudly so that all the passengers to hear, "We is aiming to change in Chicago for horses and wagon to Kansas."

We click-clacked along for nearly a day and I fell asleep. A few hours later, the Old Man shook me awake. "Grab our bags, Onion," he whispered. "We got to jump."

"Why, Captain?"

"No time for questions."

I cast a glance outside and it was nearly dawn. In the train car, the rest of the passengers was dead asleep. We moved to a seat near the car's edge and lollygagged there till the train stopped to take on water, then jumped off. We hid in the thickets on the side of the tracks a good while, waiting for the engine to get up steam and roll again, the Old Man with his hand on one of his seven-shooters. Only when the train pulled away did his hand drop off his hardware.

"Federal agents is tracking us," he said. "I want them thinking I'm out west."

I watched the train pull away slowly. It was a long stretch of straight track up the mountains, and as the train huffed up it, the Old Man stood up, dusted himself off, and stared at it a long time.

"Where are we?"

"Pennsylvania. These is the Allegheny Mountains," he said, pointing at the winding mountains in the direction of the train, which struggled up the straight track to a winding curve. "This was my boyhood home."

That was the only time I ever heard the Old Man refer to his growing-up years. He watched the train till it was a tiny dot in the mountains. When it was gone, he took a long look around. He looked downright troubled.

"This ain't no way for a general to be living. But now I know why the Lord gave me a hankering to see my old home. See these mountains?" He pointed around.

I couldn't see nothing *but* mountains, and I said, "What about 'em, Captain."

He pointed to the wide passages and craggy cliffs all around us. "A man can hide in these passes for years. There's plenty game. Plenty timber for shelter. An army of thousands couldn't dig out a small army that's well hidden. God pressed His thumb against the earth and made these passages for the poor, Onion. I ain't the first to know it. Spartacus, Toussaint-Louverture, Garibaldi, they all knowed it. It worked for them. They hid thousands of soldiers that way. These tiny passages will entrench hundreds of Negroes against an enemy of thousands. Trench warfare. You see?"

I didn't see. I was fretting that we was standing out in the cold in the middle of no place, and come night, it'd be even colder. I weren't liking that idea. But, being that he never asked my opinion, I told him truthfully, "I don't rightly know 'bout them things, Captain, having never been in no mountains myself."

He looked at me. The Old Man never smiled, but the gray eyes got soft a minute. "Well, you'll be in 'em soon enough."

We weren't far from Pittsburgh, turns out. We followed the tracks all day back down the mountain to the nearest town, waited, and caught a train to Boston. On the train, the Old Man announced his plan. "I got to raise money by speechifying. It ain't nothing to it. It's just a show. After I raise enough chips, we'll head out west again with a full purse to gather the men and raise the hive in our fight against the infernal institution. Don't tell nobody nothing 'bout our purpose in the meantime."

"Yes, Captain."

"And I might ask you to tell some of our donors about your

life of deprivation and starvation as a slave. Being hungry and all. Whipped scandalous, and them type of things. You can tell them that."

I didn't want to confess to him I weren't never hungry as a slave, nor was never whipped scandalous. Fact is, only time I was hungry and eating out of garbage barrels and sleeping out in the cold was when I was free with him. But it weren't proper to say it, so I nodded.

"And while I gives the show," he said, "you must watch the back of the hall for any federal agents. That's important. They is warm on us now."

"What do they look like?"

"Hmm. I reckon they got oily hair and is done up in proper clothing. You'll see 'em. Don't worry. I done arranged everything. Yours won't be the only eyes watching. We'll have plenty help."

True to his word, we was met up at the Boston train station by two of the finest, richest-looking white fellers I ever seen. They treated him like a king, fed us well, and drug him along to a couple of churches for some speechifying. He pretended he weren't for it at first, but they insisted it was already arranged— and he went along as though it come as a surprise. At the churches he gave boring speeches to crowds of white folks who wanted to hear all about his adventures fighting out west. I never been one for speeching and carrying on, unless course there's joy juice or paying money involved, but I must say that while the Old Man was hated out on the plains, he was a star back east. They couldn't get enough of his stories about the rebels. You would'a thunk that every Pro Slaver, including Dutch, Miss Abby, Chase, and all them other low drummers, scammers, four-flushers, and pickpockets, who mostly lived off pennies and generally didn't treat the Negro any worse than they treated each other, was a bunch of cranks, heathens, and drunks who runned around murdering one another while the Free Staters spent all day setting in church at choir practice and making paper cutout dolls on Wednesday nights. Three minutes into his talk, the Old Man had them high-siddity white folks hollering bloody murder against the rebels, nigh shouting against slavery. He weren't much of a speaker, to be honest, but for once he got the wind in his sails about our Dear Maker Who Restoreth Our Fortunes, he got 'em going, and the word spread fast, so by the time we hit the next church, all he had to say was, "I'm John Brown from Kansas, and I's fighting slavery," and they roared. They called for them rebels' heads, announced they'd trounce 'em, bounce 'em, kill 'em, deaden 'em where they stood. Some of the women broke into tears once the Old Man spoke. It made me a bit sad, truth be to tell it, to watch them hundreds of white folks crying for the Negro, for there weren't hardly ever any Negroes present at most of them gatherings, and them that was there was doodied up and quiet as a mouse. It seemed to me the whole business of the Negro's life out there weren't no different than it was out west, to my mind. It was like a big, long lynching. Everybody got to make a speech about the Negro but the Negro.

If the Old Man was hiding from a federal agent, he had a strange way of showing it. From Boston to Connecticut, New York City, Poughkeepsie, and Philadelphia, we done one show after another. It was always the same deal. He'd say, "I'm John Brown from Kansas, and I's fighting slavery," and they'd howl.

We collected quite a bit of money in this fashion, with me movin' 'bout the hall passing the hat. Sometimes I collected as much as twenty-five dollars, sometimes more, sometimes less. But the Old Man made it clear to all them followers that he was planning to head back west to fight slavery, clean, in his own fashion. Some questioned him about how he planned to do it, how he planned to fight slavery and all, who he was gonna do it with, and so forth. They put the question to him ten times, twenty times, in every town. *"How you gonna fight the Pro Slavers, Captain Brown? How you gonna conduct the war?"* He didn't tell a straight-out fib. Rather he bounced around the question. I knowed he weren't going to tell them. He never told his men or even his own sons his plans. If he weren't tellin' his own people, he weren't tellin' no group of strangers who throwed him a quarter apiece. Truth is, he didn't trust nobody with his plans, especially his own race. "These house-born city-grubbers is good for talk only, Onion," he muttered. "Talk, talk, talk. That's all they do. The Negro has heard talk for two hundred years."

I could'a heard it another two hundred years the way I was living, for I was mostly satisfied in them times. I had the Old Man to myself, and we lived high. I ate well. Slept well. In feather beds. Traveled on trains in white folks' compartments. Them Yanks treated me fine. They didn't no more notice me of being a boy under that dress and bonnet than they would notice a speck of dust in a room full of cash. I was simply a Negro to them. "Where did you find her?" was the question most asked of the Old Man. He'd shrug and say, "She is one of the many multitudes of enshackled persons whom I has freed in God's name." Them women fussed over me something fierce. They oohed and ahhed and gived me dresses, cakes, bonnets, powder, ear loops, pompons, feathers, and gauze. I was always wise enough to keep silent around white folks in them days, but there weren't no call for me to talk nohow. There ain't nothing gets a Yankee madder than a smart colored person, of which I reckon they figured there was only one in the world, Mr. Douglass. So I played dumb and tragic, and in this manner I managed to finagle a full set of boy's pantaloons, shirt, jacket, and shoes, plus twenty-five cents from a woman in Connecticut who sobbed when I told her I was aiming on freeing my enslaved brother, of which I had nar one. I hid those clothes in my gunnysack for my own purpose, for I always had my eye on movement, always kept myself ready to roll. In the back of my mind was the notion that the Old Man would one day be deadened by somebody, for he was a fool about dying. He'd say, "I'm on God's clock, Onion. I'm prepared to die fighting against the infernal institution," which was fine for him but not for me. I always made ready for the day I'd be on my own.

We slung along like that for a few weeks till spring approached, and the Old Man begun pining for the prairie. Them city parlor halls and speakings was wearing him down. "I'd like to go back west to smell the spring air and fight the infernal institution, Onion," he said, "but we still has not made enough yet to raise our army. And there is still one special interest I must tend to here." So instead of leaving from Philadelphia the way he planned, he decided to make a second pass at Boston before heading west for good.

They had him set up at a big hall there. His handlers had primed the thing. There was a fine, mighty crowd standing outside, waiting to be let in, which meant much money to be collected. But they delayed it. Me and the Old Man was standing behind the big organ pipes in the pulpit, waiting for the crowd to come in, when the Old Man asked one of his handlers who was standing about, "What's the delay for?"

The man was in a tizzy. He seemed scared. "A federal agent from Kansas has come to this area to arrest you," he said.

"When?"

"No one knows when or where, but someone spotted him at the train station this morning. You want to cancel today's event?"

Oh, that primed the Old Man. That drug him out. He loved a fight. He touched his seven-shooters. "He better not show his face in here," he said. And the others standing around allowed that they agreed, and promised that if the agent showed himself, why, he'd be jumped and shackled. But I had no trust in them Yanks. They weren't uncivilized like the raw Yanks out west, who would knock you cold and drug you along from a stirrup by one boot and beat you something scandalous like a good Pro Slaver would. These Yanks was civilized.

"There will be no arrest in here today," the Old Man said. "Open the doors."

They ran and done as he said, and the crowd filed in. But before he walked out to the pulpit to speak, the Captain pulled me aside and gived me warning. "Stand along the far wall and watch the room," he said. "Keep your eyes open for that federal agent."

"What do a federal agent look like?"

"You can smell him. A federal man smells like bear, for he uses bear grease to oil his hair and lives indoors. He don't cut stove wood or plow a mule. He'll be clean looking. Yellow and pale."

I looked into the hall. Seemed like about five hundred folks out there fit that description, not including the women. The

Old Man and his boys had taken down a bear or two in our travels, but other than eating the meat and using the fur to warm my gizzards, weren't nothing I could remember about the bear smell. But I said, "What do I do if I see him?"

"Don't say nothing or interrupt my talking. Just wave the Good Lord feather in your bonnet." That was our sign, see. That feather he gived me from the Good Lord Bird, which I gived to Frederick, and got back from Frederick after he died. I kept that thing stuffed in my bonnet flush to my face.

I allowed that I would do as he said, and he went up to the pulpit while I moved into the room.

He walked up to the podium wearing both his seven-shooters and his broadsword with a look on his face that showed he was ready to crust over on some evil. When the Old Man got to boiling and was ready to throw hot grits around and raise hell, he wouldn't get excited. He'd go the other way. He'd calm up, get holy, and his voice, normally flat like the plains, would get high and tight, curvy and jagged sharp, like the Pennsylvania mountains he favored. First thing he said was, "I has word a federal agent is on my tail. If he is present, let him show himself. I will meet him with an iron fist right here."

Blessed God if you couldn't hear a pin drop in there let me drop a corpse by the telling of it. Good God, he put a scare into them Yanks then. They growed quiet when he said that, for he feared 'em up something good. They seen his true nature. Then, after a few moments, they got their courage up, and growed mad, and booed and hissed. They flew hot as the devil, and shouted out they was ready to leap on anyone who would so much as look at the Old Man sideways. That brought me some relief, but not much, for they was cowards and talkers, whereas the Old Man, when he beat his drum wrong about somebody, he'd drug 'em over the quit line without too much tearing his hair out 'bout the whole bit. But he couldn't kill nobody in there, not with all them people there, and that gived me some comfort.

The room quieted after he shussed 'em and assured 'em no agent would dare show himself anyhow. Then he went on into his normal speech, pissing all over the Pro Slavers as usual, hollering 'bout all the killings they done, without mentioning his own, of course.

I knowed that speech like the back of my hand, having heard it many times by then, so I got bored and fell asleep. Near the end of things, I woke up and runned my eyeballs along the walls, just to be safe, and darned if I didn't spot a feller who seemed suspicious.

He stood along the back wall among several other fellers who hooted and hollered against the Pro Slavers. He didn't join them in that. Didn't gnash his teeth or grind his hands or nod his head, or cry and pull his hair and holler against the Pro Slavers like those around him did. He weren't enraptured with the Old Man. He stood stone-cold silent, cool as spring water, watching. He was a clean-cut feller. Short, stout, pale from living inside, wearing a bowler cap, white shirt, and bow tie, with a handlebar mustache. When the Old Man paused in his speech for a moment, the crowd shifted, for it growed hot in the room, and the feller removed his hat, showing a mane of thick, oily hair. By the time he pushed back a lick of that oily hair and throwed the hat back on his head, the thought had gathered in my mind. That was an oily-haired man if I ever saw one, and I ought to go over there and at least smell him for bear.

The Old Man had kicked his speech into full-out blast by
that time, for near the end of his speech he always worked his
talk up full, and was in high spirits anyway for he knowed
he was heading west after this last big throw-down. He gave
his usual proclamations against the dreaded master and the
poor slave not prospering and so forth. The crowd was loving
it, the women crying and pulling out their hair and gnashing
their teeth—it was a good show—but I was alarmed now,
watching that spy.

I weren't taking no chances. I slung my feather out my bonnet and waved it toward the podium, but the Old Man was in
high spirits and had peaked by then. He had launched into the
final part of his talk, where he busted loose to God in prayer,
which he always done at the end, and course he always done
his praying with his eyes closed.

I already done told you how long the Old Man's prayers
went. He could tear into a prayer for two hours and spout the
Bible easy as you and I can spout the alphabet, and he could do
that alone, by hisself, with nobody standing around. So imagine when he had a few hundred folks setting there listening on
his thoughts and pleas to our Great King of Kings who made
rubber and trees and honey and jam with biscuits and all them
good things. He could go on for hours, and we actually lost
money on account of that, for sometimes them Yanks got worn
out with his rumblings to our Maker and cleared the hall before the basket got passed. He growed wise to that tactic by
that time and begun to keep his speculatings short, which for
him meant still at least a half hour, his eyes shut at the pulpit,
howling at our Maker to hold him in high stead while he done
His duty of murdering the slavers and sending them to Glory

or Lucifer, though he had a devil of a time keeping it to that length.

I reckon the agent had spied the show before, 'cause he knowed the Old Man was winding down, too. He saw the Old Man close his eyes to start his Bibling and quickly slipped off the back wall and worked through the crowd gathered along the side aisle of the hall, making his way to the front. I quick waved my feather at the Old Man again, but his eyes was shut tight as he gived the Lord ninety cents on the dollar. There weren't nothing to do but move with the agent.

I came off the back wall and worked my way around the room behind him fast as I could. He was closer to the stage than I was, and movin' quick.

The Old Man must'a smelled a rat, for in the middle of his proclamations 'bout immortal souls and the afflicted, his eyes suddenly popped open and he blurted out a quick "Amen." The crowd hopped out their seats and surged to the front of the hall, making a beeline to commingle with their hero and shake his hand and get his autograph and give him coin donations and so forth.

They swarmed the agent as well, and slowed his progress. But he was still ahead of me, and I was but a colored girl, and the crowd pushed me aside in the scramble to shake the Old Man's hand. I was being thumped 'bout by Yankees trying to swarm the Old Man. I waved the Good Lord feather again but I was drowned out by taller adults all around. I caught a glimpse of a little girl up front who beat the crowd to the Old Man, holding out a paper for him to sign. He leaned down to sign it, and as he done so, the agent busted through the crowd and made it to the front of the room and was nearly on him. I jumped into the pews and leaped over the seats toward the front.

I was ten feet off when the agent was within arm's length of the Captain, who had bent down with his back to the agent to put his mark on the paper for the little girl. I crowed out, "Captain! I smell bear!"

The crowd paused a moment, and I do believe the Captain heard me, for his head snapped up and the old, stern, wrinkled face clicked to alertness. He stood and spun around in a snap, his hands on his seven-shooters and I ducked low, for that gun makes a powerful boom when it wakes up. He caught the feller cold. Had the drop on him, for the agent hadn't quite reached him yet, nor gone for his metal. He was a dead man.

"Aha!" the Old Man said.

Then, to my surprise, his hands came off his seven-shooters and his tight face uncrinkled. He stuck his hand out. "I see you has got my letters."

The stout feller with a mustache and bow tie stopped short and bowed low in his bowler cap. "Indeed!" he said. He spoke with an English accent. "Hugh Forbes at your service, General. It is an honor to meet the great warrior of slavery of whom I have heard so much. May I shake your hand?"

They shook hands. I reckon this was the "special interest" the Captain had waited on, the thing he had hung around waiting for back east before heading back to the plains.

"I has studied your great war pamphlet, Mr. Forbes," the Old Man said, "and I daresay it is excellent."

Forbes bowed low again. "You humble me, dear sir, though I do confess my military training duties are underscored by the many victories I experienced on the European continent under the legions of the great General Garibaldi himself."

"Indeed it is pertinent," the Old Man said. "For I has a plan that needs your military training and expertise." He glanced around at the folks gathered 'round them, then at me. "Let us retire to the back room here, whilst my consort counts up the funds from tonight's gatherers. There is doings of which I needs to discuss with you in private."

With that, the two went into the back room of the hall while I collected the funds. What they discussed I weren't privy to, but they commingled there the better part of three hours, and when they emerged, the hall had cleared out.

It was quiet and the streets was safe. I handed the Old Man the $158 collected from that night's doings, our best take ever. The Old Man produced another pile of bills, counted them up, placed a total of $600 in a brown bag, just 'bout every penny we'd made from our three months of giving speeches and shows up and down the East Coast, raising money for his army, and handed the bag to Mr. Forbes.

Mr. Forbes took the bag and stuffed it in his vest pocket. "I am proud to serve in the legions of a great man. A general in the score of Toussaint-Louverture, Socrates, and Hippocrates."

"I'm a captain, serving in the army of the Prince of Peace," Old Man Brown said.

"Ah, but to me you are a general, sir, and I will call you thus for I serve under nothing less."

With that, he turned and marched down the alley, military style, like a soldier, clickety-clack, erect and proud.

The Old Man watched him all the way till he reached the end of the alley. "I has been trying to find that man for two years," he announced. "That is why we lingered here so long, Onion. The Lord finally brung him to me. He will meet us in Iowa and train our men. He is from Europe."

"He is?"

"Yes indeed. A trained expert under Garibaldi himself. We has a true military trainer, Onion. Now, finally, I am ready to go to war."

Forbes reached the end of the alley, turned to the Old Man, tipped his cap, bowed, and walked away into the night.

The Old Man never saw him again.

20

Rousing the Hive

We sat in a flophouse in Chester, Pennsylvania, outside Philadelphia, for two weeks while the Old Man wrote letters, studied maps, and waited for word of the military trainer, Mr. Forbes, arriving in Iowa. When he got a letter from Mr. Kagi saying he hadn't arrived, he knowed the jig was up. He didn't mope 'bout it, but rather seen it as a positive sign. "We been had by a wicked snare, Onion. The devil is busy. But the Lord reckons we don't need training to fight our war. Being on the righteous side of His word is training enough. Besides," he announced, "my greater plan is 'bout to be unleashed. It is time to hive the queen bees. We is going to Canada."

"Why, Captain?"

"Is it the white man upon whom the Negro can depend to fight his war, Little Onion? No. It is the Negro himself. We are 'bout to unleash the true gladiators in this hellion against the infernal wickedness. The leaders of the Negro people themselves. Onward."

I weren't against it. Being that me and the Old Man traveled as man and consort, the mistress at the flophouse where we stayed made me sleep in the maids' quarters, a rat-infested sop of a room that reminded me of Kansas. I had gotten spoiled by them Yanks crying over me being a slave and filling me with hasty pudding, smoked turkey, venison, boiled pigeon, lamb, dainty fish, and pumpkin bread every chance they got. The mistress of that tavern weren't one of those. She didn't have two cents' worth of sympathy for no abolitionist, mostly 'cause she was basically a slave herself. She served sour biscuits and gravy, which was fine for herself and the Old Man, for he didn't have no taste for anything cooked, but my own tastes growed to pumpkin bread, fresh blackberries, turkey, venison, boiled pigeon, lamb, dainty fish, pumpkin bread, and butchered ham with real German sauerkraut like I had up in Boston every time I dropped word on being a slave. I was all for staking out new territory. Besides, Canada was free country. I could stay there and be done with him before he got deadened, which was my thoughts.

We took the train to Detroit, and from there met up with the Old Man's army, which had growed from nine to twelve. Included in that group was four of the Old Man's sons: Owen, of course, Salmon, plus two younger ones, Watson and Oliver. Jason and John had quit. A. D. Stevens was still there, grousing, dangerous Yankee that he was. Kagi had commanded them as the Old Man had ordered, and there was some new roughnecks: Charles Tidd, a hot-tempered feller who had served as a soldier with the federals. John Cook was still there, now carrying two six-shooters on his hips, and several others including the Old Man's sons-in-law, the Thompson boys, and the Coppoc brothers—them last two being shooting Quakers. That was the main ones. With the exception of Cook, who could talk the horns off the devil's head, they was mostly quiet, serious fellers, men of letters, so to speak. They read newspapers and books, and while they was mellow in polite company, they'd loose their business on you with a muzzle loader and blow a hole in your face in a minute. Them fellers was dangerous, but for the simple reason they had a cause. Ain't no worse thing in the world than fronting up against one of those, for a man with a cause, right or wrong, has got plenty to prove, and will make you suck sorrow if you get in the way of 'em wrongly.

We wagoneered up to Chatham, Ontario, the men in the back while the Old Man and I rode up front. He was cheerful all the way, allowing that we was heading to a special meeting. "It's the first of its type," he announced. "A convention with Negroes from all over America and Canada is hiving to make a resolution against slavery. The war begins in earnest, Onion. We will have numbers. We will have resolution. We will have *revolution! It's percolating!*"

It didn't percolate right off. Only forty-five folks percolated to Chatham, and of that number, nearly a third was the white fellers from the Old Man's army or was white fellers who picked up and joined us along the way. It was January, cold and snowy, and on account of that or whatever other duties kept them free Negroes home, it was as pitiful a convention as I ever did see. It was held in an old Masons' lodge in a single day, with lots of speeches and resolving and herebys and halooting 'bout this and that and not a bite to eat; a bunch of them fellers read declarations the Old Man had written up, and there was a lot of hollering 'bout who shot John and what the slave needed to do to prosper and get clear of the white man. There weren't nothing too good for encouragement in the whole deal from what I could see. Even the Old Man's pal Mr. Douglass didn't come, and that made the Old Man's feathers fall some.

"Frederick never plans well," he said airily, "and he will regret the lack of planning that caused him to miss one of the great moments in American history. There is great speakers and great minds present here. We is changing the course of this country as we speak, Onion."

Course, being that he was the main appointed speaker and wrote the constitution and set the bylaws and basically done the whole thing himself, that helped make the thing in his mind seem more important. It was all 'bout him, him, and him. Nobody in America could outdo John Brown when it come to tooting his own whistle. He let the Negroes have their moments, course, and after they blowed out more hot gas and done more grousing 'bout the white man and slavery in that one day than I was to hear in the next thirty years, it was his turn. It was the end of the day, and they had speechified and signed papers and made resolutions and the like, and it was the Old Man's turn to speak and show his papers and froth his mouth 'bout the whole slavery show. I was dead tired and hungry by then, course, having had nothing to eat being around him as usual, but he was the main event, and that being so, they was all licking their chops for him when he shuffled to the front of the room fluffling his papers, while the room lay quiet, full of expectation.

He wore a string tie for the occasion, and sewed three new buttons on his tattered suit, of which they was all different-colored buttons, but for him that was sporty. He stood upon the old rostrum, cleared his throat, then declared, "The day of the Negro's victory is at hand." And off he went. I ought to say here that these wasn't no ordinary Negroes the Old Man was talking with. These Negroes were upper crust. They wore bow ties and bowler caps. They had all their teeth. Their hair was clipped clean. They was schoolteachers and ministers and doctors; shaved men who knowed their letters, and, by God, the Old Man roused these sporty, free, highfalutin, big-time Negroes till they was ready to roast corn and eat earworms in his favor. He raised the rafters on that old lodge house. He had them Negroes bellowing like sheep. When he harped 'bout destroying the white man's slave yard, they hollered, "Yes!" When he railed 'bout taking the revolution to the white man, they screamed, "We is all for it!" When he honked on 'bout busting them slaves loose by force, they piped out, "Let us begin!" But when he quit his speech and held up a paper asking for volunteers to come up and sign on in his war against slavery, not a man stepped forward nor raised his hand. The room was quiet as a cotton sack.

Finally a feller in the back stood up.

"We is all for your war on slavery," he said, "but would like to know what your specific plan is."

"I can't announce it," the Old Man grumbled. "There might be spies among us. But I can tell you, it ain't a peaceable march using moral suasion."

"What's that mean?"

"I aim to purge America's sin with blood. And I will do it soon. With the help of the Negro people."

That curdled my cheese right there, and I decided Canada is where I would stay. I had my pantaloons, shirt, and shoes hidden away, plus a few pennies I'd managed to save up from our Yankee fund-raising. I figured with all them high-siddity niggers in the room, there must be at least one or two kind-hearted souls among 'em who would help me get started out new again, maybe tender me some shelter and a bit to eat till I got going enough to pull up my own knickers.

A slim feller with long sideburns and a smock coat near the front of the room stood up. "I allows that is plan enough for me," the feller said. "I will join up." His name was O. P. Anderson. A braver soul you will not meet. But I'll get to O.P. in a minute.

Next the Old Man looked around the room and asked, "Is there anyone else?"

Not a soul stirred.

Finally another feller spoke out. "If you will just tell a little of your battle plan, Captain, then I will join. I can't sign a contract knowing what kind of dangers is ahead."

"I ain't asking you to trot 'round a circle like a horse. Is you wanting to save your people or not?"

"That's just it. They're my people."

"No they're not. They're God's people."

That started some wrangling and conniption, with some arguing this way and that, some with the Old Man, others against. Finally the first feller who started the ruckus said, "I ain't afraid, Captain. I escaped slavery and run three thousand miles here on foot and horseback. But I hold my life dear. And if I'm to lose it fighting slavery, I would like to know the manner in which it is to happen."

Several others agreed with him, and allowed they'd join, too, if the Old Man would simply reveal his plan—where it would happen, when, what was the strategy, and so forth. But the Old Man was stubborn on that count, and wouldn't turn. They pressed him on it.

"Why is you holding back?" one said.

"Is there a catch?" said another.

"It's a secret conference, Captain! Ain't nobody gonna tell!"

"We don't know you!" somebody hollered. "Who are you? Why should we trust you? You is white, and got nothing to lose, whereas we stand to lose everything."

That got him, and the Old Man firmed up, he got mad, for his voice thinned out and his eyes growed steady and cold, which they did in them times. "I has proven over the course of my life that I am a man of my word," he said. "I am a friend of the Negro and I move to God's purpose. If I say I am planning a war to end slavery, that is word enough. This war will begin here but not end here. It will go on whether you join it or not. You have to meet your Maker just as I do. So go ahead: Work out on your own what you chooses to tell Him when your time to meet Him comes. I only ask"—and here he glared 'bout the room—"that whatever you do, tell no one about what you've heard here."

He looked 'bout the room. Not a soul spoke out. He nodded. "Since there is no one else signing on, our business is done. Therefore, as president of this here body and author of this here constitution, I hereby move to close this—"

"Hold a minute, Captain." Here a voice come from the back of the room.

Every head turned to see a woman. She was the only woman in the room besides yours truly, who don't count. She was a short, slender number. She wore her hair under a wrap and a simple maid's dress and apron. Her feet was covered by a pair of man's boots. She dressed like a slave, except for a colorful shawl, beaten and worn, which she carried across her arm. She had a quiet manner 'bout her, she weren't a talker, you could see that, but her eyes was dark and boiling. She moved toward the front of the room like the wind, quick, silent, smooth, taut as rope, and them fellers parted and slid their benches out the way to let her pass. There was something fearful 'bout that woman, silent, terrible, and strong, and I made up my mind to keep away from her right off. I had good practice being a girl by then. But colored women could sniff out my true nature better than most, and something told me that a powerful-looking woman like that could not be fooled with nor did she fool easily. She slipped to the front of the room with her hands folded in across her chest and faced the men. If you passed by the window of that old lodge and peeked inside, you'd'a thunk a cleaning woman was addressing a room full of professors, explaining to them why she hadn't cleaned the privy or some such thing, for the men was dressed in suits, hats, and bow ties—whereas she was dressed like a simple slave.

"My name's Harriet Tubman," she said. "And I know this man." She nodded to the Captain. "John Brown don't have to explain nothing to this plain woman. If he say he got a good plan, he got a good plan. That's more than anyone here got. He done took many a whipping for the colored, and he took it standing up. He got his own wife and children starving at home. He already gived the life of one of his sons to the cause. How many of you has gived yours? He ain't asking you to feed his children, is he? He ain't asking you to help him, is he? He's asking you to help yourself. To free yourself."

Silence in the room. She glared 'bout.

"Y'all clucking like a bunch of hens in here," she said. "You setting here warm and cozy, worrying 'bout your own skin, while there's children crying for their mothers right now. There's fathers torn apart from their wives. Mothers torn from their children. Some of you got wives, children, living in slavery. And you setting here on the doorstep of change, scared to walk through it? I ought to take a switch to some of you. Who's a man here? Be a man!"

Well, it hurt my heart to hear her talk that way, for I was wanting to be a man myself, but afraid of it, truth be told, 'cause I didn't want to die. I didn't want to be hungry. I liked somebody taking care of me. I liked being coddled by Yanks and rebels for doing nothing but shoving biscuits down my throat, and being led 'bout by the Old Man, who took care of me. And before that, Pie and Miss Abby taking care of me. Mrs. Tubman standing there so firm saying them words, reminded me of Sibonia before she met the hangman's noose, tellin' Judge Fuggett to his face: "I am the woman, and I am not ashamed or afraid to confess it." She was a fool to hang for freedom! Why fight when you can run for it? The whole business shamed me worse than if Mrs. Tubman had whipped me, and before I knowed it, I heard a terrible squawking sound in the room, the sound of a scared soul, shouting forth, hollering, "I'll follow the Captain to the ends of the earth! Count me in!"

It was several moments before I realized all that piping and squawking was my own voice, and I nearly wet myself.

"Praise God!" Mrs. Tubman said. "And a child will lead them! Praise Jesus!"

Well that got 'em all going, and before you know it, every single soul in that room stood up and stumbled over each other in their bowler hats to get to the front of the room to sign on. Clergymen, doctors, blacksmiths, barbers, teachers. Men who never handled a gun or sword. To a man they put their names to that paper, signing on, and it was done.

The room emptied thereafter, and the Captain found himself standing in the empty hall with Mrs. Tubman while I cleaned up, sweeping the floor, for he had borrowed the hall under his name and wanted to return it as he got it. He thanked her as she stood there, but she waved her hand. "I hope you do have a plan, Captain, for if you don't, we will all suffer for nothing."

"I'm working on it, with God's help," the Old Man said.

"That ain't enough. God gave you the seed. But the watering and caring of that seed is up to you. You's a farmer, Captain. You know this."

"Course," the Old Man grumbled.

"Make sure it's right," Mrs. Tubman said. "Remember. Your average Negro would rather run from slavery than fight it. You got to give 'em direct orders. With a direct, clear plan. With an exact time. And a fallback plan if the thing don't go. You can't deviate from your plan once it set. Start down the road and don't go sideways. If you deviates, your people will lose confidence and fail you. Take it from me."

"Yes, General." That's the first and only time I ever heard the Old Man capitulate to anyone, colored or white, or ever call anyone a general.

"And the map I gived you of the various routes through Virginia and Maryland, you must memorize and destroy. You got to do that."

"Course, General."

"Okay. God bless you, then. Send me the word when you is ready, and I will send as many to you as I can. And I will come myself." She gave him the address of the tavern in Canada where she was staying, and made ready to leave.

"Remember, you must be organized, Captain. Do not get

too hung up on emotional matters. Some is gonna die in this war. God don't need your prayers. He needs your action. Make your date solid. Hold tight to it. The wheres and whats of your plan, don't nobody need to know, but hold tight to the date, for folks is coming a long way. My people will be coming from a long way. And I will be coming from a long way."

"I will make it clear, General," he said. "And I will hold tight to the date."

"Good," she said. "May God bless you and keep you for what you has done and is 'bout to do."

She flung on her shawl and prepared to leave. As she did, she spotted me toward the door, sweeping the floor, hiding behind that broom more or less, for that woman had my number. She motioned to me. "Come over here, child," she said.

"I'm busy here, ma'am," I croaked.

"Git over here."

I went over, still sweeping.

She looked at me a long time, watching me sweep the floor, wearing that damn fool dress. I didn't say a word. Just kept on sweeping.

Finally she placed her small foot on the broom and stopped it. I had to look up at her then. Them eyes was staring down at me. I can't say they was kind eyes. Rather they was tight as balled fists. Full. Firm. Stirred. The wind seemed to live in that woman's face. Looking at her was like staring at a hurricane.

"You done good to speak out," she said. "To make some of these fellers stand up as men. But the wind of change got to blow in your heart, too," she said softly. "A body can be whatever they want to be in this world. It ain't no business of mine. Slavery done made a fool out of a lot of folks. Twisted 'em all different kinds of ways. I seen it happen many a time in my day. I expect it'll happen in all our tomorrows, too, for when you slave a person, you slave the one in front and the one behind."

She looked off out the window. It was snowing out there. She looked right lonely at that moment. "I had a husband once," she said. "But he was fearful. He wanted a wife and not a soldier. He became something like a woman hisself. He was fearful. Couldn't stand it. Couldn't stand being a man. But I led him to freedom land anyway."

"Yes, ma'am."

"We all got to die," she said. "But dying as your true self is always better. God'll take you however you come to Him. But it's easier on a soul to come to Him clean. You're forever free that way. From top to bottom."

With that, she turned and walked past the other side of the room toward the door, where the Old Man was busy picking up his papers, maps, and his seven-shooter. He seen she was leaving, and dropped his papers to hurry to open the door to let her out. She stood at the open door a minute, watching the snow, her eyes glancing up and down at the empty, snowy road. She studied the street carefully a long moment, looking for slave stealers, I reckon. That woman was always on the look-out. She watched the street as she spoke to him.

"Remember, Captain, whatever your plan, be on time. Don't deviate the time. Compromise life before you compromise time. Time is the one thing you can't compromise."

"Right, General."

She bid him a hasty good-bye and left, walking down the road in them boots and that colorful shawl draped on her shoulders, snow falling on the empty road around her, as me and the Old Man watched her.

Then she quickly turned back, as if she forgot something, walked to the steps where we stood, still wearing her beaten colorful shawl, and held it out for me. "Take that and hold it," she said, "for it may be useful." Then she said to the Old Man again, "Remember, Captain. Be on time. Don't compromise the time."

"Right, General."

But he did compromise the time. He blowed that one, too. And for that reason, the one person he could count on, the greatest slave emancipator in American history, the best fighter he could'a got, the one person who knowed more 'bout escaping the white man's troubling waters than any man alive, never showed up. The last he seen of her was the back of her head as she walked down the road in Chatham, Canada. At the time, I weren't sad to see her go, neither.

21

The Plan

B y the time the Old Man got back to Iowa, he was so excited, it was a pity. He left the U.S.A. for Canada with twelve men, expecting to pick up hundreds. He come back to the U.S.A. with thirteen, on account of O. P. Anderson, who joined us on the spot, as well as a few white stragglers who come along for a while and dropped off like usual when they seen that freeing the slaves was liable to get your head squared by an ax or butchered some other way. The rest of the coloreds we'd met up in Canada went back to their homes in various parts of America but had promised to come when called. Whether they was gonna be true to their word or not, the Old Man didn't seem worried, for by the time he got back to Iowa, he was downright joyful. He'd got the General behind him, that was Mrs. Tubman.

He almost weren't sensible in his excitement. He was joyful. It ain't a clean proposition when you decides to mount thirteen fellers and declare a war on *something* rather than somebody. It occurred to me then he might be slippin' and I ought to maybe take my leave when we got back home before he got too deep into whatever foolishness he planned next, for he didn't seem right. But in them days I didn't linger on any subject so long as I was shoving eggs, fried okra, and boiled partridge down my throat. Besides, the Old Man had more bad luck than any man I ever knowed, and that can't help but to make a person likable and interesting to be around. He spent long hours in his tent, praying, studying maps, compasses, and scribbling numbers. He always wrote letters like a madman, but now he wrote triple the letters he wrote before, so much that his army's main job in them first weeks in Tabor involved nothing more than sending and getting his mail. He sent his men to Pee Dee, Springdale, and Johnston City, to pick up letters from safe houses and taverns and friends and send off letters to Boston, Philadelphia, and New York. It took him hours to go through his mail, and while he done that, his men trained with wood swords and pistols. Some of that mail was letters with money from his abolitionist supporters back east. He had a group of six white fellers in New England who gave him big lumps of money. Even his friend Mr. Douglass sent him a shilling or three. But the truth of it is, most of them letters, the ones that weren't from creditors, contained not money but questions. Them white folks back east was asking for—no begging for—his plans.

"Look at this, Onion," he railed, holding up a letter. "All they do is ask questions. Talk, talk, talk, that's all they do. Armchair soldiers. Setting around while someone destroys their house and home with the infernal institution. And they call *me* insane! Whyn't they just send the money? I'm the one they trusted to take on the fight, why tie my hands behind my back by asking me how. There ain't no 'how,' Onion. One must *do*, like

Cromwell. There are spies everywhere. I'd be a fool to tell 'em my top-secret plans!" He was confounded with it. He was furious when some of his supporters declared they weren't going to send him a dime more if he didn't tell them their plans.

The ironical thing is, I reckon he would have told them his plans. He wanted to tell 'em his plans. Problem is, I don't think the Old Man knowed what his plan was hisself.

He knowed what he wanted to do. But as to the exactness of it—and I knowed many has studied it and declared this and that and the other on the subject—Old John Brown didn't know exactly what he was gonna do from sunup to sundown on the slavery question. He knowed what he *weren't* gonna do. He weren't going to go down quiet. He weren't going to have a sit-down committee meeting with the Pro Slavers and nag and commingle and jingle with 'em over punch and lemonade and go bobbing for apples with 'em. He was going down raising hell. But what kind of hell, he was waiting on the Lord to tell him what that is, is my reckonings, and the Lord weren't tellin', at least that first part of the year in Tabor. So we set 'bout Tabor in a rented cabin, the men training with swords and fussin' over spiritual matters and fetching his mail and grousing amongst themselves, waiting for him to bark out what was next. I got the ague and was on my back for a month of that time, and not long after I got well, the ague hit the Old Man. It floored him. Knocked him on his back. He didn't move for a week. Then two. Then a month. March. April. At times I thought he was gone. He'd lay there, mumbling and murmuring, saying, "Napoleon used the mountains of the Iberians! I ain't done yet!" and "Josephus, catch me if you can!" only to fall out again. Sometimes he'd sit straight up, feverish, staring at the ceiling, and holler, "Frederick. Charles! Amelia. Get that bird!" then drop off again, like he was dead. The two of his sons, Jason and John Jr., who declared they was out of the slave war and had already quit, he'd call out their names sometimes, hollering, "John! Get Jason in here!" when neither was within five hundred miles. Several of his army left, promising to return, and did not. But others replaced them. The main ones though—Kagi, Stevens, Cook, Hinton, O. P. Anderson—they stayed, training themselves with wood swords. "We promised to fight with the Old Man till death," Kagi said, "even if it's his."

Four months in that cabin gave me plenty of time to hear the Old Man's thoughts, for he was in a fever and prone to blab 'bout himself. Come to find out he'd failed at just 'bout everything. He had several businesses that failed: cattle rustling, tannery, land speculating. All gone belly up. Bills and lawsuits from his old business partners followed him everywhere. To the end of his life, the Old Man wrote letters to creditors and throwed a dollar here or there to whomever he owed money to, which was a considerable amount of people. Between his first wife, Dianthe, who he outlived, and his second wife, Mary, who he did not, he had twenty-two children. Three of them, all little ones, died in a bunch in Ritchfield, Ohio, where he worked in a tannery; one of 'em, Amelia, was scalded to death in an accident. Losing them children hurt his heart sorely, but Frederick's dying, he always seed that as murder, and it was always the biggest hurt on his heart.

We caught Frederick's murderer, Rev. Martin, by the way. Cold got the drop on him back outside Osawatomie, Kansas, six months earlier, in fall, while rolling through there out of the western territory. We come upon him sleeping in a hammock at his settlement, a small spread tucked in a valley beneath a long, sloping ridge just outside Osawatomie. The Old Man was leading his crew along the edge of that ridge with his eye out for the federals when he suddenly stopped and held up the column, peering down at a figure in his front yard laying in a hammock, dead asleep. It was Rev. Martin, all right.

The Old Man sat atop his stolen mount and stared at Rev. Martin a long time.

Owen and Kagi rode up next to him.

"That's the Rev," Owen said.

"It is," the Old Man said.

Kagi said calmly, "Let's ride down there and have a talk with him."

The Old Man stared down the ridge a long time. Then he shook his head. "No, Lieutenant. Let's ride on. We've a war to fight. I don't ride for revenge. 'Revenge,' says the Lord, 'is Mine's.' I ride against the infernal institution." And he upped and nicked his horse on the side, and we rode on.

His fever stayed on into May, then June. I nursed him during that time. I'd come in to give him soup and find him sleeping, only to bust awake in a sweat. Sometimes, when his mind came back to him, he'd brood over military books, poring over maps, land drawings, circling various towns and mountain ranges with a pencil. He seemed to edge toward getting better at them times, then suddenly bust back into full-out sickness. When he felt better, he'd wake up and pray like a fiend, two, three, four hours at a time, then drop off to peaceful sleep. When the fever got him again, he'd fall into feverish talking with our Maker. He had whole conversations with the Lord then, with backbiting arguments and sharing thoughts and biscuits with an imaginary man standing there, sometimes

throwing pieces of cornmeal or johnnycake 'bout the room, as
if he and the Maker, who was standing somewhere 'bout him,
was having a marriage spat and throwing food 'bout the
kitchen. "What do you think I am?" he'd say. "A money tree?
A fool for gold? But that's hardly a righteous request!" Or he'd
suddenly set up and blurt out, "Frederick! Ride on! Ride on,
son!" then fall out, asleep, only to wake up hours later, not
remembering a thing he'd said or done. His mind had gone off
on a jolt and fling, so to speak, it had ginned and baled hay
and gone on home, and toward July, the men got to burbling
'bout disbanding altogether. Meanwhile, he allowed no one
except me to enter his cabin to nurse and feed him and see
'bout him. It got to when I'd come out the cabin, his men
would gather 'round me and say, "Is he living, Onion?"

"Yet living. Sleeping."

"He ain't dying, is he?"

"No. Praying and reading. Eating a little."

"He got a plan?"

"Nar word."

They waited like that and didn't make a fuss with him, busy-
ing themselves under Kagi by clanking away with their swords,
reading the military pamphlet written by Colonel Forbes,
which is all the Old Man got out of that little gamer. They
played with a cat named Lulu that wandered in, and picked
corn and done other odd jobs for farmers that lived nearby.
They got to know one another in that fashion, and Kagi stuck
out in that time as a leader of men, for fighting and squabbling
erupted among them during many an idle hour of chess and
fighting with wood swords and fussin' 'bout spirituality, for
some of 'em was nonbelievers. He was a thoughtful feller, firm
and steady, and he kept them together. He talked into line the

more doubtful ones who mumbled 'bout disbanding and going back east to teach school or work jobs, and kept the rest of the rough ones in check. He didn't take no backwater off nobody, not even Stevens, and that scoundrel was rough work and would bust out the brains of anybody who looked at him sideways. Kagi could handle him, too. Come one evening in late June, I walked into the Captain's cabin bearing a bowl of turtle soup, which always seemed to revive the Old Man some, and found him setting up on his bed, looking strong and wide-awake. A huge map, the favorite one he always fiddled with, lay in his lap, along with a bunch of letters. His gray eyes was bright. His long beard flowed down his shirt, for he never cut it from that day forward after he got that ague. He seemed well. He spoke in a strong way, his voice high and tight, like it is when he is in battle. "I has spoken with God and He has given me the word, Onion," he said. "Summon the men. I'm ready to share my plan."

I gathered them up and they congregated outside his cabin. He emerged shortly after, pushing back the canvas flap covering the door, stepping before them with his usual stern expression. He stood tall, without his jacket, without a walking stick to lean on nor did he lean against the doorway, to let them know he weren't weak or sick no more. The campfire was lit before him, for dark was coming, and the prairie dust blowed leaves and tumbleweeds 'bout. In the long ridge behind his cabin, wolves howled. In his old knarled hands he held a sheaf of papers, his big map, and a compass.

"I has commingled with the Lord," he said, "and I has a battle plan which I aims to share. I knows you all wants to hear it. But first off, I wants to give thanks to our Great Redeemer, He Who sheddeth His blood on the cross of holy held high."

Here he folded his hands before him and prattled off a prayer for a good fifteen minutes. Several of his men, nonbelievers, got bored, turned on their heels, and wandered off. Kagi departed to a nearby tree, sat down under it, and fiddled with his knife. Stevens turned around and walked off, cursing. A feller named Realf produced pen and paper and commenced to scribbling poetry. The others, Christians and heathens alike, stood patiently as the Captain railed at God, the wind blowing against his face, going high and low with his prayer, up and down, round and round, asking the Redeemer for guidance, direction, chatting 'bout Paul when he wrote Corinthians and how he weren't good enough to take the strap off Jesus's shoes and so forth. He gone on with that railing and ranting at full steam, and when he finally throwed out the last "Amen," those who had departed to read their mail and monkey with their horses saw he was finally ready and returned hastily.

"Well, now," he said, "as I said before, I has commingled with our Great Redeemer, He Who hath sheddeth His blood. We has discussed this entire enterprise from top to bottom. We has wrapped our minds around each other like a cocoon wraps a boll weevil. I has heard His thoughts, and I, having heard them, I must say here that I am but a tiny peanut in the corner sill of the window of our Savior's great and powerful thoughts. But, having studied with Him and asked Him several times, going on years now, of what to do about the hellish institution of evil that exists in this land, I am certain now that He has chosen me to be an instrument of His purpose. Course, I already knowed that, just like Cromwell and Ezra the prophet of the old knowed it, for they was instruments in the same fashion, especially Ezra, who prayed and afflicted himself before God in the same fashion as I have, and when Ezra and his people were in a strait, the Lord busily and quietly engaged them to the arrangement of safety without harm. So fear not, men! God is no respecter of persons! Indeed it says in the Bible, the book of Jeremiah, 'For these are the days of vengeance and there shall—'"

"Pa!" Owen cut him off. "Out with it!"

"Hmph," the Old Man snorted. "Jesus waited an eternity to free you of the curse of mortal sin, and you didn't hear Him bellowing like a calf as you are now, son. But"—and here he cleared his throat—"I has studied the matter, and I will share with you here what you need to know. We are going to trouble Israel. We will raise the mill. And they will not soon forget us and our deeds."

With that, he turned and lifted the flap on the door of his cabin and pushed the door to go back inside. Kagi stopped him.

"Hold on!" Kagi said. "We have tarried here, hanging kettles and banging rocks with wood swords for quite a bit. Are we not men here, with the exception of the Onion? And even she, like us, is here of our own volition. We deserve more than cursory information from you, Captain, lest we go out and fight this war on our own."

"You will not succeed without my plan," the Old Man grunted.

"Perhaps," Kagi said. "But surely there is danger involved. And if I am to wager my life on any plan, I would like to know the manner of it."

"You will know it soon enough."

"Soon enough is now. Or I, for one, will announce my own plan, for I have been working on one. And I suspect the men here will hear it."

Oh, that knotted him up. The Old Man couldn't stand it.

He just plain couldn't stand having someone else be the boss or tell a plan better than his. The men were watching close now. The wrinkles in his face knotted up and he blurted out, "All right. We're leaving in two days."

"For where?" Owen said.

The Captain, still holding the canvas door cover over his head, dropped it, and it flapped across the cabin door like a giant, dirty sheet hung out to dry in the wind. He glared at them with his hands in his pockets, jaw jutting out, disgruntled to the limit. It just plain irritated him to be talked to that way, for he listened to no council but his own. But he hadn't no choice.

"We plans to strike at the heart of this infernal institution," he said. "We will attack the government itself."

A couple of fellers tittered, but Kagi and Owen did not. They knowed the Old Man better than the others, and knowed he was serious. My heart skipped a beat, but Kagi said calmly, "You mean Washington? We can't attack Washington, Captain. Not with thirteen men and the Onion."

The Old Man snorted. "I wouldn't plow that field with *your* mule, Lieutenant. Washington is where men talk. This is war. Wars is fought in the field, not where men set about eating pork and butter. In war, you strikes at the heart of the enemy. You strike his supply lines like Toussaint-Louverture struck the French on the islands around Haiti. You busts open his food chain like Schamyl the Circassian chief done against the Russians! You attacks his means like Hannibal in Europe done against the Romans! You take his weapons like Spartacus! You hives his people and arms them! You dissiminates his power to his chattel!"

"What is you talking 'bout!" Owen said.

"We is going to Virginia."

"What?"

"Harpers Ferry in Virginia. There's a federal armory there. They make guns. There's a hundred thousand rifles and muskets in that place. We will break in there and, with those weapons, arm the slaves, and allow the Negro to free himself."

Many years later, I joined a choir in a Pentecostal church after taking a liking to a minister's wife who slept around to save the wear and tear on her holy husband. I runned behind her several weeks till one morning the pastor gived a rousing sermon 'bout how the truth will set you free, and a feller stood up in the congregation and blurted out, "Pastor! I got Jesus in my heart! I'm confessing! Three of us in here has porked your wife!"

Well, the silence that followed that poor man's declaration weren't nothing compared to the quiet that fell on them roughnecks when the Old Man dropped that bomb on 'em.

To be clear on it, I weren't afraid at that moment. In fact, I felt downright comfortable, 'cause for the first time, I knowed I weren't the only person in the world who knowed the Old Man's cheese had slid off his biscuit.

Finally John Cook managed to speak. Cook was a chatty feller, dangerous, the Old Man declared many a time, for Cook was a loose talker. But chatty as he was, even Cook had to cough and snort and clear his throat a few times before he found his voice.

"Captain, Harpers Ferry, Virginia, is eight hundred miles from here. And just fifty miles from Washington, D.C. It's heavily guarded. With thousands of U.S. government troops nearby. There's militia from Maryland and Virginia all around it. I'd guess there'd be maybe ten thousand troops mustered up against us. We wouldn't last five minutes."

"The Lord will protect us from them."

"What's He gonna do, cork their rifles?" Owen asked.

The Old Man looked at Owen and shook his head. "Son, it hurts my heart that you has not taken God into your bosom in the ways I've taught you, but as you know, I let you go your own way in your beliefs—which is why you remains so thick after all these years. The Bible says he who thinketh not in the ways of the Redeemer knoweth not the safeness of the Lord. But I have thunk with Him and know His ways. We have thunk this matter through together for nearly thirty years, the Lord and I. I know every part and portion of this land of which I speak. The Blue Mountains runs diagonally through Virginia, Maryland, all the way up into Pennsylvania and down into Alabama. I know them mountains better than any man on earth. As a child, I ran through them. As a young man, I surveyed them for Oberlin College. And during that time, I considered this slavery question. I even made a journey to the European continent when I runned a tannery on the premise of inspecting the European sheep farms, but my real aim was to inspect the earthwork fortifications made by the chattel who fought against the rulers in that great continent."

"That is impressive, Captain," Kagi said, "and I don't doubt your word or study. But our aim has always been to steal slaves and trouble the waters so the country will see the folly of the infernal institution."

"Pebbles in the ocean, Lieutenant. We ain't stealing Negroes no more. We hiving 'em to fight."

"If we're gonna attack the federal government, why not take

Fort Laramie in Kansas?" Kagi said. "We can control the fight
in Kansas. We got friends there."

The Old Man raised his hand. "Our presence here on the
prarie is a feint, Lieutenant. It's meant to throw our enemy off
our trail. The fight is not out west. Kansas is the tail end of the
beast. If you were to kill a lion, would you chop off his tail?
Virginia is the queen of the slave states. We will strike at the
queen bee in order to kill the hive."

Well, they had caught their breath now and warm words
was passed. Doubts sprung up. One by one, the men chirped
out their disagreement. Even Kagi, the calmest feller among
'em and the Captain's most solid man, disagreed. "It's an impossible task," he said.

"Lieutenant Kagi, you disappoint me," the Old Man said. "I
has thought this matter through carefully. For years, I have
studied the successful opposition of the Spanish chieftains
when Spain was a Roman province. With ten thousand men,
divided into small companies, acting simultaneously yet sepa-
rately, they withstood the whole consolidated power of the
Roman Empire for years! I have studied the successful warfare of the Circassian chief Schamyl against the Russians. I
have lingered over the accounts of the wars of Toussaint-
Louverture on the Haitian islands in the 1790s. You think I
have not considered all these things? Land! Land, men! Land
is fortification! In the mountains, a small group of men, trained
as soldiers, in a series of delays, ambushes, escapes, and surprises, can hold off an enemy for years. They can hold off thousands. It is has been done. Many times."

Well, that didn't flatten them fellers out. The warm words
become hard words and rose to chirping and near shouts. No
matter what he said, they weren't listening. Several announced

they was leaving, and one, Richardson, a colored who just joined a few weeks previous—bellowing and trumpeting 'bout how he was itching to fight slavery—suddenly remembered he had cows to milk at a nearby farm where he was working. He hopped a horse, spurred that thing to a high trot, and was gone.

The Old Man watched him go.

"Anyone who wants to can leave with him," he said.

There was no takers, but still, they jawed at him some more for the better part of three hours. The Old Man listened to them all, standing at the doorway of his cabin with his hands in his pockets, the dirty canvas cover of the doorway flapping behind him in the breeze, giving his words extra punch as it slapped and knocked against the door while he spoke against their fears. He had practiced this in his mind for many years, he said, and for each worry they come up with, he had a response.

"It's an armory. It's guarded!"

"By two night watchmen only."

"How we gonna sneak out a hundred thousand guns? In a boxcar? We need ten boxcars!"

"We don't need all of 'em. Just five thousand will do."

"How we gonna get out the area?"

"We won't. We slip into the nearby mountains. The slaves will hive with us once they know where we are. They will join and fight with us."

"We don't know the routes! Are there rivers about? Roads? Trails?"

"I know the land," the Old Man said. "I have drawn it for you. Come inside and see."

They reluctantly followed him and crowded into his cabin, where he unfurled a huge, canvas map on the table, the giant map I'd seen him secreting in his jacket and scrawling at and chewing the edges on from the first day I'd met him. Atop the map, labeled Harpers Ferry, were dozens of lines which showed the armory, nearby plantations, roads, trails, mountain ranges, and even the number of slaved Negroes living on nearby plantations. He'd done a lot of work, and the men were impressed.

He held the candle over the map so the men could see it, and after they looked at it for a few moments, he pointed to it and began to speak.

"This," he said, pointing with his pencil, "is the Ferry. It is guarded by a single night watchman on either end of it. With the element of surprise, we will take them easily. Once we take them, we cut the telegraph wires here, and take the guardhouse easily, right here. The railroad tracks and the gunnery factory we hold till we load our weapons. It's that easy. We can take the whole place in the middle of the night and be done in three hours and be gone. We gather our weapons and slip into the line of mountains"—here he pointed to his map—"that surround it. These mountains pass through Maryland, Virginia, down into Tennessee and Alabama. They're thin passes. Too narrow for cannons, too tight for wide columns of troops to pass."

He put the candle down.

"I surveyed these places several times. I know them like the back of my hand. I have studied them for years, before any of you were born. Once we establish ourselves in those passes, we can easily defend against any hostile action. From there, the slaves will flock to our stead, and we can attack plantations in the plains on both sides from our mountain posts."

"Why would they join us?" Kagi asked.

The Old Man looked at him as if he'd just pulled out his teeth.

"For the same reason that this little girl"—here he pointed to me—"has risked life and limb to join us and lived out on the plains and braved battle like a man. Can't you see, Lieutenant? If a little girl will do it, a man certainly will. They will join us 'cause we will offer them something their masters cannot: their freedom. They are thirsting for the opportunity to fight for it. They are dying to be free. To free their wives. To free their children. And the courage of one will move the next. We'll arm the first five thousand, then move farther south, arming more Negroes as they join with the plunder and arms of the Pro Slavers we defeat as we go. As we move south, the planters will not be able to withstand their Negroes leaving. They will stand to lose everything. They will not be able to sleep at night worrying about their Negroes joining the masses that approach them from the north. They will quit this infernal institution forever."

He placed his pencil down.

"That, in essence," he said, "is the plan."

You had to reckon, for an insane man, he sure knowed how to cook it up, and for the first time, the looks of doubt started to fall off the men's faces, and that put me back to feeling chickenhearted, for I knowed the Old Man's schemes never worked out to the dot the way he drawed them up, but he was sure to do whatever they was, anyway.

Kagi rubbed his jaw. "There are a thousand places where it can fail," he said.

"We have already failed, Lieutenant. Slavery is an unjustifiable, barbarous, unprovoked sin before God—"

"Spare us the sermon, Pa," Owen snapped. "We ain't got to

bite off the head of the whole thing." He was nervous, and that was unsettling, for Owen was coolheaded and usually went along with his Pa's ideas, no matter how corn-headed they was.

"Do you prefer that we await the outcome of moral persuasion to end slavery, son?"

"I prefers a plan that keeps me from becoming an urn in somebody's backyard."

There was a fire going in the cabin, and the Old Man moved to pick up a log and place it on the dying fire. He stared at the campfire as he spoke. "You is here out of your own choice," he said. "Every one of you, including Onion," he said, pointing to me, "a plain and simple colored girl, which should tell you something about courage, big men that you are. But if any man here feels the plan will not work, you are welcome to leave. I bear no ill will toward any man who does so, for Lieutenant Kagi is right. It is dangerous work I propose. Once the element of surprise is done, they will come at us hard. Of that there is no doubt."

He looked 'bout. There was silence. The Old Man spoke softly now, comforting. "Don't worry. I thought it clean through. We will make our business known to the struggling Negroes in the surrounding areas beforehand, and they will hive to us. Once that is done, we can attack the armory with even greater numbers. We will seize it in minutes, hold it long enough to load our weapons, then slip out into the mountains and be gone by the time the militia get wind of it. I has it on good word that the slaves from the surrounding counties and plantations will hive to us like bees."

"On whose word?"

"On good word," he said. "There are twelve hundred coloreds living at the Ferry. There's thirty thousand coloreds within fifty miles of the Ferry, if you include Washington, D.C., Baltimore, and Virginia. They will hear of our revolt, flock to us, and demand that we arm them. The Negro is primed and ready. He need only the chance. This is what we are giving him."

"Negroes are not trained soldiers," Owen said. "They can't handle weapons."

"No man needs training to fight for his freedom, son. I have prepared for that eventuality. I have ordered two thousand pikes, simple broadswords that can be wielded by any man or woman for the purpose of destroying an enemy combatant. They are stored in various warehouses and safe houses that we will pick up along route. Others we will have sent to us in Maryland. That is why I let John and Jason quit. To prepare those weapons for us before they went home."

"It sounds easy as grazing oats the way you sell it," Cook said, "though I am not sure I am for it."

"If God wills it that you should stay back while the rest of us ride into history, I am not against it."

Cook growled, "I didn't say I was staying back."

"I gived you an out, Mr. Cook. With full redemption for your service and no hard feelings. But should you stay, I will guard your life with as much jealousy as if it were my own. And I will do that for every man here."

That calmed them down some, for he was still Old John Brown, and he was still fearsome. One by one, the Old Man checked their doubts. He had studied the question. He insisted the Ferry weren't closely guarded. It weren't a fort, but rather a factory. Weren't but two night watchmen to take out to get into it. Should the plan fail, the place was built where two rivers, the Potomac and Shenandoah, met. Both were getaways for a quick escape. The town was remote, in the mountains, with less than 2,500 people—workers, not soldiers—living there. We'd cut the telegraph wires, and without a telegraph, it would be impossible for word of our attack to pass. The two rail lines that ran through it had a train scheduled to stop there during our attack. We'd stop that train, hold it, and if necessary use it as an extra escape route if trapped. The Negroes would help us. They were there in numbers. He had suitcases full of government numbers on Negroes. They lived in the town. They lived 'bout on plantations. They had already gotten word. Thousands would flock to our stead. In three hours it would be done. In twenty-four hours we would be gone in the mountains and safe. In and out. Easy as pie.

He was as good a salesman as you could find when he wanted to be, and by the time he was done, he rosied it up so nicely you'd'a thunk the Harpers Ferry armory was just a bunch of pesters waiting to be squashed by his big, toeless old boot; the whole thing sounded easy as picking apples out an orchard. Truth is, though, it was a bold plan, outrageously stupid, and for his men, young, adventurous roughnecks who liked a cause, just the kind of adventure they signed up for. The more he sold it, the more they warmed to it. He just beat 'em down with it, till finally he yawned and said, "I am going to sleep. We are leaving in two days. If you are still here then, we ride together. If not, I understand."

A few, including Kagi, seemed to cotton to the idea. A few others did not. Kagi murmured, "We will think on it, Captain."

The Old Man looked at them, all young men, gathered around him in the firelight, big, rough, smart fellers standing around looking at him like he was Moses of old, his beard flowing down to his chest, his gray eyes sure and steady. "Sleep on it. If you wakes up tomorrow with doubts, ride out with my blessing. I only ask that those who depart to watch your tongue. To forget what you have heard here. Forget us. And remember that if you have a busy tongue, we will not forget you."

He glared around at the men. The old fire had returned now, the face hard as granite, the fists removed from his pocket, the thin, drooped body covered by the ratty soot and toeless boots standing erect. "I has more studying to do, and we will commence our battle plans tomorrow. Good night," he said.

The men wandered outside. I watched them filter off and slip away, till only one man stood. O. P. Anderson, the only colored among them, was the last to leave. O.P. was a small, slender, delicate feller, a printer, a sharp feller, but he wasn't overbuilt like the rest of the Old Man's crew. Most of the Captain's men were strong and rugged adventurers, or gruff pioneers like Stevens, who carried six-shooters on both sides and picked fights with anyone who came near him. O.P. weren't like Stevens or the rest of them at all. He was just a drylongso colored feller with good intentions. He weren't a real soldier or gunfighter, but he was there, and from the fret on his face, he looked to be scared something scandalous.

When he stepped out the cabin, he slowly lowered the canvas flap and wandered off to a nearby tree and sat. I sauntered over and sat next to him. From where we was, we could see inside the tiny window of the cabin. Inside, the Old Man could be seen standing at his table, still poring over his maps and papers, slowly folding them up, scratching a marking on a couple here and there as he put them away.

"What you think, Mr. Anderson?" I said. I was hopeful that O.P. thunk what I thunk, which is that the Old Man was crazy as a bedbug and we should skip off right away.

"I don't understand it," he said glumly.

"Understand what?"

"Understand why I'm here," he muttered. He seemed to be speaking to himself.

"You gonna leave, then?" I asked. I was hopeful.

From where he sat at the foot of the tree, O.P. looked up and stared at the Old Man, busy inside his cabin, still fiddling with his maps, muttering to himself.

"Why should I?" he said. "I'm as mad as him."

22

The Spy

Like most things with the Old Man, what was supposed to take a day took a week. And what was supposed to take two days took two weeks. And what was supposed to take two weeks took four weeks, a month, and two months. And so it went. He was supposed to leave Iowa in June. He didn't put his hat on his head and tip goodbye to that place till mid-September. By then I was long gone. He had sent me forward into the fight.

It wasn't the fight I wanted, but it was better than getting kilt or staying out on the plains. He decided to send one of his men, Mr. Cook, ahead to Harpers Ferry to serve as a spy and to spread the word of his plan amongst the Negroes there. He announced it to his lieutenant Kagi one morning in July, when I was there serving them two breakfast in the Old Man's cabin.

Kagi didn't like the plan. "Cook is a chatterbox," he said. "He's a rooster. Plus he's a ladies' man. He's sending letters to his various lady friends saying he's on a secret mission and he'll have to leave soon, and they'll never see him again. He's brandishing his gun in public and saying he killed five men in Kansas. He got ladies in Tabor fretting all over him, thinking he's gonna die on a secret mission. He'll crow our plan all over Virginia."

The Old Man considered it. "He's an irritant and he does have a long tongue," he said, "but he's a good talker and can scout the enemy and move about daily life there. Whatever he says about us ain't gonna harm God's plan for us, for no one is inclined to believe a blowhard like him anyway. I will advise him that he should use but his eyes and mouth in Virginia to our purpose and nothing more. He'd be a hindrance to us otherwise, for we have a bit more plundering to do to gather weapons and money and he don't soldier well. We have to use everyone to their best. Cook's best weapon against an enemy is his mouth."

"If you want to hive the Negroes, why not send a Negro to Virginia with him?" Kagi said.

"I has considered sending Mr. Anderson," the Old Man said, "but he's nervous about the proposition overall, and may not toe the line. He may scatter."

"I don't mean him. I mean the Onion," Kagi said. "She can pose as Cook's slave. That way she can keep an eye on Cook, and help hive the bees. She's old enough. And you can trust her."

I was standing there when them two was pondering this, and I can't say I was against the idea. I was anxious to get out of the west before the Old Man got his head blowed off. Iowa was rough living, and the U.S. Cavalry was hot on our trail. We'd had to move several times 'bout Pee Dee and Tabor to keep out of sight, and the thought of grinding over the prairie by wagon and stopping every ten minutes while the Old Man prayed, with federal dragoons riding down on us one way and

Pro Slavers hunting us another, weren't a notion that throwed a lot of sugar in my bowl. Also, I growed fond of the Captain, truth be told. I was partial to him. I'd rather he got killed or smashed up on his own time away from me and I would know he was dead later—much later would be soon enough. I knowed he was insane, and if he wanted to fight against slavery I was all for it. But I myself had no plans on doing a wink of the same. Traveling east to Virginia with Cook put me closer to the freedom line of Philadelphia, and slipping off from him would be easy, 'cause Cook never let his talking hole rest and didn't look beyond his own self much. So I piped up to the Old Man and Mr. Kagi that it would be a great idea for me to go with Mr. Cook, and I would do my best to hive the Negroes while I was there waiting for the rest to come.

The Old Man looked me over close. The thing 'bout the Captain was that he never gived you straight-out instruction, unless you was in a shooting fight, of course. But in day-to-day living, he mostly declared, "I'm going this way to fight slavery," and the men said, "Why, I'm going that way, too," and off we went. That's how it was with him. This whole business in the newspapers later 'bout him leading them young fellers around by their noses, that's hogwash. You couldn't get them ornery roughnecks to do what you wanted, for while they was roughnecks, they was sweet on a cause, and broad-minded to whoever led them to it. You couldn't get a two-hundred-dollar mule to tear them fellers away from the Old Man. They wanted to be with him 'cause they was adventurers and the Old Man never told them how to be. He was strict as the devil on the matter of religion when it come to his own self, but if your spiritual purpose took you a different way, why, he'd lecture you a bit, then let you move to your own purpose. So long as you didn't cuss, drink, or chew tobacco, and was against slavery, he was all for you. There was some straight-out rascals in his army, when I think of it. Stevens, course, was a bad-tempered and disagreeable rascal if I ever seen one, chanting to spirits and arguing about his religious beliefs with Kagi and the rest. Charlie Tidd, a white feller, and Dangerfield Newby, a colored—both of them joined up later—them two was outright dangerous and I don't know that they had a drop of religion between the two of 'em. Even Owen weren't all-the-way God-fearing to his Pa's standard. But so long as you was against slavery, why, you could do just whatever you pleased, for despite his grumpiness, the Old Man always thought the best of folks and misjudged their natures. Looking back, it was a terrible notion to send Cook to spy, and a worse notion to send me as an ambassador to rally the colored, for both of us was wanting for knowledge and wisdom, and neither of us would give a sting for nothing but ourselves. We were the two worst people he could have sent ahead.

And course he went with it.

"Splendid idea, Lieutenant Kagi," he said, "for my Onion here can be trusted. If Cook spills the beans, we will know it."

With that, the Old Man went out and stole a fine Conestoga wagon from a Pro Slaver, and had the men load it with picks, shovels, and mining tools which they spread 'bout in the back, and throwed several wooden crates in there marked Mining Tools.

"Careful with what is in these crates," the Old Man said to Cook as we loaded up, nodding at the crates marked Mining Tools. "Do not hurry along the trail. Too much bumping and grinding along and you'll meet the Great Shepherd in pieces. And watch your tongue. Any man who cannot keep from his friends that which he cannot keep to himself is a fool." To me he said, "Onion, I will miss you, for you is dutiful and our Good Lord Bird besides. But it is better that you be out of our trek east, for the enemy is close and there is dirty work ahead of us, what with the gathering of means and plunder. You will no doubt be of great assistance to Mr. Cook, who will benefit from having you at his side." And with that, me and Cook was off on that Conestoga wagon headed for Virginia, and I was one step closer to being free.

Harpers Ferry is as pretty a town as you'd want to see. It's set above two rivers that meet. The Potomac runs along the Maryland side. The Shenandoah runs along the Virginia side. The two rivers bang up against each other just outside town, and there's a peak, an overhang just at the edge of town, where you can stand right there and watch them run cockeyed and smack up against each other. One river hits the other and runs backward. It was a perfect place for Old John Brown to favor, for he was as upside down as them two rivers. On both sides of town is the beautiful blue Appalachian Mountain ranges. At the edge of those ranges was two railroad lines, one running along the Potomac side, heading toward Washington and Baltimore, and the other on the Shenandoah side, running toward west of Virginia.

Me and Cook got there in no time, sailing along in clear weather with that Conestoga wagon. Cook was a chatterbox. He was a treacherous, handsome scoundrel, with blue eyes and pretty blond curls that traveled down his face. He kept his hair 'round his face like a girl, and would converse with anyone who came along as easily as molasses can spread on a biscuit. It ain't no wonder the Old Man sent him, for he had a way 'bout him that made picking information out of folks easy work, and also his favorite subject was hisself. We got along well.

Once we got to the Ferry we moved with the aim of finding a house near the edge of town for the Old Man's army where he could also receive all the arms and so forth that the Old Man had arranged to ship down. The Old Man had been clear in his instructions, saying, "Rent something that don't attract a lot of attention."

But attention was Cook's middle name. He asked 'bout in town and when he didn't hear what he wanted, went into the town's biggest tavern, declaring he was a rich miner for a big mining outfit and I was his slave and he needed a house to rent for some miners that was on their way. "Money is no object," he said, for the Old Man had outfitted him with a pocket full of fatback. Before he left the place, every man in the tavern knowed his name. But a slave owner did come up to us and told Cook he knowed of a settlement nearby that might be up for rent. "It's the old Kennedy farm," he said. "It's a bit out of the way from the Ferry, but it might suit your purpose, for it is large." We rode out to it and Cook looked it over.

It was far from the Ferry, 'bout six miles, and it weren't cheap—thirty-five dollars a month—which Cook was sure the Old Man would squawk 'bout. The farmer had passed away and the widow weren't budging on the price. The house had two rooms downstairs, a tiny upstairs, a basement, and an out-door shack to store arms, and across the road, an old barn. It was set back 'bout three hundred yards from the road, which was good, but it was awful close to a neighbor's house on both sides. If the Old Man had been there he wouldn't have took it, 'cause anyone peeking from the neighbors' houses could look in on it and see in. The Old Man had been clear that he needed a house that was set back by itself, not around no other houses, for he'd have a lot of men hiding there and a lot of traffic going in and out, what with shipping arms and gathering men and all. But Cook had a hankering for a fat white maiden he seen hanging laundry down the road when we first rode out to scout the place, and when he seen her, he cashed in his chips on it. "This is it," he said. He paid the widow owner of the place, told her his boss of the mining company, Mr. Isaac Smith, was coming in a few weeks, and we was in.

We spent a couple of days setting up, and then Cook said, "I am going to town to joust about and get information on the layouts of the armory and the arms factory. You go roust the coloreds."

"Where are they?" I asked.

"Wherever colored are, I expect," he said, and was gone.

I didn't see him for three days. I sat there the first two days scratching my ass, figuring 'bout my own plans to run off, but I didn't know nobody and didn't know if it was safe to walk 'bout. I had to know the lay of the land before I cut, so, not knowing what to do, I sat tight. On the third day there, Cook came busting in the door, laughing and giggling with that same fat, young little blond lady we seen down the road hanging laundry, both of 'em cooing and dewy-eyed. He spied me setting there in the kitchen, and said, "Why didn't you go roust the colored like you was supposed to?"

He said this right in front of his lady friend, giving the plan away right off. I didn't know what to say, so I blurted out, "I don't know where they are."

He turned to the lady with him. "Mary, my slave here"—oh, that boiled me some, him playing it that way. Playing it to the hilt, he was, playing big, after he done gived the whole plan away—"my colored here's looking for some coloreds to congregates with. Where is the coloreds?"

"Why, they is *everywhere*, my peach," she said.

"Ain't they living someplace?"

"Sure," she giggled. "They lives everywhere out and 'bout."

"Well, as I told you, we is on a secret mission, my sweet. A very important mission. For which you can't tell a soul, as I told you," he said.

"Oh, I knows that," she said, giggling.

"And that is why we needs to know exactly where the Onion here can go find some colored friends."

She considered it. "Well, there's always some high-siddity free niggers wandering 'bout town. But they ain't worth peanuts. And then there's Colonel Lewis Washington's nigger plantation. He's the nephew of George Washington himself. And Alstad's and the Byrne brothers. They all got colored slaves, nice and proper. There's no shortage of niggers 'round here."

Cook looked at me. "Well? What you waiting for?"

That needled me, him playing big shot. But I cut out the door. I decided to try the plantations first, for I figgered an ornery and snobbish colored wouldn't be no use to the Captain. Little was I to learn they could be trusted as much as any slave and was good fighters to boot. But I'd only trusted two coloreds up to that point in my life, not counting my late Pa—Bob and Pie—and neither of them worked out to the dot. I'd got instructions from Cook's lady friend on where the Washington plantation was, and went out there first, being that it was on the Maryland side of the Potomac, not too far from where we was staying.

The house was on a wide road where the mountain flattened out. It set behind a wide wrought-iron gate, down a long curved driveway. At the front of that gate, just outside it, a slim colored woman was out gardening and raking leaves. I approached her.

"Morning," I said.

She stopped her raking and stared at me a long time. Finally she blurted out, "Morning."

It occurred to me then that she knowed I was a boy. Some colored women just had my number. But this was during bondage time. And when you in bondage, you is drowning, in a manner of speaking. You no more pay attention to the getup of the feller next to you than you do the size of his shoes if he got any, for both of you is drowning in the same river. Unless that feller is tossing you a rope to pull you ashore, his shoes ain't much of a bother. I reckon that's why few colored women I come across didn't scratch at me too much. They had their own problems. Anyway, there weren't nothing to be done 'bout it then nohow. I had an assignment. And until I figured out the lay of the land, I couldn't run off no place. I was spying for the Old Man and I was looking out for my own self, too.

"I don't know where I am," I said.

"You are where you is," she said.

"I'm just looking to get the lay of the land."

"It lay before you," she said.

We wasn't getting nowhere, so I said, "I'm wondering if you knowed anybody who wants to know their letters."

A nervous look shot across her face. She glanced over her shoulder at the big house, and kept that rake working.

"Why would somebody want to learn how to do that? Niggers got no cause to read."

"Some do," I said.

"I don't know nothing 'bout that," she said, still working that rake.

"Well, miss, I'm looking for a job."

"Learning how to read? That ain't no job. That's trouble."

"I knows how to read. I'm looking to teach someone *else* how to read. For money."

She didn't say another blooming word. She lifted that rake off the ground and showed me the back of her head. She plain walked off.

I didn't wait. I got outta sight. Jumped into the thickets right then and there, set tight, thinking she'd gone into the house to squeal to the overseer boss or, even worse, her master. I waited a few minutes, and just as I was 'bout to light out, a coach wagon driven by four huge horses dashed from the back of the house and drove hard toward the gate. That thing was movin'. Up front was a Negro driver, dressed in a fine coach jacket, a top hat, and white gloves. The wagon busted through the front gate and the Negro halted it on a dime just outside the gate where I was.

He hopped down and looked around into the thickets. Looked right at 'bout where I was. I knowed he couldn't see me, for the foliage was thick and I crouched low. "Anybody there?" he asked.

"Ain't nobody here but us chickens," I said.

"C'mon out here," he snapped. "I seen you from the window."

I done like he said. He was a thick-sprouted, broad-chested man. Close up, he looked even more splendid in tails and coachman's costume than he did from afar. His shoulders was broad, and though he was short, his face was bright and sharp, and his gloves shone in the afternoon sun. He stared at me, frowning. "The Blacksmith send you?"

"Who?"

"The Blacksmith."

"Don't know no Blacksmith."

"What's the word?"

"I can't think of none."

"What song you singing, then? 'We Can Break Bread Together'? That's the song, ain't it?"

"Got no song. I only know them Dixie songs like 'Old Coon Callaway Come On Home.'"

He looked at me, puzzled. "What is wrong with you?"

"Nothing."

"You on the gospel train?"

"The what?"

"The railroad."

"What railroad?"

He glanced behind him at the house. "You run off? You a runaway?"

"No. Not yet. Not exactly."

"Them's three answers, child," he snapped. "Which of 'em is it?"

"Pick any one you want, sir."

"I ain't got time for fooling. State your business quick. You in thick lard already, out here prowling the Colonel Washington's road without permission. You bet' not be here when he comes back. I got to fetch him in town in thirty minutes."

"Would that town be Harpers Ferry?"

He pointed down the mountain at the town. "Do that look like Philadelphia down there, child? Course that's Harpers Ferry. Every day of the week. Where else would it be?"

"Well, I come to warn you," I said. "Something's 'bout to kick off there."

"Something's always 'bout to kick off someplace."

"I mean with the white folks."

"White folks always got the kick, to everything and everybody. They got the mojo and say-so, too. What else is new? By the way, is you a sissy? You look mighty queer, child."

I ignored that, for I had work to do. "If I was to tell you that something big's coming," I said, "something very big, would you be akin to rousing the hive?"

"Rousing the what?"

"Helping me. Rouse the hive. Gather the colored people up."

"Girl, you weeding a bad hoe for satisfaction, talking that way. If you was my child, I'd warm your two little cakes with my switch and send you hooting and hollering down that road, just for popping off to my wife 'bout reading. You'll get every nigger 'round here throwed in hot water talking that way. She ain't with the cause, y'know."

"The what?"

"The cause, the gospel train, she ain't with it. Don't know nothing 'bout it. Don't wanna know. Can't know. Can't be trusted to know, you get my drift?"

"I don't know what you're talking 'bout."

"G'wan down the road, then, with your foolish self."

He climbed up on his wagon and readied up to har up his horses.

"I got news. Important news!"

"Big head, big wit. Little head, not a bit. That's you, child. You got a condition." He lifted his traces to har up his horses. "Good day."

"Old John Brown's coming," I blurted out.

That got him. Stopped him dead. There weren't a colored person east of the Mississippi who hadn't heard of John Brown. Why, he was just a saint. Magic to the colored.

He stared down at me, holding his reins still in his hands. "I ought to whip you something scandalous just for standing there and lying like you is. Spouting dangerous lies, too."

"I swear 'fore God, he's coming."

The Coachman glanced at the house. He swung the wagon 'round and faced it so that the far side of the coach door was blocked from the view of the house. "Git in there and lay down low on the floor. If you pop your head up before I tell you to, I'mma ride you straight to the deputy and say you was a stowaway and let him have you."

I done as he said. He harred up them horses, and we rode.

Ten minutes later the wagon halted, and the Coachman climbed down. "Git out," he said. He said it before the door was halfway open. He was done with me. I climbed out. We was on a mountain road in thick woods, high above Harpers Ferry, on a deserted stretch of trail.

He climbed up on the wagon and pointed behind him. "This here is the road to Chambersburg," he said. "It's 'bout twenty miles yonder. Go up there and see Henry Watson. He's a barber. Tell 'em the Coachman sent you. He'll tell you what to do next. Stay off the road and in the thickets."

"But I ain't a runaway."

"I don't know who you is, child, but git gone," the Coachman said. "You sporting trouble, popping up out of nowhere and running your talking hole full steam 'bout Old John Brown and knowing your letters and all. Old Brown's dead. One of the greatest helpers to the Negro in the world, deader than yesterday's love. You ain't worthy to speak his name, child."

"He ain't dead!"

"Dead in Kansas Territory," the Coachman said. He seemed certain. "We got a man here who reads. I was in the church the day he read that newspaper to us. I heard it myself. Old Brown was out west and had militia chasing him and the U.S. Cavalry hot on his tail and everybody and his brother, for there was a reward on him. They say he outshot 'em all, he did, but they caught him after a while and drowned him. God bless him. My master hates him. Now git."

"I can prove he ain't dead."

"How so?"

"'Cause I seen him. I knows him. I'll take you to him when he comes."

The Coachman smirked, grabbing his reins. "Why, if I was your Pa, I'd put my boot so far up your arse you'd cough out my big toe, standing there lyin'! What the devil is wrong with you, to stand there and lie like that in God's hearing? What's the great John Brown want with a little nigger sissy like you? Now put your foot in the road 'fore I warm your two little brown buns! And don't tell nobody you know me. I'm 'bout filled up with that damn gospel train today! And tell the Blacksmith if you see him, don't send me no more packages."

"Packages?"

"Packages," he said. "Yes! No more packages."

"What kind of packages?"

"Is you thick, child? Git along."

"I don't know what you're talking 'bout."

He glared down at me. "Is you on the underground or not?" he said.

"What underground?"

I was confused, and he stared down at me, hot. "Git on up the road to Chambersburg 'fore I kick you up there!"

"I can't go there. I'm staying at the Kennedy farm."

"See!" the Coachman snorted. "Caught you in another lie. Old man Kennedy drawed his last breath last year 'bout this time."

"One of Brown's men rented the house from his widow. I come to this country with him."

That cooled him some. "You mean that new chatty white feller running 'round town? The one sporting 'round with fat Miss Mary, the blond maid who lives up the road from there?"

"Him."

"He's with Old John Brown?"

"Yes sir."

"Why's he running 'round with her then? That silly nag's been boarded more than the B&O railroad."

"I don't know."

The Coachman frowned. "My brother told me to quit fooling with runaways," he grumbled. "You can't tell the straight truth from a crooked lie with 'em." He sighed. "I reckon if I was sleeping in the cold under the sky I'd be talking cockeyed, too." He groused some more, then fished in his pocket and pulled out a bunch of coins. "How much you need? All's I got is eight cents." He held it out. "Take this and git. G'wan now. Off with you. G'wan to Chambersburg."

I growed a little warm then. "Sir, I ain't here for your money," I said. "And I ain't here to go to nobody's Chambersburg. I come to warn you Old John Brown's coming. With an army. He's planning to take Harpers Ferry and start an insurrection. He told me to 'hive the bees.' That's his instruction. Said, 'Onion, you tell all the colored that I'm coming and to hive 'em up. Hive the bees.' So I'm tellin' you. And I ain't tellin' nobody no more, for it ain't worth the trouble."

With that, I turned and started down the mountain road toward Harpers Ferry, for he had rode me a ways out.

He called out to me, "Chambersburg's the other direction."

"I knows where I'm going," I said.

His coach was pointed toward Chambersburg, too, up the mountain, away from me. He harred up his horses and galloped up the mountain trail. It took him several minutes to get up the road and find a place to turn around, for he had those four horses drawing it. He got it done in a snap, and brought them horses banging down the mountain behind me at a full trot. When he reached me, he pulled them beasts to a dead stop. Stopped 'em on a dime. He could drive the shit outta that coach. He stared down at me.

"I don't know you," he said. "I don't know who you are or where you come from. But I know you ain't from this country, so your word ain't worth a pinch of snuff. But lemme ask you: If I was to ask at old Kennedy's farm 'bout you, would they know you?"

"Ain't but one feller there now. That feller I told you 'bout. His name is Mr. Cook. The Old Man sent him to spy on the town ahead of his coming, but he ought not to have sent him, for he talks too much. He's likely done spread the word to every white man in town 'bout the Captain."

"Good God, you surely fib like a winner," the Coachman said. He sat for a long moment. Then he looked around to see if the way was clear and nobody was coming. "I'mma test you," he said. He reached in his pocket and pulled out a crumpled-up piece of paper. "You say you know your letters?"

"I do."

"Well read that," he said. Sitting up in the driver's seat, he handed it down to me.

I took the paper and read it aloud. "It says, '*Dear Rufus, please give my coachman Jim four ladles and two spoons from your store and make sure he don't eat any more store-bought biscuits from you, which is charged to my account. That nigger is fat enough as it is.*'"

I handed it back to him. "It's signed, 'Col. Lewis F. Washington,'" I said. "That's your master?"

"God damn that elephant-faced old bugger," he muttered. "Never drew a short breath in his life. Never done a day's work. And feeding me boiled grits and sour biscuits. What's he expect?"

"Say what?"

He shoved the paper in his pocket. "If you *was* speaking the truth, it'd be hard to tell it," he said. "Why would the great John Brown send a sissy to do a man's job?"

"You can ask him yourself when he comes," I said, "for you is full of insults and nothing more." I started down the mountain, for there was no convincing him.

"Wait a minute."

"Nope. You been told, sir. You been warned. G'wan 'round to the Kennedy farm and see if you don't find Mr. Cook setting there talking in ways he shouldn't."

"What 'bout Miss Mary? She working with Old John Brown, too?"

"No. He just made her acquaintance."

"Sheesh, he couldn't do no better than that? That woman's face could stop a clock. What manner of man is your Mr. Cook that he runs behind her?"

"The rest of his army don't act in the manner of Mr. Cook," I said. "They coming to shoot men, not chase women. They is dangerous. They coming all the way from Iowa and they got more hardware than you ever saw, and when they load their breachloaders they drop the hammer and tell it to hurry. That's a fact, sir."

That got him, and for the first time I seen the doubt move off his face a little. "Your story is fetching, but it sounds like a lie," he said. "Still, ain't no harm in me sending somebody by old man Kennedy's farm, if that's where you say you living, to check on your fibbing. In the meantime, I reckon you ain't dumb enough to mention me or the Blacksmith or Henry Watson to nobody in town. You liable to end up on the cooling board if you do. Them two is as bad as they get. They'd bust a charge into your head and feed you to the pigs if they thunk you gived away their doings."

"They better makes sure they got all their back teeth if they do it," I said. "For when Captain Brown comes I'mma tell him you and your friends here was a hinderance, and y'all will have to deal with him. He'll curdle your cheese for treatin' me like a liar."

"What you want child, a gold medal? I don't know you from Adam. You come out the blue, spinning a heap of tall yarns for somebody so young. You lucky your lie landed with me, and not with some of these other niggers 'round here, for there's a heap of 'em would hand you over to the slave patrollers for a goosefeather pillow. I'll check your story with Mr. Cook. Either you is lying or you is not. If you lying, you had to work like the devil to dream up that yarn. If you not, you is disobeying God's orders to the limit in some kind of devilish fashion, for ain't no way on God's green earth that Old John Brown, hot as he is, is gonna come here, where all these weapons and soldiers is, to fight for the colored's freedom. He'd be putting his head right in the lion's mouth. He's a brave man if he's living, but he ain't a straight fool."

"You don't know him," I said.

But he didn't hear me. He had harred up his horses and was gone.

23

The Word

Two days later, an old colored woman bearing brooms inside a wheelbarrow pushed up to the door of the Kennedy farm and knocked. Cook was fast asleep. He woke up, grabbing his pistol, and runned to the door. He spoke with the door closed, his pistol down by his side. "Who is it?"

"Name's Becky, massa. I'm selling brooms."

"Don't want none."

"The Coachman says you did."

Cook looked at me, puzzled. "That's the feller I told you 'bout," I said. He stood there blinking a minute, half-sleep. He didn't no more remember what I told him 'bout the Coachman than a dog would remember his birthday. Fat Mary from down the road was wearing him out. He didn't get back to the house the night before till the wee hours. He come in with his disheveled clothes and his hair a mess, smelling like liquor, laughing and whistling.

"All right, then. But come in slow."

The woman walked in slowly and purposeful, pushing the barrel before her. She was old, slender, deep brown, with furried white hair, a wrinkled face, and a tattered dress. She pulled two new brooms out of the barrel and held one in each hand. "I made these myself," she said, "fashioned from the best straw and brand-new pine handles. Made from southern pine, the best kinds."

"We don't need no brooms," Mr. Cook said.

The woman took a long look around. She saw the boxes marked "Mining" and "Tools." The clean mining picks and axes, which hadn't seen a bit of dirt. She looked at me once, then again, blinking, then at Cook. "Surely the little missus here"—she nodded at me—"could use a broom to clean up after the young master."

Cook was sleepy and irritable. "We got brooms enough here."

"But if you mining and getting all dirtied up, you'll be bringing in all kinds of filth and dirt and so forth, and I wouldn't want the master to get too sullied up."

"Can't you hear?"

"I'm sorry, then. The Coachman said you'd need brooms."

"Who is that again?"

"That's the feller I told you 'bout," I piped up again. Cook looked at me and frowned. He weren't like the Old Man. He didn't quite know what to do with me. He was all right when we was on the trail out west and there weren't nobody else around to shoot the yarn with. But once he got around civilization, he didn't know whether he should act white or colored, or be a soldier or a spy, or shit or go blind. He hadn't paid me the least bit of attention since we got to the Ferry, and what attention he did pay to me weren't respectful. I was just a bother to him. It was all fun to him. I don't know but that he didn't think anything would come of the Old Man's plans, or believed him in the least, for Cook had never been in a real war, and never seen the Old Man fight. "Is she one of them you supposed to be hivin'?" he asked.

"One of 'em," I said.

"Well, hive her," he said, "and I will brew us up some coffee." He picked up a bucket and moved outside. There was a water well out back, and he stumbled out there holding that bucket, rubbing his eyes.

Becky looked at me. "We is here on a mission," I said. "I reckon the Coachman told you."

"He told me he met a strange li'l cooter on the road dressed funny, who gived him bad instructions, and was likely stretching his blanket lying."

"I wish you wouldn't call me names, for I has done you no wrong."

"I'll be calling you dead if you continues on as you is. You do much harm to yourself when you paddle 'bout, selling fool's gold. Talking 'bout a great man. And talking it into the ears of the wrong folks. The Coachman's wife don't work on the gospel train. She got a mouth like a waterfall. You putting a lot of people in danger, hooting and railing 'bout John Brown like you is."

"I already had a mouthful 'bout that from the Coachman," I said. "I don't know nothing 'bout nobody's gospel train, not in no way, form, or fashion. I ain't a runaway and ain't from these parts. I been sent forward to hive the bees. Get the colored together. That's what the Old Man sent me for."

"Why would he send you?"

"He ain't got but two coloreds in his army. The other ones he weren't too sure 'bout."

"In what way?"

"Thought they might trot off before they done what the Captain told 'em what to do."

"The Captain. Who's that?"

"I already told you. John Brown."

"And what did the Captain tell you to do?"

"Hive the bees. Ain't you heard me?"

Cook came to the kitchen, holding a pot of water. Then moved to put some kindling on the fire to make some hot water. "You hive her yet?" he said gaily. He was just a fool. He was the gayest man I ever saw. It would cost him. He'd be deadened 'cause of it, acting a fool.

"She don't believe it," I said.

"What part of it?"

"No parts of it."

He stood up and cleared his throat, agitated. "Now listen, Aunt Polly, we come all this way to fr—"

"Becky's my name, if you please."

"Becky. A great man's 'bout to come here and free your people. I just got a letter from him. He'll be here in less than three weeks. He needs to hive the bees. Free you all."

"I done heard all I need to hear about hiving and freeing," Becky said. "How's all this hiving and freeing gonna happen?"

"I can't right tell all of it. But Old John Brown is coming, surely. From out west. Freedom's nigh for you and your people. Onion here ain't lying."

"Onion?"

"That's what we call her."

"Her?"

I piped up quickly, "Miss Becky, if you ain't one to hive or get on board with what John Brown's selling, you ain't got to come."

"I didn't say that," she said. "I wants to know what he's selling. Freedom? Here? He might as well be singing to a dead hog if he thinks he's gonna come here and get away scot-free with that. There's a damn armory here."

"That's why he's coming," Cook said. "To take the armory."

"What's he gonna take it with?"

"Men."

"And what else?"

"And all the Negroes that's gonna join 'em once he takes it over."

"Mister, you talking crazy."

Cook was a braggert, and it clean plucked his feathers to talk to a person that didn't believe him or talked back to him. Especially a colored. "Am I?" he said. "Looky here."

He led her to the other room, where the stacks of the mining boxes marked Mining Tools lay 'bout. He took a crowbar to one and opened it up. Inside, stacked in neat rows, were thirty clean, brand-new Sharps rifles, one after another.

I had never seen the inside of them boxes neither, and the fullness of the thing hit me and Miss Becky at the same time. Her eyes got wide. "Glory," she said.

Cook snorted, bragging. "We got fourteen boxes here, just like this one. There's more coming by shipment. The Captain's got enough arms to furnish two thousand people."

"There ain't but ninety slaves in Harpers Ferry, mister."

That stopped him dead. The smile disappeared from his face.

"I thought there was twelve hundred colored here. That's what the man at the post office said yesterday."

"That's right. And most of 'em's free colored."

"That ain't the same," he muttered.

"It's close enough," Miss Becky said. "Free colored's connected to bondage, too. Many of 'em's married to those in bondage. I'm free, but my husband, he's a slave. Most free colored's got slave relations. They ain't for slavery. Believe me."

"Good! Then they'll fight with us."

"I ain't say that." She sat down, rubbing her head. "Coachman done sent me into a dilemma," she mumbled. Then she uttered hotly, "This is some damn trickeration!"

"You ain't got to believe," Cook said gaily. "Just tell all your friends that Old John Brown is coming in three weeks. We attack on October twenty-third. He gave me the date by letter. Spread that around."

Now, I was just a young boy dressed like a girl and foolish as a dimwit and not able to hold anybody in their wrong, stupid as I was, but still, I was a young man coming into myself, and even I weren't that dim. It occurred to me that it didn't take but one of them colored angling for a can of peaches or a nice fresh watermelon from their master to rouse the whole bit, to spill the beans, and the jig was up for everybody.

"Mr. Cook," I said. "We don't know if we can trust this woman."

"You invited her," he said.

"Suppose she tells!"

Miss Becky frowned. "You is got some nerve," she said. "You busted in on Coachman's property, damn near gave him away to his runny-mouth wife, and now you tellin' *me* who can be trusted. It's you we can't trust. You could be selling us a heap of lies, child. You better hope your yarn matches up. If not, the Blacksmith will deaden you right where you is and be done with it. Ain't nobody in this town gonna fret over a nigger child dead in an alley someplace."

"What I done to him?"

"You endangering his railroad."

"He owns a railroad?"

"The underground, child."

"Hold on," Cook said. "Your Blacksmith ain't deadening nobody. Onion here is like a child to the Old Man. She's his favorite."

"Sure. And I'm George Washington."

Now Cook got hot. "Don't get sassy with me. We coming here to rescue you. Not the other way 'round. Onion here, the Captain stole her out of slavery. She's like his kin. So you ought not to talk about your Blacksmith hurting this one here, or nobody else. Your Blacksmith won't be drawing air long, fooling with the Captain's plans. He don't want to be on the wrong side of Captain Brown."

Becky put her head in her hands. "I reckon I don't know what to believe," she said. "I don't know what to tell the Coachman."

"Is he the Negro in charge around here?" Cook asked.

"One of 'em. The main one's the Rail Man."

"Where's he at?"

"Where you think? On the railroad."

"The underground?"

"No. The real railroad. The B&O. The one that goes chug-chug. I reckon he's in Baltimore or Washington, D.C., today."

"Perfect! He can hive the bees there. How can I reach him?"

She stood up. "I'll take my leave, now. I done told you too much already, sir. For all's I know, you could be a slave stealer from New Orleans, come up here to steal souls and sell 'em off down river. You can have one of them brooms. It's a gift. Use it to sweep the lies out this place. Watch the lady next door, if you don't want deputies around. She's a nosybody. Mrs. Huffmaster's her name. And she don't like niggers nor slave stealers nor abolitionists."

As she moved toward the door, I blurted out, "You ought to check with your people. Check with your Rail Man."

"I ain't checking with nobody. It's a trick."

"G'wan, then. You'll see. We don't need you, neither." She showed me her back, but as she moved to the door, there was a coat hook there, and she noticed the beaten shawl that the General gave me in Canada hanging on it. The shawl from Harriet Tubman herself.

"Where'd you get this?" she asked.

"It's a gift," I said.

"From who?"

"One of the Captain's friends gived it to me. Said it would be useful. I just brung it 'cause . . . I used it to cover some of my things in the wagon."

"Did you now . . ." she said. She gently took the General's shawl off the coat hook. She held it in the light, then laid it on the table, her brown fingers spreading it wide. She stared carefully at the designs on it. I hadn't paid them no mind. It weren't nothing but a crude dog in a box with his feet pointed at all four corners of the box, with his snout nearly touching one of the top corners. Something in that design moved her, and she shook her head.

"I don't believe it. Where'd you meet . . . the person that gived you this?"

"I can't say, for I don't know you, neither."

"Oh, you can tell her," Cook said, runny mouth that he was.

But I didn't open my mouth a bit. Miss Becky stared at the shawl, her eyes suddenly bright and full. "If you ain't lying, child, it's a great day. Did the soul who gived you this say anything else?"

"No. Well . . . She did say don't change the time, 'cause she was coming herself. With her people. She did say that. To the Captain. Not me."

Miss Becky stood silent a minute. You'd a thunk I gived her a million dollars, for it seemed like a spell come over her. The old wrinkles in her face evened out and her lips broke into a small smile. The lines in her forehead seemed to vanish. She picked up the shawl and held it out away from her. "Can I keep this?" she asked.

"If it'll help, all right," I said.

"It helps," she said. "It helps a great deal. Oh, the Lord is in the blessing business, ain't He? He done blessed me today." She got in a hurry then, whipping the shawl onto her shoulders, gathering up her brooms and tossing them in the wheelbarrow, as me and Cook stared.

"Where you going?" Cook said.

Miss Becky paused at the door, grabbed the door handle and held it tight, staring at it as she spoke. The happiness fell off her then, and she was all business again. Serious and straight on. "Wait a few days," she said. "Just wait. And be quiet. Don't say nothing else to nobody, white or colored. If a colored comes here asking 'bout your Captain, be careful. If they don't mention the Blacksmith or the Rail Man in their first breath, draw your knife on 'em and make it count, for we is all blown. You'll get word soon."

And with that she opened the door, grabbed her wheelbarrow, and left.

24

The Rail Man

Not long after, Cook got a job at the Ferry working at the Wager House, a tavern and railroad depot right at the armory where he could annoy the folks. His hours was long. He worked into the night, while I stayed at the farm, tidied house, tried to cook, hide what I could of them crates, and pretended to be his consort. 'Bout a week after he started, Cook come back to the house one evening and said, "Somebody wants to talk with you."

"Who is it?"

"Somebody colored at the railroad."

"Can you bring 'em here?"

"Says he don't want to come here. Too dangerous."

"Whyn't he tell you what he got to tell?"

"Said it clearly. You the one he wants."

"He say anything 'bout the Blacksmith?"

Cook shrugged. "I don't know nothing 'bout that. Just said

he wanted to talk to you." I made ready to go. I was bored to tears cooped up in that house anyway.

"Not now," Cook said. "Tonight in the wee hour. One in the morning, he said. . . . Just set tight and go to bed. I'm going back to the tavern. I'll wake you up when it's time."

He didn't have to wake me up 'cause I set up. All evening, waiting, anxious, till Cook finally come in around midnight. We walked down the mountain from the Kennedy farm to the Ferry together. It was dark and drizzling as we came off the mountain. We crossed the Potomac side of the bridge, and as we done so, we saw the train had arrived, the B&O, a huge railway engine setting just outside the rifle works building at the Ferry. The locomotive set there, steaming, taking on water. The train's passenger cars was empty.

Cook led me around to the back side of the station and down the entire length of the train. When we reached the last car, he split off into the thickets and headed down toward the Potomac, to the water's edge. The Potomac runned underneath the railroad tracks. It was pretty dark down there, nothing to see but the swirling water in the moonlight. He pointed to the riverbank. "Feller wants to talk to you down there. Alone," he said. "These coloreds is distrustful."

He waited up at the top of the bank while I moved down to the bank of the Potomac. I sat there and waited.

A few minutes later, a tall, hulking figure emerged from the far end of the bank. He was a right-powerful-looking man, dressed in the neat uniform of a railroad porter. He didn't come right up on me, but rather stayed in the shadow of the railroad trestle as he come closer. When he seen me, he didn't come closer but stopped a few feet off and turned and leaned on the trestle, staring at the river. Above us, the train gived a sudden clank and burst of steam, its valves and all clacking thusly so, blowing that steam. I jumped as I heard it, and he glanced at me, then looked away back toward the river again.

"Take 'em an hour to get the steam up," he said. "Maybe two. That's all the time I got."

"You the Rail Man?"

"It don't matter what I am. Matters what you is. What are you?"

"I'm a messenger."

"So was Jesus. You ain't seen Him running 'round in a skirt and bloomer panties. Is you a girl or a boy?"

"I don't know why everyone's huffing and puffing 'bout what I am," I said. "I'm just carrying a word."

"Bringing trouble is what you doing. If a body ain't sure, it'll cost you."

"What I done wrong?"

"I understands you is looking to buy some of the Coachman's brooms. We carries them to Baltimore and beyond," he said.

"Says who?" I asked.

"Says the Blacksmith."

"Who is he, anyway?"

"You don't wanna know."

He stared across the water. By the light of the moon, I could see the outline of his face. He looked to be a friendly-faced feller, but his face was strained and tight. He weren't in no happy mood.

"Now I'll ask it again," he said. He glimpsed over his shoulder at Cook, who watched down on us, and then back at the water. "Who are you. Where you from. And what you want."

"Well, I don't reckon I know what to say to you, for I done told it twice already."

"When you roll up on a watery mouth like the Coachman's wife, hooting and hollering 'bout insurrection, you better state yourself clean."

"I weren't hollering 'bout insurrection. I just told her I knowed how to read."

"That's the same thing. You keep quiet 'bout them kinds of things 'round here. Or you'll have the Blacksmith to deal with."

"I ain't come all the way down here for you to throw threats at me. I'm speaking for the Captain. I ain't got nothing to do with it."

"With what?"

"You know what."

"No, I don't. Tell me."

"Why's every colored 'round here talking in circles?"

"'Cause the white man shoots straight—with real bullets, child. 'Specially if a Negro's thick enough to talk insurrection!"

"It weren't my idea."

"I don't care whose idea it is. You in it now. And if your man—if your man is who you says he is—if your man's on the line 'bout rousting out the colored, he come to the wrong town. Ain't but a hundred here at most will roll with him, if that."

"Why's that?"

"Ain't but twelve hundred colored here. A good number of 'em's women and children. The rest would fatten hogs under a tree with their own offspring 'fore they even raised an eyebrow to the white man. Shit. If Old John Brown wanted some coloreds to fight in his favor, he could'a gone sixty miles east to Baltimore, or Washington, or, or even the eastern shore of Maryland. Them coloreds there read the papers. They got boats.

Guns. Some of 'em's watermen. People who can move people. That would'a been sugar in his bowl. Even in southern Virginia, down in cotton country. There's plantations down there loaded fat with colored who'll do anything to get out. But here?" He shook his head, he glanced over his back at the Ferry. "He's in the wrong country. We's outnumbered. Surrounded on all sides by whites in every county."

"There's guns here," I said. "That's why he's coming. He wants the guns from the armory to arm the colored."

"Please. These niggers 'round here wouldn't know a rifle from a load of greens. They can't handle nobody's rifle. They won't let a nigger near them guns."

"He got pikes. And swords. A lot of 'em. Thousands of 'em."

The Rail Man snorted bitterly. "It ain't gonna matter. First shot he fires, these white folks is gonna burn him."

"You ain't seen him when he's battlin'."

"Don't matter. They'll pull his head off his body and when they're done, they'll air out every colored within a hundred miles just to make 'em forget we ever saw Old John in these parts. They hate that man. If he's living. Which I don't think he is."

"Go on, then. I'm tired of fending and proving. When he comes, you'll see. I seen his planning. He got maps full of colors and drawings where the coloreds is gonna come from. He says they'll come from everywhere: New York, Philadelphia, Pittsburgh. He got it all planned out. It's a surprise attack."

The Rail Man waved his hand, disgusted. "It ain't no surprise here," he snorted.

"You knowed he was coming?"

"I never liked the idea from first I heard it. Never thought he'd be stupid enough to try it, either."

That's the first time I ever heard anyone outside the Old Man's circle mention the plan. "Where'd you hear it from?"

"The General. That's why I'm here."

My heart skipped a beat. "Is she coming?"

"I hope not. She'll get her head blowed off."

"How you know so much?"

For the first time, he turned to me. He sucked his teeth. "Your Captain, God bless him, he's gonna go home in threes when they done with him here. And whatever colored is stupid enough to follow him's gonna get shot to pieces, God damn him."

"Why you so mad? He ain't done nothing to you."

"I got a wife and three children in bondage here," he snapped. "These white folks is gonna donate every bullet they got to elephant-hunt the Negro once they kill Old John Brown. They'll be right raw for years. And whatever coloreds they don't stick in a death wedge in the ground they'll send off. They'll sell every soul in bondage 'round here who even looks colored. Right down the river to New Orleans they'll go, God damn him. I ain't saved up enough to buy my children yet. I only got enough for one. I got to decide now. Today. If he comes—"

He shut up. That ate at him. Just tore at him and he looked away. I seen he was troubled, so I said, "You ain't got to worry. I seen plenty more Negroes who promised to come. Up at a big meeting in Canada. They speeched 'bout it all day. They was angry. Lots of 'em. These were big-time fellers. Reading men. Men of letters. They promised to come—"

"Oh, hogwash!" he snorted. "Them uppity, long-breathed niggers ain't got enough sand in the lot of 'em to fill a God-damned thimble!"

He fumed, looking away, then pointed to the train on the trestle above us. "That train there," he said, "that's the B&O line. It rolls outta Washington, D.C., and Baltimore every day. Rolls north a bit and connects up with the train out of Philadelphia and New York City twice a week. I seen every single colored that's ever been on that train for the last nine years. And I can tell you, half of them Negro leaders of your'n can't afford a ticket on that train that would take 'em more'n ten yards. And them that could, they'd blow their wives' head off with a pistol for a single glass of the white man's milk."

He sighed angrily, blowing through his nose now. "Oh, they talk a good game, writing stories for the abolitionist papers and such. But writing stories in the paper and making speeches ain't the same as being out here doing the job. On the line. On the front line. The freedom line. They talk a whole heap, them stuffed-shirt, tidy-looking, tea-drinking, gizzard lickers, running around New England in their fine silk shirts, letting white folks wipe their tears and all. Box Car Brown. Frederick Douglass. Shit! I know a colored feller in Chambersburg worth twenty of them blowhards."

"Henry Watson?"

"Forget names. You ask too many questions and know too God-damned much now."

"You ought not to use God's name in vain. Not when the Captain comes."

"I ain't studying him. I been working the gospel train for years. I know his doings. Been hearing of 'em for as long as I been doing this. I like the Captain. I love him. Many a night I prayed for him. And now he . . ." He groused and cursed some more. "He's deader than yesterday's dinner, is what it is. How many's in his army?"

"Well, last count there was . . . sixteen or so."

The Rail Man laughed. "That ain't hardly enough for dice. The Old Man's lost his buttons. At least I ain't the only one that's crazy." He sat down at the water's edge now, then tossed a rock in the water. It made a tiny splash. The moon shone down on him brightly. He looked terrifically sad. "Gimme the rest," he said.

"Of what?"

"The plan."

I gived it to him from soup to nuts. He listened closely. I told him all 'bout taking the night watchman in the front and back entrance, then fleeing to the mountains. After I was finished, he nodded. He seemed calmer. "Well, the Ferry can be took, that much the Captain's right 'bout. There ain't but two watchmen. But it's the second part I don't get. Where's he expecting his coloreds to come from, Africa?"

"It's in the plan," I said, but I felt like sheep bleating.

He shook his head. "John Brown is a great man. God bless him. He ain't lacking in courage, that's for sure. But God's wisdom has escaped him this time. I can't tell him how to do his business, but he's wrong."

"He says he's studied it for years."

"He ain't the first person who's studied insurrection. Coloreds been studying it for a hundred years. His plan can't work. It ain't practical."

"Could you make it so, then? Being that you's a big wheel in the gospel train around here? You know which coloreds would fight, don't you?"

"I can't make two hundred coloreds get up outta Baltimore and Washington, D.C., and come up here. He needs at least that many to bust out the armory and get to the mountains once he's got what he wants. Where's he gonna get them kind of numbers? He'd need to run souls from Baltimore up through Detroit and down to Alabama."

"Ain't that what you do?"

"Running one or two souls 'cross the freedom line to Philadelphia is one thing. Running two hundred souls from D.C. and Baltimore this way is another. That's impossible. He'd have to spread the word far and wide, all the way down to Alabama to make sure he gets them kind of numbers. The gospel train can carry a word fast, but not that fast. Not in three weeks."

"You saying it can't be done?"

"I'm saying it can't be done in three weeks. Takes a letter a solid week to get from here to Pittsburgh. Sometimes a rumor travels faster'n a letter—"

He thought a minute.

"You say he's throwing big metal at 'em in three weeks?"

"October twenty-third. In three weeks."

"There ain't no time, really. It's a God-damn shame. Criminal, really. Except . . ." He fingered his jaw, thinking. "Y'know what? Tell you what. Pass the word on to the Old Captain thusly—you let him decide on it. For if I speaks it, and someone asks it of me, I'm bound by the Lord's word to tell the truth, and I don't want that. I'm a good friend of the mayor of this town, Fontaine Beckham. He's a good friend to the colored, and to me. I got to be able to tell him, if he asks, 'Mr. Mayor, I knows nothing 'bout this whole bit.' I can't lie to him. Y'understand?"

I nodded.

"Pass word to the Old Man thusly: There's hundreds of coloreds in Baltimore and Washington, D.C., itching for a chance to fight slavery. But they got no telegraph and gets no letters."

"So?"

"So how would you pass word fast to thousands of folks who got no telegraph and gets no letters? What's the fastest way from point A to point B?"

"I don't know."

"The railroad, child. That gets you to the city. But then you got to get to the colored. And I know just how to do it. Listen. I knows a few in Baltimore runs a numbers game. They collect numbers every day from both those in bondage and those that's free. They pays out to the winner no matter what. Hundreds plays it every single day. I plays it myself. If you can get the Old Man to give me some money to grease them feller's palms, the numbers men will spread the word fast. It'll go everywhere within a day or two, for them types don't fear the law. And if there's a penny in it for them, that's all they care 'bout."

"How much money?"

"'Bout two hundred and fifty oughta do it. That's twenty-five apiece. Some for them in Washington and some for the men in Baltimore. There's ten of 'em I can think of."

"Two hundred and fifty dollars! The Old Man ain't got five dollars."

"Well, that's what he got to work with. Get me that money and I'll spread it around in Baltimore and D.C. And if he throws in another two hundred fifty, I'll have a set of wagons and horses to throw at it, so them fellers that wants to join him—I expect it'll be women, too, lots of 'em—they'll ride here. Ain't but a day's ride from here."

"How many wagons?"

"Five oughta do it."

"Where they gonna come from?"

"They'll follow the tracks. Tracks cut a pretty straight path here from Baltimore. A dirt trail follows it along. There's a couple of bad patches of trail—I'll school the Negroes on it—but the trail is all right. The train don't travel but twenty or thirty miles an hour. It stops every fifteen minutes to pick up passengers or water. They'll be able to keep up all right. They won't fall far behind."

He paused a moment, staring out at the water, nodding, thinking, hatching it in his head as he spoke it. "I'll ride in here on the train. It comes in at one twenty-five a.m. every night, the B&O out of Baltimore. Remember that. One twenty-five in the a.m. The B&O. I'll be on it. When you and the Old Man's army give me the signal, I'll signal the fellers in the wagons on the road that it's time to move in."

"That sounds a little thin to me, Mr. Rail Man."

"You got a better plan?"

"No."

"That's it, then. Tell the Captain he's got to stop the train at one twenty-five, just before it crosses the B&O Bridge. I'll get you the rest of what to do later. I got to git. Tell the Old Man to send me five hundred dollars. I'll be back in two days on the next run. One twenty-five a.m. sharp. Meet me right here at that time. After that, don't never speak to me again."

He turned and left. I ran up to Cook, who stood at the top of the bank. Cook watched him leave.

"Well?"

"He says we'll need five hundred dollars to hive the bees."

"Five hundred dollars? Ungrateful wretches. Suppose he takes off with it. We coming to unslave them. How do you like that? The Old Man'll never pay it."

But when he found out, the Old Man did pay it, and a lot

more. Too bad he did, too, for it cost him big-time, and by then the whole thing was blowed wide open and there weren't no way of sending it backward, which I wish he could have, on account of a few mistakes I made, which cost everybody, including the Rail Man, pretty heavy.

25

Annie

Cook wrote the Old Man directly with the Rail Man's request, and within a week, a colored man from Chambersburg rolled up to the house in a wagon, knocked on the door, and handed Cook a box labeled Mining Tools. He left without a word. Inside the box was a few tools, supplies, five hundred dollars in a sack, and a letter from the Old Man tellin' him the army was arriving within a week. The Old Man wrote that his army would sprinkle in, by twos and threes, at night, so as not to attract suspicion.

Cook throwed the money sack into a lunch pail with some vittles and gived it to me, and I slung out to the Ferry to wait for the B&O train out of Baltimore at one twenty-five a.m. The Rail Man was the last to come off the train after the passengers and crew left out. I hailed him and gived him the lunch pail, tellin' him out loud that it was lunch for the journey back to Baltimore—just in case anyone was within hearing. He took it without a word and moved on.

Two weeks later, the Old Man arrived alone, gruff and stern

as usual. He fluffed 'bout the farm for a few minutes, checking the supplies and the roads and other matters thereabout, before he sat down and let Cook give him the lay of the land.

"I take it you has been shy of speaking our business," he said to Cook.

"Quiet as a mouse," Cook said.

"Good, for my army is coming soon."

Later that day, the first of them arrived—and she was quite a surprise.

She was a girl, a white girl, sixteen, with dark hair and steady brown eyes that seemed to hold lots of surprises and a ready laugh behind them. She wore her hair pinned back in a bun, a yellow ribbon 'round her neck, and a simple farm-girl dress. Her name was Annie, and she was one of the Old Man's older daughters. The Old Man had twelve living children altogether, but I reckon Annie had to be the best of the female lot. She was pretty as the day was long, quiet in nature, modest, obedient, and pious as the Old Man was. That took her out of my world, course, being that if a woman weren't a low-down dirty stinker who drank rotgut and smoked cigars and throwed poker cards, there weren't nothing she could do to mash my button, but Annie was easy on the eyes and a welcome surprise. She arrived in quiet fashion with Martha, sixteen, who was the wife of his son Oliver, who came trickling in to join us with the rest of the Old Man's army from Iowa.

The Old Man introduced me to the girls and announced, "I knows you is not partial to housework, Onion, being more of a soldier than a home cooker. But it is time you learn the ways of women as well. These two is to help you put the house in shape. You three can tend to the men's needs and make the farm look normal to the neighbors."

It was a fine notion, for the Old Man knowed my girl limits and that I couldn't cook for a pinch of snuff, but when he announced the sleeping arrangements, my feathers fell. We three girls was to sleep downstairs in the house, while the men slept upstairs. I agreed course, but the minute he hopped upstairs, Annie moved to the kitchen, drawed water for a bath, throwed her clothes off, and hopped into the tub, which caused me to scat from the kitchen and slam the door shut behind me, standing in the drawing room with my back to the door.

"Oh, you is a shy thing," she said from behind the door.

"Yes I is, Annie," I said from the other side, "and I appreciate your understanding. For I is ashamed to undress around white folks, being colored and all, and having my mind on the upcoming freeing of my people. I don't yet know the ways of white people, having lived around the colored so long."

"But Father says you was a friend to my dear brother Frederick!" Annie shouted from the tub behind the door. "And you has lived on with Father and his men for the better part of three years."

"Yes, I has, but that was on the trail," I shouted back from my side. "I needs time to ready myself for indoors living and being free, for my people don't know how yet to live civilized, being slaved and all. Therefore, I am glad you is here, to show me the ways of righteousness behind God's doings in my life as a free person."

Oh, I was a scoundrel, for she bit the whole thing off. "Oh, that is so sweet of you," she said. I heard her splashing and scrubbing and finally getting out the tub. "I will be glad to do it. We can read the Bible together and rejoice in learning and sharing the Lord's word and knowledge, and all His ways of encouragement and doings."

It was all a lie course, for I weren't no more interested in the Bible than a hog knows a holiday. I decided to keep out the house, knowing them arrangements just wouldn't do, for while she was a bit dowdy compared to the swinging lowlifes I lusted after out west—in fact right dusty-looking in bonnet and hat when she come in, from days of riding from the family's home in upstate New York—I glimpsed a good part of the inner package when she throwed herself in that tub, and there was enough there, by God, ripe and plump, to build as much of a fire 'round as I could imagine. I couldn't stand it, for I was then fourteen, near as I can tell it, and had yet to experience nature's ways, and what I knowed of it filled me with dread and wanting and confusion, thanks to Pie. I had to fill my mind with other doings lest my true nature show itself. I didn't have a decent bone in my body, God seed it, so I resolved to keep off from her and out the house "hiving the bees" as much as possible.

That didn't look to be easy, for we was charged to look after the Old Man's army, which begun arriving in twos and threes right after the girls did. Luckily the Old Man needed me to consort and help him with his maps and papers, for that afternoon he rescued me from the kitchen by calling me to the drawing room directly to assist him in his drawings and plans. As Annie and Martha scampered 'bout the kitchen, preparing it for big work, he pulled several large canvas scrolls out his box and said, "We has finally raised the ante. The war begins in earnest. Help me spread these maps on the floor, Onion."

His maps, papers, and letters had sprouted some in size. The small packet of papers, news clippings, bills, letters, and maps he once crammed into his saddlebags back in Kansas had growed to piles of papers thick as the Bible. His maps was scrolled on large canvas paper, unfurled to nearly as tall as me. I helped him spread them on the floor and sharpened his pencils and fed him cups of tea as he set on his hands and knees poring over them, scribbling and planning, while the girls fed us both. The Old Man never ate much. Usually he gobbled down a raw onion, which he bit into like an apple and washed down with black coffee, a conglomeration which made his breath ripe enough to draw the wrinkles out a shirt and starch it clean. Sometimes he threw a little hominy down his gizzards just for variation, but whatever he didn't eat, I polished off for him, for food was always scarce around him. And with more men arriving by the day, I knowed by then to furnish my innards as much as possible for the day when there wouldn't be no furnishings to line it, which I expected wouldn't be far off.

We worked like that for a day or two till one afternoon, poring over his map, he said to me, "Has Mr. Cook held his tongue whilst you was here?"

I couldn't lie. But I didn't want to discourage him, so I said, "More or less, Captain. But not to the limit."

Staring at his map on all fours, the Old Man nodded. "As I figured. It doesn't matter. Our army will be here in full within a week. Once they're here, we will gather the pikes and go to arms. I goes as Isaac Smith in public 'round here, Onion, don't forget it. If anyone asks, I'm a miner, which is true, for I mines the souls of men, the conscience of a nation, the gold of the insane institution! Now, give me my report on the colored, which you and Cook has no doubt been hoeing and cultivating and hiving."

I gived him the clean side of it, that I had found the Rail Man. I left out the part 'bout the Coachman's wife and her maybe spilling the beans. "You has done a good job, Onion," he said. "Hiving the bees is the most important part of our strategy. They will come, no doubt, by the thousands, and we must be ready for them. Now, in lieu of cooking and cleaning for our army, I suggest you continue your work. Hive on, my child. Spread the word among your people. You are majestic!"

He weren't nothing but enthusiastic, and I didn't have the heart to blurt out to him that the coloreds wasn't sharing his enthusiasm one bit. The Rail Man hadn't said a word to me since I gived him that money to spread the word among numbers runners in Baltimore and Washington. The Coachman avoided me. I saw Becky in town one afternoon, and she damn near fell off the wooden sidewalk scrambling to get out my way. I reckon I was bad luck to them. Somehow the word had gotten out on me, and the colored in town runned the other way every time they seen me coming. I had my hands full at home, too, running from Annie, who seen me as needing her religious training and liked to go naked every couple of days while the men were out, plopping into the tub anytime she pleased, causing me to scamper out the room on one pretense or another. At one point she announced it was time for me to wash my hair, which had gotten scandalous nappy and frizzy. I normally kept it tucked under a rag or a bonnet for weeks, but she got an eyeful of it one afternoon and insisted. When I refused, she allowed she'd find a wig for me, and one evening ventured to the Ferry and returned with a book she brought forth from the town library called *London Curls*. She read off a list of wigs that would work for me: "The brigadier, the spencer, the giddy feather top, the cauliflower. The staircase. Which is best for you?" she asked.

"The Onion," I allowed.

She burst into laughter and let it go. She had a laugh that made a feller's heart jump, and that for me was dangerous, for I growed to liking her company a bit, so I took to making myself even scarcer. I made it a point to sleep next to the stove at night, away from her and Martha, and always made sure to be the last soul on the first floor to go to sleep at night and the first out the door in the morning.

I kept myself on the go that way, hiving the bees without much success. The colored of Harpers Ferry lived on the far side of the Potomac railroad tracks. I hung around them for days, looking for coloreds to talk to. Course they avoided me like the plague. Word had gotten around to them 'bout the Old Man's plot by then. I never did figure out how, but the colored wanted no parts of it nor me, and when they seen me, moved off quick. I was especially moved to discouragement one morning when the Old Man sent me on an errand to the lumber mill. I couldn't find it, and when I rolled up to a colored woman on the road to ask for directions, before I could open my mouth, she said, "Scatter thee, varmint. I ain't got nothing to do with you and your kind! You gonna get us all murdered!" and off she went.

That moved me to discouragement badly. But it weren't all bad news. After Kagi arrived, he met up on his own with the Rail Man, and I reckon his cool manner calmed the Rail Man some, for Kagi reported they'd gone over various plans to get the colored to the Ferry from points east and thereabouts, and the Rail Man seemed to have it worked out right and promised to deliver. That pleased the Old Man no end. He announced to the others, "Luckily for us, the Onion has been diligent in her work, hiving."

I cannot say I agreed with him there, for I hadn't done nothing but fumble 'bout. It didn't matter to me what he said then, to be truthful, for I had my own problems. As the days passed, Annie became a powerful force in my heart. I didn't want it to happen, course, never seen it coming, which is how these things work, but even in all my running around outside, it couldn't help but that the three of us, Annie, Martha, and myself, was kept busy as bees in the house once the Old Man's army rolled in. There weren't no time to make a clean break with all that scrambling around, and my idea of running off to Philadelphia, which was always my plan, got lost in all that busywork. There just weren't no time. The men come pouring in, a trickle at first, in the dead of the night, by twos and threes, then more steadily and in bigger numbers. The old players came first: Kagi, Stevens, Tidd, O. P. Anderson. Then some new ones—Francis Merriam—a wild-eyed feller a bit off his rocker. Stewart Taylor, a bad-tempered soul, and the rest, the Thompson brothers and the Coppocs, the two shooting Quaker brothers. Lastly, two Negroes arrived, Lewis Leary and John Copeland, two stalwart, strong-willed, handsome fellers who hailed from Oberlin, Ohio. Their arrival perked the Old Man's ears toward the colored again, for them two was college fellers and arrived out of nowhere, having heard the fight for freedom was coming through the colored grapevine. He got much encouragement from seeing them pop into place, and one evening he looked up from his map and asked me how the hiving 'bout the Ferry was going.

"Going fine, Captain. They hiving hard."

What else was there to say to him? He was a lunatic by then. Hardly eating, not sleeping, poring over maps and census numbers and papers and scribbling letters and getting more letters in the mail than seemed possible for one man to get. Some of them letters was full of money, which he gived to the girls to buy food and provisions. Others was urging him to leave Virginia. My mind was so confused in them days, I didn't know whether I was coming or going. There weren't no room to think. The tiny house was like a train station and armed camp put together: There was guns to ready, ammo to figure, troop strength to discuss. They dispatched me all over, to the Ferry and back, here and there in the valley and all around it to get supplies, count men, spy on the rifle works, tell how many windows was in the engine house at the Ferry, fetch newspapers from the local general store, and count the number of people in it and the like. The Old Man and Kagi begun several late-night runs back and forth to Chambersburg, Pennsylvania, 'bout fifteen miles, to collect other arms by wagon, which he had shipped to secret addresses in Chambersburg. It was just too much work. Annie and Martha was a cooking and washing service and entertainment sensations, for the men had to stay cooped upstairs in the house all day playing checkers and reading books, and them two kept them amused and entertained, in addition to the three of us scurrying 'bout downstairs preparing food.

This went on for nearly six weeks. The only solace from that madness was to hive the colored, which got me out the house, or at times, to set out on the porch with Annie in the evenings. That was one of her jobs, to set there serving as lookout and to keep the house looking normal and keep the downstairs presentable to make sure that nobody wandered in and found the hundreds of guns and pikes laying around in crates. Many an evening she asked me to set out on the porch with her, for none of the men was allowed to show themselves, and besides, she saw it as her business to educate me as to the ways of the Bible and living a Christian life. We spent them hours reading the Bible together in the dusk and discussing its passages. I come to enjoy them talks, for even though I'd gotten used to living a lie—being a girl—it come to me this way: Being a Negro's a lie, anyway. Nobody sees the real you. Nobody knows who you are inside. You just judged on what you are on the outside whatever your color. Mulatto, colored, black, it don't matter. You just a Negro to the world. But somehow, setting on the bench of that porch, conversating with her, watching the sun go down over the mountains above the Ferry, made me forget 'bout what was covering me and the fact that the Old Man was aiming to get us all minced to pieces. I come to the understanding that maybe what was on the inside was more important, and that your outer covering didn't count so much as folks thought it did, colored or white, man or woman.

"What do you want to be someday?" Annie asked me one evening as we set out on the porch at sunset.

"What you mean?"

"When this is all done."

"When what is all done?"

"When this war is over. And the Negro is free."

"Well, I'll likely be a . . ." I didn't know what to say, for I weren't thinking of the whole bit succeeding. Running to freedom up north was easier, but I had no absolute plans on it that very moment, for setting with her made every minute feel joyous, and time passed quickly and all my plans for the future seemed far off and not important. So I said, "I'll likely buy a fiddle and sing songs the rest of my life. For I enjoys music."

"Henrietta!" she scolded naughtily. "You never allowed you can sing."

"Why, you has never asked."

"Well, sing for me then."

I sung for her "Dixie" and "When the Coons Go Marching Home."

We was setting on a swinging bench that the Old Man set up, hung from the ceiling, and as I sat next to her and throwed my singing at her, her face softened, her whole body seemed to grow soft as a marshmallow, settling in that swinging chair, listening. "You sing beautiful," she said. "But I don't favor them rebel songs. Sing a religious song. Something for the Lord."

So I sang "Keeping His Bread" and "Nearer, My God, to Thee."

Well, that done her in. She got just dumbstruck happy by them songs. They buttered her up to privilege, practically. She set there swinging back and forth, looking righteously spent, and soft as biscuit dough, her eyes looking moist and dewy. She squirmed a little closer to me.

"Gosh, that is beautiful," she said. "Oh, I do so love the Lord. Sing another."

So I sang "Love Is a Twilight Star" and "Sally Got a Furry Pie for Me," which is an old rebel song from back in Kansas, but I changed "furry pie" to "johnnycake," and that just cleaned her up. Knocked her out. She got right syrupy, and her brown eyes—by God, them things was pretty as stars and big as quarters—set upon me and she put her arm around me on that bench and looked at me with them big eyes that liked to suck my insides out, and said, "Why, that is the most beautiful song I have ever heard in my life. It just makes my heart flutter. Would that you was a boy, Henrietta. Why, I'd marry you!" And she kissed me on the cheek.

Well, that just ruint my oats, her grazing on me like that, and I made it my purpose right then and there to never go near her again, for I was a fool for her, just a fool, and I knowed no good was gonna come of them feelings.

It was a good thing the Old Man set Annie on the porch as lookout, for a constant source of trouble lived just down the road, and was it not for Annie, we'd have been discovered right off. As it was, it set the whole caboodle off in the worst way. And as usual, it was a woman behind it.

Her name was Mrs. Huffmaster, a bit of trouble that Becky had mentioned. She was a barefoot, nosy, dirty-to-the-corn white woman who walked the road with three snot-nosed, biscuit-eating, cob-headed children, poking her nose in every yard but her own. She wandered that road before our headquarters every day, and it weren't long before she invited herself onto the front porch.

Annie normally seen her through the window and dived for the door just before Mrs. Huffmaster could get to the porch so she could hold her out there. Annie told Mrs. Huffmaster and the neighbors that her Pa and Cook runned his mining business on the other side of the valley, which was the excuse for them renting the old farm. But that didn't satisfy that old hag, for she was a nosybody who gobbled up gossip. One morning Mrs. Huffmaster slipped up onto the porch before Annie seen her and knocked on the door, aiming to push it open and step inside. Annie spied her at the last second through the window just as Mrs. Huffmaster's foot hit the porch deck, and she leaned on the door, pinning it shut. It was a good thing, too, for

Tidd and Kagi had just unpacked a carton of Sharps rifles and primers, and had Mrs. Huffmaster walked in, she would have stumbled over enough rifles and cartridges laying on the floor to pack a troop of U.S. Cavalry. Annie kept the door shut as Mrs. Huffmaster pushed against it, while me, Kagi, and Tidd scampered around, putting them guns back in the crate.

"Annie, is that you?" the old hag said.

"I'm not proper, Mrs. Huffmaster," Annie said. Her face was white as a sheet.

"What's the matter with this door?"

"I will be right out," Annie sang.

After a few hot minutes, we got them things put up and Annie slipped out the door, pulling me along with her for support, keeping the woman on the porch.

"Mrs. Huffmaster, we is not prepared for guests," she said, fluffing herself and setting in her bench on the porch, pulling me next to her. "Would you like some lemonade? I'll be happy to get you some."

"Ain't thirsty," Mrs. Huffmaster said. She had the face of a horse after eating. She looked around, trying to peek in the window. She smelled a rat.

There was fifteen men setting in that house upstairs, quiet as mice. They never went out during the day, only at night, and they set there in silence while Annie chewed the fat and run that nosybody off. Still, that woman knowed something was up, and from that day forward, she made it her business to stop off at the house anytime. She lived just down the road, and made it known that Cook had already got her dander up by romancing one of the neighbors' daughters, who her brother had expected to marry. She took that as an affront of some kind, and made it her business to come by the house each day at different times, with her ragged, barefoot, dirty children trailing behind her like ducklings, poking her nose around and picking at Annie. She was a rough, uncouth woman who belonged more in Kansas Territory than back east. She constantly picked on Annie, who was refined and sweet and pretty as a peeled onion. Annie knowed it weren't her business to ruffle that woman's feathers in any way, so she took it standing up, calm as lettuce.

It got so that each afternoon at some point Mrs. Huffmaster would stomp onto the front porch where Annie and I sat and bark out, "What is you doin' today?" and "Where's my pie?" Just straight out bullying and poking. One morning she stomped up there and said, "That is a lot of shirts you is hanging out on your back line there."

"Yes, ma'am," Annie said. "My Pa and brothers has a host of shirts. Changes 'em twice a week, sometimes more. Keeps my hands busy all day washing 'em. Ain't that horrible?"

"'Deed it is, especially when but one shirt will serve my husband two or three weeks. How you get so many shirts?"

"Oh, by and by. My father bought them."

"And what does he do again?"

"Why, he's a miner, Mrs. Huffmaster. And there's a couple of his workers live here, work for him. You know that."

"And by the way, where is your Pa and them digging again?"

"Oh, I don't ask their business," Annie said.

"And your Mr. Cook sure do have a way with girls, being that he romanced Mary up the road. Does he work in the mine, too?"

"I reckon he does."

"Then why's he working the tavern down at the Ferry?"

"I don't know all his business, Mrs. Huffmaster. But he is a dandy talker," Annie said. "Maybe he got two jobs. One talking and one digging."

And on and on it went. Time and again Mrs. Huffmaster invited herself inside the house, and each time Annie would put her off by saying, "Oh, I can't finish cooking yet," or point to me and say, "Oh, Henrietta here is 'bout to take a bath," or some such thing. But that lady was moved to devilment. After a while she stopped being friendly altogether, and her questions took on a different tone. "Who is the nigger?" she said to Annie one afternoon when she come upon me and Annie setting out reading the Bible and conversating.

"Why, that's Henrietta, Mrs. Huffmaster. She's a member of the family."

"A slave or free?"

"Why, she's a . . ." and Annie didn't know what to say, so I said, "Why, I'm in bondage, missus. But a happier person in this world you cannot find."

She glared at me and said, "I didn't ask if you was happy."

"Yes, ma'am."

"But if you is in bondage, why is you hanging 'bout the railroad down at the Ferry all the time, trying to roust the niggers up? That's the talk 'round town 'bout you," she said.

That stumped me. "I done no such thing," I lied.

"Is you lying, nigger?"

Well, I was stumped. And Annie sat there, calm, with a straight face, but I could see the blood rushing to her cheeks, and see the cheerfulness back out of her face, and the angry calm lock itself into place instead—like it did with all them Browns. Once them Browns got to whirring up, once they got their blood to boiling, they got quiet and calm. And dangerous.

"Now, Mrs. Huffmaster," she said. "Henrietta is my dear

friend. And part of my family. And I don't appreciate you speaking to her in such an unkind manner."

Mrs. Huffmaster shrugged. "You can talk to your niggers however you like. But you better get your story straight. My husband was at the tavern at the Ferry, and he overheard Mr. Cook say that your Pa ain't a miner or slave owner at all, but an abolitionist. And that the darkies is planning something big. Now your nigger here is saying y'all *is* slave owners. And Cook says y'all is not. Which is it?"

"I reckon you is not privy to how we live. For it is none of your business," Annie said.

"You got a smart mouth for someone so young."

Well, that woman weren't of the notion that she was talking to a Brown. Man or woman, them Browns didn't knuck to nobody once they got on their hind legs 'bout something. Annie was a young thing, but she flew hot and stood up in a snap, her eyes a-blazing, and for a minute you seen her true nature, cool as ice on the outer part, but a firm, crazy wildness inside there somewhere; that's what drove them Browns. They was strange creatures. Pure outdoor people. They didn't think like normal folks. They thunk more like animals, driven by ideas of purity. I reckon that's why they thought the colored man was equal to the white man. That was her Pa's nature, surely, jumping 'round inside her.

"I'll thank you to step off my porch now," she said. "And make it quick, or I'll help you to it."

Well, she throwed down the gauntlet, and I reckon it was coming anyway. That woman left in a huff.

We watched her go, and when she crossed the muddy road out of sight, Annie blurted out, "Father will be angry with me," and burst into tears.

It was all I could do to keep myself from hugging her then, for my feelings for her was deep, way down deep. She was strong and courageous, a true woman, so kind and decent in her thinking, just like the Old Man. But I couldn't bring myself to it. For if I'd a pressed up against her and held her in my arms, she'd'a knowed my true nature. She'd'a felt my heart banging, she'd'a felt the love busting outta me, and she'd'a knowed I was a man.

26

The Things Heaven Sent

Not a week after Annie put her foot in Mrs. Huff-master's duff, the Captain upped and laid down the date. "We move on October twenty-third," he announced. That was a date he'd already called out, and writ-ten letters 'bout, and told loudmouth Cook and anybody else he reckoned would need to know it, so it weren't no great se-cret. But I reckoned it made him feel better to announce it to the men lest they forget or wanted to hightail out of it before the whole deal begun in earnest.

October twenty-third. Remember that date. At the time, that was two Sundays distant.

The men was happy, for while the girls slept downstairs and was right comfortable, yours truly included, the men was packed like rats in the upstairs attic. There was fifteen up there in that tiny space sleeping on mattresses, playing chess, exercis-ing, reading books and newspapers. They was squeezed tighter than Dick's hatband, and had to keep quiet all day lest the neighbors or Mrs. Huffmaster hear them. During thunder-storms they jumped up and down and hollered at the top of their lungs to get their feelings out. At night a few even roamed the yard, but they couldn't venture far or go to the village, and they had gotten so they couldn't stand it. They took to squabbling, especially Stevens, who was disagreeable any-way, and throwed up his fists at any slight. The Old Man brung 'em in too early, is what it was, but he had no place to store 'em. He hadn't planned on keeping 'em cooped up there that long. They come in September. By October it'd been a month. When he announced they was ready to make their charge on October twenty-third, that was three more weeks. Seven weeks total. That's a long time.

Kagi mentioned this to him, but the Old Man said, "They've soldiered this far. They can stand another couple of weeks." He weren't studying them. He had become fixated on the colored.

Everything depended on their coming, and while he tried not to show he was concerned, he was wound up tight on it—and ought to have been. He had written to all his colored friends from Canada who promised to high heaven they was gonna come. Not too many had written back. He set still through the summer and into September, waiting on them. In early Octo-ber, he got thunderstruck with an idea and announced he and Kagi was gonna ride to Chambersburg to see his old friend, Mr. Douglass. He decided to take me along as well. "Mr. Douglass is fond of you, Onion. He has asked about you in his letters, and you will make a good attraction for him to come join us."

Now, the Old Man knowed nothing 'bout Mr. Douglass's drinking and fresh ways, chasing me 'round his study and all as he done, and he weren't gonna know, for one thing you learns when you is a girl is that most women's hearts is full of secrets.

And this one was gonna stay with me. But I liked the idea of going to Chambersburg, for I had never been there. Plus, anything to get me out the house and away from my true love was a welcome change, for I was heartbroken on the matter of Annie and was happy to get away from her anytime.

We rode up to Chambersburg in evening, early October, in a horse-drawn, open-backed wagon. We got there in a jiffy. It weren't but fourteen miles. First the Captain called on some colored friends up there, Henry Watson, and a doctor named Martin Delany. Mr. Delany had helped ship arms through to the Ferry, apparently at much danger to himself. And I had a feeling that Mr. Watson was the feller the Rail Man had referred to when he said, "I know a feller in Chambersburg who's worth twenty of them blowhards," for he was a cool customer. He was an average-size man, dark skinned, slender, and smart. He was cutting hair in his barbershop on the colored edge of town when we come up on him. When he seen the Old Man, he shooed the colored out his shop, closed it down, brung us to his house in the back of it, and produced food, drink, and twelve pistols in a bag marked Dry Goods, which he handed the Old Man without a word. Then he handed the Old Man fifty dollars. "This is from the Freemasons," he said tersely. His missus was standing behind him as he done all this, closed up his shop and so forth, and she piped out, "And their wives."

"Oh, yes. And their wives."

He explained to the Old Man that he'd set up the meeting with Mr. Douglass in a rock quarry at the south edge of town. Frederick Douglass was big doings in them days. He couldn't just walk into town without nobody knowing. He was like the colored president.

Mr. Watson gived the Old Man directions on how to get

there. The Old Man took 'em, then Watson said, "I am troubled that the colored may not come." He seemed worried.

The Old Man smiled and patted Mr. Watson on the shoulder. "They will roust, surely, Mr. Watson. Don't fret on it. I will mention your worries to our fearless leader."

Watson smirked. "I don't know 'bout him. He gived me a mouthful 'bout finding a safe place. Seems he's slanting every which way on the question of your purpose."

"I will speak to him. Calm his doubts."

Mrs. Watson was standing behind them as they talked, and she blurted out to the Old Man, "We got five men for your purpose. Five we can trust. Young. Without children or wives."

"Thank you," he said.

"One of them," she managed to choke out, "one of them's our eldest son."

The Old Man patted her on the back. Just patted her on the back for courage as she cried a little bit. "The Lord will not forsake us. He is behind our charge," he said. "Take courage." He gathered up the guns and money they gived him, shook their hands, and left.

Turns out them five fellers never had to come after all, the way it all worked out, for by the time they was geared up to go, the only place for them to head was due north as fast as their legs could carry them. White folks got insane after the Old Man done his bit, they went on a rampage and attacked coloreds for miles. They was scared outta their minds. I reckon in some fashion, they ain't been the same since.

I hears that much has been said 'bout the last meeting between the Old Man and Mr. Douglass. I done heard tell of ten or twenty different variations in different books written on the subject, and various men of letters working their talking holes on the matter. Truth be to tell it, there weren't but four grown men there when the whole thing happened, and none lived long enough to tell their account of it, except for Mr. Douglass himself. He lived a long life afterward, and being that he's a speechifier, he explained it every which way other than in a straight line.

But I was there, too, and I seen it differently.

The Old Man came to that meeting disguised as a fisherman, wearing an oilskin jacket and a fisherman's hat. I don't know why. No disguise would'a worked by then, for he was red hot. His white beard and hard stare was plastered on every wanted poster from Pittsburgh to Alabama. In fact, most of the colored in Chambersburg knowed 'bout that supposed secret meeting, for they must've been two or three dozen that turned out in the dead middle of the night as we rolled in the wagon toward the rock quarry. They whispered greetings from the thickets on the side of the road, some held out blankets, boiled eggs, bread, and candles. They said, "God bless you, Mr. Brown" and "Evening, Mr. Brown" and "I'm all for you, Mr. Brown."

None said they was coming to fight at the Ferry though, and the Old Man didn't ask it of 'em. But he seen how they held him. And it moved him. He was a half hour late for meeting Mr. Douglass on account of having to stop every ten minutes to howdy the colored, accepting food and pennies and whatever they had for him. They loved the Old Man. And their love for him gived him power. It was a kind of last hurrah for him, turned out, for they wouldn't have time to thank him later on, being that after he moved to the business of killing and deadening white folks at breakneck speed, the white man turned on them something vicious and drove lots of 'em clear outta town, guilty and innocent alike. But they juiced him good, and he was fired up by the time we turned into the rock quarry and bumped down the path toward the back of it. "By gosh, Onion, we will push the infernal institution to ruination!" he cried. "God's willing it!"

The quarry had a big, wide, long ditch at the back of it, big enough for a wagon to roll through. We rolled into that thing smooth business, and an old colored man silently pointed us right through it to the back. At the back of it, standing there, was Mr. Douglass himself.

Mr. Douglass brung with him a stout, dark-skinned Negro with fine curly hair. Called himself Shields Green, though Mr. Douglass called him "Emperor." Emperor held himself that way, too—straight-backed, firm, and quiet.

Mr. Douglass didn't look at me twice, nor did he hardly greet Mr. Kagi. His face was drawed serious, and after them two embraced, he stood there and listened in dead silence as the Old Man gave him the whole deal: the plan, the attack, the colored flocking to his stead, the army hiding in the mountains, white and colored together, holing up in the mountain passes so tight that the federals and militia couldn't get in. Meanwhile Kagi and the Emperor stood quiet. Not a peep was said by either.

When the Old Man was done, Mr. Douglass said, "What have I said to you to make you think such a plan will work? You are walking into a steel trap. This is the United States Armory you are talking about. They will bring federals from Washington, D.C., at the first shot. You will not be there two minutes before they will have you."

"But you and I has spoken of it for years," the Old Man said. "I have planned it to the limit. You yourself at one time pointed out it could be done."

"I said no such thing," Mr. Douglass said. "I said it *should* be done. But what *should* be and *could* be are two different things."

The Old Man pleaded with Mr. Douglass to come. "Come with me, Frederick. I need to hive the bees, and with you there, every Negro will come, surely. The slave needs to take his liberty."

"Yes. But not by suicide!"

They argued 'bout it some more. Finally the Old Man placed his arm around Mr. Douglass. "Frederick. I promise you. Come with me and I will guard you with my life. Nothing will happen to you."

But, standing there in his frock coat, Mr. Douglass weren't up to it. He had too many highballs. Too many boiled pigeons and meat jellies and buttered apple pies. He was a man of parlor talk, of silk shirts and fine hats, linen suits and ties. He was a man of words and speeches. "I cannot do it, John."

The Old Man put on his hat and moved to the wagon. "We will take our leave, then."

"Good luck to you, old friend," Mr. Douglass said, but the Old Man had already turned away and climbed into the wagon. Me and Kagi followed. Then Mr. Douglass turned to the feller with him, Shields Green. He said, "Emperor, what is your plan?"

Emperor shrugged and said simply, "I guess I'll go with the Old Man." And without another word, Emperor climbed into the wagon next to Kagi.

The Old Man harred up his horses, backed away from Mr. Douglass, turned that wagon 'round, and took his leave. He never spoke to Frederick Douglass or ever mentioned his name again.

All the way back to Harpers Ferry he was silent. I could feel his disappointment. It seemed to surge out of him. The way he held the traces, drove them horses at half-trot through the night, the moon behind him, the silhouette of his beard against the moon, his beard shaking as the horses clopped along, his thin lips pursed tight, he seemed like a ghost. He was just knocked down. I guess we all has our share of them things, when the cotton turns yellow and the boll weevil eats out your crops and you just shook down with disappointment. His great heartbreak was his friend Mr. Douglass. Mine's was his daughter. There weren't no way for them things to go but for how God made 'em to go, for everything God made, all His things, all His treasures, all the things heaven sent ain't meant to be enjoyed in this world. That's a thing *he* said, not me, for I weren't a believer in them times. But a spell come over me that night, watching him eat that bad news. A little bit of a change. For the Captain took that news across the jibs and brung hisself back to Harpers Ferry knowing he was done in. He knowed he was gonna lose fighting for the Negro, *on account* of the Negro, and he brung hisself to it anyway, for he trusted in the Lord's word. That's strong stuff. I felt God in my heart for the first time at that moment. I didn't tell *him*, for there weren't no use bothering the Old Man with that truth, 'cause if I'd'a done that, I'd'a had to tell him the other part of it, which is that even as I found God, God was talking to me, too, just like He done him, and God the Father was tellin' me to get the hell out. And plus, I loved his daughter besides. I didn't want to throw that on him. I knowed a thing or two right then. Learned it on the spot. Knowed from the first, really, that there weren't no way Mr. Douglass could'a brung hisself to fight a real war. He was a speeching parlor man. Just like I knowed there weren't no way I could'a brung myself to be a real man, with a real woman, and a white woman besides. Some things in this world just ain't meant to be, not in the times we want 'em to, and the heart has to hold it in this world as a remembrance, a promise for the world that's to come. There's a prize at the end of all of it, but still, that's a heavy load to bear.

27

Escape

Things was a hot mess the moment we hit the door of the farm back at the Ferry. Time we walked in, the Captain's son Oliver and Annie were waiting at the door for him. Annie said, "Mrs. Huffmaster called in the sheriff."

"What?"

"Says she saw one of the coloreds in the yard. She went to the sheriff and denounced us as abolitionists. Brung the sheriff by."

"What happened?"

"I told him you'd be back Monday. He tried to get in but I wouldn't let him. Then Oliver came down from upstairs and told him to get off. He was angry when he left. He gave me a mouthful 'bout abolitionists running slaves north. He said, 'If your Pa's running a mining company, where's he mining? If he's got to move his mining goods, where the cows and the wagons he's using for that purpose?' He says he's coming back with a bunch of deputies to search the house."

"When?"

"Saturday next."

The Old Man thunk over it a moment.

"Was one of our men in the yard? One of the Negroes?" Kagi asked.

"It doesn't matter. Just wait a minute," the Old Man said.

He lingered a long moment before speaking, standing there, swaying a little. He looked nearly insane by then. His beard flowed nearly to his belt buckle. His suit was ragged to near pieces. He still wore the fisherman's hat from his disguise, and beneath it his face looked like a wrinkled mop. He had all kinds of problems going on. The curtain was pulled back off the thing. Several men had written letters home to their mamas saying good-bye, causing all kinds of suspicion, with the mamas writing to the Old Man saying, "Send my boy home." His daughter-in-law Martha, Oliver's wife, was pregnant and bawling every half hour; some of the white folks who'd given him money for his fight against slavery now wanted it back; others had written letters tellin' congressmen and government folks 'bout what they'd heard; his money people in Boston was bugging him 'bout how big his army was. He had all kinds of problems with the weapons, too. Had forty thousand primers without the right caps. The house was loaded with men who was tightly wound up and cooped in that tiny attic that was so crowded it was unbearable. The weight of the thing would'a knocked any man insane. But he weren't a normal man, being that he was already part insane in a manner of speaking. Still, he seemed put out.

He stood there, swaying a minute, and said, "That is not a problem. We'll move on Sunday."

"That's in four days!" Kagi exclaimed.

"If we don't go now, we may never go."

"We can't move in four days! We got everybody coming on the twenty-third!"

"Them that's coming will be here in four days."

"The twenty-third is only a week from Sunday."

"We haven't got a week," the Old Man snorted. "We move this Sunday, October sixteenth. Whoever wants to write home, do it now. Tell the men."

Kagi didn't need to do that, for several was gathered 'round listening and had already written home, being cooped up in the attic with nothing to do but write. "How we gonna pass the word to the colored?" Stevens asked.

"We don't need to. Most of the colored that's supposed to be here will come. We got five from Chambersburg, five from Boston that Merriman's promised. Plus the men from around here. Plus those from Canada."

"I wouldn't count the men from Canada," Kagi said. "Not without Douglass."

The Old Man frowned. "We still got twenty-nine overall men to my count," he said.

"Fourteen who ain't present and accounted for," Kagi said.

The Old Man shrugged. "They'll hive from everywhere once we get started. The Bible says, 'He who moves without trust cannot be trusted.' Trust in God, Lieutenant."

"I don't believe in God."

"Doesn't matter. He believes in you."

"What about the General?"

"I just got a letter from her," the Old Man said. "She's ill and can't come. She gave us the Rail Man. That's enough. He'll spread the word among her people."

He turned to me. "Onion, hurry down to the Ferry and wait

for the train. When the B&O comes in, tell the Rail Man we're movin' on the sixteenth, not the twenty-third. That's a week early."

"I better do that," Kagi said.

"No," the Old Man said. "They're onto us now. You'll be stopped and questioned. They won't bother with a colored girl. I need you men here. We got a lot to do. Got to fetch the rest of the Sharps rifles and prep 'em. Got to get the tow balls and primers ready, got the pikes to unpack. And we got to get Annie and Martha up the highway within a day, two at most. Onion will ready them when she gets back. For she's going with them. I'll not have women here when we make our charge."

That made my heart leap with happiness.

"How will they go?" Kagi asked.

"My son Salmon'll take 'em up to Philadelphia. They can take the train to upstate New York from there. No more time to talk, Lieutenant. Let's move."

I hustled down the rail yard at the Ferry singing like a bird, happy as all get-out. I waited under the bank for the one twenty-five B&O, hoping it weren't late, for I didn't want to be left behind. I weren't gonna miss my ride out of there in no way, shape, form, or fashion. I would let them drop me off in Philadelphia. I had waited a long time to get there. I could leave guilt-free. The Old Man had gived me his blessing.

Thanks be to God, that thing rolled in on time. I waited till all the passengers emptied. The train had to huff and chug up another few feet to take on water, and when it stopped at the water tower, I runned down to seek out the Rail Man. I saw him near the back of the train, movin' passengers' bags into the station and onto waiting wagons. I waited till he was done. He moved to the other side of the train near the caboose and congregated with another colored porter. I approached him there, and when the other porter seen me coming, that feller slipped away. He knowed my deal and I was arsenic to him, but the Rail Man seen me, and without a word nodded to the spot under the bank where we met before and stepped back onto the train.

I rushed down to the bank and waited for him, standing in the shadow of the trestle, so as not to be seen. He came down shortly and he was hot. He placed his back on the trestle post and he talked with his back to me. But he was still hot. "Didn't I tell you not to come here?" he said.

"Change of plans. The Old Man's rolling in four days."

"Four days? You funning me!" he said.

"I ain't," I said. "I'm just tellin' you."

"Tell him I can't get that many people together in four days. I just got the ball rolling."

"Bring what you got, then, for he is dedicated to that time," I said.

"I need another week. The twenty-third is what he said."

"The twenty-third is out. He's going this Sunday."

"The General is sick. Don't he know that?"

"That ain't my problem."

"Course it ain't. All's you worried 'bout is your own skin, you little ferret."

"You raising a ruckus with the wrong person. Whyn't you pick on somebody your own size?"

"Watch your mouth or I'll level you off, ya varmint."

"Least I ain't a thief. For all I know, you done took the Old Man's money for nothing and gonna not show up like the rest."

The Rail Man was a big man, and he had his back to me. But now he turned and grabbed me by the dress and lifted me clear off the ground.

"One more cockeyed word out that fast little hole in your face, you little snit, and I'll throw you in the river."

"I'm just tellin' you what the Old Man said! He said he's movin' in four days!"

"I heard it! Saddle your tongue with the rest. I'll have here who I can. Tell your Old Man to stop the train before it gets to the bridge on the Potomac. Don't let it get across. Stop it there and give me a password."

"What's that?"

"A word. A sign. Ain't they got passwords and all they use on your side?"

"Nobody said nothing 'bout that."

He placed me down. "Shit. Some kind of damn operation this is."

"So can I tell the Captain you know?"

"Tell 'em I know. Tell 'em I'll bring who I can."

"What else?"

"Tell 'em we need a password. And stop the train before it gets on the bridge. Not at the station. Otherwise the passengers will get out. Stop it at the bridge and I'll come out and see what's the matter. I'll hold a lantern out. I'll walk along the train and say whatever password we figure on. Can you remember that? Stop the train before the bridge."

"Yeah."

"Tell you what, since you're thick, I'll give you a password. It's got to be something normal. So I'll say, 'Who goes there?' And whoever is there will say, 'Jesus is walkin'.' Can you remember that?"

"Who goes there? Jesus is walkin'. I got it."

"Don't forget. 'Who goes there?' and 'Jesus is walkin'.' If they don't say that, then by God I ain't gonna wave the lamp for them that's behind me. I'll have a baggage car full of colored behind me, and maybe a wagonload coming alongside the trail as well. I'd have got more but I can't roust 'em up in four days' time."

"Understood."

"After I wave that lamp from the tracks, the colored'll know what to do. They'll jump off the back, come up, take the conductor and engineer, and hold 'em as prisoners for the Captain. The rest will take a few rail tools I give 'em and destroy the tracks behind the train so it can't back up. I'll hold the train for that."

"How you gonna do that?"

"There's another colored porter and a colored coalman, too. They're with us. In a fashion."

"What's that mean?"

"Means they know 'bout it and staying out the way. Everybody in this world ain't a fool like me. But they're trustworthy. If they wasn't, you'd'a been deadened already. Hanging 'round the station like you is, runnin' off at the mouth. Every colored at the Ferry knows what's going on. Anyway, them two will hold the train under the pretense of being dumb niggers, long enough for the colored in the baggage car and wagons to get out. Understood?"

"All right, then."

"Once them niggers clear the train, I'm out. You pass that word to the Old Man. Tell him thus: Once they're off the train, the Rail Man is out. And without that password, too, I ain't movin'. 'Who goes there?' and 'Jesus is walkin'.' I don't hear them words, that lamp won't swing from my hand. If that lamp don't swing, them niggers won't move. And it's done, whatever it is. Anyway, my part ends right there, no matter how the cut comes or goes. You understand?"

"I got it."

"All right. Git along, then, ya half-assed rascal. You's an odd something. Slavery done made some odd weasels outta us, and I surely hope you don't see the end of your days looking the way you do now. If you see me again in life on the road or any-place else in this man's world, never speak to me again or even nod in my direction. I wish I never met you."

And with that, he moved off quick, slipping down the bank and under the trestle, up the slope to the hissing train and climbed on it. By the time I hustled across the covered bridge back onto the Maryland side and made my way up to the road that followed the Potomac along toward the Kennedy farm, that thing was chugging toward Virginia and out of sight.

When I got back to the house, it was chaos. That place was rolling like a military fort under fire. The fellers scrambled 'bout every which way, toting crates, suitcases, guns, powder, muskets, boxes of ammunition. They was relieved to get movin', having been crushed in that tiny space so long it was a pity, and so they moved at full speed, busting with pep and excitement. Annie and Martha scurried 'bout, ready to leave, too. Everyone in that small farmhouse moved with purpose, pushing and shoving past me, while I lingered a bit. I moved to slow purpose them next two days, for I wanted to say good-bye to the Old Man.

He weren't studyin' me. He was in his glory, movin' through

the place like a hurricane. He was covered in soot and gunpowder, racing from upstairs to downstairs and back again, giving orders. "Mr. Tidd, dip them tow balls in oil so we can fire the bridges with 'em. Mr. Copeland, throw more cartridges into that rifle box there. Move with speed, men. Quick. We are in the right and will resist the universe!" I watched him the better part of two days as he ducked from one room to the next, ignoring me altogether. I gived up after the second day and slipped into a corner of the kitchen to feed my face, for I was always hungry and it was near time to leave. I got in there just in time to see Annie slip in and sit down, exhausted. She looked out the window a minute, not noticing me, and the look on her face made me just plain forget 'bout where I was.

She sat there near the stove, glum, then slowly picked up a few pots and pans and things to pack up, trying to keep a brave face on. Not a single one of them Browns ever lacked confidence in their Pa, I'll say that for 'em. Just like him, they believed in the Negro being free and equal and all. Course they was out of their minds at the time, but they can be excused, being that they all growed-up religious fools, following the Bible to the letter. But Annie was wound down. She was feeling low. I couldn't bear seeing her so spent, so I slipped over to her, and when she seen me she said, "I got a terrible feeling, Onion."

"Ain't no need to worry 'bout nothing," I said.

"I knows I shouldn't. But it's hard to be brave about it, Onion." Then she smiled. "I'm glad you coming with me and Martha."

Why, I was so happy my heart could bust, but course I couldn't say it, so I downplayed it like usual. "Yes, I am, too," was all I could say.

"Help me get the rest of the things here?"

"Course."

As we moved 'bout, making ready to leave, I begun to think on what my plans was. Annie and Martha lived on the Old Man's claim in upstate New York near Canada. I couldn't go up there with them. That would be too hard for me to be near Annie. I decided I would ride the wagon to Pennsylvania country and get off there, with the aim of getting to Philadelphia— if we could make it that far north. It weren't a sure thing, for no matter how you sliced it, I was endangering 'em, surely. We would be rolling through slave country, and since we was traveling with speed, would have to move by day, which was dangerous, for the closer you got to the freedom line of Pennsylvania, the more slave patrols was likely to stop and confront Salmon 'bout whether he was transporting slaves. Salmon was young and strong-headed. He was like his Pa. He wouldn't suffer no fools or slave patrols to stop him while he moved his sister and sister-in-law to safety, and he wouldn't surrender me, neither. Plus he'd have to get back. He'd shoot first.

"I have to fetch some hay," I told Annie, "for it's better that I ride under the hay in the back of the wagon till we get to Pennsylvania."

"That's two days," she said. "Better you sit up with us and pretend to be in bondage."

But, seeing her pretty face staring at me so kind and innocent, I was losing my taste for pretending. I cut out for the shed without a word. There was some hay stored there, and I brung it to the Conestoga we was preparing to get movin' on. I'd have to ride under the hay, in the wagon, in broad daylight till night for the better part of two days. Better to hide that way than out in the open. But, honest to Jesus, I was getting worn out with hiding by that time. Hiding in every way, I was, and I growed tired of it.

We loaded up the wagon the day before the big attack and left without ceremony. The Captain gave Annie a letter and said, "This is for your Ma and your sisters and brothers. I will see you soon or in the by and by, Lord willing." To me he said, "Good-bye, Onion. You has fought the good fight and I will see you soon as your people is free, if God wills it." I wished him luck, and we was off. I jumped inside the bottom of the wagon in the hay. They covered me with a plank that spanned along the side of the wagon and placed Annie on it, while Salmon, who was driving, sat up front with his sister-in-law Martha, Oliver's wife.

Annie was sitting right above me as we moved out, and I could hear her throw out a tear or two amid the clattering of the wagon. After a while she stopped bawling and piped out, "Your people will be free when this is all done, Onion."

"Yes, they will."

"And you can go off and get a fiddle and sing and follows your dreams all you want. You can go on about your whole life singing when it's all done."

I wanted to say to her that I would like to stay where she was going and sing for her the rest of my life. Sing sonnets and religious songs and all them dowdy tunes with the Lord in 'em that she favored; I'd work whatever song she wanted if she asked me to. I wanted to tell her I was gonna turn 'bout, turn over a new leaf, be a new person, be the man that I really was. But I couldn't, for it weren't in me to be a man. I was but a coward, living a lie. When you thunk on it, it weren't a bad lie. Being a Negro means showing your best face to the white man every day. You know his wants, his needs, and watch him proper. But he don't know your wants. He don't know your needs or feelings or what's inside you, for you ain't equal to him in no measure. You just a nigger to him. A thing: like a dog or a shovel or a horse. Your needs and wants got no track, whether you is a girl or a boy, a woman or a man, or shy, or fat, or don't eat biscuits, or can't suffer the change of weather easily. What difference do it make? None to him, for you is living on the bottom rail.

But to you, inside, it do make a difference, and that put me out to the part. A body can't prosper if a person don't know who they are. That makes you poor as a pea, not knowing who you are inside. That's worse than being anything in the world on the outside. Sibonia back in Pikesville showed me that. I reckon that business of Sibonia throwed me off track for life, watching her and her sister Libby take it 'round the neck in Missouri. "Be a man!" she said to that young feller when he fell down on the steps of the scaffold when they was ready to hang him. "Be a man!" They put him to sleep like the rest, strung him up like a shirt on a laundry line, but he done okay. He took it. He reminded me of the Old Man. He had a face change up there on that scaffold before they done him in, like he seen something nobody else could see. That's an expression that lived on the Old Man's face. The Old Man was a lunatic, but he was a good, kind lunatic, and he couldn't no more be a sane man in his transactions with his fellow white man than you and I can bark like a dog, for he didn't speak their language. He was a Bible man. A God man. Crazy as a bedbug. Pure to the truth, which will drive any man off his rocker. But at least he knowed he was crazy. At least he knowed who he was. That's more than I could say for myself.

I rumbled these things in my head while I lay in the bottom of that wagon under the hay like the silly goose I was, offering a pocketful of nothing to myself 'bout what I was supposed to be or what songs I was gonna sing. Annie's Pa was a hero to me. It was him who held the weight of the thing, had the weight of my people on his shoulders. It was him who left house and home behind for something he believed in. I didn't have nothing to believe in. I was just a nigger trying to eat.

"I reckon I will sing a bit once this war is over," I managed to say to Annie. "Sing here and there."

Annie looked away, bleary-eyed, as a thought struck her. "I forgot to tell Pa about the azaleas," she suddenly blurted out.

"The what?"

"The azaleas. I planted some in the yard, and they come up purple. Father told me to tell him if that happened. Said that was a good sign."

"Well, likely he'll see them."

"No. He don't look back there. They're deep in the yard, near the thickets." And she broke down and howled again.

"It's just a flower, Annie," I said.

"No, it's not. Father said a good sign is signals from heaven. Good omens is important. Like Frederick's Good Lord Bird. That's why he always used those feathers for his army. They're not just feathers. Or passwords. They're omens. They're things you don't forget easily, even in times of trouble. You remember your good omens in times of trouble. You can't forget them."

A horrible, dread feeling come over me as she said that, for I suddenly remembered that I clean forgot to tell the Captain the password the Rail Man told me to pass on to him at the bridge when they stopped the train. He'd said to tell them the password. He'd say, "Who goes there?" and they'd pass it back,

"Jesus is walkin.'" And if he didn't hear that password, he weren't gonna bring his men on.

"Good God," I said.

"I know," she howled. "It's just a bad omen."

I didn't say nothing to her but I lay there as she howled, and God knows it, my heart was pounding something dreadful. To hell with it, was my thinking. Weren't no way in the world I was gonna crawl out from under that hay, walk that toll road in daylight, privy to every paddie slave snatcher between Virginia and Pennsylvania and go back to the Ferry and get shot to pieces. We'd ridden nearly three hours. I felt the sun's heat bouncing off the ground into the bottom of the wagon where I lay. We had to be near Chambersburg by then, just near the Virginia line, smack dab in slave country.

Annie howled a bit more, then steadied herself. "I know you're thinking of Philadelphia, Onion. But I'm wondering . . . I'm wondering if you'll come to North Elba with me," she said. "Maybe we could start a school together. I know your heart. North Elba is quiet country. Free country. We could start a school together. We could use—I could use a friend." And she busted into tears again.

Well, that done it. I lay under that hay thinking I weren't no better than them speechifying, low-life reverends and doctors up in Canada who promised to show up for the Old Man's war and likely wouldn't. The whole bit shamed me, just pushed up against me something terrible as she howled. It pushed on me harder with each mile we went, pressing on my heart like a stone. What was I gonna do in Philadelphia? Who was gonna love me? I'd be alone. But in upstate New York, how long could I go on before she'd find out who I was? She'd know it before long. Besides, how can somebody love you if you don't know

who you is? I had thoroughly been a girl so long by then that
I'd grown to like it, got used to it, got used to not having to lift
things, and have folks make excuses for me on account of me
not being strong enough, or fast enough, or powerful enough
like a boy, on account of my size. But that's the thing. You can
play one part in life, but you can't be that thing. You just playing it. You're not real. I was a Negro above all else, and Negroes
plays their part, too: Hiding. Smiling. Pretending bondage is
okay till they're free, and then what? Free to do what? To be
like the white man? Is he so right? Not according to the Old
Man. It occurred to me then that you is everything you are in
this life at every moment. And that includes loving somebody.
If you can't be your own self, how can you love somebody?
How can you be free? That pressed on my heart like a vise right
then. Just mashed me down. I was head over heels for that girl,
I loved her with all my heart, I confess it here, and her father's
charge would be against me for the rest of my life if he got
killed on account of the Rail Man not hearing the right password. Curse that son of a bitch father of hers! And the Rail
Man, too! That self-righteous, ignorant, risk-taking, elephant-
looking bum! And all them slave-fightin' no-gooders! It would
be on my head. The thought of the Captain getting deadened
on account of me made me feel ten times worse than Annie not
loving me, which if she'd'a knowed what I was, she'd'a been disgusted with me, a nigger, playing a girl, not man enough to be
a man, loving her and all, and she wouldn't love me back in
the least, or even like me, no matter how much she felt for me
at that moment as a full-hearted girlfriend. She was loving a
mirage. And I'd have her father's blood on my hands the rest of
my life, laying there like a coward under the hay and not being
a natural man, man enough to go back and tell him the words

that might help him live five minutes longer, for while he was a fool, his life was dear to him as mine's was to me, and he'd risked that life many times on my account. God damn it to hell.

To have the Captain's blood on my hands on account of something I was supposed to do, it was just too much. I couldn't stand it.

The plank she was setting on was propped on two boards. With both hands I pushed it a foot or so forward and burst out the hay and sat up.

"I got to go," I said.

"What?"

"Tell Salmon to stop."

"We can't. We in slave country. Get back in that hay!"

"I won't."

Before she could move to it, I slid out from under the plank, pulled the bonnet off my head, and ripped the dress down to my waist. Her mouth opened in shock.

"I love you, Annie. I won't ever see you again."

With one swift motion, I grabbed my gunnysack and leaped out the back of the wagon, rolling on the road, her shocked cry echoing into the woods and trees around me. Salmon harred up the wagon and yelled back for me, but he might as well been hollering down an empty hole. I was up the road and gone.

28

Attack

I runned down the road like the wind, and caught a ride with an old colored man from Frederick, Maryland, who was driving his master's wagon to the Ferry to pick up a shipment of lumber. It took us a full day to roll back for he was sharp, and had to roll past slave patrollers while stating his marse's business. He dropped me off a few miles from the Ferry on the Maryland side and I done the rest on foot. I made it to the farmhouse late, several hours after dark.

The house was dark as I approached and I couldn't see no candlelight. It was drizzling and there was no moon. I had no timepiece, but I guessed it was close to midnight.

I burst in the door and they were gone. I turned toward the door, and a figure blocked it and a rifle barrel met me right in the face. A light was thrown on me, and behind it stood three of the Old Man's army: Barclay Coppoc, one of the shooting Quakers, Owen, and Francis Merriam, a one-eyed batty feller, crazy as a weasel, who had joined up late in the doings. All three was holding rifles and armed to the teeth with sidearms and broadswords.

"What you doing here?" Owen asked.

"I forgot to give your Pa the password for the Rail Man."

"Father didn't have a password for him."

"That's just it. The Rail Man had one for me to give him."

"It's too late. They left four hours ago."

"I got to tell him."

"Sit tight."

"For what?"

"They'll figure it out. We could use you here. We is guarding the arms and waiting for the colored to hive," Owen said.

"Well, that is the dumbest thing I ever heard in my life, Owen. Can't you wake up to it?"

I looked at Owen, I swear 'fore God he tried to keep a straight face on it. "I'm dead set against slavery, and anyone who ain't is a fool," he said. "They'll come. And I will set here and wait till then," he said. I guess this was his way of showing his faith in his Pa, and also getting out the deal. The farm was five miles from the Ferry, and I reckon the Old Man left him 'cause Owen had seen enough of his crazy Pa's doings. He'd been all through the Kansas Wars and seen the worst of it. Those other two up there, the Old Man probably left them there to relieve them from the action, for Coppoc weren't but twenty, and Merriam was thick as mud in his mind.

"Did the B&O come yet?" I asked.

"I don't know. Haven't heard it."

"What time is it?"

"One ten in the a.m."

"It don't come till one twenty-five. I got to warn him," I said. I moved toward the door.

"Wait," Owen said. "I'm done pulling you out the fire, Onion. Set here." But I was out the door and gone.

It was a five-mile run down to the Ferry, pitch-black with a drizzling rain. Had I stayed on the old colored man's wagon and not got off at the Kennedy farm, I could'a ridden right into town and made it in better time, I reckon. But that old man was long gone. I had my satchel throwed around my back with everything I owned, including a change of boy clothes. I was planning on lighting out when it was done. The Rail Man would give me a ride. He weren't staying, he said as much. Had I any sense I would'a throwed a revolver in my sack. There was a dozen of 'em laying in the farmhouse, two setting on the windowsill when I walked in there, likely loaded and primed. But I didn't think of it.

I came hard down that hill, and didn't hear a bit of firing as I came down it, so no shooting had started. But when I hit the bottom and runned along the Potomac, I heard a train whistling and saw a dim light on the other side, 'bout a mile off to the east, curving 'round the edge of the mountain. That was the B&O, not wasting no time, coming out of Baltimore.

I throwed myself down the road fast as my legs could go, running toward the bridge that crossed the Potomac River.

The train got to the other side just before I did. I heard the hissing of the brakes as it stopped short, just as I put my foot on the far side of the bridge coming over. I seen it halted there, setting, hissing, through the bridge span trestles as I ran. The train had stopped 'bout a few yards shy of the station, just as the Rail Man said it would. Normally it stopped at the station, discharged passengers, then moved up a few yards to the water tower to take on water, then headed over the Shenandoah Bridge, where it headed down to Wheeling, Virginia. That weren't normal, for the train to stop there, which meant the Old Man's army had already started their war.

The Shenandoah was a covered bridge, with a wagon road running on one side of it and the train tracks on the other. From my side atop the B&O Bridge, I seen two fellers with rifles approaching the train from the Shenandoah Bridge side where it was stalled, 'bout a quarter mile off from me. I was still making it, running across the B&O Bridge, the train stopped dead, setting there, hissing steam, the lantern at the front of it, dangling over the cowcatcher.

From the bridge as I got closer, I recognized the two figures as Oliver and Stewart Taylor, walking along the sides of the train, holding rifles to the engine master and coal slinger as they climbed down the train. They climbed down right into Oliver's hands, they did. He and Taylor moved them along toward the back of the train, but what with the hissing and clanking of the engine, and being where I was, running hard, I couldn't hear what was said. But I was busting it, running hard, almost there, and as I got closer, I could hear their voices talking a little bit.

I was just 'bout across the bridge when I saw the wide, tall silhouette of the Rail Man emerge from a side door of a passenger compartment and climb down the steps. He come down the steps slowly, carefully, reached up, shut the train door behind him, and set off down the tracks on foot. He come right at Oliver, holding a lantern at his side. He didn't wave it. Just held the lantern steady at his side, walking toward Oliver and Taylor, who was walking away from him toward the Ferry with their prisoners. Oliver looked over his shoulder and saw the Rail Man, and he motioned Taylor to keep going with the two prisoners while he broke off and turned back toward the Rail

Man, his rifle at his hip. He didn't raise it, but he held it steady there as he came toward the Rail Man.

I runned hard to get there, giving it every string I had. I humped off the bridge on the Ferry side and turned and followed the tracks toward them and hollered as I come. They weren't but two hundred yards off or so, but that train was clanking and banging, and I was in the dark, running down the tracks, and when I seen Oliver close in on the Rail Man, I hollered out, "Oliver! Oliver! Hold it!"

Oliver didn't hear me. He glanced over his shoulder for just a second, then turned back to the Rail Man.

I was close enough to hear as I come now. The Rail Man kept coming at Oliver, and I heard him shout out, "Who goes there?"

"Stay where you are," Oliver said.

The Rail Man kept coming, said it again, "Who goes there?"

"Stay there!" Oliver snapped.

I hollered out, "Jesus is walkin'!" but I weren't close enough, and neither of them heard me. Oliver didn't turn his back this time, for the Rail Man was on him, not five feet off, still holding that lamp at his side. And he was a big man, and I reckon on account of his size and him coming toward Oliver in that fashion, not being afraid, well, Oliver shouldered his rifle. Oliver was young, only twenty, but he was a Brown, and once them Browns moved on intent, there weren't no stopping. I screamed, "Oliver!"

He turned again. And this time seen me coming at him. "Onion?" he said.

It was dark and I don't know if he seen me clear or not. But the Rail Man did not see me at all. He weren't more than five feet from Oliver, still holding that lamp, and he said to Oliver again, "Who goes there!" impatient this time, and a little nervous. He was trying to give him the word, you see, waiting for it.

Oliver spun back toward him with the rifle on his shoulder now and hissed, "Don't take another step!"

I don't know if the Rail Man got Oliver's intent wrong or not, but he showed his back to Oliver. Just spun around and walked away from him, brisk-like. Oliver still had his gun trained on him, and I reckon Oliver would have let him walk back onto the train if the Rail Man had gone on and done that. But instead, the Rail Man did an odd thing. He stopped and blowed out that lantern, then, instead of walking back onto the train, turned to walk toward the railroad office, which was just a few yards off the track there. Didn't head toward the train. Went toward the rail office. That killed him right there.

"Halt!" Oliver called out. He called it twice, and the second time he called it, the Rail Man dropped the lamp and stepped up toward the office. Double-stepped now.

God knows it, he never did wave that lantern. Or maybe he was disgusted that we wasn't smart enough to know the password, or he just weren't sure what was happening, but when he dropped that lantern and made toward the office, Oliver must'a figured he was going for help, so he let that Sharps speak to him. He cut loose on him once.

That Sharps rifle, them old ones during that time, they barked so loud it was a pity. That thing choked out some fire and offered up a bang so big you could hear it echoing all along the sides of both rivers; it bounced off them mountains like a calling from on high, the sound of that boom traveling across the river and bouncing down the Appalachian valley and up the Potomac like a bowling ball. Sounded big as God's thunder, it did, just made a terrible noise, and it busted a ball straight into the Rail Man's back.

The Rail Man was a big man, over six hands tall. But that ball got his attention. It stood him up. He stood still a few seconds, then moved again like he wasn't hit, kept going toward the railroad office, staggering a bit, stepping over the tracks as he done so, then collapsed at the front door of the railroad station on his face. He flopped down like a bunch of rags, his feet flopping into the air.

Two white men flung open the door and drug him in just as I reached Oliver. He turned to me and said, "Onion! What you doing here?"

"He was with us!" I gasped. "He was flocking the colored!"

"He should'a said it. You seen it. I told him to halt! He didn't say a blamed word!"

There weren't no use in tellin' him now. It was my mistake and I planned to keep it. The Rail Man was dead anyway. He was the first man killed at Harpers Ferry. A colored.

The white folks runned with that later on. They laughed 'bout it. Said, "Oh, John Brown's first shot to free the niggers at Harpers Ferry killed a nigger." But the fact is, the Rail Man didn't die right off. He lived for twenty-four hours more. Lived longer than Oliver did, it turns out. He had a whole day to tell his story after he was shot, for he bled to death and was conscious before he died, and his wife and children and even his friend the mayor called on him, and he spoke to them all, but he never did tell a soul what he done or who he really was.

I later heard tell that his real name was Haywood Shepherd. The white folks at Harpers Ferry gived him a military funeral when the whole thing was done. They buried him like a hero, for he was one of their niggers. He died with thirty-five hundred dollars in the bank. They never did figure out how he got that much money, being a baggage handler, and what he planned to use it for. But I knowed.

If the Old Man hadn't changed dates on him, making it so the Rail Man gave his password to the wrong person, he'd'a lived another day to spend all that money he saved on freeing his kin. But he brung his words to the wrong man, and the wrong movement.

It was an honest mistake, made in the heat of that moment. And I don't beat myself over the head with it. Fact is, it weren't me who blowed out the Rail Man's lantern and dropped it that night. It was the Rail Man himself that done it. Had he calmed down and waited another second he would'a seen me and waved that thing up and down. But it was hard buying that whole bit deep inside, truth be to tell it, for a lot was wasted.

I told Oliver standing there, "It's my fault."

"There'll be time enough to count lost chickens later," he said. "We got to move."

"You don't understand."

"Understand later, Onion. We got to roll!"

But I couldn't move, for a sight over Oliver's shoulder froze me in my tracks. I was standing before him, looking down the track behind him, and what I seen made my two little walnuts, packed inside my dress, shrivel up in panic.

In the dim light of the tavern that lit the track, dozens of coloreds, maybe sixty or seventy, poured out of two baggage cars. It was Monday morning in the wee hours, and some was still dressed in Sunday church clothes, for I reckon they'd gone to church the day before. Men in white shirts, and women in dresses. Men, women, children, some in their Sunday best, and others with no shoes, some holding sticks and pikes and even an old rifle or two. They jumped out of them baggage cars like they was on fire, the whole herd of 'em, turning and running off on foot, making tracks back toward Baltimore and Washington, D.C., as fast as their feet could go. They was waiting on the Rail Man to wave that lamp. And when he didn't, they took the tall timber and went home. It didn't take much for a colored to think he'd been tricked by anyone, white or colored, in them days.

Oliver turned and looked back there just as the last of them leaped out the baggage car and hit the tracks running, then turned back to me, puzzled, and said, "What's going on?"

I watched the last of them disappear, dodging in and out of the trees, jumping into the thickets, a few sprinting down the tracks, and said, "We is doomed."

29

A Bowl of Confusion

I slunk behind Oliver and Taylor as they left the bridge in a hurry with the engineer and coal slinger as prisoners. They marched the two them past the Gault House on Shenandoah Street and straight into the gates of the armory inside the ferry gate, which was unguarded. On the way there, Oliver explained that the cat was out the bag. Cook and Tidd had already cut the town's telegraph wires, his older brother Watson, another one of the Captain's sons, and one of the Thompson boys was guarding the Shenandoah Bridge. The rest had overcome the two watchmen, stolen into the armory buildings, and seized them. Two fellers took up in the arsenal, where the guns was guarded. The train was held up. Kagi and John Copeland, the colored soldier, had the rifle works—that's where the guns was made. The rest of the Old Man's army of seventeen men was scattered 'bout in various buildings across the grounds.

"There weren't but two guards," Oliver said. "We took them by surprise. We sprung the trap perfect."

We brung the prisoners into the Engine Works Building, the entrance guarded by two of the Old Man's soldiers, and when we walked in, the Captain was busy giving orders. When he turned and seen me walk in, I thought he'd be disappointed and angry that I disobeyed his orders. But he was used to crazy conglomerations and things going cockeyed. Instead of being angry, the expression on his face was one of joy. "I knowed it. The Lord of Hosts foresees our victory!" he declared. "Our war is won, for our good omen the Onion has returned! As the book of Isaiah says, 'Woe to the wicked. And say ye to the righteous that it shall be well with him!'"

The men around him cheered and chuckled, except, I noted, O. P. Anderson and the Emperor. They was the only two colored in the room. They looked just plain fertilized, put out, right unnerved.

The Old Man clapped me on the back. "I see you is dressed for victory, Onion," he said, for I still had my gunnysack with me. "You come well prepared. We is headed for the mountains shortly. Soon as the colored hives, we will be off. There is a lot of work yet ahead." And with that he turned away and begun giving orders again, tellin' someone to go get the three men at the farm to ready a nearby schoolhouse to gather in the colored. He was just plumb full of orders, tellin' this one to go this way and the other one to go that way. There weren't nothing for me to do, really, except to set tight. There was already several eight or nine prisoners in the room, and they looked downright glum. Some of them were still shaking the sleep out their eyes, for it was near two a.m. and they'd been woken in some form or fashion. To my recollection, of them that was in the room was a husband and wife seized when taking a shortcut home through the armory from the Gault tavern in town, two armory workers, two railroad workers, and a drunk who lay asleep on the floor most of the time, but woke up long enough to declare that he was the cook at the Gault House tavern.

The Old Man ignored them, course, marching past them, giving orders, just happy as you please. He was as peachy as I'd ever seen him, and for the first time in a long while, the wrinkles in his face creaked and twisted amongst themselves and wrapped around his nose like spaghetti, and the whole conglomeration broke open into a look of—how can I say it—downright satisfaction. He weren't capable of a smile, not a true, wide-open, get-your-drawers-out-the-window smile, showing that row of them gigantic, corn-colored front chompers of his I seen from time to time when he chewed bear or pig guts. But he was one hundred percent stretched out in terms of overall satisfaction. He had accomplished something important. You could see it in his face. It hit me heavy then. He had actually done it. He had taken Harpers Ferry.

When I look back, it hadn't taken him more than five hours to do the whole bit from soup to nuts. From the time they walked in there at nine o'clock until that moment the train arrived just after one a.m., was five hours total. It went off smooth as taffy till I got there. They cut the telegraph wires, overcome two old guards, walked past two saloons that was well lit full of Pro Slavers, and walked dead into the armory. That armory covered quite a bit of ground, a good ten acres, with several buildings that done various facets of the rifle-making business, barrels, muskets, ammo, hammers, and so forth. They broke open every building in the grounds that was locked and took 'em over. The main one was Hall's Rifle Works. The Old Man

stuck his best soldiers in there, Lieutenant Kagi and the colored man from Oberlin, John Copeland. A. D. Stevens, who
was disagreeable but probably the best fighting soldier among
his men, Brown kept with him.

My arrival seemed to pound things up higher, for after a
few minutes of tellin' this feller to do this and that feller to do
that and giving a few orders that didn't have no sense to them,
for the thing was done, the Old Man stopped and looked 'bout
and said gravely, "Men! We are, for the moment, in control of
a hundred thousand guns. That is more than enough for our
new army, when they come."

The men cheered again, and when all the cheering died
down, the Old Man turned around and looked for Oliver, who
had come into the Engine Works with me. "Where's Oliver?"
he asked.

"Gone back to guard the train," Taylor said.

"Oh, yes!" the Old Man said. He turned to me. "Did you see
the Rail Man?"

Well, I didn't have the courage to break the bad news to
him. Just couldn't do it in a hard way. So I said, "In a fashion."

"Where is he?"

"Oliver took care of him."

"Did the Rail Man hive the bees?"

"Why, yes he did, Captain."

O. P. Anderson and the Emperor, the two Negroes, they
come over when they heard me answer to the affirmative.

"You sure?" O.P. said. "You mean the colored came?"

"Bunches."

The Old Man was mirthful. "God hath mercy and delivered
the fruit!" he said, and he stood up, bowed his head, and held
his arms outward, palms up, got holy right there. He clasped his

hands in prayer. "Didn't He say, 'Withhold not good from them to whom it is due,'" he near shouted, "'when it is in the power of thine hand to do it'?" and off he went, prowling his thanks 'bout the book of Ecclesiastes and so forth. He stood there burbling and mumbling the Bible a good five minutes while O.P. and the Emperor chased me 'round the room, asking questions, for I walked away then. I just wanted to avoid the whole thing.

"How many of 'em was it?" O.P. asked.

"A bunch."

"Where they at?" the Emperor asked.

"Up the road."

"They run off?" O.P. asked.

"I wouldn't call it running," I said.

"What would you call it, then?"

"I calls it a little misunderstanding."

O.P. grabbed me by the neck. "Onion, you better play square here."

"Well, there was some confusion," I said.

The Old Man was standing nearby, mumbling and murmuring deep in prayer, his eyes closed, babbling on, but one of his eyes popped open when he heard that. "What kind of confusion?"

Just as he said that, there was a loud knock on the door.

"Who's inside there?" a voice shouted.

The Old Man runned to the window, followed by the rest of us. Outside, at the front door of the engine house was two white fellers, railroad workers, both of 'em looked drunk to the point of sneezing gut water, probably had just walked out the Gault House tavern on nearby Shenandoah Street.

The Old Man cleared his throat and stuck his head through

the window. "I'm Osawatomie John Brown of Kansas," he declared. He liked to use his full Indian name when he was warring. "And I come to free the Negro people."

"You come to what?"

"I come to free the Negro people."

The fellers laughed. "Is you the same feller that shot the Negro?" one asked.

"What Negro?"

"The one over yonder in the railroad yard. Doc says he's dying. Said they saw a nigger girl shoot him. They're plenty hot 'bout it. And where's Williams? He's supposed to be on duty."

The Old Man turned to me. "Someone shot over there?"

"Where's Williams?" the feller outside said again. "He's supposed to be on duty. Open this damn door, ya fool!"

"Check with your own people about your man," the Old Man shouted back through the window.

O.P. tapped the Captain on the shoulder and piped up, "Williams is in here, Captain. He's one of the armory guards."

The Old Man glanced at the guard, Williams, who sat on a bench, looking glum. He leaned out the window. "Pardon me," he said. "We got him in here."

"Well, let him out."

"When you let the Negro people go, we'll let him out."

"Quit fooling, ya sawface idiot. Let him out."

The Old Man stuck his Sharps rifle out the window. "I'll thank you to take your leave," he said, "and tell your superiors that Old Osawatomie John Brown's here at the federal armory. With hostages. And I aims to free the Negro people from their enslavement."

Suddenly Williams, the armory guard who was setting

along the wall bench, got up and stuck his head out a window near him and hollered, "Fergus, he ain't fooling. They got a hundred armed niggers in here, and they got me prisoner!"

I don't know but that them fellers saw one of their own yelping out the window, or if it was what he said 'bout them armed coloreds, or if it was the Old Man's rifle that done it, but they scattered in quick time.

In ten minutes, fifteen fellers was standing out there at a safe distance, mostly drunks from the Gault House saloon across the street, haggling and arguing among themselves, for only two of 'em had weapons, and in every building they'd run to inside the armory gates to fetch a gun from, they found a rifle pointed out the window at them with someone tellin' them to get the hell off and away. One of them broke off from the rest gathered out front, tiptoed close enough to the front door of the engine house to be heard, and shouted, "Quit fooling and let Williams the hell out, whoever you is, or we'll fetch the deputy."

"Fetch him," the Old Man said.

"We'll fetch him, all right. And if you so much as touch our man, you cracker-eatin' snit, we'll bust a hole in you big enough to drive a mule through."

Stevens growled, "I had enough of this." He stuck his carbine through the window and busted off a charge over their heads. "We has come to free the Negro people," he shouted. "Now spread the word. And if you don't come back with some food, we'll kill the prisoners."

The Old Man frowned at Stevens. "Why'd you say that?"

Stevens shrugged. "I'm hungry," he said.

We watched the men scramble out the gate, busting off

in every direction, running up the hill into the village and the heights of jumbling, mashed-up houses that set beyond it, hollering as they went.

Well, it started slow and seemed to stay slow. Morning come, and outside the armory walls by the dawn's light, you could see the town waking up, and despite all that yelling from the night before, not a soul among them seemed to know what to do. People walked back and forth up and down the street to work like it weren't nothing, but at the train station, there was some growing activity. Several gathered there, I reckon, wondering where the engineer and coal man was, for the B&O locomotive engine sat there dead in the water, the engine quit, dried up, for it was plumb out of water and the engineer was gone from it, being that he and the coal man was our prisoners. Next to the Gault House, there was general confusion, and at the Wager House next to that—that was a saloon and hotel just like the Gault—there was some milling around as well. Several of those 'bout was passengers who got off the train and wandered up to the station, wondering what had happened. Several passengers held their luggage, motioning and gesturing and so forth, and I reckon they was tellin' different stories, and I heard tell that several had murmured they seen a bunch of Negroes running off out the baggage car. But there was a festive atmosphere to the whole thing, to be honest. Folks standing 'round, gossiping. In fact, several workmen walked past the crowd, straight into the armory gate that morning to go to work, thinking nothing of it, and walked right into the barrels of the Captain's men, who said, "We has come to free the Negro. And you is our prisoner."

Several didn't believe it, but they was hustled into the engine house sure enough, and by ten a.m. we had damn near fifty people in there, milling around. They weren't disbelieving so much like the others from the night before, for the Captain put the Emperor to watch them, and the Emperor was dreadful serious to look at. He was a dark-skinned, proud-looking Negro with a thick chest and wore a dead-serious expression, sporting that Sharps rifle. He was all business.

By eleven a.m. the Old Man begun making one mistake after another. I say that now, looking back. But at the time it didn't seem so bad. He was delaying, see, waiting for the Negro. Many a fool has done that, waiting for the Negro to do something, including the Negro himself. And that's gone on a hundred years. But the Old Man didn't have a hundred years. He had but a few hours, and it cost him.

He stared out the window at the train and the angry passengers spilling off it, more and more of 'em, huffing and puffing, mad 'bout their delay, not knowing what was going on. He turned to Taylor and said, "I sees no reason to hold up all them people from doing their business and their travels, for they has paid for those train tickets. Turn loose the engineer and the coal man."

Taylor done as he was told, cut the train engineer and coal man loose, following behind them to the train so as to give word to Oliver, who was holding the train at the bridge, to let the train roll on.

In doing so, in letting that train go, the Old Man released 'bout two hundred hostages.

The engineer and coal man didn't stop at the gate, not with Taylor following behind them, for he hustled them 'round the other side of the trestle bridge out the back entrance of the armory, direct to the steam engine. They got the steam up in thirty minutes, the passengers clattered on board, and they had that train rolling to Wheeling, Virginia, full out in record time.

"They'll stop at the first town and telegraph the news out," Stevens said.

"I see no reason to hold up the U.S. Mail," the Old Man said. "Besides, we wants the world to know what we're doing here."

Well, the world did know by noon, for what begun as a festive event that morning with fellers taking shots of rotgut and chatting amongst themselves with gossip, had now wheedled down to disbelief, to irritation to finally cursing and gathering near the armory walls. We could hear them hollering rumors and guesses to one another 'bout the cause of the Old Man's holding up the engine house. One man said a crazed group of robbers was trying to bust open the armory's vault. Another hollered that a doctor killed his wife and was hiding there. Another ventured that a nigger girl lost her mind and killed her master and run into the engine house for protection. Another said the B&O train was sabotaged by a baggage handler over a love affair. Everything but what the Old Man had declared. The notion that a group of white fellers had taken over the country's biggest armory to help free the colored race was just too much for 'em to handle, I reckon.

Finally, they sent an emissary to talk to the Old Man, an important-looking feller in a linen suit and bowler hat, likely a politician of sorts. He marched a few feet into the gate, shouted out at the Old Man to cut out the fooling and stop being a sot, and was met by a rifle shot over his head. That drummer whistled out the gate so fast his hat pulled off his head, and he was back across the road before that thing hit the ground.

Finally around one o'clock, a very old man, dressed like a common worker, broke from the crowd of mumblers and ruffled bystanders standing at the gate at a safe distance across the road in front of the Gault House, shuffled slowly across Shenandoah Street, walked dead into the armory, strode to the front of the engine house door, and knocked. The Old Man peeked at him through the window, his Sharps at the ready. It was full daylight now, and nobody had slept. The Old Man's face was lined and tight.

"We understands you is Old John Brown of Osawatomie, Kansas," the old man said politely. "Is that right?"

"That be me."

"Well, seeing you close, you is old all right," the feller said.

"I'm fifty-nine," the Old Man said. "How old are you?"

"I has got you by eight years, sir. I'm sixty-seven. Now, you has got my younger brother in there. He's sixty-two. And I'd appreciate if you'd let him out, for he is ill."

"What's his name?"

"Odgin Hayes."

The Old Man turned to the room. "Who here's Odgin Hayes?"

Three old fellers raised their hands and stood up.

The Captain frowned. "That won't work," he said. And he commenced to giving all three a lecture on the Bible and the book of Kings, 'bout how Solomon had two women each claiming the same baby, till the king said, I'll cut the baby in two and give you both half, and one woman said, give it to the other mother, for I can't stand to see my baby cut in two, so the king gived it to *her*, for he knowed she was the real mother.

That shamed 'em, or maybe it was the part 'bout being cut in two, or maybe him giving the lecture using his broadsword to make points in this way and that. Whatever it was, two of 'em confessed outright they was lying and sat down, and the real Odgin stayed standing up, and the Old Man let him out.

The old feller outside appreciated the gesture and said so, but as he walked across the armory back out to Shenandoah Street, the crowd had growed now, and several fellers in militia uniforms could be seen milling around, waving swords and guns. The Gault House and the Wager House, both saloons, was doing booming business, and the crowd was full-out drunk, boisterous and unruly, cursing and so forth.

Meanwhile, the prisoners inside, not to mention Stevens, was getting hungry and begun bellowing 'bout food. The Old Man seen this and said, "Hold on." He hollered out the window at the gate. "Gentlemen. The people here is hungry. I got fifty prisoners here who has not ate since last night, and neither has my men. I'll exchange one of my prisoners for breakfast."

"Who you sending out?" someone hollered.

The Old Man named a feller, the drunk who had staggered in the night before and been captured and announced he was the cook at the Gault House.

"Don't send that souse," somebody shouted. "He can't cook to save his life. Keep him in there."

There was laughing, but then more grumbling and cursing, and finally they agreed on letting the feller out. The cook shuffled over to the Gault House, and in a couple of hours come back with three men carrying plates of food, which he gived out to the prisoners, and a bottle of whiskey. Then he took a drink and went to sleep again. He forgot all 'bout going free.

By now it was near four p.m. The sun was high overhead, and the crowd outside was hot. Apparently the doctor who had treated the Rail Man spread word to the town that the Rail Man was dying. Several men on horseback was seen galloping up through Bolivar Heights—you could see them running up the roads to the houses tucked up there just above the armory, and you could hear them yelling rumors that echoed down the hill: shouts that the armory was taken by a Negro insurrection. That made the thing electric. All the fun went out of it then. The drunk cursing turned to ranting and full-out cussing and swearing and talking 'bout people's mothers and the raping of white women, and several rifles and guns could be seen brandished among the crowd, but there weren't no firing from them yet.

Then, at the far end of the armory, across from the rifle works, several townspeople came sprinting out an unguarded building, holding rifles they had stolen. Kagi, Leary, and Copeland, guarding the rifle works at the far end of the yard, saw them through their window and opened up on them.

The crowd outside the gate quickly scattered, and now they opened up. The Old Man's men returned the fire, which splattered the windows and pinged into the brick walls around the townsmen. They quickly re-formed into groups. Two militia companies in different uniforms, some fully uniformed and others in only hats and coats, suddenly appeared out of nowhere and assembled in raggedy fashion around the arsenal yard. Them fools had every kind of gun they could dig up: squirrel guns, muskets, fowling pieces, six-shooters, old muskets, and even a few rusty swords. Half a dozen of them crossed the Potomac above the Ferry, walked down the pass next to the Chesapeake and Ohio Canal, and attacked Oliver and Taylor on the bridge, who engaged them. Another group came over on

the Shenandoah opposite the rifle works. A third went to capture the Shenandoah Bridge, firing on two of the Old Man's
fellers who was guarding that. Kagi and Copeland suddenly
had their hands full down at the far end of the armory with
another group down there that had stolen them rifles. And just
like that, it was full out. It had started.

The militia and civilians outside the main gate, they huddled for a minute, then assembled in a group and marched, and
I mean marched, I'd say a good thirty of 'em, marched right
inside the armory gate, firing on the engine house as they came,
sending shots through every window.

Inside the engine house, the Old Man kicked into action.
"Men! Be cool! Don't waste powder and shot. Aim low. Make
every shot count. They will expect us to retreat right away.
Take careful aim." The men did as he said, and, from the windows, busted enough charges at them militia to push them
back ten yards, scattering them back out the armory gate and
onto Shenandoah road in no time.

That firing was too much for them Virginians and they
stayed out the gate, but not that far this time, not across the
road. Their numbers growed by the second, too. More could be
seen coming from the hills above, some running on foot, others
on horseback. Out the window, I saw Kagi emerge from the
rifle works and shoot his way through the yard, past the entrance gate with Copeland covering him, trying to make his way
over. It was hot work getting to the engine house, but he managed it at a full sprint. The Emperor opened the door for him
and slammed it shut behind him.

Kagi was calm, but his face was red and alert with alarm.
"We got a chance to pull out now," he said. "They movin' a

group to take both bridges. They'll have the B&O Bridge in a few minutes if we don't hurry. And if they take Shenandoah Bridge, we're trapped."

The Old Man didn't bat an eyelash. He sent Taylor to cover the B&O Bridge, told Kagi to go back to his position with Dangerfield Newby, a colored, then said to Stevens and O. P. Anderson, "Take Onion back to the farmhouse and bring in the coloreds. They is no doubt hiving there and anxious to join in the fight for their freedom. It is time to take this war to the next level."

O.P. and Stevens gathered themselves on the quick. O.P. wore a look on his face that said he weren't sorry to leave, and neither was I. I had a bad feeling 'bout things, for I knowed then that the Old Man was losing his buttons. I weren't in the mood to say good-bye to him then, even though I hadn't fully confessed to him 'bout the Rail Man being shot dead. It didn't seem to matter then, for the thing was winging out of control in a worse way than even I imagined, and my arse was on the line, and while it's a small arse and was covered with a dress and petticoat for the better part of three years up to that point, it did cover my backside, and thus I was always fond of it. I was used to the Old Man losing touch and getting holy once the shooting started. That weren't the problem. The problem was: 'Bout a hundred armed white fellers screaming outside the gate, tanked, seeing double, and the mob growing by the second. I might mention here that for the first time in my life, the feeling of holy sanctimony begun creeping into my spirit. I felt myself reaching to the Lord a little. It might'a been 'cause I had the urge to piss and no place to do it without giving myself away, for that was always a problem in them days—that, and always having to dress like I was going hunting every night when I gone to bed. But I think it was a little more. The Old Man tried to press sanctification on me many a day, but I ignored him in the years previous. It weren't nothing to me but words. But, watching that crowd outside muster up, I growed chickenhearted from that affair, scared right down to my little dangling rascal and his twin little giddies. I found myself muttering, "Lord, 'scuse me a minute. I has not had a high tolerance for the Word before but . . ." Kagi heard me and scowled a minute, for he was a strong man, a man of courage, but even a strong man can have his courage moved and overtested. I seen real concern in his normally cool face this time, and heard his voice crack when he said it. He gived it to the Old Man straight: "Get out now before it's too late, Captain." But the Old Man ignored him, for he'd heard me call out God's name, and that tickled him. He said, "Precious Jesus! Onion has discovered Thee! Success is at hand!" He turned to Kagi, calm as a bowl of turtle soup, and said, "G'wan back to the armory. Reinforcements is coming."

Kagi done like he said while O.P. and Stevens grabbed a couple of extra balls and cartridges for their rifles, throwed them in their pockets, and moved to the back window. I followed. The window faced the back wall of the armory. They busted a few shots out the window, which sent a couple of Virginians who'd wandered back there scrambling, and we three crawled through it and out. We made for the back wall, which led to the bottom of the river at the B&O Bridge. We was over that wall in no time. We runned through an open lot and sprinted across the bridge and made it across only 'cause Oliver and Taylor was giving fits to a small group of the enemy who

was trying to drive them off it. We made it with bullets pinging everywhere, and within seconds crossed the bridge to the
Maryland side. From there we hustled past two more of
the Old Man's men, crossed the road, and in seconds was
climbing through thick thickets up the mountain toward the
Kennedy farm—in the clear.

We stopped at a clearing 'bout a half mile up. We could see
from our vantage point the crowds and militia growing outside
the armory, groups of men now, charging into the armory in
fours and fives, firing into the engine house, then backpedaling
as the Old Man and his men answered 'em—dropping one or
two Virginians each time. The wounded lay in the clear in the
armory yard, moaning, just feet from their fellow fighters, some
of whom had quit breathing altogether, and the rest of their
brothers who stood crowded at the entranceway on Shenandoah Street, cursing angrily, afraid to come in and get them.
Oh, it was a hot mess.

We watched, terrified. I knowed I weren't going back over
to the Ferry. The crowd outside the armory had growed to
nearly two hundred now and more coming, most of 'em holding bottles of gut sauce in one hand and rifles in the other.
Behind them, in the town itself and at Bolivar Heights above
it, dozens of folk could be seen fleeing up the hills and out of
Harpers Ferry, most of 'em colored, and a good deal of white
folk, too.

Stevens kept going up the hill while O.P. and I stood for a
moment together, watching.

"You going back there?" I asked O.P.

"If I do," he muttered, "I'm walking on my hands."

"What we gonna do?"

"I don't know," he said. "But I wouldn't go back there if Jesus Christ Himself was down there."

I silently agreed. We turned and climbed up the mountain, following Stevens, making our way up toward the farmhouse fast as we could go.

30

Un-Hiving the Bees

We found Cook on a quiet dirt road near the Kennedy farm in a state of excitement. Before we could say a word, he blurted out, "We has hived some bees!" He led us to a nearby schoolhouse, where Tidd and Owen stood over two white men and 'bout ten slaves. The coloreds sat on the porch of the schoolhouse, looking bewildered and like they had just got out of bed. Cook pointed to one of the white men setting among 'em under the barrel of Owen's rifle. "That's Colonel Lewis Washington," he said.

"Who's he?" O.P. asked.

"He's the great-nephew of George Washington."

"*The* George Washington?"

"Correct." He grabbed a shiny, powerful-looking sword lying on the porch floor. "We got this from the mantle of his fireplace." He turned to O.P. and said, "I presents to you the sword of his great-uncle. It was a gift to Washington from Frederick the Great."

O.P. looked at that broadsword like it was poison. "Why I got to have it?" he asked.

"The Old Man would want you to. It's symbolic."

"I . . . I ain't got no use for it," O.P. said.

Cook frowned. Stevens snatched it and holstered it in his belt.

I walked over to Colonel Washington to have a look. He was a tall, slender white man in a nightshirt, still wearing his sleeping cap on his head, his face unshaven. He was trembling like a deer. He looked so glum and scared, it was a pity.

"When we busted in his house, he thought we was thieves," Tidd snorted. "He said, 'Take my whiskey! Take my slaves. But leave me alone.' He squawked like a baby." Tidd leaned down to Colonel Washington. "Be a man!" he barked. "Be a man!"

That got Stevens going, and he was an aggravating soul if I ever saw one. He was overall the best soldier I ever saw, but he was the devilment when it come to wagging his fists and digging into a fight. He strutted over to Colonel Washington and glared down at him, hulking over him. The colonel just shrank beneath him, setting underneath that big feller. "Some colonel you are," Stevens said. "Ready to trade your slaves for your own wretched life. You ain't worth a pea thrasher, much less a bottle of whiskey."

Oh, that riled the colonel, Stevens scratching at him that way, but the colonel held his tongue, for he seen Stevens was mad.

Tidd and Owen produced pikes and rifles and begun handing them out to the coloreds, who, truth be told, looked downright bewildered. Two got up and took them gingerly. Then another grabbed one. "What is the matter with you?" Tidd said. "Ain't you ready to fight for your freedom?" They said nothing, befuddled by the whole bit. Two of 'em looked like they had just got out of bed. One turned away and refused the weapons handed to him. The rest, after a bit of burbling and showing how chickenhearted they felt 'bout the whole affair, went along more or less, taking whatever weapon was offered and holding them like they was hot potatoes. But I took a notice to one of 'em sitting at the end of the row of the coloreds. He was seated on the floor, this feller in a nightshirt and pantaloons, with his suspenders hung low. He looked familiar, and in my excitement and fear it took me a long minute before I recognized the Coachman.

He weren't dressed so splendid now, for he weren't wearing his pretty coachman's outfit with white gloves, as I seen him before, but it was him, all right.

I started toward him, then turned away, for he seen me and I got the understanding that he didn't want me to recognize him. I knowed he had some secrets and thought it better to pretend not to know him, with his master there. I didn't want to get him in trouble. If a feller had the impression that the bottom rail was gonna be on top, he'd act far different if he'd'a knowed that at some point the white man was gonna get the Ferry back and sling the Negro every which way. I seen what was going on down at the Ferry and he did not. Neither did Tidd, Cook, or the rest of the Old Man's soldiers who stayed back up at the farm. But I saw O.P. pull Tidd aside and give him a mouthful. Tidd said nothing. But the Coachman watched them both, and while he didn't hear what nar a one of them was saying, I guess he made up his mind at that moment that he weren't going to play dumb and was going for the whole hog.

He stood up and said, "I am ready to fight," and grabbed his pike when it was offered. "I needs a pistol as well." They gave him one of them, too, and some ammunition.

His master, Colonel Washington, was setting on the floor of the schoolhouse porch, watching this, and when he seen the Coachman take them weapons, he couldn't help hisself. He got snappy. He said, "Why, Jim, sit down!"

The Coachman walked over to Colonel Washington and stood over him with a terrible look on his face.

"I ain't taking another word from you," he said. "I been taking words from you for twenty-two years."

That flummoxed Colonel Washington. Just dropped him. He got hot right there. He stammered, "Why, you ungrateful black bastard! I been good to you. I been good to your family!"

"You skunk!" the Coachman cried. He raised his pike to deaden him right there, and only Stevens and O.P. grabbing him stopped him.

They struggled with him mightily. Stevens was a heavy man, a big mule-strong feller, as tough a man as there was, but he could barely hold the Coachman. "That's enough!" Stevens hollered. "That's enough. There's fight enough at the Ferry." They wrestled him back away from the colonel, but the Coachman couldn't stand it.

"He's as big a skunk as ever sneaked in the woods!" the Coachman cried. "He sold my mother off!" and he went at Colonel Washington again even harder this time, and this time even Stevens, big as he was, couldn't handle him. It took all four of them—Tidd, Stevens, Cook, and O.P.—to keep him from killing his former master. They had to grapple with him for several minutes. The Coachman gave all four of them all they could handle, and when they finally pinned him back, Stevens was so hot, he pulled his hardware and stuck it in the Coachman's face.

"You do that again, I'll air you out myself," he said. "I'll *not* have you spilling blood here. This is a war of liberation, not retribution."

"I don't care what name you calls it," the Coachman said. "You keep him away from me."

By God, the thing had winged so far out of control, it weren't funny. Stevens turned to O.P. and said, "We got to move these people now. Let's move them to the Ferry. The Captain needs reinforcements. I'll tend to the others. You keep him away from the colonel." He nodded at the Coachman.

O.P. weren't for it. "You know what's waiting for us at the Ferry."

"We got orders," Stevens said, "and I aims to follow 'em."

"How we gonna get to the Ferry? We'd have to fight our way in. It's closed off by now."

Stevens peered at Washington out the corner of his eye. "We ain't got to fight our way in. We can walk in. I got a plan."

The road from the schoolhouse on the Maryland side going down to the Ferry is a dangerous one. It's a steep, sharp hill. At the top of it, the road arcs like the curve of an egg. You bounce high over that, and from there you can see the Ferry and the Potomac clear, then you hit that hill and fly down that till you hit the bottom. Right there, at the bottom, is the Potomac River. You got to turn left hard to follow the road to the bridge back over to the Ferry. You can't take that hill too fast coming off that mountain, 'cause if you come down too fast, it's too steep to stop. Many a wagon, I reckon, has bent and broken an axle or two at the bottom, trying to take that turn too fast. You got to take that thing with your horses reined up tight and your brake pulled in hard, otherwise you'll end up in the Potomac.

The Coachman took that road in Colonel Washington's four-horse coach like the devil was whipping him. He bounced down that hill so fast, it felt like the wind was gonna pull me off. Stevens, Colonel Washington, and the other slave owner rode inside, while the slaves, me, and O.P. rode the running boards, hanging on for dear life.

'Bout a half mile from the bottom, before that dangerous turn come up, Stevens—thank God for him—he hollered out the window to the Coachman to har them horses and stop the wagon, which the Coachman done.

I was standing on the running board, watching, with my head at the window. Stevens, sitting next to Washington, removed his revolver from his holster, primed it, pulled the hammer back, and stuck it into Washington's side. Then he covered it with his coat so it couldn't be seen.

"We is going across the B&O Bridge," he said. "If we get stopped by militia there, you'll get us through," he said.

"They won't let us!" Colonel Washington said. Ooooo, he growed chickenhearted right there. Big man like that, crowing like a bird.

"Surely they will," Stevens said. "You're a colonel in the militia. You just say, 'I have made arrangements to exchange myself and my Negroes for the white prisoners inside the engine house.' That's all you say."

"I can't do it."

"Yes, you can. If you open your mouth in any other direction at the bridge, I'll bust a charge in you. Nothing will happen to you if you follow my directions."

He stuck his head out the window and said to the Coachman, "Let's go."

The Coachman didn't hesitate. He harred up them horses and sent that wagon raking down that road again. I hung on from my fingernails down, glum as could be. I would'a jumped off that thing when it stopped, but there weren't no scampering off with Stevens around. And now, with that thing up to speed again, if I'd'a jumped off on that hill, I'd'a been busted into a million pieces by them wagon's wheels, which was thick across as my four fingers, if Stevens didn't shoot me first, he was so mad.

I just weren't fixated on that particular way of dying, the method of it, being throwed off a wagon or getting aired out for trying to run, but it occurred to me I might be crossing the quit line anyway once we hit the bottom of the hill, for I was on the side where it would fall if it overturned if the Coachman tried to pull into the turn going too fast. Blessed God, that upset me, and I don't know why. So I fixed my mind on jumping. That turn at the bottom was sharp enough to pull them wheels off. I knowed the Coachman'd have to slow down to make that sharp twist left and head toward the Ferry. He'd *have* to break it down some kind of way. I figured to make my move then. Leap off.

O.P. had the same idea. He said, "I'm jumping when we get to the bottom."

There was a slight curve just before we hit bottom, and as

we came around it and made it hard for the river, we both seen we was fixed for disappointment. There was militia in formation on the road, marching right through the intersection, just as the Coachman was making for it.

He seen them militia, and didn't brake much, God bless him, he hit that T-intersection straight on, hard as them horses could stand it, drove right into the middle of the militia, busted 'em up, scattered 'em like flies. Then he backed up, turned left, and stung them horses up with his whip and put it on 'em. That nigger could drive a mule up a gnat's ass. Put some distance between us and them fellers in an instant, and he needed to, for once they recovered and seen all them raggedy niggers hanging off Colonel Washington's fancy coach without no explanation, they drawed their hardware and cut loose. Sent balls a-whizzing. But the Coachman outdistanced them, and we lost them in the curve of the mountain road.

We could see the Ferry from where we was. We was still across the river from it. But we seen the smoke and could hear the firing. It looked hot. The road in front of us was spotted with militia hurrying to and fro, but they was from different companies and different counties, dressed in different uniforms, and they didn't know one from the other and let us pass without a word. They had no idea the ones from behind us was firing at us, for the blasting of the ones behind us melted into the shooting coming from across the Potomac. Nobody knowed who was doing what. The Coachman played it smart. He drove right past them, hollering, "I got the colonel here. I got Colonel Washington! He's exchanging hisself for the hostages!" They moved aside to let us pass. There weren't no stopping him, which made it bad for me, for I couldn't drop off that thing with all that militia around. I had to hang on.

Sure as God would have it, when we got to the B&O Bridge—that thing was loaded with militia, creaking down under the weight of 'em—Colonel Washington done just as he was told, followed orders to the dot, and we was waved through. Some even cheered as we passed, hollering, "The colonel's here! Hooray!" They didn't give it a thought, for a good number of 'em was drunk. Couldn't have been less than a hundred men on that bridge, the very same bridge that Oliver and Taylor guarded just a day before by themselves in total darkness and weren't a soul on it. The Old Man had blowed his chance to get out.

As we crossed the bridge, I had a clear sight of the armory from above. By God, there was three hundred militiamen down there if there was one, milling around the gate and walls and more coming from town and Bolivar Heights above it, cramming at the entrance, lining the riverbank, all along the sides of the armory walls. All white men. Not a single colored in sight. The armory walls was surrounded. We was riding into death.

I got light-headed on God then. The devil flew off my back and the Lord latched Hisself to my heart. I said, "Jesus! The blood." I said them words and felt His spirit pass through me. My heart felt like it busted out the penitentiary, my soul swelled up, and everything 'bout me, the trees, the bridge, the town, became clear. I then and there decided if I ever cleared things, I would tell the Old Man what I'd felt, clear it with him 'bout all that religious blabbing he'd done, that it weren't for naught, and also clear it with him 'bout not saying nothing 'bout the Rail Man and a few other assorted lies I told. I didn't think I'd have the chance, to be honest, which I reckon means I weren't totally given to the spirit. But I thunk on the notion anyway.

As we cleared the bridge and the wagon turned toward the armory, I turned to O.P., who was hanging on the running board by his fingernails. I said, "Good-bye, O.P."

"Good-bye," he said, and he done something that just knocked me out. He dropped off that wagon to his death and rolled down the bank into the Potomac. Rolled like a potato into the water, and that was the last I seen of him. Must'a been a good twenty feet. Rolled into the water. He weren't going back to the armory to get shot up. He chose his own death. Chalk up a second colored to the Old Man's scheme. To count, I'd seen with my own eyes the first two folks deadened in the Old Man's army on account of him freeing the colored was the colored themselves.

We come to the armory gate with the Coachman hollering all the way that we had Colonel Washington, rolled right through that mob, and busted into the yard clear. The mob weren't going to stop us. The colonel was in the wagon. They knowed his coach and knowed who he was. I reckoned they parted on account of an important man being inside there, but when we come through the gate and hit the yard clean, I seen the real reason why.

That yard was dead as a cornfield. Quiet as a mouse pissing on cotton.

What I couldn't see from the bridge, I seen from the ground in front of the engine house. The Old Man had been busy. There was several dead men laying out in the open, white men and a couple of colored, too, all within shooting range of the engine house and buildings around it. The Old Man weren't fooling. That's why them militia congregated outside the armory gate and walls. They was still scared to go inside. He'd been beating 'em off.

The Coachman wheeled that wagon around a couple of chewed-up dead fellers and finally got tired of steering around them and just aimed the wagon straight for the engine house, bouncing over the heads of a couple of the dead—it didn't bother them nohow, they didn't feel nothing. He stopped dead directly in front of the engine house, those inside flung the door open, and we rushed inside, the door closing behind us.

That place stunk something ferocious. There was thirty or so hostages in there. Whites was gathered on one side of the room and the colored on another side, separated by a wall, but it weren't a continuous wall to the ceiling, so you could move between the two sides. Nar privy was on either side of the room, and if you thunk whites and coloreds was different, you ain't got a big put up to the truth when you get a whiff of their nature doings and comes to the understanding that one pea don't grow to no higher grade than the other. That place reminded me of them Kansas taverns, but worse. It was downright infernal.

The Captain stood by a window, holding a rifle and his seven-shooter, looking calm as a corn shoot, but a little beaten down, truth be to tell it. His face, old and wrinkled even in normal times, was covered in grit and powder. His white beard looked like it'd been dipped in a bag of dirt, and his jacket was flecked with holes and gunpowder burns. He'd been up thirty hours without sleep and no food. Still, compared to the rest of his men, he looked fit as a fiddle. The others, young men, Oliver, Watson—who had been flushed off the Shenandoah—Taylor, looked clean run out, their faces white, pale as ghosts. They knowed what they was looking at. Only the Emperor seemed calm. That was a bodacious Negro there. And other than O.P., a braver man I never saw.

Stevens handed the Old Man Colonel Washington's sword, which the Captain held high. "That is righteous," he said. He turned to Colonel Washington's slaves who had just come off the wagon and entered the Engine Works and said, "In the name of the Provisional Government of the United States, I, President John Brown emeritus elected, *E pluribus unum,* with all rights and privileges hereto, selected by a Congress of your brethren, I hereby pronounces you is all *free.* Go in peace, my brother Negroes!"

Them Negroes looked downright befuddled, of course. Weren't but eight of 'em. Plus a few more lined up against the wall as hostages already, and they weren't going nowhere, so that added to their confusion. Them Negroes didn't move nor spout a blaming word between 'em.

Since nobody said nothing, the Old Man added, "Course if you want, since we is all here fighting a war against slavery. If you wants to join us in battling for your freedom, why, we is all for that, too. And for that cause, and for the cause of your freedom in the days ahead, so that no one can wrest it from you, we is going to arm you."

"We done that," Stevens said. "But their pikes fell off in the ride down."

"Oh. Well, we got more. Where's O.P. and the others?"

"I don't know," Stevens said. "I thought they was on the wagon. I reckon they're hiving more bees."

The Old Man nodded. "Yes, of course!" he said, looking at the flock we just brought in. He went down the line of Negroes, shaking a hand or two, welcoming them. The Negroes looked glum, which he ignored course, talking to Stevens as he shook their hands. "This is working exactly the way I figured it, Stevens. Prayer works, Stevens. Spiritualist that you is, you really ought to become a believer. Remind me to share with you a few words from our Maker when there is time, for I knows you have it in you yet to turn to the ways of our Great Humbler."

He had plain gone off the deep end, of course. O.P. weren't hiving nothing but the bottom of the Potomac. Cook, Tidd, Merriam, and Owen, they'd taken the tall timber back at the Kennedy farm. They was gone, I was sure. I never held that against them, by the way. They valued their skin. There was weak spots in them men, and I knowed all 'bout that, for I had weak spots myself—all over. I weren't against 'em.

The Old Man suddenly noticed me standing there and said, "Stevens, why is Onion here?"

"She come back to the Ferry on her own," Stevens said.

The Old Man didn't like it. "She ought not be here," he said. "The fighting's gotten a bit dirty. She ought to be hiving more bees in safety."

"She wanted to come," Stevens said.

That was a damn lie. I hadn't said a thing 'bout going back to the Ferry. Stevens gived orders at the schoolhouse, and like usual, I done what he said.

The Old Man placed his hand on my shoulder and said, "It does my heart good to see you here, Onion, for we needs children to witness the liberation of your people and to tell stories of it to future generations of Negroes and whites alike. This day will be remembered. Besides, you is always a good omen. I have never lost a battle when you is about."

He forgot all 'bout Osawatomie, where they deadened Frederick and sent him packing, but that was the Old Man's nature. He never remembered nothing but what he wanted to, and didn't tell himself nothing but what he only really wanted to believe.

He got downright wistful standing there. "God has blessed us, Onion, for you is a good and courageous girl. Having you with me at this moment of my greatest triumph is like having my Frederick here, who gived his life in favor of the Negro, even though he didn't know his head from his hindquarters. You has always gived him such joy. It gives me cause to thank our Redeemer and how much He hath given to all of us." And here he closed his eyes, folded his hands across his chest, and busted into prayer, chanting his thanks to our Great Redeemer Who walked the road to Jericho and so forth, praying 'bout Fred being so lucky as to ride with the angels, and while he said it, he didn't want to forget to mention some others of his twenty-two children, the ones who'd died from sickness and those who yet had gone to glory: the ones who died first, little Fred, Marcy when she was two, William who died of fever, Ruth who got burned; then he runned down the list of the living ones, then his cousin's children, and his Pa and Ma, thanking God for accepting them on high and teaching him the Lord's way. All this with his men standing 'round and the hostages behind him, watching, and a good three hundred white fellers outside, milling around looped and shit-faced, passing ammo and gearing up to make another charge.

There weren't no Owen to bust him out of that trance— Owen's the only one had the guts to do it, to my knowledge— for the Old Man's prayers was serious business, and I seen him pull his heater out on any fool game enough to break off his conversations between him and his Maker. Even his main fellers Kagi and Stevens was scared to do it, and when they done it, they went 'bout it roundabout with no success, breaking drinking glasses at his feet, coughing, hacking, harring up spit, chopping wood, and when that didn't work, they had target practice and blowed off caps right next to his ear, and still they couldn't break him out of one of his prayer spells. But my arse, or what was left of it, was on the line, and I valued it dearly, so I said, "Captain, I is thirsty! And there is some business at hand. I'm feeling Jesus."

That snapped him out of his trance. He stood up straightaway, tossed out two or three amens, throwed his arms out wide and said, "Thank Him, Onion! Thank Him! You is on the right road. Give Onion some water, men!" Then he drawed himself up to his full height, pulled out from his belt and held up the sword from Frederick the Great, admiring it, then placed it across his chest. "May this new acceptance of the Son of Man in Onion's heart serve as a symbol of inspiration to us in our fight for justice for the Negro. May it give us even greater force. Let it inspire us to lend ourselves even more wholly to the cause, and give our enemies something to cry about. Now, men. On to it. We is not done yet!"

Well, he didn't say nothing 'bout busting out of there. Them's the words I was looking for. He didn't breathe a word of that.

He ordered the men and the slaves to chink out the walls, and they got busy. A feller named Phil, a slave feller, got some of the slaves together—there was 'bout twenty-five colored in there in all, some who had come or been gathered thereabouts along with those we brung, plus five white masters who set tight, not movin'—and them coloreds got busy. They chinked out some expert holes with pikes and loaded up the rifles. Lined 'em up one by one so the Old Man's men could grab one after the other without having to load 'em up, and we prepared for perfect slumber.

31

Last Stand

The mob outside the gate waited a good hour or so for Colonel Washington to work whatever magic he had supposedly had, to exchange hisself and his Negroes for the white hostages. When it didn't happen by the second hour, someone hollered out, "Where's our colonel? How many hostages is you giving up for our colonel and his niggers?"

The Old Man stuck his face in the window and hollered, "None. If you want your colonel, come and get him."

Oh, they throwed a hissy fit all over again. There was some hollerin', fussin', and huddlin' up, and after a few minutes they walked 'bout two hundred militia through the gate, in uniform, marched 'em in there in formation, turned 'em against the engine house, and told 'em, "Fire!" By God, when they cut loose, it felt like a giant monster kicked the building. The whole engine house shook. Just a roaring and banging. Bricks and mortar chinked everywhere, from the roof pillars on down. Their firing blowed big pieces of brick mortar right clear through the walls of the Engine Works, and even tore off a big piece of the timber that held up the roof, it came crashing down.

But they didn't overtake us. The Old Man's men were well trained and they held steady, firing through the holes in the brick made by the militia's firing, with him hollering, "Calm. Aim low. Make 'em pay dear." They powered the militia with balls and drove 'em back outside the gate.

The militias gathered outside the walls again, and they was so drunk and mad now it was a pity. All that laughing and joking from the day before was gone now, replaced with full-out rage and frustration in every appearance. Some of them growed chickenhearted from that first charge, for several of their brothers had been hurt or deadened by the Captain's men, and they peeled off and hauled ass away from the group. But more was coming down to the gate, and after a few minutes, they regrouped and come through the gate again in even greater numbers, for more men had arrived outside the armory to replace those that fell. Still, the Old Man's men held them off. And that company drew back. They milled around out there by the safety of the gate, yelling and hollering, promising to string the Old Man up by his privates. Shortly after, they brung in a second company from somewhere 'bout. Different uniforms. Marched another two hundred or so into the gate, madder than the first, cussing and hooting, turned 'em on the building, and by the time they busted off their caps, the Old Man's crew had diced, sliced, and gutted out a good number of 'em, and they broke loose for the gate running faster than the first, leaving a few more gutted or dead 'bout the yard. And each time the Virginians moved to fetch one of their wounded, one of the Old Man's men poked his Sharps out the chinks in the brick wall and made 'em pay for them thoughts. That just got 'em hotter. They was burning up.

The white hostages, meantime, was dead quiet and terrified. The Old Man put the Coachman and the Emperor in charge of minding 'em, and had a good twenty-five slaves in there running 'bout busy. They wasn't bewildered no more, them coloreds was with it. And not a peep was heard out of any of them white masters.

Now we wasn't far from their saviors. We could hear the militia talking and yelling outside, screaming and cussing. That crowd growed bigger and bigger, and with that come more confusion to 'em. They'd say let's go this way, try this, and someone would shout that plan down, then someone else would holler, "My cousin Rufus is wounded in the yard. We got to get him out," and someone would say, "You get him!" and a fight would break out among 'em, and a captain would shout more directions, and they'd have to break up the fighting among themselves. They was just discombobulated. And while they done this, the Captain was ordering his men and the colored helpers, in calm fashion, "Reload, people. Aim low. Line the rifles on the walls loaded so you can grab one after you fire the first. We are hurting the enemy." The men and them slaves was firing and reloading so fast, so efficient, seemed like a machine. Old John Brown knowed his business when it come to fighting a war. They could have used him in the great war that was to come, I'll say that.

But his luck couldn't hold. It runned out like it always done with him. In stitches. Clean out, the way it always did with him.

It begun when a chunky white feller come out to talk to the

Old Man and try to smooth things. He seemed to be some kind of boss. He came into the armory a few times, said I'm coming in peace, and let's work this out. But each time he came in, he didn't venture too far in. Would stick his head in and scoot out. He weren't armed, and after he poked his head and begged his way in a few times, the Old Man told his men, "Don't shoot him," and he hollered at the little feller, "Keep off. Keep back. We come to free the Negro." But that feller kept fiddling with coming back and forth, sticking his head in, then going back out. He never come all the way in. I heard him out there trying to calm the men down outside the gate at one point, for they'd become a mob. Weren't nobody in control of them. He tried that a couple of times and gave up on that and got to scooting a little farther into the armory again, just peeking in, then scampering back to safety like a little mouse. Finally he got his nerve up and come in too close. He runned behind a water tank in the yard, and when he got in there, he peeked his head out from behind that water tank, and one of the Old Man's men in the other armory buildings—I believe Ed Coppoc done it—got a bead on him and fired twice and got him. Dropped his game. The man fell and stopped paying taxes right there. Done.

That feller's death drove that mob outside into a frenzy. They was already spiked by then—them two saloons at the gate was doing big business—but that feller's death drove them straight cross-eyed. Made 'em into a straight-out mob. Turns out he was the mayor of Harpers Ferry. Fontaine Beckham. Friend to the Rail Man and liked by all, white and colored. Coppoc couldn't'a knowed it. There was a lot of confusion.

The mayor's body lay there with the rest of the dead for a couple of hours, while the Virginians outside whooped and hollered and banged their drums and played the fife and promised the Old Man they was gonna come in there and cut him to pieces and make him eat his bloomers. They railed and promised to make his eyeballs into marshmallows. But nothing happened. Dusk come. It weren't quite dark, but it got quiet out there, quiet as midnight. Something was happening out there in the dusk. They stopped hollering and quieted up. I couldn't see them then, for it growed dark, but somebody must'a come there, a captain or somebody, and got them sorted out and better organized. They set there for 'bout ten minutes that way, murmuring quietly 'bout such and so and such and such, like little kids whispering, real quiet, not making a whole lot of noise.

The Old Man, watching through the window, drew back. He lit a lantern and shook his head. "That's it," he said. "We has them neutralized. Jesus's grace is more powerful than what any man can do. Of that you can be certain, men."

Just then they busted through that gate in a horde, four hundred men, the newspaper said later—so many you couldn't see between 'em, a stampede, firing as they come, in a full-out, ass-and-hindquarters, band-beatin', honest-to-goodness charge.

We couldn't take it. We didn't have the numbers and was spread too thin around the armory. Kagi and the two coloreds from Oberlin, Leary and Copeland, was at the far end in the rifle works building, and they was the first to fall. They was driven out the back windows of the building and fled into the banks of the Shenandoah, where they both got hit. Kagi took a ball to the head and dropped down dead. Leary got hit in the back and followed him. Copeland got farther into the river, managed to climb on a rock in the middle of the river, and was stranded there. A Virginian waded out there and climbed on the rock with him. Both men drawed revolvers and fired. Both guns snapped, too wet to fire. Copeland surrendered. He'd hang in a month.

Meantime, they overrun a man named Leeman in the armory. He dashed out the side door and jumped into the Potomac and tried to swim across. Militiamen spotted him from the bridges and fired. Wounded him but didn't kill him. He drifted downstream a few feet and managed to pull himself up onto a rock. Another Virginian climbed out to him, holding his pistol out the water to keep it dry. He climbed onto the rock where Leeman lay sprawled on his back. Leeman hollered, "Don't shoot! I surrender!" The feller smiled, leveled his gun, and blasted Leeman's face off. Leeman lay sprawled on that rock for hours. He was used as target practice by them men. They got wasted on gut sauce and happily pumped him full of balls like he was a pillow.

One of the Thompson boys, Will, the younger one, got out the armory some kind of way and got trapped on the second floor of the Gault House hotel, across the road from the armory. They burst in on him, drug him downstairs, kept him prisoner for a few minutes, then took him to the B&O Bridge and made ready to shoot him. But a captain runned over and said, "Take this prisoner inside the hotel."

"The lady who owns the hotel don't want him," they said.

"Why not?"

"She said she don't want her carpet mussed up," they said.

"Tell her I ordered it. He ain't gonna muss her carpet."

Them men didn't pay that captain no mind. They pushed him off, stood Thompson up on the bridge, backed off him, and blistered him full of holes right there. "Now he'll muss up her carpet," they said.

Thompson fell into the water. It was shallow water down there, and from where we was, you could see him floating the next morning, his face staring up out the water, his eyes wide, asleep forever, as his body bobbed up and down, his boots licking the bank.

We was holding 'em off at the engine house, but it was a full-out gunfight. From a corner of the yard, the rifle works building, the last man living out there, the colored man Dangerfield Newby, seen us making a fight of it and tried to make it for us.

Newby had a wife and nine children in slavery just thirty miles off. He'd been holed up in the rifle works with Kagi and the others. When Kagi and his men made for the Shenandoah River, Newby smartly held up and let the rest chase them others. While they done that, he jumped out a window on the Potomac River side and sprinted across the armory toward the engine house on the back side of the armory. That smart nigger was making time, too. He aimed to get to us.

A white feller from the back of the water tower seen him and throwed a bead on him. Newby saw him, drawed his rifle and dropped him, and kept coming.

He had almost made it to the engine house when a feller from a house across the street leaned through an upper-story window and laid an answer on Newby with a squirrel gun loaded with a six-inch nail. That nail plugged straight into Newby's neck like a spear. Blood burst out his neck and the ground caught him, and he was dead before he got there.

We was fully shooting out cap for cap with them when this

happened, so nobody could do nothing but watch, but the mob paid attention to his dying. He was the first colored they could get a hold of, and they was thirsty for him. They grabbed him, pulled his body out the entrance and into the street. They kicked him, pummeled him. Then a man ran up to him and cut off his ears. Another pulled off his pants and cut off his private parts. Another poked sticks into the bullet wound. Then they drug him up the road to a hog pen and tossed him in there, and the hogs rooted on him, one of them pulling out something long and elastic from his stomach area, one end of it being in the hog's mouth and the other in Newby's body.

The sight of Newby getting rooted by them hogs seemed to incite the Old Man's men to cussing and shooting, and they fired into the militia with deadly effect, for they had worked in right close on us in numbers, and now the Captain's men, furious, drove them back. They done it to effect for a few minutes, but there weren't no chance. They had us then. They closed the door. We was surrounded. Without Kagi and the others to cover us from the other end of the yard, there was no more driving them out the gate. They was at all points 'bout us, but they lingered now, stopped their charges and hung where they was, just out of rifle range. Didn't come no closer. The Old Man's army had stopped 'em where they was, but more flooded into the yard on both ends, and they couldn't be driven out the gate now. They was right there, 'bout two hundred yards off. We was defeated.

I found the Lord full out then. It's true I found Him earlier that day, but I never full out accepted Him in total until that time, being that my Pa was thickly scandalous in the preaching department and the Old Man bored me to tears with the Word, but God works like He wants to. He outright laid on me full-out then, for He'd given me a warning before that He was coming into my heart in full, and He came right then on me full blast. If you think looking at three hundred boiling-mad, half-cocked Virginians holding every kind of breech-loader under God's sun staring back at you with murder in their eyes is a ticket to redemption, you is on the dot. I seen what they done to Newby, and every colored in that engine house knowed whatever devilment Newby got, we was two trips short of, for Newby was lucky. He got his while he was dead, and the rest of us was conjured to get it wide awake and alive, if we lived long enough to get it in that fashion. I found the Lord surely. I called on Jesus outright. A feeling come over me. I sat in a corner, covered my head, pulled out from my bonnet my Good Lord Bird feather, and held that thing tight, just a-praying, and saying, "Lord, let me be Your angel."

The Old Man didn't hear me, though. He was busy conjuring up ideas, for the men in the room had dropped away from the walls and windows to surround him, as he backed off from his window and wiped his beard thoughtfully. "We has them where we wants them," he announced cheerfully. He turned to Stevens and said, "Take Watson out with a prisoner and tell them we will begin exchanging our men for Negroes. By now Cook and the others has hived some more bees at the schoolhouse and the farm. On our signal, they will begin their attack from the rear with the Negroes, thus provoking our escape. It is time to move into the mountains."

Stevens didn't want to do it. "The time to move into the mountains was about noon," he said. "Yesterday."

"Have faith, Lieutenant. The game is not up yet."

Stevens grumbled and roughly grabbed a hostage and nodded at young Watson, who dutifully followed. The engine house door was actually three double doors, and they had roped them all shut. They unwrapped the rope from the center door, slowly pushed it open, and walked out.

The Old Man put his face to the window. "We is negotiating hostages in exchange for safe passage of my Negro army," he shouted. Then he added, "In good faith."

He was answered by a blast of grape that drove him back from the window and knocked him clear onto the floor. The Frederick the Great sword which he'd stuck in his belt, the one we'd captured from Colonel Washington, clattered away.

The Old Man weren't badly wounded nor dead, but by the time he dusted himself off and got his sword back in his belt and went back to look out the window, Stevens lay on the ground outside badly wounded, and Watson was gut shot, banging desperately on the door of the engine house with a death wound.

The men opened the door for Watson, who came tumbling in there, spilling blood and guts. He lay on the floor, and the Old Man went over to him. He looked at his son, gut shot and moaning, just stood over him. It hurt him. You could see it. He shook his head.

"They just don't understand," he said.

He knelt over his son and felt his head, then his neck pulse. Watson's eyes was shut, but he was still breathing.

"You done your duty well, son."

"Thank you, Father," Watson said.

"Die like a man," he said.

"Yes, Father."

It would take Watson ten hours, but he done just as his Father asked him to.

32

Getting Gone

Night came. The militia had retreated again, this time with their wounded and with Stevens, who was still living. They lit lanterns outside and it got deathly quiet. All the shouts and hollering outside was pushed across the street and gone. The mob was moved away from the armory gates. Some kind of new order had come over out there. Something else was going on. The Old Man ordered the Emperor to climb up to the hole in the roof blowed out by the fallen timber to take a look, which he done.

He came back down and said, "The federals is out there, from Washington, D.C. I seen their flag and their uniforms." The Old Man shrugged.

They sent over a man, who walked over to one of those wooden doors that was lashed shut. He stuck his eye in a chink hole in the door and knocked. He called out, "I want Mr. Smith." That was the name the Old Man used at the Kennedy farm when he went around in disguise at the Ferry.

The Old Man came to the door but didn't open it. "What is it?"

The big eye peered inside. "I am Lieutenant Jeb Stuart of the United States Cavalry. I have orders here from my commander, Brevet Colonel Robert E. Lee. Colonel Lee is outside the gates and demands your surrender."

"I demands freedom for the Negro race of people that is living in bondage in this land."

Stuart might as well have been singing to a dead hog. "What is it you want at this direct moment, sir, in addition to that demand?" he asked.

"Nothing else. If you can cede that immediately, we will withdraw. But I don't think it's in your power to do so."

"Who am I speaking with? Can you show your face?"

The wood door had a panel in it for seeing. The Old Man slid it back. Stuart blinked a moment in surprise, then stood back and scratched his head. "Why, ain't you Old Osawatomie Brown? Who given us so much trouble in Kansas Territory?"

"I am."

"You are surrounded by twelve hundred federal troops. You have to surrender."

"I will not. I will exchange the prisoners I have in return for the safe passage of me and my men across the B&O Bridge. That is a possibility."

"That cannot be arranged," Stuart said.

"Then our business is done."

Stuart stood there a moment, disbelieving.

"Well, go on, then," the Old Man said. "Our business is finished, unless you yourself can free the Negro from bondage." He slammed the porthole shut.

Stuart went back to the gate and disappeared. But inside the engine house, the hostages begun to sense the change in things. The bottom rail had been on top the whole night, but the minute they got a sense the Old Man was doomed, them slave owners started chirping out their views. There was five of 'em setting along the wall together, including Colonel Washington, and he started chirping at the Captain, which gived the rest courage to start in on him also.

"You're committing treason," he said.

"You'll hang, old man," said another.

"You ought to give yourself up. You'll get a fair trial," said another.

The Emperor strode over to them. "Shut up," he barked.

They shrank back, except for Colonel Washington. He was snippy to the end. "You're gonna look good ducking through a hangman's noose, you impudent nigger."

"If that's the case, then I'll spot you," the Emperor said, "and blast you now in spite of redemption."

"You'll do no such thing," the Old Man said. The Captain stood by the window, alone, staring out thoughtfully. He spoke to the Emperor without looking at him. "Emperor, come over here."

The Emperor came over to the corner and the Old Man placed his arms around the colored man's shoulders and whispered to him. Whispered to him quite a long time. From the back, I saw the Emperor's shoulders bunch up and he shook his head several times in "no" fashion. The Old Man whispered to him some more, in a firm fashion, then left him to watch the window again, leaving the Emperor to himself.

The Emperor suddenly seemed spent. He drifted away from the Old Man and stopped in the farthest corner of the engine house, away from the prisoners. He seemed, for the first time, downright glum. The wind gone right out of him at that moment, and he stared out the window into the night.

It growed quiet now.

Up to that point there was so much going on in the engine house, there weren't no time to think of what it all meant. But now that darkness fell and it was quiet outside the armory and inside it too, there was time to think of consequences. There was 'bout twenty-five colored in that room. Of that number I reckon at least nine, ten, maybe more, was gonna hang surely and knowed it: Phil, the Coachman, three Negro women, and four Negro men, all of them was enthusiastic helping the Old Man's army, loading weapons, chinking out holes, organizing ammunition. The white hostages in that room would squeal on them surely. Only God knows what their names was, but their masters knowed 'em. They was in trouble, for they got right busy fighting for their freedom once they figured what the game was. They was doomed. Weren't no bargaining left for them. Of the rest, I'd say maybe half of that number, five or six, helped but was less enthusiastic 'bout fighting. They done it but had to be ordered to do it. They knowed their masters was watching and was never enthusiastic. And then the last of them, that last five, they wouldn't hang, for they sucked up to their masters to the limit. They didn't do nothing but what they was forced to do. A couple even fell asleep during the fighting.

Now that the thing was swinging the other way, them last five was setting pretty. But the ones in the middle, them that was on the fence and had half a chance to live, they swung back toward their masters something terrible. They sucked up to 'em full stride, angling to get back to their good graces. One of 'em, a feller named Otis, said, "Marse, this is a bad dream." His

marse ignored him. Didn't say a word to him. I can't blame that
Negro for sucking up the way he done. He knowed he was dead
up a hog's ass if his master put a bad word out on him, and the
master weren't playing his hold card. Not yet. They wasn't out
the woods yet.

The rest of the Negroes that was doomed, they watched the
Emperor. He come to be kind of the leader to them, for they'd
seen his courage through the night, and their eyes followed
him after the Old Man spoke to him. He stood at the window,
staring out, thinking. It was pitch-black in there, you couldn't
see a thing 'cept what little light the moon let into the port-
holes, for the Old Man wouldn't let anyone light a lantern. The
Emperor just stared out, then he paced a little, then stared out
some more. Coachman, Phil, and the other Negroes who was
sure to hang followed him with their eyes. They all followed
him, for they believed in his courage.

After a little while the Emperor called them over to his corner, and they bunched around him. I came, too, for I knowed
whatever punishment awaited them was mine's, too. You could
feel their despair as they gathered around him close and listened, for he spoke in a whisper.

"Just before light, the Old Man's gonna start a shoot-up out
front and let the colored out the back window. If you want out,
you can climb out the back window when the shooting starts,
make for the river, and be gone."

"What 'bout my wife?" the Coachman asked. "She's still in
bondage at the colonel's house."

"I can't tell you what to do 'bout that," the Emperor said.
"But if you is caught, make up a lie. Say you was a hostage. You
gonna swing for sure otherwise."

He was silent, letting this sink in.

"The Old Man's giving us an out," he said. "Take it or not. He and those that's left got some tow balls dipped in oil which he'll fire. He'll throw them out into the yard to make a lot of smoke, then shoot behind it. You can do your best to get gone out the back window and over the back wall when that happens. Whoever here wants to try it can do it."

"Is you gonna try it?" the Coachman asked.

The Emperor didn't answer. "Y'all oughta sleep some," he said.

They all reckoned they would, and retired to sleep for a couple of hours, for no one had slept in more than forty hours hence. That raid started on a Sunday. It was now Monday night going to Tuesday.

Most of the room slept, but I couldn't, for I knowed what was coming, too. The Emperor didn't sleep, neither. He stood by the window, staring out, listening to Watson groaning his death moans. Of all the coloreds in the Old Man's army, the Emperor weren't my favorite. I didn't know him that well, but he weren't short on courage. I went over to him.

"You gonna make a try for freedom, Emperor?"

"I am free," he said.

"You mean you a free Negro?"

He smiled in the dark light. I could see his white teeth, but he didn't say more.

"I'm wondering," I said, "if there's some way I can't swing."

He looked at me and smirked. I could see his face by the light of the moon through the porthole window. He was a dark man, chocolate skinned, with wide lips, curly hair, and a smooth face. I could see his silhouette. His head stood still in the window, and the breeze that blowed off his face seemed cool and refreshing. It was like the wind seemed to part around his face. He leaned over to me and said softly, "You don't get it, do ya?"

"I get it."

"Then why you asking questions to answers you already know? They gonna hang every colored in here. Hell, if you even looked at them white hostages funny you'll hang—and you done more than that, surely."

"They don't know me," I said.

"They know you sure as God's standing over the world. They know you just as well as they know me. You ought to take it standing up."

I swallowed hard. I had to do it. Couldn't stand it, but I had to do it.

"What if one of us is different from what they know?" I whispered.

"Ain't no difference between us when it come to the white man."

"Yes, there is," I said. I grabbed his hand and stuck it right on my privates in the dark. Just to let him touch my secrets. I felt him take in his breath, then he snatched his hand back.

"They don't know me," I said.

There was a long pause. Then the Emperor chuckled. "Good God. That ain't hardly a conflageration," he said.

"A what?" For the Emperor couldn't read, and he come up with words that didn't make no sense.

"A conflageration. A parade. You ain't got enough fruit there to squeeze," he snorted. "You'd have to work all night just to find them peanuts," and he chortled in the dark some more. He just couldn't stop chuckling.

That weren't funny to me. But I'd already thunk it through.

I needed some boy clothes. There was but two in the engine house whose clothes I could take, and no one would notice. A colored slave who got shot and died that previous afternoon, and Watson, the Old Man's boy, who was not quite dead but almost there. The slave was too big for me, plus he was hit by a ball in the chest and his clothes was soiled with his blood. But they was nice clothes—he was obviously an inside slave—and they would have to do. Blood or not.

"I wonder if you do me a favor," I said. "If I could just get a pair of pantaloons and shirt off that feller there," I whispered, nodding at the slave, whose silhouette could be seen in the moonlight. "Maybe with your help, I could slip them on and move out with the rest of the colored. When the Old Man lets us out."

The Emperor thought 'bout it a long moment.

"Don't you wanna die like a man?"

"That's just it," I said. "I'm but fourteen. How can I die like a man if I ain't lived like one yet? I ain't had nature's way with a girl once. I ain't yet kissed a girl. I think a feller ought to have the chance to be himself at least one time in this world, 'fore he moves on to the next. If not just to praise His name as his own self, rather than as somebody else. For I done found the Lord."

There was a long silence. The Emperor rubbed his jaw a moment. "Set here," he said.

He went over and woke the Coachman and Phil and pulled them into a corner. There was some whispering between the three, and by God if I didn't hear them chortling and laughing. I couldn't see them in the dark but I could hear them, and I couldn't get past that. Them three laughing at me, so I said, "What's so funny!"

I heard the footsteps of the Emperor's boots coming to me.

I felt a pair of pantaloons shoved in my face in the dark. And a shirt.

"If them federals find you out, they'll splatter you all over the creek. But it'd cause a regular frolic in here among us if you was to get out clear."

The shirt was huge, and the pants, when I put them on, were even bigger. "Whose pants is these?" I asked.

"The Coachman's."

"What's the Coachman gonna wear? He's gonna run out the window in his drawers?"

"What do you care?" he said. For the first time I noticed he was shirtless. "He ain't going nowhere. Neither is Phil. And here"—he stuffed in my hand a worn-out old feather—"this is the last of the Good Lord Bird. The Old Man gived it to me. His last feather. I'm the only one he gived one to, I think."

"I already got my feather. I don't need yours, Emperor."

"Keep it."

"What 'bout these pants? They're huge."

"You fit 'em good enough. The white man don't care what you wear. You just another shabby nigger to him. Just play it smart. At dawn, when the Captain gives the order, we'll fire them tow balls, throw a couple out the front and back, and send a few charges out the window, and then you get gone out that window quick. Them white folks ain't gonna pay you no more attention than they do a hole in the ground if you can get clear of the Ferry. Tell 'em you belongs to Mr. Harold Gourhand. Mr. H. Gourhand, got it? He's a white man lives near the Kennedy farm. The Coachman knows him. He says Gourhand's got a slave boy 'bout your age and size, and both of 'em's out of town."

"Somebody'll know him!"

"No, they won't. The federals out there, they ain't from this country. They're from Washington, D.C. They won't know the difference. They can't tell one of us from the other anyway."

At dawn, the Old Man gived the order. They fired the tow balls, tossed 'em, and commenced blasting out the window, letting the colored slip out the back window of the engine house. I went right along with 'em, four of us altogether went, and we more or less fell right into the arms of the U.S. Cavalry. They was on us the second we hit the ground, and pulled us clear of the engine house while their brothers fired on it something fierce. At the back gate, under the railroad tracks, they gathered around us, asking 'bout the white folks inside, and asking where is you from, and who does you belong to, and is the white folks hurt. That was the main thing they wanted to know, was the white folks hurt. When we said no, they asked was we part of the Old Man's army. To a man we swore up and down we was not. You never seen such ignorant Negroes in your life. By God, we acted like they was our saviors, and dropped to our knees and prayed and cried and thanked God for bringing them to save us and so forth.

They took pity on us, them federal marshals, and the Emperor was right. They had cleared the entire area around the armory of local militia. The soldiers doing the asking weren't locals from the Ferry. They was federal men who come up from Washington, D.C., and they bought our story, though they was suspicious enough. But, see, the fight was still raging while they questioned us, and they wanted to go back and get the local prize, which was the Old Man hisself, so they let us take our leave. But one soldier, he smelled a rat. He asked me, "Who do you belong to?" I used the name Master Gourhand and told him where Master Gourhand lived, up near Bolivar Heights, near the Kennedy farm.

He said, "I'll give you a ride there."

I hopped aboard his mount and got me a ride clear up to the Kennedy farm. I directed him there, hoping none of the enemy knowed yet 'bout the Old Man using it as his headquarters. Luckily they didn't, for when we reached it, it was all quiet up there.

We charged into the yard on horseback, me riding behind the federal, and when we charged in there, who but O. P. Anderson was standing out front, drawing water from the well with another colored slave he'd picked up someplace. That fool was yet living. He had no rifle and was dressed like a slave. You couldn't tell him from the other slave. His hair uncombed, he was dressed as poor as the other feller, looking rough as an orange peel. Them two could'a been brothers.

But the sight of me without my bonnet, dressed in men's clothing, just knocked O.P. out.

"Whose nigger is this?" the soldier said.

O.P. blinked the shock out his face. He had trouble with his tongue for a moment.

"Huh?"

"He said he lives 'round these parts with a Mr. Gourhand," the soldier said. "Poor creature was kidnapped and was held prisoner at the Ferry."

O.P. seemed to have trouble speaking, then finally got right with the program. "I has heard the news, master," he said, "and I am glad you brung this child back. I will wake the master and tell him."

"There ain't no need," Owen said, coming out the cabin and

stepping on the porch. "I is the master and I is awake." I reckon he was hiding inside along with Tidd, a feller named Hazlett, and Cook. I got nervous then, for I'm sure them three had drawed a bead on that soldier from inside the house the minute he clomped up there. Owen stepping outside likely saved that soldier's life, for them men had grabbed a few hours' sleep and was bent on leaving in a hurry.

Owen stepped off the porch, took a step toward me and suddenly recognized me—seen me dressed as a boy for the first time. He didn't have to play it slick. His shock was genuine. He liked to fell out. "Onion!" he said. "By God! Is that you?"

The soldier seen it weren't no ruse then. He was a nice feller. "This nigger's had quite a night. He says he belongs to Mr. Gourhand, who lives up the road, but I understand he is out of town."

"That is correct," Owen said, rolling with the lie. "But if you will hand his colored over to me, I will keep him safe for Mr. Gourhand, for it is a dangerous time to be about, what with what is going on 'round here. I thank you for bringing her back to me," Owen said.

The soldier smirked. "Her?" he said. "That's a *he*, sir," he scolded. "Can't y'all tell your niggers one from the other? No wonder y'all got insurrections all 'round here. You treat your colored so damn bad you don't know one from the other. We'd never treat our niggers this way in Alabama."

And with that, he turned on his mount and took off.

I didn't have time to give 'em the full word on the Old Man's situation, and didn't need to. They didn't need to ask. They knowed what happened. And neither did they ask 'bout my new look as a boy. They were in a hurry and making ready to run for their lives. They had slept a few hours from sheer exhaustion, but now that it was light it was time to go. They packed up on the quick and we took the tall timber together—me, O.P., Owen, Tidd, Cook, Hazlett, and Merriam. Straight up the mountain behind the Kennedy farm we went, with the sun coming up behind us. There was some fussin' and fightin' when we got to the top of the mountain, for everyone except O.P. wanted to take the mountain route direct north, and O.P. said he knowed another way. A safer way and more roundabout. Southwest through Charles Town and then farther west via the Underground Railroad to Martinsburg and then over to Chambersburg. But the others weren't for it. Said Charles Town would be too out of the way and we were too hot. O.P. gived 'em a mouthful on it and that brought on more hard words, for there weren't a lot of time, not with patrols likely rolling by then. So them five went their own way, direct up toward Chambersburg, while O.P. went southwest for Charles Town. I decided to cast my lot with him.

It was a good thing, for Cook and Hazlett got caught up in Pennsylvania a day or two later. Owen and Merriam and Tidd somehow got away. I never did see any of them ever again. I heard Merriam killed hisself in Europe. But I never did see Owen again, though I heard he lived a long life.

Me and O.P. got free through Mr. George Caldwell and his wife, Connie, who got us through Charles Town. They're dead now, so it don't hurt none giving 'em up. There was lots working on that underground gospel train that nobody knowed 'bout. A colored farmer drove us by wagon to Mr. Caldwell's barbershop, and when Mr. Caldwell found out who we were, he and his wife decided to split us up. We was too hot. They sent O.P.

off with a wagonload of coffins to Philadelphia driven by two Methodist abolitionists, and I don't know what happened to him, whether he died or not, for I never heard from him again. Me, I was kept with the Caldwells. I had to sit with them, wait it out underneath their house and in the back room of Mr. Caldwell's barbershop for four months before rolling ahead. It was on account of being 'bout the back room of the barbershop that I learned what happened to the Old Man.

Seems that Jeb Stuart and the U.S. Cavalry busted in the engine house with killing on their minds just minutes after I got out, and got to it. They overrun the engine house, killed Dauphin, Thompson, brother of Will, the Coachman, Phil, and Taylor. Watson and Oliver, both the Old Man's boys, was done in. Killed every one in there, good and bad, all but the Emperor. The Emperor somehow lived, long enough to hang anyway.

And as for the Old Man?

Well, Old John Brown lived, too. They tried killing him, according to Mr. Caldwell. When they busted down the door, a lieutenant runned a sword right into the Old Man's head as the Captain was trying to reload. Mr. Caldwell said the Lord saved him. The lieutenant was called to emergency duty on account of the uprising and was in a hurry when he left his house. He was so hot to get out, he grabbed the wrong sword off his mantelpiece as he runned out the door. He snatched up his military parade sword instead of his regular broadsword. Had he used a regular sword, he would'a deadened the Old Man easily. "But the Lord didn't want him killed," Mr. Caldwell said proudly. "He still got more work for him."

That may be true, but Providence laid down a hard hand for the Negroes in Charles Town in them days following the

Old Man's defeat, for he was jailed and scheduled to be put on trial. I lived hidden in the back room of Mr. Caldwell's barbershop during them weeks and heard it all. Charles Town was just up the road from Harpers Ferry, and white folks there was in a state of panic that bordered on insanity. They was plain terrified. Every day the constable would bust into Mr. Caldwell's shop and rouse up Negro customers. He drug two or three men out at a time, brung them to the jail to question them 'bout the insurrection, then jailed some and released some. Even the most trusted Negroes in the slave owner's houses was put out in the fields to work, for their masters didn't trust them to work in the house, thinking their slaves would turn on 'em and kill 'em. Dozens of slaved Negroes was sold south, and dozens more run off, thinking they'd *be* sold. One colored slave come into Mr. Caldwell's shop, complaining that if a rat's tail touched the wall in his master's house in the middle of the night, the entire house was roused, guns was grabbed, and this feller would be sent downstairs first to go see 'bout it. The white newspaper said that Baltimore arms dealers sold ten thousand guns to Virginians during Old John Brown's trial. One Negro in the barbershop joked, "The Colt Company ought to do something nice for Captain Brown's family." Several fires were set on Charles Town plantations, and nobody knowed who done it. And a story in the Charles Town paper said that slave owners was complaining that their horses and sheep was dying suddenly, as if they'd been poisoned. I'd heard that one, too, whispered in the back of Mr. Caldwell's barbershop. And when I heard it, I said to Mr. Caldwell, "Would that all these fellers doing that devilment today had showed up at the Ferry. It would have been a different game."

"No," he said. "It had to end the way it did. Old John Brown

knows what he's doing. They should'a killed him. He's raising
more hell now writing letters and talking than he ever did with
a gun."

And that was true. They put the Old Man and his men in
jail in Charles Town, the ones from his army that lived through
the fight: Hazlett, Cook, Stevens, the two coloreds, John Cope-
man, and the Emperor, and by the time the Captain got done
writing letters and getting visitors from his friends in New
England, why, he was a star all over again. The whole country
was talking 'bout him. I hear tell the last six weeks of his life
the Old Man got more folks moved 'bout the slavery question
than he ever did spilling blood back in Kansas, or in all them
speeches he gave up in New England. Folks was listening now
that white blood was spilled on the floor. And it weren't just
any old white blood. John Brown was a Christian man. A bit
off his biscuit, but a better Christian you never saw. And he
had lots of friends, white and colored. I do believe he done
more against slavery in them last six weeks with letter writings
and talking than he ever done raising one gun or sword.

They set a quick trial for him, convicted him right off, and
set a date for the Old Man to hang, and all the while that Old
Man kept writing letters and squawking and hollering 'bout
slavery, sounding off like the devil to every newspaper in America that would listen, and they was listening, for them insurrections scared the devil out the white man. It set the table for the
war that was to come, is what it did, for nothing scared the
South more than the idea of niggers running 'round with guns
and wanting to be free.

But I wasn't thinking them thoughts back then. Them fall
nights become long for me. And lonesome. I was a boy for the
first time in years, and being a boy, with the end of November

coming, that meant in five weeks' time it would be January, and I would be fifteen. I never knowed my true birth date, but like most coloreds, I celebrated it on the first of the year. I wanted to move on. Five weeks after the insurrection, in late November, I caught Mr. Caldwell one evening when he come to the back of the shop to give me some bacon, biscuits, and gravy and asked 'bout me maybe leaving for Philadelphia.

"You can't go yet," he said. "Too hot. They haven't hung the Captain yet."

"How is he? He's yet living and yet well?"

"That he is. In the jailhouse as always. Set to hang on December second. That's in a week."

I thunk on it a moment. It hurt my heart a little to think of it. So I said, "It would do me well, I reckon, for me to see him."

He shook his head. "I ain't hiding you here for my safety and satisfaction," he said. "I got enough risk just taking care of you."

"But the Old Man always thunk I brought him good luck," I said. "I rode with him for four years. I was friends to his sons and family and even one of his daughters. I'm a friendly face. It might help him, being that he ain't never gonna see his wife and his children on this side no more, to see a friendly face."

"Sorry," he said.

He sat on that thought a few days. I didn't ask it. *He* said it. He come to me a few days later and said, "I thunk on it and I changed my mind. It would be a help to him to see you. It would help him through his last days, to know you is yet living. I'm doing this for him. Not you. I will arrange it."

He called on a few persons, and a few days later he brung an old Negro man named Clarence back behind the shop to where I was hid. Clarence was a white-haired old feller, slow movin' but thoughtful and smart. He cleaned the jailhouse where the Old Man and the others was kept. He set down with Mr. Caldwell, and Mr. Caldwell discussed the whole thing. The old man listened thoughtfully.

"I gots an in with the captain of the jailhouse, Captain John Avis," Clarence said. "I knowed Captain Avis since he was a boy. He's a good man. A fair man. And he's grown fond of Old John Brown. Still, Captain Avis ain't gonna just let this boy walk in there," he said.

"Can't I come with you as a helper?" I asked.

"I don't need a helper. And I don't need no trouble."

"Clarence, think on what the Captain has done for the Negro," Mr. Caldwell said. "Think of your own children. Think of Captain Brown's children. For he has plenty, and won't never see them nor his wife no more on this side of the world."

The old man thought for quite some time. Didn't say a word. Just thunk on it, rubbing his fingers together. Mr. Caldwell's words moved him some. Finally he said, "It is a lot of activity in there. The Old Man's popular. A lot of people coming and going during the day. Lots more for me to do with them leaving things, gifts and letters and all sorts of stuff. The Old Man's got a lot of northern friends. Captain Avis don't seem bothered by it none."

"So can I go?" I asked.

"Lemme think on it. I might mention it to Captain Avis."

Three days later, in the wee hours of the second of December, 1859, Clarence and Mr. Caldwell came into the basement of the barbershop and roused me from sleep.

"We moves tonight," Clarence said. "The Old Man is hanging tomorrow. His wife come down from New York and just left him. Avis'll look the other way. He's right touched by it all."

Mr. Caldwell said, "That's fine and good, but you got to move from here now, child. It's gonna be too hot for me if you is found out and come back here." He gave me a few dollars to get started in Philadelphia, a railroad train ticket from the Ferry to Philadelphia, a few rags, and some food. I thanked him and was gone.

It was close to dawn but not quite. Me and Mr. Clarence drove in an old wagon and mule to the jailhouse. Mr. Clarence gave me a bucket, a mop, and cleaning brushes, and we how-died the militia out front and walked past them and into the jailhouse smooth as taffy. The other prisoners was dead asleep. Captain John Avis was there, setting at a desk in front, scribbling his notes, and he looked at me and didn't say a word. Just nodded at Clarence, and looked back down at his papers. We walked down to the back section of the house where the prisoners were, way to the end corridor, and on the right, in the last cell, setting up on his cot writing notes by the light of a small stone fireplace, was the Old Man.

He stopped writing and peered into the darkness as I stood in the hallway outside his cell, holding that bucket, for he couldn't see me clear. Finally he spoke out.

"Who is there?"

"It's me. Onion."

I stepped out the shadows wearing pantaloons and a shirt, and holding a bucket.

The Old Man looked at me a long time. Didn't say a word 'bout what he seen. Just stared. Then he said, "C'mon in, Onion. The captain don't lock the door."

I come in and set on the bed. He looked exhausted. His neck and face was charred from some kind of wound, and he limped as he moved to put a piece of wood on the fire. He moved gamely as he sat back on his cot. "How is you feeling, Onion?"

"I'm fine, Captain."

"It does my heart good to see you," he said.

"Is you all right, Captain?"

"I am fine, Onion."

I didn't right know what to say to him at that moment, so I nodded at the open cell door. "You could escape easily, couldn't you, Captain? There's plenty talk 'bout rousing up new men from all parts and taking you back out. Couldn't you bust out and we could stir up another army and do it like the old days, like Kansas?"

The Old Man, stern as always, shook his head. "Why would I do that? I am the luckiest man in the world."

"It don't seem that way."

"There is an eternity behind and an eternity before, Onion. That little speck at the center, however long, is life. And that is but comparatively a minute," he said. "I has done what the Lord has asked me to do in the little time I had. That was my purpose. To hive the colored."

I couldn't stand it. He was a failure. He didn't hive nobody. He didn't free nobody, and that spun my guts a bit to see him in that state, for I did love the Old Man, but he was dying cockeyed, and I didn't want that. So I said, "The slaves never hived, Captain. That was my fault."

I started to tell him 'bout the Rail Man, but he put up his hand.

"Hiving takes a while. Sometimes bees don't hive for years."

"You saying they will?"

"I'm saying God's mercy will spread its light on the world. Just like He spread His mercy to you. It done my heart good to see you accept God in that engine house, Onion. That alone, that one life freed toward our King of Peace, is worth a thousand bullets and all the pain in the world. I won't live to see the change God wants. But I hope you do. Some of it anyway. By God, I feels a prayer hatching, Onion." And he stood up and grabbed my hands and prayed for a good half hour, holding my hands in his wrinkled paws, his head down, pow-wowing with his Maker 'bout this and that, thanking Him for making me true to myself, and all sorts of other business, praying for his jailer and hoping the jailer gets paid and don't get robbed and nobody breaks outta jail on his watch, and throwing in a good word for them that jailed him and killed his boys. I let him go on.

After 'bout a half hour he was done, and sat back down on his bed, tired. It was getting light outside. I could see just a peek of dawn was through the window. It was time for me to go.

"But, Captain, you never asked me why I . . . went 'bout as I did."

The old face, crinkled and dented with canals running every which way, pushed and shoved up against itself for a while, till a big old smile busted out from beneath 'em all, and his gray eyes fairly glowed. It was the first time I ever saw him smile free. A true smile. It was like looking at the face of God. And I knowed then, for the first time, that him being the person to lead the colored to freedom weren't no lunacy. It was something he knowed true inside him. I saw it clear for the first time. I knowed then, too, that he knowed what I was—from the very first.

"Whatever you is, Onion," he said, "be it full. God is no respecter of persons. I loves you, Onion. Look in on my family from time to time."

He reached into his shirt pocket and pulled out a Good Lord Bird feather. "The Good Lord Bird don't run in a flock. He flies alone. You know why? He's searching. Looking for the right tree. And when he sees that tree, that dead tree that's taking all the nutrition and good things from the forest floor. He goes out and he gnaws at it, and he gnaws at it till that thing gets tired and falls down. And the dirt from it raises the other trees. It gives them good things to eat. It makes 'em strong. Gives 'em life. And the circle goes 'round."

He gave me that feather, and set back on his cot, and gone back to his writing, writing another letter, I expect.

I opened the cell door, closed it quietly, and walked out the jailhouse. I never saw him again.

The sun was coming up when I come out the jailhouse and climbed in old Clarence's wagon. The air was clear. The fresh breeze was blowing. It was December, but a warm day for a hanging. Charles Town was just waking up. On the road to the Ferry to catch the train to Philadelphia, military men on horseback, a long line of 'em, approached us, riding by twos, carrying flags and wearing colorful uniforms, the line stretching far as the eye could see. They rode past us in the other direction, headed down toward the field past the jailhouse, where the scaffold was already built, waiting for the Old Man. I was glad I weren't going back to Mr. Caldwell's place. He gave me my walking papers. Give me money, food, a train ticket to Philadelphia, and from there I was on my own. I didn't stick around for the hanging. There was enough military there to crowd a field and beyond. I hear tell no colored was allowed within three miles of that hanging. They say the Old Man was taken out by a wagon, made to sit on his own coffin, and driven over from the jailhouse by Captain Avis, his jailer. He told the captain, "This is beautiful country, Captain Avis. I never knowed how beautiful this was till today." And when he got on the scaffold, told the hangman to make it snappy when he hung him. But like always he had bad luck, and they made him wait a full fifteen minutes with his face hooded and his hands tied while the whole military formation of white folks lined up by the thousands, militia from all over the United States, and U.S. Cavalry from Washington, D.C., and other important people from all over who come to watch him hang: Robert E. Lee, Jeb Stuart, Stonewall Jackson. Them last two would be deadened by the Yanks in the coming years in the very war the Old Man helped start, and Lee would be defeated. And a whole host of others who came there to watch him hang would be deadened, too. I reckon when they got to heaven, they'd be right surprised to find the Old Man waiting for 'em, Bible in hand, lecturing 'em on the evils of slavery. By the time he'd done with 'em, they probably wished they'd gone the other way.

But it was a funny thing. I don't think they'd have to wait that long. For we rode past a colored church as we moved out of Charles Town, and inside the church you could hear the Negroes singing, singing 'bout Gabriel's trumpet. That was the Old Man's favorite song. "Blow Ye Trumpet." Them Negroes was far away from the doings on the plaza where the Old Man was to hang, way out from it. But they sang it loud and clear....

Blow ye trumpet blow
Blow ye trumpet blow....

You could hear their voices for a long way, seemed like they lifted up and carried all the way into the sky, lingering in the air long afterward. And up above the church, high above it, a strange black-and-white bird circled 'round, looking for a tree to roost on, a bad tree, I expect, so he could alight upon it and get busy, so that it would someday fall and feed the others.

The End

Acknowledgments

Deeply grateful to all those who, over the years, have kept the memory of John Brown alive.

James McBride
Solebury Township, Pa.

James McBride is an accomplished musician and author of the National Book Award–winning *The Good Lord Bird*, the #1 bestselling American classic *The Color of Water*, and the bestsellers *Song Yet Sung* and *Miracle at St. Anna*, which was turned into a film by Spike Lee. McBride is a Distinguished Writer in Residence at New York University.

James McBride's books bring to life the American experience.

His classic memoir, *The Color of Water*, heralded a new voice in American literature and is still beloved and a hallmark text, nearly twenty years after publication.

McBride's novels—including *The Miracle at St. Anna*, *Song Yet Sung*, and National Book Award winner *The Good Lord Bird*—chronicle unexpected stories from American history. From Buffalo Soldiers in World War II to runaway slaves on the Eastern Shore of Maryland to John Brown's Harpers Ferry antislavery raid, McBride's stories captivate, surprise, and move.

T338-1213

The acclaimed landmark memoir that spent years on the *New York Times* bestseller list

As a boy in Brooklyn's Red Hook projects, James McBride knew his mother was different. But when he asked about it, she'd simply say, "I'm light-skinned." Later he wondered if he was different too, and asked his mother if he was black or white. "You're a human being," she snapped. "Educate yourself or you'll be a nobody!" And when James asked what color God was, she said, "God is the color of water."

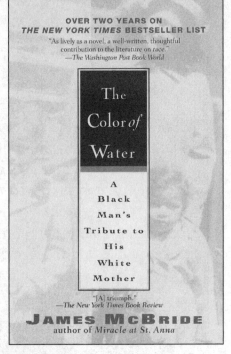

As an adult, McBride finally persuaded his mother to tell her remarkable story—of a rabbi's daughter, born in Poland and raised in the South, who fled to Harlem, married a black man, founded a Baptist church, and put twelve children through college. *The Color of Water* is a tribute to McBride's mother, an eloquent exploration of what family really means, and a groundbreaking literary phenomenon that transcends racial and religious boundaries.

"[A] triumph."   —*The New York Times Book Review*

"As lively as a novel, a well-written, thoughtful contribution to the literature on race."   —*The Washington Post Book World*

James McBride's novel displays his extraordinary gift for storytelling in a universal tale of courage and redemption, inspired by a little-known historic event

As World War II draws to an end, four Buffalo Soldiers from the United States Army's Negro 92nd Division find themselves separated from their unit and behind enemy lines in Italy. Risking their lives for a country in which they are treated with less respect than the enemy they are fighting, the soldiers discover humanity in the small Tuscan village of St. Anna di Stazzema. Even in the face of unspeakable tragedy, they learn to see the small miracles of life.

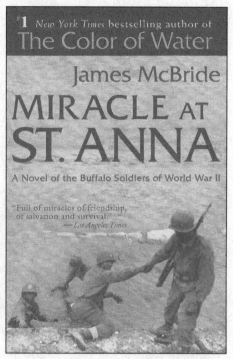

#1 *New York Times* bestselling author of
The Color of Water

James McBride

MIRACLE AT
ST. ANNA

A Novel of the Buffalo Soldiers of World War II

"Full of miracles of friendship, of salvation and survival."
—*Los Angeles Times*

"Full of miracles of friendship, of salvation and survival."

—*Los Angeles Times*

"Searingly, soaringly beautiful…The book's central theme, its essence, is a celebration of the human capacity for love."

—*The Baltimore Sun*

A riveting Civil War–era tale of haunting choices, set on the Eastern Shore of Maryland

A group of slaves breaks free in the labyrinthine swamps of Maryland, setting loose a drama of violence and hope among slave catchers, plantation owners, watermen, fellow slaves, and free blacks. Among them is Liz Spocott, a runaway slave, near death, wracked by disturbing visions of the future, and armed with "the Code," a fiercely guarded cryptic means of communication for slaves on the run. As she makes her desperate flight among the denizens of the swampy peninsula, Liz's extraordinary dreams of tomorrow create a freedom-seeking furor among the community.

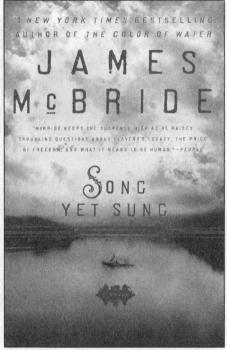

"Gripping, affecting and beautifully paced, *Song Yet Sung* illuminates, in the most dramatic fashion, a deeply troubled, vastly complicated moment in American history."   —*O, The Oprah Magazine*

"McBride keeps the suspense high as he raises troubling questions about slavery's legacy, the price of freedom, and what it means to be human."   —*People*

T341-0713

An instant classic by a master storyteller

An antique-toy collector makes two astonishing discoveries. Five boys in a Pennsylvania town learn that secrets can hide in plain sight. A Ph.D. candidate uncovers a long-hidden promise. In *Five-Carat Soul*, James McBride brings to vivid life a captivating cast of characters with extraordinary stories to tell. Spanning centuries and defying categorization, these stories are full of the

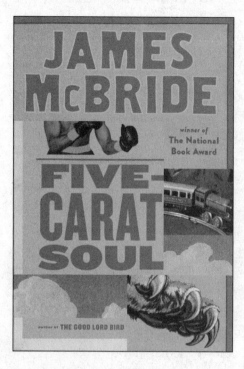

humor and humanity that are the hallmarks of McBride's work—and that make them a pleasure to read.

"A pinball machine zinging with sharp dialogue, breathtaking plot twists and naughty humor . . . McBride at his brave and joyous best." —*The New York Times Book Review*

"McBride has the comic energy and antic spirit of Richard Pryor."

—*Chicago Tribune*

T340-0713